LEGACY
OF THE
NINE REALMS

FLAMES
of
CHAOS

AMELIA HUTCHINS

Authored By: Amelia Hutchins
Cover Art Design: Covers by Combs
Copy edited by: Melissa Burg
Edited by: E & F Indie Services
Published by: Amelia Hutchins
Published in (United States of America)
10 9 8 7 6 5 4 3 2 1

Dedication

To everyone just trying to tread water, you got this. Your chaos shines brightly, don't dull it for anyone. Let your flames burn wildly, and rattle the world with your inner beast. Set the world on fire, and rise from the ashes smiling. You are brutally beautiful in your own way.

Also by Amelia Hutchins

Legacy of the Nine Realms
Flames of Chaos
Ashes of Chaos *Spring 2020*

The Fae Chronicles
Fighting Destiny
Taunting Destiny
Escaping Destiny
Seducing Destiny
Unraveling Destiny
Embracing Destiny - *Coming 2020 (Final Book)*

The Elite Guards
A Demon's Dark Embrace
Claiming the Dragon King
The Winter Court
A Demon's Plaything

A Guardian's Diary
Darkest Before Dawn
Death before Dawn

Also by Amelia Hutchins

If you're following the series for the Fae Chronicles, Elite Guards, and Monsters, reading order is as follows:

Fighting Destiny

Taunting Destiny

Escaping Destiny

Seducing Destiny

A Demon's Dark Embrace

Playing with Monsters

Unraveling Destiny

Sleeping with Monsters

Claiming the Dragon King

Oh, Holy Knight

Becoming his Monster

A Demon's Plaything

The Winter Court

If She's Wicked

Embracing Destiny 2020

Warning!

Stop!! Read the warning below before purchasing this book.

Warning: This book is **dark**. It's **sexy, hot, and intense**. The author is human, as you are. Is the book perfect? It's as perfect as I could make it. Are there mistakes? Probably, then again, even **New York Times top published** books have minimal mistakes because, like me, they have **human editors**. There are words in this book that won't be found in the standard dictionary because they were created to set the stage for a paranormal-urban fantasy world. Words in this novel are common in paranormal books and give better descriptions to the action in the story than can be found in standard dictionaries. They are intentional and not mistakes.

About the hero: chances are you may **not** fall instantly in **love** with him, that's because **I don't write men you instantly love**; you grow to love them. I don't believe in **instant love**. I write flawed, raw, caveman-like **assholes** that eventually let you see their redeeming qualities. They are **aggressive, assholes**, one step above a caveman when we meet them. You may *not* even like him by the time you finish this book, but I promise you will **love** him by the end of this **series**.

Warning!
(cont'd)

About the heroine: There is a chance that you might think she's a bit naïve or weak, but then again, who starts out as a badass? Badass women are a product of growth, and I am going to put her through **hell**, and you get to watch **her** come up **swinging** every time I knock her on her ass. That's just how I do things. How she reacts to the set of circumstances she is put through may not be how you as the reader, or I, as the author would react to that same situation. Everyone reacts differently to circumstances and how Aria Hecate responds to her challenges, is how I see her as a character and as a person.

I don't write love stories: I write fast-paced, knock you on your ass, *make you sit on the edge of your seat wondering what is going to happen next* books. If you're looking for cookie-cutter romance, this isn't for you. If you can't handle the ride, ***unbuckle your seatbelt and get out of the roller-coaster car now***. **If not, you've been warned.** If nothing outlined above bothers you, carry on and **enjoy the ride!**

LEGACY
OF THE
NINE REALMS

FLAMES
of
CHAOS

LEGACY
OF THE
NINE REALMS

FLAMES
of
CHAOS

CHAPTER
1

Exhaling a long, shaky breath, I stared at the lights of the city below the cliff I stood upon. Haven Falls, a city of immortal beings that weren't even from the Human Realm. A place that haunted my dreams and lived in every nightmare I'd ever had. It was nestled between winding valleys, hidden within them to remain a secret from the mortals whose realm we lived in. I'd stood in the same spot long enough for the day to become night. The town had turned from a bustling hub of activity to a lighted dreamscape.

I'd been twelve when my Aunt Aurora had taken us away from here, away from the cruel brutality of the immortal realms from which we'd come. This place held no appeal and no good memories for me. It was the center of everything I hated; everything I wished to burn down and feel the ashes of the wreckage between my toes. I'd dreamt once I had burned it down, leaving those who stood aside and watched me being tortured, brutalized, and terrorized by my mother, in ashes.

My sisters didn't share my vision of this place, nor had they endured what my mother put me through trying to end my life. They relished being home, seeing their old friends while helping me search for my twin, who had been missing several months now without a single sign of her.

My eyes lifted toward the galaxies of stars above and then lowered to fall on the oldest of my sisters as she moved to where I stood.

Sabine was everything gentle and motherly to us since she was the oldest and had been present for every set of twins being born, and also because our mother was a heartless bitch. We had to learn quickly to depend on one another in order to survive. Stopping beside me, she peered up at the stars before she spoke.

"Once we enter the town, they'll know we are back," she muttered in a hushed tone, pushing her golden curls away from her face as the wind picked up, mirroring the internal struggle her words created within me.

"They already know we are here," I countered, sensing eyes that viewed us as we stood in the crisp evening air, staring out at the town. "We are being watched and have been since the moment we exited the cars."

"They can watch us all they want. Someone here knows what happened to Amara, and we're not leaving here until we find her."

Frowning, I considered her words. Amara had been withdrawn from me for a while now, and I wasn't so sure she wanted to be found. It hadn't been unusual for her to be missing for an extended period, but this one felt different. It felt wrong, and everything inside of me said to find her before it was too late to save her.

Turning, I took in the stares of my sisters, who had rallied behind me to come find Amara. Every single one of them refused to stay behind, and I loved them more for it. We were of the original family of witches, born from the same blood that ran through Hecate, the Goddess of Witches. She was my grandmother, and because of her, we had a duty to this town, one we'd escaped from until now. We'd left our mother, Freya, here to deal with the fallout, but Freya was wishy-washy and had a bad reputation for shirking her duties. She vanished soon after we did. *Shocker.*

Amara, my sister who I had a love-hate relationship with for the last few years, had come back to Haven Falls to secure our family's place on the council within the Nine Realms when word had reached us that Freya had vanished without a word. It would have been troubling if it was anything new, but it wasn't. Freya loved men, and she cared little about propriety or reputation when she took them as lovers. She hated being part of the council that oversaw the immortals entering the Human Realm from the Nine Realms.

Only those with the purest of bloodlines could sit on the council of the Nine Realms. Together they decided whether immortals were safe enough to enter the Human Realm and if they could maintain our secrets. In the center of town is the portal between this realm and the entrance to the Nine Realms. Those coming through had to check in with the council, gaining papers that made them legal to be here.

Amara came back to Haven Falls on her own,

offering to hold the seat among the council. I pleaded with her to reconsider, but she refused. She'd reminded me that no immortal passing through the portal could gain entrance unless a witch of Hecate bloodline voted with the others. Still, it could have been anyone else. She'd come back soon after that, but more often than not, she missed meetings. She withdrew from everything and everyone, which made waves in this town. Amara had even withdrawn from magic, unwilling to do spells that called for the coven, claiming she was drained or sick on the days they needed them.

Upon her return to the Human Realm, she checked in weekly, letting us know everything was fine. Then weeks turned into months, and then nothing. It was as if she just vanished. We'd called her phone, leaving voice messages and text messages to no avail. Then the day came when her phone was disconnected. Calls to the original families held little to no hope. No one had seen her in weeks, and even worse, the store we ran was closed down. The bond I shared with Amara had severed as if she'd just ceased to exist. For me, it was debilitating to be unable to reach out and sense the presence of my twin. It felt like a part of me was missing, and no matter how much I tried, I couldn't reconnect it.

"Someone in this town has to know what happened to her," my sister Luna said, slipping her hand into mine and squeezing it reassuringly. "They'll regret it if they touched one of our own. There are enough of us to wage war if they so much as harmed a hair on her pretty head."

Enough of us.

My family was composed of all females, eight sets of twins. Hecate had cursed her line to birth multiples, all female offspring. She'd ensured we would never be alone, but that came at a heavy price. Any female who carried a male child learned quickly the cost of doing so. My mother was the daughter of Hecate, purest of blood, and yet she birthed twin daughters without a care of what happened after we'd detached from her womb. Her sisters Hysteria and Aurora had been the ones to deal with the repercussions of her overactive libido.

Freya had wanted an army of witches, but she didn't want the responsibility that came with birthing that army herself. Instead, she left us with her sisters, who loved us like their own children, Aurora more so than Hysteria. Hysteria had entered the portal and hasn't been heard of since. Hecate herself birthed two sets of twins. Freya and Aurora and Hysteria and Kamara. Kamara had been lost centuries ago or left on her own. Nobody knew what happened to her, other than she'd vanished and hadn't been seen or heard of since.

"We may have to consider the fact that she might have gone with our mother," Kinvara stated, shrugging when I stared at her, brow raised in a questioning look.

"I have considered it, but Amara isn't that stupid." I frowned, knowing it was a viable explanation, but that wouldn't make Amara safe. "I don't think she'd be stupid enough to trust our murderous mother."

"I don't think our mother would try to murder Amara," Sabine pointed out. "She's cold-blooded for sure, but she isn't a murderer. Maybe she wanted Amara with her to lure men to her bed, but murder? I don't think she would do something like that to her own child."

"Seriously?" I snorted. "That bitch tried to murder me frequently. Hell, she tried to abort Amara and me from her womb. If Aurora hadn't stepped in during every attempt on my life, I would be dead. I was a *child*."

Sabine frowned, nodding at the anger and hatred that dripped from my words. "She was crazed after she came back. Something was off, Aria. I don't know why she did what she did to you, but whatever the reason, know that she wasn't the same when she returned from the Nine Realms, heavily pregnant with you and Amara."

"It doesn't excuse her actions, Sabine. She tried to murder me."

"Yes, and Aurora saved you. She never tried to murder Amara directly. She only aimed for her when you were both in her womb, so not sure you can assume she'd go for her now. That is what we are saying, and since we left this place, she hasn't been able to find you. Aurora made certain we were untraceable."

Our mother, God love her, wasn't selective about the creatures she took between her thighs. Freya also never kept track of who had fathered us, making it impossible to know what we were until the change began within us; then, we handled it on our own. Aine and Luna had glowing blue eyes, marking them alpha wolves, alerting us to their heritage. Sabine and Callista were nymphs or sirens, but it was hard to tell since there wasn't much difference between the two species. We'd resorted to calling them hookers because it made them laugh when we did. Kinvara and Valeria were succubi, the result of our mother getting busy with a horde of incubus demons on one of her trips into the Nine Realms. She'd created her own twisted version of Noah's ark, but with daughters.

Our father's blood only determined half of what we

were; our mothers, the other. Unlike my sisters, who had realized what they were by their sixteenth birthday, I had no idea what I was. Where they depended on nature to cast magic or spells, I wielded it from someplace else. It was exhilarating when I used magic, but there was a call to something darker within me that preened proudly when I did. As if something deadly slumbered within me and had yet to awaken fully.

"Cars are coming from the east," Luna stated, staring in that direction. She tilted her head, listening as we all followed her gaze.

"Friend or foe, Luna?" Sabine asked softly as if she feared they would hear her.

"Silly sister," I chuckled darkly. "They're all foe." I watched the dark highway behind us and then narrowed my gaze as headlights finally came into view.

Luna sniffed the air and smirked generously. "I smell men, and nice smelling ones at that. Alpha wolves or something else similar to the genetic makeup. I smell raw power and violence in the air that screams of danger. Eight men or so," she said, sniffing once more before nodding. "I'm thinking foe."

"But we like men," Aine said as her own nose lifted, inhaling deeply. "Especially ones that smell like these creatures. Meow, mommas, get ready. Get your game faces on." She fluffed her hair and fixed her breasts before speaking again. "Definitely foe, but I can use some hate fucking about now."

"How do you know they're foe?" Sabine asked, worrying her lip between her teeth as she waited for their answer.

AMELIA HUTCHINS

"Easy, Aria just said they're all foe," Luna snorted, rolling her eyes as she adjusted her breasts and compared hers with her twin, Aine's. She withdrew a tube of lip gloss, slathering it on her lips as we all studied her prepping for sex.

"You guys are disturbing sometimes," I muttered.

I reached up, hooking my silver hair behind my ears, not that it would help with the wind howling around us. I didn't need a mirror to know my eyes would be bluer than green with the lack of sleep I'd had in the last twenty-four hours. I'd had nightmares and had given up trying to sleep at the thought of returning to this place.

The car's pulled up, aiming high-beams directly at us. It forced those who were sensitive to light to cover their eyes as it shined over us. I silently inspected the men unloading from the black SUVs, moving toward us in a dark, lethal way that couldn't be concealed, no matter what mask of civility they'd donned to enter this realm.

My eyes locked onto the tallest male, inspecting him as muscles pushed against the shirt he wore. He was a good head taller than the others. Power exuded from him, pushing against my flesh as he reached up and pushed light brown hair away from his face. Ocean-colored eyes slid over the lot of us before they moved back to me, lifting his nose, inhaling our scents.

"You're unwelcome here. Leave, and you can live; stay, and you die," he announced with an accent I couldn't place. He was sex in the purest form, and even I couldn't tear my eyes off him—or couldn't until Kinvara snorted.

8

"Is that how you welcome ladies to town?" she asked, her pheromones filling the air to tempt him to her. *Hussy.*

"I won't ask again, ladies."

"You don't have the authority to tell us to leave," I said, pulling his lethal glare back to me and off of my sister. I crossed my arms over my chest, daring him to tell me I was wrong. When I got mad, I dug my heels in deep and didn't give an inch of room for anyone to push me around.

CHAPTER
2

He smiled coldly, studying my face while I did the same to him. His power wrapped around me threateningly. It was debilitating power that tightened around my throat, causing the hair on my neck to rise in warning. The smirk on his sinful mouth told me he had done it on purpose, knowing it wasn't something that could be ignored. His intense gaze swallowed me whole, drowning me slowly as it beckoned me into the deep waters, white-capped waves that promised to consume me.

"Oh, but I do, little girl," he chuckled darkly. "I am the king here. That means I hold all the power over any who enter Haven Falls and my jurisdiction," he snorted, stepping closer to where I stood, silently taking him in. He stopped mere inches away from me and sniffed the air again.

I inhaled his scent, barely containing the shiver that raced down my spine. It was a mixture of sandalwood and a hint of whiskey. The button-up shirt he wore did little to conceal the contours of his body, which I studied absently. Not too beefed up, but more than a swimmer's build. His arms were lightly tattooed, with writing in ancient languages, if I wasn't mistaken. He wore jeans that hugged powerful legs ending at black Doc Martin shit-kickers. I pulled my gaze from his body and rested it on his face, taking in the sharp jawline that was lightly dusted in a five o'clock shadow. His mouth was full, sensual, and pulled back tightly to reveal a smile that was all teeth.

"Are you finished eye-fucking me?" he asked darkly, his voice sending a shiver racing down my spine.

"Maybe," I said before giving myself a mental shake. "Since when does Haven Falls need a king?" His eyes did a slow perusal of my body, stopping briefly over the top I wore, which crisscrossed over my chest, exposing my midriff and sides, leaving a little more cleavage than I was comfortable with being exposed to his heated stare. My skirt was slit up the sides of my legs, revealing both thighs before it stopped at my hips. The boots I wore matched his, but they were more for comfort than kicking ass. Slowly, his eyes lifted to my breasts once more before stopping on my face.

"Since I took control of it," he growled. The sound of his voice slithered over my flesh, wrapping around my throat until air no longer could enter my airway. "Who the fuck would you be, little girl?"

"Aria Hecate, daughter of Freya Hecate, born of Hecate," I smirked impishly, watching as his eyes narrowed, and the tick in his jaw hammered at the mention of my last name. "These are my sisters, and I assure you, even as the king, you don't have the authority to remove us."

He chuckled seductively, closing the distance until he was in my space, breathing my air until there wasn't enough for the two of us to inhale. His breath fanned my flesh; his proximity forced my neck to careen to hold his stare. He lifted his hand and brushed a single finger over my cheek as he stared me down.

"Hecate," he hissed as if the name was something vile stuck to the tip of his tongue. "Fucking witches." Snorting, he stared me dead in the eye as if he'd be happier with his large hands around my throat.

"Well, not sure on the fucking part, but we're definitely witches."

"And what is your other half, Aria Hecate? Your mother was a whore, one who slept with any creature brave enough to crawl between her thighs."

"Me? Who knows, because as you've so delicately pointed out, my mother is a whore," I noted, studying the way his eyes narrowed on me as he lifted his nose, inhaling deeply. "You want to sniff my ass too?" I assumed he was an alpha wolf, but the power radiating off of him wasn't anything I'd felt before.

"You should leave before it's too late, witch." His men chuckled behind him, and I narrowed my eyes on him, letting my eyes slide down his frame before coming up to frown as if he were lacking. "Your kind is nothing but fucking trouble."

"You don't know me, so I suggest you stop stereotyping me with other witches. I'm not leaving because some asshole tells me to leave. I have it on good authority that, at this moment, no Hecate witch sits on the council, which means there is a line to get into this realm that isn't getting pushed through. Tell me I'm wrong, oh great King of Haven Falls?" He stared me down with coldness in his gaze that sent ice humming through my veins. "Without one on the council, the covenant cannot award citizenship to immortals wishing to enter this realm. They need our bloodline present to approve those applications, and the process calls for a vote from each original bloodline, or did that change when you proclaimed yourself a king?" I waited for him to say something to counter it, but his eyes just gazed into mine, until I swallowed hard, my confidence shaking as he continued to watch me chillingly. "Mmm, didn't think so. Not even a self-proclaimed king has the authority to overthrow the covenant."

"Aria," he said, tasting my name on his tongue while I smirked. I had expected him to argue, not to step closer and lift my chin. His touch sent butterflies racing through my insides. "I don't care who the fuck you are, or what last name you throw around. I own this fucking town. I will eat you for breakfast, little girl, and I enjoy eating pretty things."

"I hope that's not a metaphor for eating pussy! Aria is a virgin, and someone has to pop that overly ripe cherry!" Kinvara shouted, and I turned, staring at her. The entire clearing was dead silent after her words had filled it.

I blushed as the male studied me, noting the reddening in my cheeks. He smirked wolfishly, which caused my eyes to lower to his sensual mouth. I pulled my face away from his touch, shooting Kinvara a deadly glare as she shrugged innocently.

"Hey, I'm all for you getting that cherry eaten. Gods know you need to get some before you explode," she offered, wincing.

"Shut up, Kinvara, you're not helping the situation," Sabine groaned.

He inspected me, unnerving me with the intensity of his stare. Lightning crashed above us, and I peered up, staring at the sky covered in dense clouds. It struck again beside us, causing my eyes to narrow as my sisters jumped. The male had yet to look away from me, and when my gaze moved back to his eyes, there was something sinister within them. The wind picked up, howling eerily, sending my hair whipping against my face. I turned my back to the male, staring at where the lightning continued to strike without stopping. I stepped back absently, unable to shake the feeling that something was in the woods, watching us.

I bumped into something hard and unmoving. I looked over my shoulder before staring up into stormy eyes that narrowed on me as he inhaled once more. The heat of his body slithered over my bare flesh, but the power he exuded was worse than the heat. Tearing my gaze from his, I watched as a dark shadow slipped from the forest.

"What the hell is that?" I whispered, barely loud enough to be heard over the crashing of the lightning as it hit the ground.

"You tell me, Aria," he demanded, touching my waist, causing my skin to pebble into goosebumps from the single brush of his fingers.

"Mine," it hissed as if it was the ugly little bugger,

Gollum, from *Lord of the Rings*. "Aria Hecate is mine!" it screeched, causing me to tilt my head.

"Pass," I muttered. "That's not ominous or anything."

"Come to me, Aria. Let me taste your sweetness, little one," it continued.

I didn't need an invitation. I exploded into action, running toward the creature as power erupted around me. It smiled, waving its hand, beckoning me closer. I stopped where it had been, turning in a full circle only to find not a single trace of the beckoning creature. My hands lifted, uprooting trees from where they attached to the ground, holding them suspended in the air as I peered around, finding no sign of the creature. Slowly and methodically, I placed the trees back into the ground. Lightning crashed beside me, and I turned, inhaling the scent of burned ozone before veering toward my sisters, running right into a chest that smelled of heavenly male.

I peered up, frowning at him suspiciously. His hands captured my waist, pulling me against him as he peered down. "Let me go now," I stated coldly.

"Witch, huh?" he hissed. "Witches do not control the elements, nor do they have enough power on tap to uproot hundreds of trees, let alone to place them back into the ground."

"You don't get to fondle me or ask me questions. I don't even know your name," I ground out, studying him as his touch sent a pulse of electrical current racing through me.

"It's Knox. What the fuck are you, Aria?"

"Mmm, what the hell are *you*? Not an alpha wolf; your eyes aren't blue enough. Not an incubus, because you're not oozing enough sex for me to toss my clothes down and beg you to touch me. Not a demon, because you don't carry their scent. The writing on your arms suggest you aren't from here, so who the fuck are you, Knox? And why are you in my town?"

"I asked you first."

"Wouldn't you like to know," I whispered, licking my lips as he watched. "Let me go, asshole. I can already tell that I'm not going to like you. So, unless you plan on stealing a base, get the fuck off of me. I'm not into baseball."

"Afraid of the bat, or just not good playing with balls?"

"It's the balls. I always seem to make them explode unexpectedly. No one seems to like it when their balls explode prematurely."

"That depends on within whom they explode."

I stuttered for a retort and then clamped my mouth closed, blinking at his statement. Well, that backfired. "Keep your balls away from me."

"Afraid you may like my dick?" he asked, lifting his hand to push away a stray strand of hair. "Be a good girl, and I may even let you suck it."

"You two going to fuck, or you want a few more minutes alone?" Luna asked, watching us.

I ignored her, pulling my arm from Knox's hold before I sidled up next to him, watching as he studied me. "I wouldn't suck your dick if it contained the last air molecule in the entire universe, *puppy*. You're not man enough to handle me, anyway. You're probably like every other male on this planet who thinks bitches should bow down and worship that tiny little thing between your legs. I don't fucking bow to anyone. I sure as fuck don't bow to "some self-conceited, self-absorbed, self-appointed king" to a town that should be burned to ashes and destroyed, asshole," I muttered as I turned, marching back to where my sisters stood, listening to everything we said. "Let's go before something else welcomes us back or tries to kill us."

"I suggest you be at the council meeting tomorrow and learn the new laws of Haven Falls. If you fuck with me, little girl, I will fuck you back. I don't have mercy when I fuck my enemies. If you don't like the new laws, you can get the fuck out of my town."

"Who says I would ever want mercy from you?" I snorted as I spun on him, lifting a brow in question. "You don't scare me, Knox. You don't even register on the scale of things I fear."

"Yeah, let's test that fucking theory, shall we?" he asked. A loud crashing noise exploded, and the world vanished around me.

CHAPTER
3

I grabbed on to Knox as the world stopped spinning and buried my face against him. I knew he'd moved us in a way that only certain immortals could, a gift from the gods to the strongest, most powerful of creatures.

My breathing intensified, growing rapid as I struggled to calm my reaction to being up too high above the ground. The air was thinner, which meant we were high above the town, in the highest peak of the tallest mountain, teetering on something I couldn't see. My feet couldn't find anything to stand on, and when I peered up, sea-blue eyes studied me with interest.

"Scared yet?" he uttered huskily.

"What the hell are you?" I whispered, peering down the precarious height of the drop as my heart kicked into rapid beats. Knox lifted his hand to cup my cheek, and I held on tighter as rocks slid off the cliff he held me over.

"What the hell are *you*, Aria?" he countered curiously, studying me as he brushed his thumb over my cheek.

"I don't know," I replied through quivering lips, my body reacted to the fear of being held over the edge, and yet not. Knox held me there, my feet never touching the ground, but I didn't fear falling with him holding me. "My mother never told me, other than I was evil."

"Are you afraid of me?" he asked, lowering his mouth to brush his lips over mine, sending a wealth of heat rushing through me. "Because you should be terrified of me," he chuckled darkly as his chest rattled, echoing through the mountains. "You have no idea what scared is. If you were smart, Aria, you'd run now. You enter my town, you play by my rules. I own everything and everyone. You won't like me or the changes I have made."

"I guessed that already. I don't want to be here, but shit happens, and here we are. You may own everything, but you don't own everyone. You don't own me, Knox. Or should I call you *Your Majesty*?" I snorted as he glared at me. "Don't expect me to bow, Knox. I get on my knees for no one."

"Mmm, you'd look so much better on your knees with something in that smart little mouth of yours. Too bad you're a witch."

"What the hell did witches ever do to you?" I snapped, exasperated with his slurs against us. Not all witches were the same, and to box us all into one group was shit.

"Everything, I hate everything about you and your kind," he snarled, exposing raw emotion that made my heart squeeze in warning. "You're the epitome of evil, wrecking lives just because you have the power to do so. You murder the innocent and destroy lives so fucking easily because you never have to wait around to see the end results."

"Don't hold back on me now," I said, grinning at him.

"You're all worthless bitches who destroy everything you touch. Not to mention you fuck anything and anyone willing to breed your poisonous wombs."

"I've murdered no one in my life. I also haven't felt the urge to want a man, nor wreck his life to take him by force. No man has touched me, Knox, nor will I lower myself to resort to murder to get fucked. Don't stereotype me. I'm not like other witches, of that you can be certain. I do, however, leave destruction in my wake when someone hurts one of my own. How about we make a deal right here, right now? You stay the fuck away from me, and I'll stay away from you."

"This town isn't big enough for that to happen, Aria."

"You'd be surprised at what I can do in small spaces."

"You stink of the need to be bent over and fucked."

"Then plug your nose, because it won't be you who bends me over," I snapped, hating that my nipples were hard from the electricity that was rushing through us.

Butterflies were having a party within my stomach, and something was happening to my brain. Usually, I was smarter than this. Normally, I didn't flirt with death. This man was a predator, which kind I wasn't sure of, but there were sharp edges to his persona that screamed it. The way he watched me for any minute reaction stuck in my craw, and then there was my reaction to him.

I didn't notice things about men, never cared to, and yet I already knew his eyes held flecks of sapphire in their oceanic depths. Knox's hair wasn't brown; it was a sandy blonde, appearing darker beneath the shadows of the moon's pale light. His body was built for speed, not strength. He was strong and didn't need strength from his physique to accomplish his goals because he was intelligent.

"Either kiss me or put me back on the ground. I have shit to get done tonight, Knox."

He smiled, lowering his eyes to linger on my mouth before he once again moved us to the ground, but he did more than that; he froze time and space. I felt his mouth brushing against mine even though I couldn't see him, then exhaled as I watched the dark SUV driving away from us. He'd taken me back and frozen time. He'd frozen time on *me*! No one had ever been able to use magic on me, which had puzzled everyone, but then we had no idea who fathered Amara or me. I swallowed down fear and turned, staring at my sisters, who watched me back.

"He freaking froze me," I admitted through trembling lips.

"That isn't good."

"No, that's not good at all." I stared at the taillights, wondering who the hell he really was. I wasn't leaving until I figured out what happened to my sister. I refused to be chased out of town by some dick who got off on being a bully.

"His presence here is troubling," Sabine announced, forcing us all to turn toward her. "You know how we have to enter the Nine Realms and show our presence there? The House of Witches may be where Amara has gone. I've heard of a plan before, where if one of us was to remain in the Nine Realms, or show up when it wasn't time, an assassin would be sent out to hunt them. What if he is here looking for Amara, and she is hiding?"

I chewed my lip absently, wondering if what she said was true. It wasn't impossible. I mean, we were supposed to send another Hecate witch to the House of Witches soon. It was a show of force, reminding the people of why they held the castle, and to show our approval for the king and queen we'd chosen to rule in our place. It also reinforced the magic of the court, something only our bloodline could do since we created the land. Without us returning there once a year, magic would fade from existence in the Nine Realms.

Each original bloodline had a duty to return to the Nine Realms once a year. This reinforced their power to the land while showing strength behind the rules, assuring the people the kings and queens of our choosing could lead in our stead. It reinforced their rule while replenishing the magic.

"You think she went back early?" I was unable to shake the fear that slithered down my spine.

"She was always eager to go, Aria. It's a possibility. It makes more sense than her being with Freya."

"Sabine, it is against the covenant to enter the Nine Realms without gaining a pass, and we already know she didn't get one. There are guards posted everywhere.

How would she even get in?" I asked, a million scenarios running through my head. "I also don't think Knox is an assassin. Assassins don't announce their presence, they just kill you. Knox is…deadly, but he isn't exactly hiding it or his power. He just froze me in time and then took me to the top of a cliff, dangling me over the edge. Knox is a king, of which realm is anyone's guess. I am not marking him off as a suspect, but something about him is calling to me, and that terrifies me."

"Calls to you, how?" Sabine asked, narrowing her eyes on me.

"I don't know, almost like he senses whatever is within me, and it senses him. The noise he made, I felt the back of my throat starting to move as if it would echo the sound. I've never felt an intense need to do anything other than magic, but whatever he did, altered something within me. Almost as if he sensed it and awoken it from slumber."

"You're almost twenty-five, so if he is awakening whatever your other half is, let him. We will need all the help we can get to find Amara." Sabine scrutinized me carefully and then motioned to the car. "Let's go home, ladies."

I watched my sisters loading into the cars and exhaled slowly. Knox was different, and not in a good way. I had responded to his touch, and I never responded to any man's touch. My body sizzled with excitement and fear. It was red-hot, as if embers had ignited into flames and were burning within me. That would be a problem, one I'd have to handle with delicate steps.

I wasn't about to end up dead while searching for Amara, not if she'd been willing to leave us. I hated that it was a possibility, or that she had vanished without a trace. People didn't just vanish; they didn't just disappear without leaving a trail. She'd left a trail; I just had to find it and figure out what had happened to my twin sister. She could be out there right now, wishing I had come sooner to save her.

"Are you getting in?" Sabine asked, and I nodded, moving to the car.

CHAPTER
4

We pulled up to an ancient mansion, the House of Magic, around one in the morning. The enormous weeping willow trees I'd spent endless summers beneath seemed to wave a friendly hello as I jumped out of the SUV and eyed the house. The wards hummed in our presence; runes danced in an erotic sway as they settled into place to open the house for us.

Everyone waited, holding their breath as I stepped over the wards and into the front yard. We controlled the house with living magic, which meant it could either accept you or reject you. Occasionally, it would sense we weren't full witches and would lock us out.

I turned to tell everyone it was safe when a large house caught my eye. It was massive and sat on the corner of the block, with property boarding the edge of ours. It hadn't been here the last time we were, because I would have remembered something so beautiful. It almost looked out of place, putting the rest of the houses on the large block to shame.

The gate spread around the house, adorned with the symbol of a K surrounded by ravens in flight to mimic a circle. Who the hell built a house on our block of that magnitude without being taken to task for the monstrosity of it?

The other houses were all set in front of their properties that stretched for miles and miles behind the actual block. They'd built them to mirror human homes in case the barrier protecting Haven Falls was breached or failed. You could walk through a basic yard before reaching the front of the mansion, but what spread out behind each was an oasis of landmasses.

"So, the wards are still in place. The house is undisturbed. Amara's car isn't here, which may mean she left willingly," Luna pointed out. "I don't smell human flesh rotting, but there's some bad fruit inside and something else I can't pinpoint from outside."

I eyed Luna before shaking it off internally. I'd be a liar if I said I wasn't preparing for the worst. Amara wasn't flakey. She was the one who went to town to defend our family—or had until recently. She was my sister, the one I'd shared a womb. She didn't leave without telling me, and she sure as hell wouldn't leave us to worry about her.

Starting toward the house, I whispered the spell to unlock the door and flick on the porch light, but the light didn't come on. Inside, I whispered the spell to ignite the candles, and nothing happened. Swallowing, I scrunched up my face.

"There's no power." I felt along the wall before

stubbing my toe on something hard. "Shit," I groaned. Reaching, I tried the next switch, but again nothing happened. "There's no power or candles."

"It's the House of Magic. What the hell do you mean there are no candles?" Sabine asked incredulously.

"The other houses have power, how is it we don't?" Kinvara asked, standing beside me, which caused me to jump in the darkness.

"Jesus! Don't do that," I huffed, holding my hand against my heart. "I'll try the breaker, but we may have to wait until morning and call someone to have it replaced. Someone should run to the shop to get candles and food. I'm starving."

"And beer, or wine, maybe both," Luna said. "I can't see shit here."

"It's the wards; they're blocking everything but your magic. Only the Hecate bloodline magic works within the property lines." Sabine had been a little over twenty when we left here. It made her the oldest, or at least the oldest that we knew of. "I'll take a few with me to the store and see what we can find."

"I'll try the electrical box," I muttered.

"I'm going too!" Kinvara screamed, and Luna and the others followed Sabine, leaving me alone in the darkness.

"Thanks, assholes." I followed the wall based on my memory and opened the basement door. I slowly worked my way down the stairs, feeling the steps before I trusted myself enough to put both feet on them.

On flat ground, I whispered the spell to ignite the

flames within the candles once more, but the basement remained dark. The altar was down here, which consisted of candles, meaning either someone had been inside the mansion, or no one had for some time. My hand slid over the wall, finding the metal box and opening it as my nail broke from yanking on it. "Son of a bitch," I groaned, smelling the blood from the broken nail, which had split past the cuticle.

Nothing happened when I flipped on the basement breaker. I then tried the main breaker switch yelping as sparks shot from the box, causing strange noises to sound from outside the house.

Groaning louder, I started toward the stairs, taking the same path until I reached the top of the steps and entered the kitchen. Power sizzled over my flesh as I searched the darkness, finding nothing out of the ordinary. Shutting the downstairs door, I peeked out the back window, noting that now all the houses sat in the dark.

"Shit," I muttered, rubbing my temples in frustration. My hands settled on the counter briefly before I spun around, sensing the disturbance again. I swung blindly, intending to hit whatever or whoever was in front of me and slipped on something wet on the floor. I slipped again, dropping to my knees, fumbling, and grasping on to anything I could get a hold of as I went to the floor.

I latched my fingers onto something solid, and it didn't give. Exhaling, I lifted myself up on the cloth, only to realize it was attached to something hard. It also smelled of sensual, masculinity, and if I let go, I'd be flat on the floor, at Knox's freaking feet.

CHAPTER
5

The entire house was bathed in shadows. I still held on to the body I'd grasped on to as I fell. Closing my eyes, I fought for any strength to get to my damn feet without falling flat on my ass again. Heat burned my cheeks, and I popped my eyes open, peering up at him with the hope that his eyesight was as bad as mine in the dark.

"You lied, Aria," a rich, deep voice said in front of me.

"What, what are you doing here?" I snapped angrily.

"You're on your knees, and it's a very good look on you."

"Why are you in my *house*?"

"You blew the power out in mine and everyone else's," he growled irritably.

"Not likely, they only allow the original families to live on this block, Knox. You are not an original," I mumbled.

"Light a fucking candle, witch."

"There isn't a candle in the entire house, jerk." I righted my top, relieved that he hadn't been able to see most of my breasts that became exposed in my fall. My skirt was askew, but it wasn't revealing anything indecently, so I ignored it.

A lighter flicked, and a candle flame danced to life in his hand. He sat it on the counter before instructing a male I hadn't even noticed was there to retrieve more from their house. Frowning, I had been about to point out we didn't need their charity when his brow lifted, as if he had read my thought, or knew my intention. My mouth closed as my shoulders slumped in defeat.

He picked up the candle and held it in front of his face, and I gaped at him openly. On the side of the road, beneath the moon's fluorescent light, he'd been decent to gaze at. In the soft glow of the candlelight? He was sex incarnate, primal, predatory, and all wrapped into one dangerous package. Knox was frightening to be with alone. He was the type of creature virgins sacrificed their lives for with the mere thoughts of sex once they reached the promised lands. His dark hair was ruffled, and he was shirtless, as if I'd interrupted him mid-virginal sacrifice.

My eyes slid over his chiseled abs, pausing on the ravens drawn in stages of flight on his hip. The man had been created from the paintbrush of a skilled artist, dripped with masculinity. He was then sent out into the world with the sole purpose of dropping female panties or melting them. My gaze lifted, locking with his as a guilty flush made my cheeks heat with embarrassment.

"Electrical box?" he asked with a slightly raised

eyebrow as if I bored him with my endless gawking.

I turned, intending to show him the way, and slipped on the floor, only for him to catch my arm and then pull me toward him until my flesh touched his, igniting with heat as if he'd set me on fire.

"Can you try not to break your pretty neck until I leave?" he snapped.

I righted my frame, inwardly giving myself a mental shake for acting like an idiot in front of him. He kneeled down, exposing the powerful lines of his back and the ravens that flowed from his hip to his shoulder blade. I leaned over him, staring down at the red substance on the floor, and narrowed my gaze on it as he pushed a finger through it and brought it up to his nose.

"There is blood covering the entire floor," he announced.

"What?" I asked, staring at my dress that was now covered in blood, which the candlelight exposed. I stared at my palms and groaned loudly. "That's not right. The wards were up. I only disturbed them when I entered the yard," I mused, thinking out loud. The blood was cold but fresh enough to still be wet. I pulled my hair out of my ponytail and fixed it, oblivious to the fact I was covering the silver strands in crimson. It was something I did when I was nervous or worried. "No one was inside the house. I was the first one in." I shook my head absently, staring back down at the blood.

"You might want to stop touching yourself. You're starting to look like a murder victim; it's giving me a fucking hard-on."

"Shit," I groaned, wiping it off on my ruined dress.

"The box is this way." I replayed his words as I bent over to undo my boots so I wasn't traipsing blood through the house. The plastic soles were shit on slick surfaces, and I was clumsy enough on my own. Once I'd set the boots on the counter, I tiptoed around the trail of blood and then paused as my gaze followed it to the basement door. "That's impossible. I was just down there and didn't slip in blood."

"I'm surprised you didn't break your bloody neck," he muttered, grabbing my hand as he made his way to the door. "Stop fighting me." He pulled me closer to him, uncaring that I was trying to take my hand from his.

"Right? Because I know you so well, don't I? I'm about to walk into a dark basement with you, and for all I know, you could be a serial killer."

"It wasn't human blood, Aria. If I wanted to kill you, I'd have fucking done it already. I wouldn't drag you into the basement and kill you there. I'd do it right fucking here to make a statement."

"That's exactly what a killer would say. You know it's always the blonde who dies first, right?"

"Your hair is silver, not blonde."

"Yeah, well, maybe holding hands with you disturbs my feminine sensibilities."

"Are you afraid of being alone with me in the dark, little girl?"

"Absolutely," I said, nodding as a smile spread over his face. "You know I'm not that little, right? I'm five-three, which is only a smidge under the average for women." He turned around, looming over me as he peered down, locking eyes with me, making me feel tiny and insignificant.

"Are you always this annoying?"

"I'm not annoying. I'm nervous. I don't enjoy being alone with you. I don't like the dark. Darkness doesn't bother me per se, but dark places unnerve me."

"Witches aren't afraid of the dark," he breathed.

"Yeah, normal witches don't have mothers who lock them in dark cells telling them evil belongs in the shadows. That which is born of darkness must be returned to the darkness from which it came; I did." I chewed my lip, unwilling to meet his stare as my internal scream sounded of the child I'd been, terrified of the darkness. Amara had found me, freeing me, much to Freya's ire. She'd always found me, and yet I couldn't sense her to help her now.

"That's a sad story, little witch," he mumbled absently.

"It's life," I retorted. "Let's go."

"In a hurry to be alone with me now?" he asked, hiking a dark brow up his forehead.

His skin was bronzed, probably from long vacations in the tropics sipping drinks with fancy umbrellas. Unlike my pale skin that barely tanned at all. The last vacation I'd had was to the kiddy pool we'd bought and set up lounge chairs around, sunbathing while we drank margaritas, pretending we were in the Bahamas.

Knox turned, moving down the stairway slowly as I followed close behind him. He'd yet to release my hand, which I was sure he held because it bothered me.

Once we reached solid ground, the wind picked up and blew the candle out. I quickly whispered the spell to ignite the flame and watched as it leapt to life.

He moved to the box, opening it before he held the candle up and exposed the wire. Rats. Not figuratively, but literally. The wiring had been chewed apart, exposing wires that had touched together and shorted out because of it. I expelled the air from my lungs and then screamed as something ran over my bare foot. I spun around, backing up until I was against Knox's frame.

"The little witch fears rats too?" he purred against the shell of my ear.

"They're rodents and carry the plague."

Lips brushed my ear, sending heat swirling through my entire body until every nerve ending exploded to life within me. "You're right, you're not normal. Aria the witch, afraid of the dark and rats," he murmured before I felt his nose touching my hair, inhaling it. "You smell of blood and roses."

I turned my head, staring at him. "I thought you didn't like witches?"

"I don't, but you don't smell like a witch. You don't act like one or wield magic as you should. You're a puzzle, and I like to tear puzzles apart."

"You figured all that out in the little time you've known me? You don't know me. You know nothing about me."

"You don't like the dark if there are walls around you, boxing you in. Your shampoo is rose-scented, and you add your own concoction to it to enhance the scent.

You don't pull from nature to wield magic, you just fucking use it without thought. Your eyes are turquoise, but when you're turned on, they're more blue than green. When you're angry, they're more green than blue. I'd hate to look into them when you cried because they're the kind of eyes that expose a soul and everything within it when you're wounded. You're five-foot-three, almost the national average for women but a smidge shorter. And you have pretty titties with little pink nipples that get hard at the sound of my voice when it is lowered. You're also a virgin. I know that not because of what your sister said, but because you reek of the need to be bent over and made into a woman."

"They do not!" I snapped, crossing my arms over my chest. "And I do not."

"Prove to me that they're not hard right now." His voice escaped his throat as a mix of lust and gravel that had my nipples hard enough to cut glass.

"Most of that stuff I have told you myself," I said, changing the subject as his eyes lowered with a smirk covering his mouth.

He shrugged his broad shoulders. "I still know it, and it is true." He looked around the room and paused as he took in the skeletal remains on the ancient altar. "Family?"

"Hecate's mate," I admitted softly since it was widely known he was in here. Or, we assumed it was who was in the basement, powering the house. Supposedly, it was Mom and Aurora's father. "The lore says that he sacrificed his life to protect his line. Some say it is Merlin himself, but I don't buy it. Hecate is the reason witches shed their inhibitions and rut like wild animals, never sticking to one male more often than not. She wanted to ensure her line never died out, so she spelled the blood to fuck like rabbits."

"And you?" he asked.

"I don't throw myself at men." I was uncertain of why I was divulging anything to him. "I am an anomaly, according to my sisters. It may be whatever I am from my father's line, but then I have no idea what or who he was."

"Because you're still a virgin," he chuckled darkly.

"That's really none of your business, and just because my sister said I was, doesn't mean I am."

"You are definitely a virgin, Aria. I can smell it on you. Your pureness, the scent of an untouched woman, is very rare. You fucking reek of it. This town will eat you alive, like a lamb to the slaughter."

"They'll try," I agreed with his assessment of the town absently before locking my gaze to his. "And they'll die. I am no lamb. I have the blood of a goddess coursing through my veins. Whatever my father added to my genes, it's powerful. Do try to leave the state of my pussy off your tongue, and out of your mouth. Keep that in mind when you are watching me, Knox."

"Why did you and your sisters really come back to Haven Falls?" he countered, catching me off guard.

"It wasn't by choice. This is the last place I ever wanted to be. My sisters are here, so I am too. Are you done interrogating me, because my sisters are home?" No sooner had I said it then the sound of laughter and chatter sounded upstairs. "Next time bring whiskey if you plan to act helpful to interrogate me, Knox. You're the king, you should know that getting a maiden to lower her guard and expose her secrets takes more than being shirtless and disarming her with a smile. You want me to spill secrets, work for it."

"Hey, we brought beer and candles! I don't think we impressed the other families, either. Most are outside, glaring at us," Valeria shouted down the stairs. "Ew, there's blood everywhere."

"Rodent blood," Luna disclosed in a bored tone. "Lots of it, too!"

"They sound fun." Knox didn't look away from me, even though I'd just called him out.

"They're the life of the party," I muttered, watching him closely.

"Are they now? One might think you would be with your inability to stay upright sober." Bright blue eyes watched me as my gaze narrowed, and a smile covered my mouth softly. I wasn't stupid; I could see him using his phone to snap photos in the darkened basement.

"You can put your phone away now. The house won't allow you to snap photos of the altar. It protects itself from intruders and spilling secrets. Goodnight, Knox." I turned, heading up the stairs without a backward glance as he followed behind me.

I accepted a beer from Luna as Knox breached the doorway, causing all chatter in the house to silent instantly. Every eye turned from his naked chest to where I sat with my bottle of Corona perched at my lips. He nodded to them, turning to me.

"There are no electricians in Haven Falls. The nearest one is two towns over, but your little altar might be an issue since he's human. Brander, my brother, is good with wiring. I'll send him over in the morning, so you stop killing the power for the entire fucking block. Goodnight, Aria."

"Night, Knox," I stated, staring at the muscles that rippled in his back with every step he took toward the door. When he vanished from sight, Luna snorted and patted me on the back.

"Girl, you better let him pluck that cherry. You don't see men like that these days. If you're not going to fuck him, let us know. He's yummy."

"You can have him," I stated. "I'm going to bed."

CHAPTER
6

Brander showed up before the sun even appeared in the sky. I opened the door, staring at him as I cleared the sleep from my eyes. We'd spent the entire night in the front room, getting drunk. Not because we'd been afraid of the dark, but because we spent most nights drunk together to ignore our personal issues. It was just easier.

The truth about witches was, we liked to party a lot. We liked to be loud and let loose. It was just easier to ignore the intense strain magic had on us than dealing with it. We compartmentalized it, stowing it away until it became too hard to contain, and we ended up letting it out at the worst time possible. That could be dangerous, considering we were supposed to keep our existence secret from the humans.

It was residue from being created, being manufactured into the most perfect magic casters this realm had ever known, or would ever know. Hecate herself was a party-driven goddess. She'd enjoyed living life fast and hard, and held back very little from the realms she'd lived within.

"You must be Brander?" Sleepily, I covered my mouth to protect him from my morning breath as I yawned.

"I am. I hear your wires got chewed, and you need some assistance?" I'd changed last night, unwilling to sleep in the dress I'd bought for my homecoming. In hindsight, that had been a terrible idea because Brander's heated gaze slid down my body before looking over my shoulder into the front room where limbs mixed in a mess of bodies, whistling low in his throat. "Lord have mercy, how many of you are there?"

"Sixteen; eight sets of twins." Crossing my arms over my black *Snitches Get Stitches* tank top, I studied him.

Brander didn't look a damn thing like Knox, other than being the same ungodly height. Where Knox's hair seemed to absorb the light and become lighter or darker based on it, Brander's was jet black and shined with a blue hue that made his blue eyes stand out more, if it was even possible. Brander's skin was lighter, as if he didn't spend his time in the sun and instead preferred the indoors. He had similar tattoos on his arms, but each one had been done in a different color of ink. The top he wore was dark blue, hiding little of the sleek build that pulsed beneath the fabric. I stepped aside, indicating he should enter.

"The electrical box is this way." He narrowed his baby blues on me, and I noted his hands were empty. "Did you bring tools?"

"I need to peek at the mess first. See what I'll need to get the job done."

I nodded, realizing it made sense for him to look at what was wrong before dragging his tools around. At the kitchen, I frowned at the dried blood and observed as he moved past it without blinking despite there being a fair amount.

It still made no sense why there was fresh rodent blood in the house when we arrived. I also couldn't explain the creature that had vanished without leaving a magical trail or a thumbprint in the air when we had arrived. I'd been unable to sense anything, other than the scent of cinnamon, which had been so faint I hadn't been sure it had been there.

Once down the staircase, I stepped aside, noting his eyes slowly took in the heavily lit altar that was being prepared for tonight.

Homecomings meant increasing the power to the altar, strengthening the connection from it to the house, which would protect us if the need arose. The skeletal figure had been refreshed, dusted off, and bathed in fresh, clean water. Quartz and Amethyst stones now circled the surrounding floor, with candles placed in the pentagram to strengthen the spell using the five-pointed star.

On the altar, next to the skeleton, were shards of Moonstones for protection and obsidian crystals for grounding magic and adding power, as well as protection for energy. Smaller, polished rocks in an impressive array of colors were styled into symbols, as a single piece of vellum sat rolled into a scroll in the skeleton's hands.

Tilting his head to the side, Brander looked at the altar before turning back to look at me. "The fuck you guys into?"

"It's strengthening the house." I ignited the sage that sat in small rose quart bowls. "Sorry, that may stink a bit. Are your senses heightened? I can extinguish it if they are." I was fishing, searching for any clue that would fill me in on what Knox was.

"I don't mind a little sage now and then, little witchy." Shrugging, he moved to the box to study the wiring.

Standing behind him, I stared at the damage done to the wires. "There's no way a rat did that kind of damage."

The wires weren't exposed, they were gnawed through, tied together to short the entire house the moment someone flipped the breaker. I had somehow narrowly escaped being electrocuted last night. Okay, maybe that was a little dramatic since I'd had rubber soles on my boots, but someone had dripped blood from the kitchen to the electrical panel. Gauging from the appearance and damage to the panel, they'd drained a giant rodent right in front of it, creating a pool of blood for some lucky asshole to stand in as they flipped the breaker.

"No, a rat couldn't have done this. This was done by a human. You see how the wires are braided? They intended to knock out the power to the house, but I'm guessing something stopped them before they succeeded in doing so. The nasty pool of blood, right there? That would have fried the poor bastard who flipped the switch since the power isn't off at the main breaker, it's just been redirected. This won't be an easy fix. See here?" Brander pointed at one of the wires behind the box. "They cut the power to something, probably a room. You will need some serious rewiring considering the age of this box."

"How much will that run us?" I asked, chewing my lip absently.

"Knox said to fix it." Rubbing his thumb over his mouth, he calculated the materials cost in his head. "Probably about three something, or so."

"Three hundred dollars?" That wasn't as bad as I had thought it would be.

Laughing, he shook his head. "No, it's going to run you about three thousand or so. Not too much, considering the amount of damage."

"No, that's not bad," I swallowed hard, hating the way my stomach flipped with the idea of finding that much money without touching the Hecate account our mother used. If we used that account, she'd know right where we were. I could overdraw a different account, but I had no idea where I'd get the money to pay it back. The shop hadn't made money since Amara vanished, and no deposits had been posted since she'd arrived here. It was another reason we'd come back. "I'll get it." Brander's lips curved into a dark smirk with my words.

Giving the skeleton a once over, he started up the stairs. "I'll be back tomorrow to pick up the money."

"Thank you." Glancing one more time at the box, I started up the stairs after him. Reaching the kitchen, I looked at Brander before I spoke. "Is Knox home?"

"Yeah, he's the prick who woke me up and sent me

over at the asscrack of dawn to assist you ladies."

"Thanks, Brander…?" I paused before tilting my head innocently. "I don't know your last name."

"I didn't offer it," he shrugged, smirking, and left the house before I could question him more.

Great, more shit to deal with for coming back to this place of hell. Like we weren't having enough issues coming home?

CHAPTER
7

I explained the situation to the others, and instead of listening to everyone complain about the lack of power in the middle of summer, I made my way to my room where I washed in a bucket of cold water from the creek out back to freshen up, since there apparently was no water either. Two hours later, I stared into the mirror, impressed that I looked even somewhat alive. No coffee had been brewed, no breakfast had been cooked, and the little water I'd gotten from the creek was ice-cold this early in the morning.

As if this homecoming hadn't been a mental fuck of ungodly proportions, it had also been the most inconvenient, sour event of the last twelve years of my life. I picked up my phone, staring at the red battery that flashed on the screen's corner, and set it back down.

On the dresser was a bottle of three hundred-year-old scotch, which had once been wasting away in the cellar. It was the one bottle I'd been saving for a celebration, but considering the clusterfuck we were in, I doubted that would happen anytime soon.

I couldn't change the situation, but I could be thankful for the asshole that was extending an olive branch, even if it was laced with thorns. Knox had been right; we couldn't call in an actual electrician since the altar couldn't be moved no matter what happened to the house. We had built the mansion around the altar. Add-on after add-on had been built until Freya and Aurora were happy with the result, which to a sane person was a mess.

The altar had been the central power source of the house before they added electricity. Instead of placing the electrical panel away from the altar, they'd damn near placed it on top of it. The floors were mazes of doors and hallways. Trying to find your bedroom drunk? Damn near impossible to achieve. It wasn't unheard of to end up in your sister's bedroom on the floor because you ended up lost in the maze.

I slipped on soft black sandals and took one last glance at the black skater dress I wore, checking my reflection before grabbing the aged bottle of scotch and heading downstairs. Fifteen minutes of zigzagging through the doors and hallways, I paused in the front room. No one had moved yet, not even Aine, who had Luna's foot in her face.

Exiting the house, I paused briefly to take in the people who sat on their porches, watching me. Welcome to Freakville, population unknown.

I closed the front door behind me, whispering a spell to seal it against harm before I started toward the largest house on the block. Okay, I wasn't sure it could be considered most impressive since it was gated and appeared to be larger than the entire block, which was saying something since all the houses here were huge mansions. It sat back further, hidden behind gates and shrubbery, unlike the others.

At the gate, I pushed the intercom button and waited, staring as the gate opened without a single noise. I walked up the driveway, noting the articulate landscaping and fountains that made up his yard. Parked in front of the house was the dark SUV he'd showed up in last night, and beside it sat a Bugatti Chiron Sport, which cost more than I'd made in my entire life. It wasn't shocking that it was a pretty ocean-blue in coloring, or that it said King One on the license plate.

I grabbed the metal knocker and pounded three times before stepping back. A man in a black tux opened the door before I'd even made it the full step back. He had keen gray eyes, and his graying dark hair was pulled back into a ponytail, away from his face.

"You're unexpected," he said, annoyed by my presence.

"I came by to apologize to Knox about last night, and to thank him for his help," I offered in the way of explaining my unannounced presence.

"Who is it, Greer?" A cultivated feminine voice asked.

"A guest for the master." Clearly annoyed, he stepped back, pushing the door open so she could see me.

"I see," she stated.

The woman had midnight-colored hair that hung in soft waves to her ass. Her eyes were outlined in dark kohl, and ruby red lips pursed with something more than disdain as she took me in. Her outfit, if you could call it that, was a sheer nightgown that left little to the imagination. Emerald green eyes studied me before settling on the bottle of scotch and then turning as power exuded into the room.

"Who is it?" Knox asked, coming down the stairs in lounge pants that probably cost more than my entire wardrobe.

"The trash has come calling, darling," she said in a sickly sweet voice. "Take it out, please. It stinks."

I bit my tongue while plastering a smile on my face to keep from returning the insult. I was on a peace-keeping mission, and calling her dirty names wouldn't achieve that goal. Knox leaned against the wall on the large, opulent staircase and studied me before his gaze dropped to the bottle of scotch.

"What the fuck do you want?"

"I came to apologize for last night. I think we got off on the wrong foot." I noted the way his stare locked with the female before slowly settling back on me. "I brought a peace offering."

Knox watched me carefully. "I doubt you have a right foot to stand on."

"Obviously, this was a mistake," I turned to leave only to find the door closed before I could get through it.

"Leaving so soon, Aria?" Knox asked huskily.

Magic exploded through me, making me jolt as it hit me. It was dark magic, slithering through my entire body as the witch watched with a look of triumphant victory shining in her eyes as my whole body trembled from the turbulent force of it.

I coughed on something, grabbing my throat as I spun on my heel, staring at the female who smirked, regarding me as I began gagging while something worked its way up my throat. I coughed again, dropping the bottle of scotch to shatter across the floor as I reached into my mouth, pulling a slithering, slimy snake from my throat before tossing it onto the marble floor. I stepped closer, smashing it until blood exploded, disturbing the otherwise pristine white marble floor.

"Lacey, what did I tell you about snakes in my house?" Knox asked in a soft, tender tone.

"Open the fucking door!" I snapped at Greer.

"Not unless the master says it is time."

"Your master and his *witch* can get bent. Open the door unless your master is willing to break the covenant of the original bloodlines. Open the fucking door."

"Let her go, Greer." Knox grinned roguishly. "Before she cries."

The door opened with magic, and men started pouring into the room. One stopped in front of me while the others passed by as if I didn't even exist.

"Jasper?" I asked in a whisper, past the swelling in my throat.

"Hells bells, Aria Hecate? You grew up." Peering at something over my shoulder, he looked back at me. "You grew up real nice, pretty girl."

"Where's your mom?" I asked, knowing his mother

was one of the few here who were decent.

"Dead," he shrugged as if it didn't bother him. "She couldn't keep her head on, I guess you could say."

I stared at him as the others crowded around me. Turning, I looked at one man whose eyes glowed amber. He had platinum hair and a pulse of power that unnerved me.

"Aren't you fucking delicious-smelling, baby girl? You smell...*nice*," he said, and I stepped back, feeling a pull from his magic. "Come to me. I want to taste your cunt."

"Does that ever work? You say, 'come here, girl, take them panties off, and I'll lick that slit right good,' and she says, 'oh, baby boy, fuck me?' Because I don't foresee that happening, do you? You and your twisted master can get bent without me. You guys are assholes." I stepped around the few who had blocked my path and headed for the gate to escape the house of horrors.

"Where are you going, baby girl? Daddy is hungry!" he called as the others laughed.

"To neutral ground, prick. Come play with me there," I called over my shoulder, slipping through the gates. The moment my foot hit the concrete, he blocked my path. I smiled coldly, staring him down as the world around us darkened and thunder sliced through the clear blue skies. His gaze lifted, and I punched him without warning, hitting him right in the throat. "Don't fuck with a witch when she's pissed off." The sensation of magic slithered over my flesh, and I turned, staring at the witch who had yet to step from the curb. "You, I'll be seeing you soon." Pulling her magic to me as my hair floated with the intense power of mine mingling with hers, I shot it back at her, and she dropped to her knees, screaming. My gaze lifted, finding Knox regarding me silently.

Turning on my heel, I left the street and moved down the sidewalk, ignoring the peeping neighbors who stared at me coldly as one of them left his yard, heading toward me. He closed the distance quickly, and I let my magic gather around me in silent warning. He didn't heed the warning, and continued coming toward me as if he planned to attack.

"The fuck are you looking at, asshole?" I demanded when the alpha stepped directly into my path. "You want some?" I asked, holding my arms up as he smirked at me.

"Fucking witch," he sneered.

I laughed coldly. "Yeah, we're back. We're all back, asshole. You want some, come get some; I'm not hard to find. Step to it if you think you're big enough, wolf, or get the fuck out of my way, asshole."

"Aria, are you starting a war already? We've not even been here for twenty-four hours, yet," Sabine said, standing with the others as they watched me posturing with the werewolf.

"No, it wasn't my intention. I didn't go looking for a fight, but I sure as fuck don't intend to back down from one," I paused, turning to stare at Knox. "I don't bow to anyone."

CHAPTER
8

Inside the mansion, I paced with pent up rage at having magic cast on me again. It wasn't something that ever happened to me, and now in less than twenty-four hours, it had happened twice. Both times, *he* had been present. I'd been stupid to think I could extend a peace offering with someone as pigheaded as that gutter swine.

"What were you thinking?" Sabine asked as Callista shook her head in silent warning.

"I thought I could extend an offer of peace! How was I supposed to know that he would allow me to be attacked in his own home! His witch cast on me, and it *worked!* A snake came out of my mouth, and not just any freaking *snake*, a black mamba. It could have freaking killed me! Then that other asshole asked to taste my cunt. And I *wanted* him to! I was defenseless, surrounded by them, and yeah, I freaking panicked."

"You're immune to magic," Callista pointed out.

"No, I *was* immune to magic. I'm not here." I paused. "If I'm not immune, Amara wasn't either. It could mean she's in his house, and nothing would penetrate it."

"You don't know that for sure, sweetie." Standing calmly beside me, Callista smiled sadly. "There's no proof, and we can't just point blame at them. You know the laws, and the council will not respond without proof."

"Knox isn't even from the original families. Who the hell is he? We've heard nothing about him, nor does he offer anything to us. The original families are all around us, the same members we grew up with. He wasn't here back then, was he?"

"No, Aria, but that alone should scare you. He came from nowhere, and every original family is at his side? You have to damn near be a god for that to happen."

"He isn't a god. The prick just wishes he was." Knocking sounded at the door, and I frowned. "I'm going to my room to wash the snake off of me. Good luck at the meeting tonight." I left the front room before anyone could argue it.

Inside my bedroom, I stripped out of the dress and tossed it onto the bed. Using magic, I rinsed my body and shivered as the magical residue clung to my flesh.

I'd reacted badly. Fear made me act with violence, it always had. Today had been no different. I'd never felt that exposed or vulnerable in my entire life, and I'd walked right into it. Moving to the closet, I opened the door and stared at the clothes I'd once owned that wouldn't ever fit me again. Not that I'd grown much since twelve, but my breasts had filled in, and my gothic phase hadn't been pleasant, nor were the clothes I'd worn.

A Tiffany-blue-colored box caught my eye, and I bent over to retrieve it as the door opened. I waited for them to speak, but they didn't, and I didn't bother to turn around because anger was humming through me.

"I'm not going to the meeting or dealing with the council today. With my luck, I'd just piss that pompous asshole off more than I already have. He's infuriating, and so condescending. Can you believe the audacity of that prick? I have been saving that bottle since I was twelve. It's now on his floor, smothered in mamba guts and utterly wasted."

I opened the box, and sorrow socked me in the gut as childhood pictures of Amara and me sat staring at me from in the box. I closed the lid, fighting the need to scream in frustration before I tossed the box down and closed my eyes, rubbing them before I groaned softly.

"I can believe the audacity of that prick," a sensual masculine voice said, making my spine stiffen. I turned, staring at Knox, where he watched me from his perch against the doorframe inside my room.

"Get out!" I could feel my face heating with anger as he continued watching me with a sinful smirk gracing his lips.

"You came onto unsanctioned ground today. That was a stupid move, little witch." He slowly walked toward me, and I stepped out of the closet, glaring at him as I waited for the house to protect me, sure it would send this asshole to his knees and make *him* bow to *me*. "You should know better than to walk onto foreign soil, Aria. You walked into my world, and you weren't invited. The rules that apply to those of the original families? They don't fucking apply on my land, nor yours."

"Screw you." I inhaled his scent as my back touched against the wall, and I stared up at him, turning to judge the distance to the door and my chances of making it out of the room before he caught me.

"You won't get there before I reach you, little girl. Promise," he uttered huskily.

His eyes leisurely slid over my body, and I winced, remembering I was damn near naked from stripping to get rid of the slimy feel of magic and snake from my skin. I was dressed in nothing but thin black lace panties and a matching bra. He paused to stand in front of me, slowly bringing his gaze back to mine.

"You hurt my fucking brother today when you punched him," he accused huskily.

"Oh, my bad," I swallowed hard, biting my lip nervously as his power sizzled over my flesh until my eyes wanted to roll back in my head. Whatever he was, he was powerful. It wasn't just power, it was raw, carnal power that tugged at my own, seeking permission to play. I felt it pushing against my barrier, itching my scalp as he tried to gain access to my mind and couldn't.

It pissed him off, his eyes narrowing as more power was used to assault my thoughts, and then my mouth opened as pain lanced through my head. My lips trembled, and my knees threatened to give out, but his knee pushed between my legs, holding me up as my head fell back, leaning against the wall. Pain split against my temples, and I fought it, holding him out of my mind. His head lowered until his forehead was against mine, his hand cupping my cheek, holding my face to his as his eyes searched my mind.

"Give me your secrets, little witch," he demanded hoarsely.

"Fuck. You. Knox," I whimpered, and a moan slipped from my throat, followed by a growl rumbling from deep in his chest as his lips brushed against mine softly. The feather-soft brush of his mouth against mine sent heat pooling between my thighs. "Go fuck your witch," I snapped, fighting against his magic. "Mister *I Don't Fuck Witches*, hypocritical prick."

"You're strong, Aria. Not stronger than me, though." He pushed his elbow against my throat, applying pressure as magic slammed into me, jarring my body and causing my teeth to chatter. "Do you know what the difference between you and Lacey is? I fucking own her. She breathes because I allow it. She is here to help me, and the moment she slips up and shows her true colors? She's finished drawing breath. She serves a purpose in my realm, and sucks a mean dick."

"Oversharing isn't caring, asshole." I slammed my magic into him and watched as he didn't even budge or blink at the magical onslaught I shot at him. "What the fuck are you?"

"The same can be asked of you?" Standing back abruptly, he watched me as I hit the ground hard on my knees before him. I gazed up, discovering him peering down at me with naked heat in his stare. "You look good on your knees, Aria."

Gasping for air, I crawled away from him with my ass pointed up in the air. I struggled to my hands and knees yelping as his hand touched the curve of my ass, finding the ravens that started on my thigh, wrapping around my leg to my navel, then further up my body. I spun around, moving to throw a punch which he easily deflected. I faked a right and threw a left punch. He dodged it, watching as he slowly stalked me again.

"How did the creature in the woods know your name?"

"I don't know."

"You're lying to me."

"I don't know!" I hissed, crying out as my knees touched the bed, and I fell back onto it. I bounced and turned, trying to escape him only for my legs to be yanked out from beneath me. He flipped me over roughly and watched as I sat up, intending to fight him. "I don't know how he knew my name, or what he was! Shouldn't you know since you're the almighty fucking king?" He smirked coldly, staring between my thighs where my lady parts were barely hidden.

"That's a pretty manicured pussy, but curious to find on a virgin. Are you just perpetually prepared to get fucked, or were you hoping I'd drink enough scotch to land in that silken trap between your thighs? You did tell me to bring some next time if I intended to interrogate you, didn't you?"

"Purely being sarcastic," I snapped. "I was born with a version of alopecia that only seems to be everywhere but my head. My aunt said it is why my hair turned silver," I admitted since it wasn't crucial to anything other than my girlie pride.

"It wasn't silver as a child?" Dropping my legs, he stepped back, crossing his arms over his chest as he stared at me.

"It was black," I shrugged. "On my fifth birthday, it turned silver overnight, and Amara's turned from blond to black. Almost like we changed places, but we aren't identical twins."

"What else happened?"

"Nothing," I lied.

"Liar," he hissed through his teeth. "Lie to me again, and you won't like what happens, but I assure you, I will."

"No offense, prick, but I'm not a huge fan of what is happening right now."

"That sassy little mouth of yours will get you fucked someday."

"Not by you," I snorted.

"I wasn't talking about your pussy."

"I'm difficult to kill."

"You're a fucking lamb in a city of hungry wolves, little girl. Eventually, someone will eat you whole. This isn't the city you grew up in. It's not a nice place anymore."

"Oh yeah, Knox? And when did it change? When you got here?" I asked, standing up to glare at him. "I'm willing to bet my tits that the moment you showed up was when shit started to get twisted around here."

"You think I care what your thought process is

or what you assume happened? Let me assure you I do not. I'm not your friend, Aria. And I'd be careful betting those pretty titties to strangers, because you might fucking lose, and I sure as hell collect my debts, especially when they're so fucking perky. No, little witch, I'm the one they call to clean shit up when it goes wrong, and this place is all wrong. I didn't become King because I wanted it; I became a king because I was fucking born one. Last chance to get out, but I have a feeling you're too fucking stupid to take my advice."

"I'm not leaving. I was born here, and I know that this is where I die. I'm not afraid of dying, but I'm no fucking lamb either. I am here because I have no other choice. My sister came here, and now she is missing. I won't leave without her."

"You won't leave here alive, no one does. At least you made peace with that." He slammed me against the bed, chuckling as he knocked the wind from my lungs, peering into my eyes while speaking in a strange language, causing the world to spin around me. He watched as his elbow blocked my airway, and I bucked against him, fighting whatever the hell he was doing to me. My legs dropped open, and he pushed against my core, inhaling as heat banked in his depths.

"Stop," I whispered hoarsely as he watched me through heated eyes that dropped to my lips before moving back up to lock with mine.

"Give me your secrets, and this ends."

"I don't have any secrets." His knee pressed against my core, and I whimpered from the pressure. Heat rushed through me as he continued pressing harder as his nostrils flared, watching as I shook with the slight compression. My body grew wet with need, and my cheeks heated with embarrassment.

"Everyone has secrets, Aria, everyone."

Footsteps sounded down the hallway, and he peered over his shoulder, listening as they continued toward the door. He exploded into ravens and vanished out the glass doors of the balcony as I lay there, struggling to put myself back together.

Whatever Knox was, he was evil. He held the kind of power creatures either craved or ran from. It had taken everything within me to keep him out of my head. Every wall I'd slammed up, he'd battered down. I'd felt him touching me without his hands upon my flesh. I'd felt his lust, his need to dominate and savage me as he'd lowered his own walls to bust through mine. He'd been too busy searching my mind even to notice I was in his, staring at a fortified crypt in his mind with more defenses than any bank vault known to mankind. Whatever he was, I was damn sure going to figure it out and bring the man to his knees.

My door opened, and the girls poured through, searching the room before eyeing the curtains that still moved from his sudden escape. Black feathers covered the floor, and my body was covered in red welts, which would bruise before morning.

"What the hell happened?" Sabine asked.

"Knox is immune to the house's defenses. He was in here," I uttered hoarsely.

"Were you doing *things*?" Callista asked carefully.

"He was throwing me around a bit if that is what you mean." I pulled the blankets over my body and shivered violently. "The house didn't even sense him, or that I was in danger."

"That's a fucking problem," Luna snapped angrily. "That needs to be remedied."

"He's immune to my magic," I continued. "He isn't like us; he isn't like any of us."

"Witches?" Callista clarified.

"No, I mean *all* of us. All the original families are susceptible to each other's powers. Knox didn't blink when I cast magic on him. He didn't fucking budge. I don't think he's one of us, and worse, I think he knows more than we do about what happened to Amara, and I intend to find out everything he knows. There's also the fact that I am susceptible to it around him. His witch was able to cast on me, and I've always been immune to all magic except for those who share our bloodline."

"You're saying that around him, you're not immune to magic?"

"That's exactly what I am saying. It's like he's my kryptonite."

CHAPTER
9

I stood in the crumpled, wilted, and very inadequate herb garden that sat behind the mansion. It was another glaring sign that Amara had been gone more than a few weeks. Her room had been pristine, and that wasn't like her at all. I was the OCD clean freak; she was the messy one.

I'd skimmed over her wardrobe, picking out a few things to borrow since we were the same size, and also because Aurora hadn't sent the truck with our clothes or household items, and we had no running water. Pushing my fingers into the soil, I fed life to plants until the garden bloomed with fresh herbs and the air scented of their mixed aromas.

Grabbing the water bucket, I moved down the wide creek that gurgled deep into the large, opulent backyard. Most families had miles and miles of luxury that covered their property, but we had nature. Witches preferred nature, needing it to draw magic from. The alpha wolves, well, they too had nature, but they used it to turn beneath the full moon. As a child, Luna and Aine could join the young male wolves to run freely, protected beneath the moon.

Bending down at the deepest part of the creek, I filled the bucket with water and then frowned when the heated water touched my hand. I stared at the creek before slowly looking around the thickly covered terrain, blocking anyone else's view with the greenery and dense vegetation.

Slowly walking back to the garden, I poured the bucket into the trench I'd dug and set it aside, retrieving dried herbs I'd picked to use tonight. Dusting off my hands, I started toward the house silently. Inside, I collected a few items and made the trek back to the creek.

I stripped down to my panties and headed toward the water with the shampoo and conditioner I'd made, gently setting them down on the flat rock that sat in the creek, pushing water in two different directions toward the adjoining properties. Pulling my panties off inside the water was tricky, but I managed it before tossing the wet undies toward the pile of clothes on the muddy bank.

The sky above me was crystal blue without a cloud in the sky. Birds chirped all around me as I soaked in the water. I leaned against the rock, resting my arms on it as I watched the house, knowing eventually, someone else would discover my little oasis, and then everyone would be in the creek, bathing with me.

Having fifteen sisters meant having nothing that was actually yours alone. Not that it bothered me; quite the opposite. I didn't have to deal with friends flaking off on me, because my friends were my sisters. I just enjoyed the solitude of being alone every once in a while. I dipped beneath the water, coming up with a bubble of laughter in my throat as a memory of Amara and me playing in the creek surfaced.

We'd spent a lot of time away from the others, craving the solitude that was elusive with the fourteen other girls around us. We'd spent countless hours down here, making mud pies, or mud shakes that we'd pretended were crafted from the finest bakeries in the Nine Realms.

She'd always wanted to be a chef or to own a bakery. In contrast, I'd wanted a bookstore that sold tonics and potions on the side, with the most extensive crystal collection in this realm. We'd made plans to save up for both, only we'd never invested our money into anything, because the moment we'd deposited into our account, Freya had taken it for the joint account we all could draw from. We hadn't been allowed to dream, not if anything we wanted wasn't with the others.

Reaching for the shampoo, I lathered my hair, inhaling the rose-scented herbs to calm my nerves from the last few days. I rinsed it out, following it with the homemade conditioner. After that, I used the soap, slowly rubbing it over my body as my eyes slipped closed. Then oceanic eyes filled my mind, forcing my eyes to open wide in horror. That wasn't happening, I told my subconscious. Not in a million years.

Something moved in the bushes, and I turned, staring at where the leaves rustled from being disturbed. I searched them for a few minutes, watching the other bushes deeper within it for any more disturbances.

"Is someone there?" I asked, waiting for whoever it was to move again. I didn't expect an answer, but I figured they would have to keep moving to escape the yard. I slipped deeper into the water until it fully concealed my body, with only my chin sticking out as my heartbeat hitched and raced faster.

My hands covered my breasts while I stared into the brush, waiting for whoever was in them to hightail it out of there. I sent magic searching, parting shrubbery while I mentally searched without leaving the water. My magic sensed no presence, finding nothing larger than a bird that sat on a branch within the thicket. I spun around to place the soap onto the rock when feet came into view. My gaze landed on the black Doc Martin boots and slowly lifted until they locked with ocean-blue eyes.

"Brave, bathing naked out here, alone," he muttered, crouching down to pick up the bottle of soap, opening the cap to sniff it. "Are you pretending to be a water nymph? Or a sprite?" he asked before closing the lid to look at me. "Which one are you today, Aria?"

"Get the hell off my land, Knox."

"Why would I do that? I own this entire town. So technically, I own your property too. Not to mention, you're causing quite the commotion with your scent. I just saved you from being eaten by a wolf, little lamb."

"There was no one there," I hissed.

"That you could see," he smirked wolfishly.

His eyes watched me sharply. I stood there, uncertain how to get to the bank without him seeing more of me than he already had. Knox seemed to come to the same idea because his smile turned wicked, and his eyes smoldered with heat.

"Turn around," I growled irritably, fighting to remain calm.

Knox's eyes left mine to stare into the brush, causing me to follow his gaze. I turned around as the air was displaced, and something moved just beyond the bushes. Something was there, something powerful, and yet my eyes couldn't see it. As if it wasn't in this realm and just beyond the portal that was thinnest here.

Splashing sounded behind me, and arms moved me until my line of sight was blocked by his body. The hair on my neck stood up, and a violent shiver rushed down my spine.

Knox growled, and something inside of me mirrored his rattle that sounded from within his chest. He peered over his shoulder, studying my face before something slammed against him, sending my naked back smashing into the rock. I cried out as pain burned my spine. I watched in horror as crimson covered the water in which I stood.

He materialized blades from thin air to cut into a monstrous-sized beast that came into sight a moment before his blades cut through it, severing it in half. My hands drop from shielding my breasts as more waves began in the water, moving directly toward us just below the surface.

Sinking into the water, I opened my eyes and stared in horror as canine legs rushed toward us, yet when I lifted from it, I saw nothing. *Invisible above the water's surface.* Sinking down again, I sent my magic slamming into the creatures, watching as it hit them hard enough to sever limbs. Rising from the water's heated depths, I gazed in the direction the creatures had been, staring at the lifeless bodies that now floated on the surface.

Hands grabbed my shoulders, and I screamed, spinning around to stare into striking blue eyes that narrowed on me. Knox pulled me to him as I stood motionless and in shock. His hands pushed me beneath the red water, and he followed, pinning me down to the rocks of the creek bed. I gasped, choking on the water that filled my lungs.

He shook his head, pulling me out of the water effortlessly. "Breathe, and fucking hold it!" he demanded, and I did without questioning him.

Once more, we sunk into the water, and he held me there, staring in the direction from where the creatures had appeared. His hand slipped around my waist, holding my naked body as his gaze slowly moved down to where my breasts bobbed with the waves of the water. My hand rose to slap him, which happened in slow motion and didn't do much other than to cause a wicked grin to lift over his smug lips. I started to push up for air, but he held me to him, pulling my mouth to his, breathing air into my starving, burning lungs.

The moment his lips touched mine, shocks shot through me until my eyes grew heavy with the need to explore his lips further. I pulled back, staring at him with confusion and anger at myself for falling for his shit. I started toward the surface again, only for him to shove me away from his body as claws shredded his arm where I had just been hiding.

Magic erupted from me, assaulting the creature that

attacked him until blood and parts of it floated to the surface. Knox stood, grabbing me without asking. I hissed as he connected with my breast, sending a shiver of fear and excitement rushing through me. He didn't stop until I was sitting on the rock, with his back to my front side.

"Get on my back, now." He stated through gritted teeth.

"What the hell were those things?" I quickly wrapped my arms and legs around him.

"Get on before more show up, woman!"

"I am on," I argued, yelping as he started out of the water.

All around us, bloody parts of dead wolf-like creatures floated in the creek, which seemed to have grown in size since I'd entered it. He reached back, holding on to my thighs as he made his way to the bank, and then bent down without warning, grabbing my wet, discarded panties.

"Next time, shower in the fucking house," he warned.

"We don't have running water, jerk. Besides, I've played in this creek countless times before today and have never been attacked."

"When you were a child," he argued. "You weren't of breeding age, and the portals hadn't been weakening between the realms. Either fucking listen to what I say, or get the fuck out of here before you end up eaten."

"I was fighting right beside you, you pompous asshole. I saved *your* life!" I hissed vehemently, and he snorted.

"The fuck you did," he laughed. "The only reason I was here was because even I could smell your female pheromones alerting the entire Nine Realms that there was a bitch in heat."

"I'm not in heat, asshole."

"You are, you so fucking are," he scoffed. "You reek of it, your sisters do too. That means every monster that is itching to get into this realm will be making a move to breed you witches. As if you weren't a nuisance enough as is," muttering, he started in the opposite direction of the back door to the mansion.

"Wait," I growled in exasperation. "Where are you taking me?"

"To my house."

"Oh, hell, no, you're not!" I fought to get down from his back even though he held my legs. "Put me down!" I demanded, abruptly getting my wish. Knox dropped me to the ground as he turned, staring at me with a look that said he wanted to snap my neck and be done with it. "You aren't taking me anywhere."

"You think that was all of them? You're sadly mistaken, Aria. Those were weak parasites making a move to land easy pussy. You were out in the open, exposed, and easy to reach."

"You could have warned us that the portals were weakening. You didn't see fit to warn us, though, did you?" I argued, growing acutely aware that I was stark-ass naked, and he either didn't care or was pretending not to notice. His nostrils flared a moment before he ripped his bloodied shirt off his back, exposing claw marks that were jagged in the skin they'd ripped open. "You're hurt," I whispered.

"Put the fucking shirt on, now."

I slipped it on, noting it smelled of him and was soaking wet as it clung to my flesh like a second skin. His stare dropped to my breasts, noting the peaked tips of my nipples and then the curve of my thighs.

"Your house isn't fucking safe yet. Your sisters are being collected, and you will be at my house until you can gather the items needed to do the blessing on this one. Sabine agreed since she was actually at the fucking council meeting and has been filled in on everything that's been happening. You weren't there, big fucking surprise."

"I was trying not to see *you*."

The temperature dropped as he smiled coldly. His arm still dripped blood, and I noted the abundance of it splattering the ground. Knox stepped closer, and I stepped back, watching the tick in his jaw while it hammered with his anger.

"You have no fucking electricity, no water, and no protection. You're ripe for plundering, and as we speak, monsters are lining up to fucking wreck that virgin pussy. Aria, you have five minutes to collect anything you need for the next twenty-four hours before I drag your naked ass to my house, kicking and screaming without your fucking consent."

"Fine," I stated, glaring daggers at him. "I'll be right back," I muttered, not trusting him. I paused as he moved to follow me. "I don't need a bodyguard."

"Oh, but you do!" he snapped.

"Does your arm hurt?"

"I'll live."

"Pity that," I muttered beneath my breath as we started back toward the house.

CHAPTER
10

Inside the house, my sisters sat on the couches with men surrounding them. I paused as every set of eyes turned to look at Knox and me as we entered. Sabine rose, moving swiftly to where I stood, searching me for injury.

"Are you okay? I should have come outside before preparing the crystals to tell you what was happening." She rushed the words out, searching every inch of me before exhaling. "Why are you naked?"

"I was bathing in the creek," I admitted. "The garden was dead, so I fixed it to procure the herbs needed for the blessing."

Sighing, Sabine watched me closely. "A lot is happening here that we were left in the dark about."

"Like monsters entering through illegal portals? Got that memo firsthand," I snorted.

"The portals between Nine Realms are closed because something was attacking and weakening the portals to the Human Realm. It is allowing creatures and beings from the Nine Realms to escape. They seek to take advantage of the law stating that if they breed with an original bloodline while in this realm, they can stay because their offspring will connect them to this realm. It's open season on immortals that have been given safe passage into this realm, Aria."

"Then, we strengthen the portals. That is the job of witches from the original line. That is why we were included."

"Yes, but to bring the portals down in their current state, they'd need a witch with Hecate blood running through their veins."

"Two minutes," Knox said curtly, cutting Sabine off, causing my eyes to turn and hold his.

If what they said was true, it wasn't just bad; it was a catastrophe in the making. I chewed my lip, studying Sabine before I dropped my eyes to the bags rested at their feet. Without saying another word, I started through the house, noting the shadow that followed me. I'd roll my eyes, but my head hurt enough, and the scrape on my back was raw and ached.

Once we reached my bedroom, I grabbed the duffle bag I'd yet to unpack and turned to eye him. "If this is some kind of game to get us to leave town, it won't work. I don't care what is here or who is coming for us. My sister is here somewhere, and either you or someone else knows where Amara is."

"She may be dead already, or with the other missing members of the original families that have vanished without a fucking trace. She alone couldn't bless this house or reinforce it against an attack. I warned your sister to leave town; she refused. I couldn't fucking demand people leave, and I sure as fuck didn't plan to babysit the mess unfolding here.

"My job is simple, fix the fucking portals and get this place stable enough to open the fucking portals in the Nine Realms again. You and your sisters? You are nothing but more trouble for me to deal with. You just brought thirteen wombs to Haven Falls that are fertile and just begging to be bred. Two more are en route, according to your sister. That's fifteen unclaimed bitches that can be forced to carry babes for those seeking to enter this realm before we fix the portals."

"You can't fix it without me, and Amara isn't dead. I'd feel it, and yeah, she may be missing, but she sure in the fuck isn't dead, so don't say it again. Let's go."

"Put your pants on and stop making it so easy for them to sniff your cunt."

"Wow, crude much?" I growled low in my chest before I dropped the duffle and bent over with his shirt concealing my naked backside to dig through the bag. I pulled out lacy panties and a pair of black *PINK* joggers, standing back up to stare at him.

"Turn around, please," I said hoarsely with emotions pushing through my mind with a tightening in my chest that unnerved me. Knox didn't argue and gave me his back while I pushed my legs through both items and yanked them up before he changed his mind. "I'm done." I hated the tremor in my tone from imaging my sister somewhere being tortured, or worse, raped.

Knox didn't wait for me to follow him as he led the

way out of the bedroom and into the hallway. Snorting, he turned at each doorway, heading down a new hallway without me needing to show him where to go. It told me he knew the layout of the house, and that bothered me. It also worried me he seemed to be able to pop into existence with little thought and often did when I was vulnerable or exposed. My magic had worked with him this time, as if he'd allowed me to keep it.

"Why did you save me?"

Shaking his head, he growled at me through gritted teeth. "It wasn't my idea to save you. Your sisters refused to leave without you."

"You can stop me from using magic, how?" I demanded and then cried out as he pushed me against the wall without me even seeing the asshole move.

"I am not playing fifty fucking questions with you, little lamb. You should be dead right now or bent over being fucked, neither of which is my fucking problem. Someone wants you alive, someone who needs their fucking head checked if they think you and your sisters are worth saving. Do me a favor and shut your pretty fucking mouth and walk." Snarling, he marched forward, his chest rattling low as a growl escaped his lips. My chest echoed the sound, and he peered down, smirking as if he thought it was cute. Bastard.

"You're a prick." I pushed him out of my way and marched down the hall with my wet hair trailing droplets over the carpet.

The moment we reached the front room, I headed toward the door when a man stepped in front of me. He gazed down at me through ice-blue eyes and inhaled deeply. The smile that covered his mouth wasn't friendly; in fact, it was anything but. He lifted his gaze over my head and then stepped back the same moment something slammed against the front door. My hand raised, and I prepared for impact as the second noise came, shaking the entire house. The door flew open, and a male stood in our path.

"You're mine," he hissed.

"Hard pass." I lifted my fingers and snapped them, causing his spine to sever and his body to twist before dropping to the ground, lifeless. I stepped over him, whispering a spell that turned the corpse to dust. On the front steps, I paused, turning to peer over my shoulder, where Knox watched me silently from inside the house. "Five minutes is up, let's go."

His mansion was opulent, I noted as they showed us to the foyer where we were told to wait. The men who stood around the room watched us warily, noting every minuscule move we made. Luna eventually sat in one of the chairs while I frowned, pulling the shirt away from the scratch on my spine from the rock. It seemed like hours passed in complete silence before Knox reemerged with his witch close on his heels.

"Sabine, this is Lacey," Knox announced. "She can help you with what you need for the blessing."

"Pass," I grumbled.

"Aria?" Sabine hissed, glaring at me over her shoulder.

"She's his witch, not one of us. She's not gathering shit to help us. I told you, no one here is a friend. Everyone is a foe. Don't trust her, Sabine. We can gather what we need without her help. There's also the fact that she cast her magic on me, declaring her enemy to our bloodline."

"I am very skilled in witchcraft," Lacey sneered.

"You're skilled in something, sweetheart, but it isn't true witchcraft. You are filled with darkness, and the house needs light. We don't need our house to be influenced by your magic. Pass."

"I know more than you, witchling," she insisted.

"Mugwort, the uterus of a dying woman, the hair of a true hybrid wolf, and the saliva of a dire wolf," I smirked. "Go fetch it, darling."

"Dire wolves have been extinct for hundreds of years," she argued, smirking with a fire burning in her emerald depths.

"Oh, sweetheart, you are special, aren't you? They're extinct in this realm, yes," I agreed through a smile that was all teeth. "The ingredients to bless the House of Magic aren't collected purely from this realm because we, ourselves, are not of this realm. You have to bleed a little to earn the respect of our grandfather. Only those of the Hecate line can enter the portal where the dire wolves still roam. Since, at one time, they were Hecate's preferred choice of familiar and are protected by her. The uterus must be from a witch, not an old dying witch either, and she must donate it of her own free will. Hybrids…That one is tricky, but then they're suckers for the chance to breed witches," I shrugged, knowing that wouldn't be a problem for her. "Mugwort, it needs to be from the cliffs of the Drahgar's keep. Tell me, Lacey. Are you still willing to procure the items? I, for one, am all for watching you be torn apart. Shit, I'll even make the popcorn."

"We assumed you needed basic items."

"You being a basic bitch, I can believe it."

"Stop it, and play nice, Aria," Callista chided with a look of warning.

"I am being nice. I just saved Lacey's life," I offered with a smirk.

My gaze dropped to the floor, feeling Knox's stare on my face. I was freezing, still damp from bathing in the creek. I had bloody bits in my hair that I could now smell since the adrenaline had ebbed. I absently rubbed my arm, having been the only one not to set my heavy bag on the floor yet. I shuffled it onto my other shoulder and winced as my spine burned.

"Sabine," I frowned as my voice seemed to echo through the room.

"Yes?"

"I need you to check my spine," I whispered, even though everyone would still hear me.

She moved around me, lifting the shirt and then inhaled sharply. "What the hell did you do?"

"It hit the rock in the creek when we were attacked. How bad is it?" I waited, feeling her hands as she pushed my shirt back down and stepped back.

"It's not… Uh, it's not that bad."

"Liar," I groaned. "I really wish we'd just stayed home and not come to this cursed freaking town right now."

"None of us were letting you come to find Amara alone, Aria. I just need some moss, and you'll be good as new. I'm guessing the rock, as you called it, which is actually black tourmaline, needs a good cleaning."

"Did it mess up the tattoo?" I needed to know if it touched the birds on my spine. It was one of the first tattoos I'd gotten. It was called either an 'unkindness' or a 'conspiracy' when there were more than two ravens together. They were also highly intelligent birds, and many had no idea just how smart they really were. In fact, they were in the top ten smartest animals in this realm. I'd gotten it because the symbol had called to me, beckoning me to get it.

"No, it didn't touch your unkindness, apparently."

"Good, I would hate to go soft now." Turning, I stared pointedly at Knox, who watched us silently. "Do we sleep on the floor then?" I asked, unwilling to stand around any longer.

"Fucking witches," he grumbled.

"Breeding witches," Brander said, staring at Luna like she was dinner, and he was about to ring the bell.

"Basic fucking rules, ladies." Knox had spat out the word *ladies* like it was sour on his tongue. "No magic in my domain, none, not even to heal Aria. Your house may be the House of Magic, but I assure you that mine is less forgiving when the rules are broken. The top floor is off-limits, stay the fuck out of it.

"The chef is not your personal bitch, and we serve dinner when I get hungry, and only then. Do not wander around alone at night. In fact, do not leave your rooms until morning. We will assemble in the breakfast room then, and go over the shit Aria missed while being childish and trying to avoid me. Afterward, we will begin to collect the shit you need to bless your house so you can get the fuck out of mine. No fucking…period. Keep your legs closed."

"Seriously?" one of his men asked until Knox leveled him with a killing glare. "We breed them, less fucking trouble," the other man offered, shrugging.

"Keep your dick in your jeans, Killian. Witches aren't worth the fucking trouble of breeding." Growling at Killian, Knox turned to look at us. "Your rooms are on the second floor; I suggest you rest up before tomorrow."

My gaze moved to Lacey, who smiled at Knox even though he'd basically just called her worthless. I snorted, which caused those fierce blue eyes to seek mine out.

"Something to say, Aria?" Knox asked.

"If I did, I'd say it," I offered crossly.

"Shower, and throw the shirt into the trash when you're done," he said before dismissing us and vanishing through huge, wood-carved doors depicting dragons in a battle against one another. This would be a long night.

CHAPTER
11

The bedroom they showed me to was huge. The bed alone was big enough to hold a party. It had black bedding with red silk curtains that enclosed the bed, keeping bugs from getting to the orgy, or so I assumed. There was a large crimson-colored couch that lined the entire wall, which backed up my theory that they often used the room for orgies. I set my bag on the bed and retrieved silk pants and a soft white camisole top before heading into the bathroom.

I peered at my tired reflection in the mirror and frowned at the paleness of my skin, comparing it to Lacey's golden glow, undoubtedly blessed by the sun gods. Where my hair clung in pale silver strands, hers glistened with radiance as the black caught the freaking light.

My saving grace was my turquoise eyes, gently slanted upward and framed by dark, thick lashes that didn't need makeup to stand out. My lips had a natural pout to them and were a dull pink color instead of some natural cheery freaking perfection, which I was sure Lacey would have beneath the slather of red lipstick she wore. My face was heart-shaped, and a natural blush filled my cheeks, which my sisters loved, but I wasn't a fan of. It tended to make it look as if I was perpetually blushing all the time.

I stripped out of Knox's shirt, tossing it into the garbage before I turned, staring at the angry red welt that sliced down my skin, with only a small cut at the base of it. It wasn't too bad but burned like fire ants were attacking it. I leaned over, turning on the water to the shower and waiting for it to heat up.

Steam curled through the air, rising to the ceiling in a steady stream. I removed the joggers and folded them on the counter before stepping beneath the water, hissing as it scalded my flesh. I swallowed a curse before turning on the cold water and placing my hand beneath the spray. After a moment, I could stand beneath the water and let it wash off the filth from the battle, wincing as pink water ran off my body. I turned, crying out as water sprayed the wound on my back. Closing my eyes, I ignored the pain, washing the wound to prevent it from becoming infected.

"I can heal that for you," a familiar female voice said.

"Get out of this room, now, Lacey," I growled in warning. "I don't need your help."

"No, you're a tough girl, but you're in a man's world here, darling. Just because my line isn't as powerful as yours, Aria Hecate, doesn't make me useless."

"No, you allowing a man to debase you and speak

about you like crap does, though. You wielded magic against me, you drew first blood. Witches never attack their own kind unless they wish for war. Now get the fuck out."

"You have no idea the predators hunting you, or the one whose roof you are sleeping beneath. I do; I can help you." Her voice held urgency, and yet I tasted the lie in it. "You're in danger, you all are. Not just from what's coming through the portals, but from the…" She paused as footsteps sounded in the room.

"Lacey," Knox's rich baritone filled the room.

"Aria's wounded, and I thought she should know she's in danger from the cut getting infected," she lied.

I listened as her breathing remained even, unhindered by the lie she spoke to him. Power radiated through the room, and silence reigned. I poked my head out, finding the room empty, closing the curtain before making quick work of the shower, exiting it to dress for bed. In the bedroom, Knox leaned silently against the doorframe, watching me with a spot of blood on his shirt. Swallowing hard, I lifted my eyes from it to his.

"I need to see your back."

"No, you do not," I scoffed. "It can wait until tomorrow when we leave here."

"I wasn't fucking asking." Growling, he pushed off the wall and began to move toward me slowly.

Ignoring him as he prowled closer, I folded the towel, searching the room for a hamper, and shook my head, moving back into the bathroom to set it on the counter. Picking up my clothes, I pushed them into a separate pouch of the duffle bag and took a quick look around the room. Sitting on the bed, I turned away from him, lifting my camisole so he could look at the damage.

Warm fingers touched my spine, and I leaned forward, moving away from his touch and the connection I felt. Pressure on the bed had me moving to stand up to escape him, but he held my shoulder, trapping me to the spot.

"Flighty little thing, aren't you, Aria?" His other hand pushed my hair over my shoulder, exposing my neck and shoulder.

His hand released my shoulder to trace his fingers down the scrape on my flesh, and I whimpered as magic slithered down my spine. My nipples responded to his touch, causing me to stare down at their raised peaks. My core clenched, and I pulled away, staring at him. His eyes were predatory. They dropped to the shirt I wore. His lips twisting into a sardonic smirk before he stood, moving into the bathroom. He returned with a garbage bag containing his shirt.

Knox stood in the doorway between the bathroom and the bedroom, studying me carefully. It was unnerving. Like a lion watching its prey as it decided how best to bring it down by landing a killing move. His smile grew wider, meaner, as he continued staring at me.

"You could just take a picture, and then it wouldn't be so damn creepy." I glared at him as my lips tugged into a frown.

I didn't drop my gaze from his, even though everything inside of me demanded I do. As if my internal senses knew I was staring death in the face and wasn't happy I was stupid enough to do so. His nostrils flared as the tick in his jaw started up, and I smirked. He hated being challenged, and he definitely hated me throwing one down.

"If you want, you can lie down with me, and we can do a selfie," I offered with bravado, but it was empty because I was terrified of this man.

He consumed the air, eating it up as if he owned it. His power slithered over my flesh in a never-ending rush that felt like I was standing in the middle of an electrical storm, waiting to be struck down at any moment.

Worse than any of that shit? My body responded to him, where it had never responded to a male before. I hadn't just kept my virginity because I'd wanted to, no. No man had ever made my body respond, and yet Knox made it hum to life like it was a song being sung on Broadway and was about to be a big hit.

My legs clenched together, drawing his eyes even from the subtle movement most men wouldn't have noticed—but not him. Knox noticed, his stare smoldered with heat banking in it before slowly moving up my body to settle on the thin camisole that did nothing to hide the erect nipples brushing against it.

"No selfie, then?" I chuckled, turning to grab the blanket when the sound of the bag hitting the floor echoed in the silent room. I turned in time to face him as he slammed me against the bed, his hand holding my throat, closing it off as he peered down into my eyes.

"Keep fucking taunting me, little lamb. I'll show you why shepherds hid their flocks from the wolves at night. You'll see what happens when those sweet, succulent, little creatures are separated from the flock. They end up fucked so hard that not even the rest of the sheep can scent what the fuck is left of it in the morning."

"Wolves can't fuck sheep, Knox," I uttered through the pressure he held on my throat. "It's anatomically impossible."

He pushed harder against my throat as his head dipped over my chest. I groaned as his teeth clamped down on a nipple, biting it hard enough to sting. My hips lifted as he held my nipple, clenched painfully between his teeth. Hot breath ignited my flesh, and I moaned when he released it, staring at me where my shirt had become sheer enough to see the pink flesh of the swollen nipple.

"You bit my nipple," I pointed out as his hand released my throat and I gasped for air, sucking it in until I coughed from the burn in my lungs.

Knox stood up slowly, glaring down at me as if he was as shocked as I was at what he'd done. He turned in a quick, fluid motion, grabbing the bag that held the shirt, and vanished from the room without a word.

"Night?" I called before dropping back onto the bed, staring in confusion at the ceiling. What the hell just happened? Slowly sitting up, I peered down at my chest and touched the swollen nipple.

Pulling the shirt away from it, I glared at the red mark where his teeth had left an impression in the flesh. "Jerk, who bites someone's nipple?" I huffed, dropping back to the bed. "Dick."

CHAPTER
12

Turning and tossing on the mattress made sleeping impossible. It was smoldering in the room, forcing me to kick off the covers and groan as sweat beaded over my flesh, making my skin sticky and causing my clothes to cling to me. Sitting up, I pulled the camisole away from my stomach and fanned my face.

A shadow moved in the room's corner, and I swallowed hard, standing from the bed to investigate it. Knox stepped from the shadows, wearing dark sweatpants that did little to hide the muscular outline of his thighs, among other things.

"You need to leave," I warned, sitting back down on the bed.

He didn't speak as he prowled closer, watching me through cold eyes as he loomed above me, making me feel small and vulnerable. He crawled onto the bed, forcing me back as he lowered his mouth to my throat, tracing the wildly beating pulse with his tongue. He sucked my skin into his mouth, nipping against the artery that was running blood at an increased rate to my throbbing temples.

"Knox," I warned, but a deep rattle and a low growl in his chest stilled the warning.

His tongue pushed against my throat, sending a wealth of heat unfurling in my belly. His hand pushed beneath my shirt, slowly exploring the contour of my stomach before finding the globe of my breast and squeezing. Knees pushed my thighs apart, and a moan escaped my throat as his finger traced my nipple before pinching the puckered flesh.

I knew I should stop him, push him away from me, and yet I didn't. His hand slowly pushed down my belly, dipping into the silk pants I wore, and I trembled violently the moment his fingers brushed my clitoris.

His head lifted, watching me through hooded eyes before his mouth claimed mine softly at first before it turned demanding. His tongue fought mine, taking an effort to remember that air was needed to sustain life.

The combination of his tongue in perfect rhythm with his fingers was erotic. My legs dropped open, and his fingertips trailed over my opening leisurely, like he was learning me, discovering my body. Knox's finger slipped into my body, and I gasped against his mouth, even as I ground into his touch. Another finger pushed into my needy core, and I arched against the fullness as he growled huskily, lifting his mouth until I fought to claim it.

He watched me while he created a storm within my body, threatening to wreck me. My shirt was up, exposing the hardened nipples that begged to be sucked by him, but he sat back, forcing his fingers deeper into my body before his thumb began working lazily against my clit.

Knox pushed the band of his sweatpants down, exposing a monstrous-sized cock that glistened with a bead of arousal on the thickened tip. His free hand moved, using his thumb to wipe the cum from his velvet flesh before he brought it to my mouth, pushing it between my lips. I moaned, licking his thumb before I sucked it deeper into my mouth.

What the hell was I doing? I should have been kicking this prick out of the room, but I wasn't. Instead, I was sucking his thumb as he slowly brought me toward the edge of release. Fingers withdrew, and he settled between my thighs. I started to sit up, fully intending to end this before it got too far out of control, but everything changed.

Thick black wings extended from his spine, and his body covered in lines that pulsed with ancient magic. Pure, dark magic of the evilest form filled the room as I opened my mouth past his thumb to argue what he was doing to my body. Claws extended, filling my mouth and cunt as he watched me closely. It hurt, aching until everything inside of me rebelled at what was being done to my body.

"Knox, no," I uttered hoarsely as the fingers withdrew from my body. I watched him lift the claw he'd just fucked me with to his mouth, licking it clean with a forked tongue.

My hands fisted the sheets to retreat. The scream that sat at the back of my throat bubbled to the front, and his wicked eyes watched me before they stared down at where he was about to join us.

He fisted his massive cock, rubbing it over my opening and watched as I struggled to escape him, but it was as if invisible hands held me to the bed, keeping me prisoner while he studied me as I trembled with fear.

"Little lamb, I will slaughter you and eat you whole," he chuckled through a multilayered voice. He pushed the generous tip of his cock into my body, watching my eyes grow wide with horror.

Nails dragged over my stomach, and blood rushed to the surface of the wounds he'd made. His other hand reached into my stomach, and I screamed. I kept screaming until he withdrew something small and unmoving from me. In his hands was a child, a winged child with a plentiful wail. I shook my head, fighting the invisible hands that held me until I rolled off the bed, landing with a thud.

I stood up immediately, intending to run, and paused. My hand touched my flat stomach and felt it was wet. I lifted my hand, but it was clean of blood, then my gaze moved to the bed, finding the sheets askew from the nightmare. It had seemed so real. I exhaled slowly and then turned my head as a scream ripped through the hallway.

I heard it again and slowly moved to the door, listening as the sound of a bed slamming against a wall filled the empty hallway. My eyes closed when realization slapped me in the face as Lacey's sounds of pleasure exploded again.

The bed was pounding against the wall, and each

time it hit, she screamed louder until I was positive she'd lose her voice come morning. Snorting, I closed my door and ignored the screams until they became too much to handle.

Leaving the room, I searched for something to pass the hours until morning, noting a soft glow from a door at the far end of the hallway. I started toward it, ignoring the noises that Knox and Lacey made that were both obnoxious and grotesque. My bare feet padded on the marble floor and paused as growling sounded from behind me.

Exhaling slowly, I silently turned around, still taking steps in the opposite direction. The growling noise grew louder while the screams from Lacey turned weaker until they changed into wet screams as if she were being ripped apart. The hair on my neck stood up, and the sound of the door opening forced me to turn back toward the open door.

I rushed into the room before closing the door silently behind me as my heart raced in my chest. I pushed my hair free from the band that held it out of my face before I turned around, looking at the walls lined with ancient tomes.

Books were something I'd always loved. I'd been unable to pass a bookstore without looking inside, even if only to touch the books with the tips of my fingers, much to the many storekeepers' annoyance when I walked out bookless. I could never get enough books or read enough words to escape the reality of the world. Everything I knew of romance, I'd learned from books.

Knox had thousands of them just waiting to be plucked from the extensive shelves lining the walls as far as the eye could see. Stepping closer, I reached out, running my fingers over the ancient spines and inhaling their earthy scent. Skimming the titles, I smiled to myself, noting he had a vast selection of human literature along with older, more primitive, and priceless tomes from the Nine Realms.

The Nine Realms were ageless, each was created from an original bloodline and governed as a group by the original families. They existed long before this or any of the other realms were even dreamt of, let alone created. To have literature from the Nine Realms was telling because only those of the highest statue or rank were given those books to keep safe. I withdrew one of the hefty tomes, thumbing through the pages while absently chewing my lip as my gaze took in the ancient beasts that had once roamed Norvalla.

Norvalla, the furthest of the Nine Realms from this one, was similar to the fae version of the Court of Night, or Nightmares. Evil lived within that realm, and all rumors said it was the worst of the Nine Realms in which to be sentenced, minus being sent to the Void of Nothingness, which served as a prison for the Nine Realms. Some realms were beautiful, unreal realms that bespoke of magical creatures and ethereal, endless beauty. Then there was Norvalla, and that was the one place that called to me and raised my curiosity. Pushing the book back into its place, I stared at the rare wood that held it.

I gasped, realizing the shelves of his library were built from the ancient white oak trees that only grew within Norvalla, and my heart skipped a beat. He not only had thousands of books and thesauruses from that realm, but he also had hundreds of customized shelves brought in from the furthest of the Nine Realms. Who the hell was he? And the books he'd chosen? Books I could get lost in for years!

You could tell a lot about a person by what type of books they displayed on their shelves. You collected books you enjoyed, books you treasured and wanted to keep close by to sink into a large Chesterfield couch and escape the world. It was like getting a rare glimpse into the soul by snooping through someone's private book collection. What they read told you a lot about a person and their personality, if they preferred fantasy or fiction to nonfiction, they needed an escape from the mundane. Nonfiction readers preferred to live in the now, to know facts the narrator or writer had studied in vivid detail. I preferred romance or fantasy to escape and live a thousand lives I'd never experience without the author giving me the chance to climb inside their soul, making their books my home for a little while.

Turning to stare deeper into the room, I noted they had built every shelf from white oak, and my mind raced with how someone or anyone could achieve bringing back that much wood. Rows of books filled the area, mirroring a library, and yet the design was created with efficiency in mind. Each corner held the carved head of a mythical beast, and I studied them until the room began to change, growing darker with every step I took. The temperature dropped, causing my bare arms to chill. The lighting was dimmer as if this side of the room lacked the candles or illumination that the opening interior held.

My breathing was the only sound I heard, other

than the padding of my feet, as I moved deeper into the luxurious room. My breath became puffs of steam, causing me to stop and take in my surroundings. I spun in a full circle, frowning at the rows of shelves that blocked my way back.

They had moved! Sucking my bottom lip between my teeth, I considered going back to see if they would move again, but my curiosity was piqued, and I needed to know what else was in this room. The room itself seemed to go on forever as if I'd stepped into another realm instead of a library. If I'd had bread crumbs, I'd have placed them on my path to help me find my way back, but Knox's library was like the candy house, and fuck if I wasn't willing to be eaten by an old hag to search through more of it.

Giving in to the curiosity that drove me, I started moving deeper into the room regardless of the temperature plummeting. My feet touched something slick, and I barely escaped slipping. Stepping back, I crouched low and ran my fingers over the floor, noting it was covered in thick ice. It wasn't just any ice; no, it was beautiful, mirroring the purity of high-quality quartz crystals that this realm produced. My hand lifted to my nose and inhaled slowly, deeply as the scent of midnight roses filled my lungs.

Holy shit.

Knox had ice from the highest peaks in the Dark Mountains, which separated two of the Nine Realms: Norvalla, and the Beast Kingdom. The ice was infused with the rich, intoxicating scent of the rare black midnight blooming rose that only grew within the mountain range. The rose's scent was prized among witches; even my Aunt Aurora had craved the precious essential oil the rose produced.

The mountain pass in which they bloomed was rumored to be guarded by monsters so hideous and strong no witch had gotten more than a drop of the essence. Aurora, however, had a small vial she treasured that she wore around her throat and never took off. She'd only ever let us girls smell it once, and I'd craved it ever since.

Standing, I carefully moved over the floor, wondering what else he held within his treasure trove. Knox seemed to be a collector of rare things, which didn't surprise me in the least. It surprised me he had a vast, history-rich library filled with rare things that shouldn't exist in this realm. He'd brought back frost, the frost that had grown to cover his floors. Frost from the Dark Mountains was a living thing, and unlike the snow or ice in this realm, it would never melt. It would continue growing until everything it could reach was covered.

Rounding a corner, I paused. Crystals covered the floor in intricate patterns. My fingers itched to touch the huge sphere of citrine that was the size of my head or bigger. The imperfection of it shone beautifully beneath the light that glowed through it. Rainbows reflected from the surface, shining over the walls to create a perfect show of ethereal beauty. Large high-quality quartz towers stood around it, adding their rainbow-like kaleidoscope lights to cover the ceiling. Everywhere I looked, there were crystals of the highest quality that sang to the witch within me to touch, and yet it was considered impolite to do so since they absorbed a person's negativity and every emotion they felt at the time that they touched it. Knox had more crystals than we did; spheres, double-sided points, tumblers, and skulls, all carved perfectly with craftsmanship I'd never seen achieved.

I hated him more because of it, and also because I wanted them all.

Continuing on, I almost wept with relief when my frozen feet touched carpet, but not just any carpet. It was the finest silk from North Attleborough, a small town within Norvalla, known for their mastery of fabrics. It was expensive, and yet so exquisite that I couldn't help but stretch my toes in it. I wanted to lie on it, roll around on it, and rejoice that my breath no longer escaped in clouds of steam or that my feet were no longer in danger of frostbite.

Refraining from making a total idiot of myself, I spun in a wide circle once more, gasping when I realized there were no more bookcases or shelves, and the way back looked like a rainbow filled ice tunnel with no end in sight. What the hell was this place? Stepping further into the room, the sensation of being watched filled me with foreboding, causing my gaze to lift to the tallest part of the newest room's wall where statues of gargoyles in perfect condition sat peering down.

"Aren't you beautiful?" I whispered, barely loud enough to be heard as if I feared being scolded by the librarian of this place? At least it wouldn't be Knox discovering me snooping, since he was currently balls deep in Lacey, judging by the lewd noises from the room next to mine.

Whoever had captured the likeness of the gargoyles

had to have perfected them. Even from where I stood below, I could see the love and quality the artist had put into each one. They looked alive, which I knew couldn't be since, even within the Nine Realms, they were extinct. The crackling of flames drew my attention back to the floor, and I shivered from the icy fingers of the chill one last time before moving toward the fire to warm up.

On my way to the fireplace, I frowned, taking in the large opulent couch carved of quartz weighing more than any creature could lift easily. It was covered in luxurious crimson velvet that popped against the light-colored carpet.

The fireplace was massive and set back in the wall, surrounded by large black onyx, reflecting the fire's dancing flames. It wasn't just beautiful. It was exquisite and hard to believe someone like Knox would relish such beautiful things in his home.

The man was an enigma. He had rare yet deadly things in his library, containing so much knowledge within the tomes lining the walls that you'd never tire of reading them. I groaned with bliss as the fire heated my flesh, warming me quickly from the walk through the iciness he'd brought here with him.

If he wasn't such a prick, I'd ask if I could read some of his treasured books, and yet I knew without asking that the answer would be a perfect no, said from his smug lips. I hoped he choked on Lacey's juices, or got stuck inside her for waking me up. Although, if he hadn't, I wouldn't have stumbled across his library or been privy to see the rare, beautiful items it held.

I turned, looking through the rest of the room, and

paused as the man of my thoughts met my gaze, peering over a book as he lounged in the matching couch to the one I'd passed. His hair was mussed, ruffled from reclining on the sofa on a mountain of pillows that were probably as soft as the carpet. Oceanic blue eyes narrowed with anger as they locked with mine over the book he was reading. Knox shirtless, with messed up hair, was dangerous.

"You were told not to leave your room."

"I know." Feeling guilty, I watched him carefully. "I couldn't sleep, and there was a light on in this room." I'd willingly broken his rule, and worse, I was alone with him. I'd assumed he'd been otherwise occupied with Lacey since it was her screams that had been coming from the room next to mine.

"I told you not to leave your room, Aria. You broke the rules," he chided, watching me through a dark, languid stare that made me feel naked and exposed as if he could see through me, watching the nightmare I'd had of him vividly through my eyes.

"I had a nightmare, and then Lacey's screams wouldn't let me sleep. They were gross and highly annoying. Apparently, your house gives me nightmares, and your girlfriend slipped and landed on someone else's dick. Maybe she got bored with yours," I offered, dropping my stare to the book he read, *Genealogy of the Hecate Bloodline.* "That is not going to offer you much help on getting her back. Whoever she landed on, they sound rather talented." Why was I still talking? His lips pulled back in a cold smile, and he tilted his head, dragging his gaze down the sheer silk pajamas I wore, clinging to my skin now covered in a subtle sheen of sweat from standing by the fire too long.

"You are either very brave or very stupid, little lamb."

CHAPTER
13

I could tell by Knox's icy glare and the narrowing of it that he was annoyed with my presence in the library. I hadn't planned to invade his space, but I was here now, and I wasn't ready to leave. He could demand that I go back to my room, but I wasn't in the mood to back down from a challenge.

He wasn't going to tell me what to do and expect me to follow his demands blindly. I was a woman, after all. His glare intensified as if he was deciding how best to cut me up and discard of my pieces.

He started to get up from the couch, but I moved toward him, taking the book from his hands, and sat beside him, staring at the page he'd been reading. Frowning, I double-checked the title before turning my head.

"Everything in this library to read, and you chose this? Seriously, Knox," I muttered, noting the page he'd been reading. He sat back on his mountain of pillows and studied me as I read about, well, me. "Of all the beautiful tomes in this place and you read about me? I'm flattered."

Aria Primrose Hecate, born to Freya Hecate, the firstborn female of Hecate. Aria's father is unknown, her bloodline pure and untainted, and yet tests could not conclude which secondary bloodline created Aria or Amara. Unlike Freya's other daughters, Aria spends her time in isolation, learning her craft with diligence and intelligence the others in the line do not possess. She is clean of male influence, having been able to ignore the fae males who used their magic on her at the tender age of ten.

She marked among the highest scale of magic and possesses a darkness mixed with light magic that is both worrisome and intriguing and should be monitored. More tests are needed to learn the father's bloodline. Still, without Freya agreeing to them, it will need to wait until Aria has fully entered into puberty, which is onset and developing slower than the average witch. This should also be closely monitored.

Nature responds to Aria in ways it has never before responded to other witches, she is unlike anything previously studied, adding to the intrigue. Amara, her twin, doesn't exhibit these traits, nor does she pull from the darkness her twin contains. Amara is sweet and rather docile compared to Aria's standoffish behavior, her natural defense to push people away. In all accounts, Aria is promised to darkness, where Amara is promised to light. Yet no proof exhibited magic from their perspective directional magical link have been proved or exhibited. Further investigation was requested, yet denied from the Oracle's.

Conclusion of this witch: dangerous, deadly, and feral. Should she continue to pull magic to her from her home realm, it is our conclusion she should be eliminated or sent back, to protect this realm from the mutation of creatures mating illegally.

Out of the Hecate line, she is the most troublesome but also the most powerful child born out of all nine sets of twins born to Freya's line. It should be noted that one male born to Freya was also close in magic and strength to Aria, and yet she excels where he failed in mental capabilities.

Okay, so it hadn't *all* been wrong, but it was creepy to know they'd been testing us in school without us knowing or feeling it. On the page beside my bio—if you could call it that—was a picture of me in a lacy summer dress that made me look washed out in the gray and black photo. The photographer had snapped the photo the moment my eyes had lifted from the white rose I held, and I didn't look happy at all. I looked utterly pissed and hostile at whoever had been behind the lens. I was no older than ten in the photo, according to the tiny writing beneath it. It was also taken a few days after one of the attempts on my life, by my *perfect* mother.

"It's wrong, I don't push people away. I trip and then walk over them," I muttered, passing the book back to him.

"Is it, or do you not like what they wrote about you?" Tossing the book aside, he crossed his arms over his chest, as if he hadn't a care in the world.

"It states my mother had nine sets of twins. She birthed eight; I know because we kept each other alive when she abandoned us. It also says she had a male child, but the Hecate line doesn't birth male offspring. We birth bitches, and we birth them easily. Most witches don't have that issue, the birthing of male offspring. It's widely known that we only birth female witches, Knox; therefore, your book is incorrect."

"Is it?" he countered.

"What are you?" I whispered breathlessly, ignoring his question as his power slithered over my flesh, sending everything within me on high alert. It wasn't something he did on cue; it came in waves as if he couldn't always prevent it from escaping his hold. "Why do you have ice from the Dark Mountain in this realm or white oak from Norvalla? Have you been there?" I asked, watching the tick in his jaw as it started to move with his anger.

"Go to bed, Aria."

"Have you been there? Are there monsters as big as they say? Tell me, Knox," I whispered as the scholar in me begged to know more. "The Dark Mountains, are there actual monsters who protect the roses? Can you get to the roses? Is it as beautiful and wild as they say it is in books?"

He remained silent, watching me as his chest lifted and fell with what I was sure was an annoyance. Rolling my eyes, I lifted from the couch and moved toward the fire, staring into the flames.

"Most people wish to see the beauty of the Nine Realms, but I want to learn its secrets. I want to see Norvalla and taste the rapids of Valania as I stand on crystal quartz larger than human houses. I crave a realm in which I was created and yet have never seen. They only allowed us into the Nine Realms if something happened to the rulers who stood in our stead until we reached a certain age. Not that I had ever been permitted to enter, sadly." I watched the flickering flame, noting the white oak within the fireplace. "You're burning white oak?" I felt an overwhelming need to reach in and protect it from the flames that burned with gusto.

"You think I would waste white oak in a fire?" His voice was directly behind me, causing me to spin around on a gasp.

I hadn't heard him move. I hadn't felt him nearing me, and yet he was so close that our flesh almost touched. His dark head lowered, more sinister in the flame's light that burned in his pretty eyes. I licked my lips nervously, preparing to bolt if the need arose. He smirked as if he'd read my mind and didn't give an inch as he stood before me, inhaling deeply, causing his nostrils to flare.

"I don't presume to know what you would or wouldn't do." The wood burned hot, sending heat kissing over my flesh like it was reaching for him as I swallowed past the narrowing of my larynx while sweat dripped down my spine.

"Look again," he said hoarsely.

I hesitated to turn my back on him, but his presence dominated the space. The room had been beautiful and lavish before I'd noticed him here. Now his presence consumed the eye, holding it prisoner and swallowing the fine details. There was the room before Knox and the room after, and there was a huge difference in space between the two. My chest rose and fell silently before I turned, peering down at the flames that licked the wood.

The flames caressed and danced against the wood, and yet there was no char mark from the fire. It wasn't burning. It was slowly carving the face of a woman that took a moment for the eye to catch the details. The pouty lips were the first thing I could see, the point of her chin and the beginning of a nose which sat in a heart-shaped face that the fire carved with the skill of a master woodworker.

It felt like forever that I stood motionless, watching the flame work as sweat dripped from my body, sending a fine droplet down the side of my face. Reaching up, I wiped it away and began to spin around, only for Knox to twine his fingers through my hair and yank my head back until I was staring at the ceiling.

"You shouldn't have fucking left your room," he hissed, holding me as his nose rubbed against the side of my neck. His other hand slipped around my stomach, and I didn't move, didn't dare to. I was in his domain, and no one else knew I was here. "You really don't listen, do you?"

"Not normally, no," I admitted thickly, my voice escaping my throat as a breathless noise. My body burned from the fire, and sweat slowly ran between my breasts as he held me in front of it.

"Go back to bed before you end up eaten."

"I can't sleep over Lacey's screaming."

"Are you sure it was Lacey and not one of your sisters self-soothing her needs?" he whispered, running his hand up my flat belly. I was trapped by his body; there was no way out without magic to combat him or escape.

"Self-soothing?" I questioned, unfamiliar with the term even though I got his meaning.

"Playing with their messy cunts." Releasing my hair as he turned me around, staring at me through dark eyes that were slits of molten color. "Fucking their needy, aching cunts with their fingers since they can't get dick in my domain," he chuckled.

"I get it." I took a step away from the fire and angling my body to run if needed. My eyes slid from his to the darkened way from which I came, but it was pitch black, as if no longer a hallway but rather something else. Did I dare run and pray to the goddess he didn't catch me?

"You wouldn't make it." Watching the perplexity cross my face as it pinched my features, he chuckled, knowing he was right.

I took another step away from him, watching as he mirrored my movements. Unlike my body, his was tense and ready to pounce, while mine was ready to get the fuck out of here. My lip trembled with fear, sensing that whatever he was, it was deadlier than I'd first assumed. I was sure if I looked up what was the worst way to die, there would be a picture of Knox beside it.

The couch touched the back of my calves, and his hands came up, pushing me down as I gasped, my ass landing on the velvet cushion. My pajamas were soaked from perspiration clinging to my flesh and outlining every inch of me to his predatory gaze. Something rattled in his chest, and I shivered, not daring to take my eyes from his, as if my life depended on it.

"Are you scared?" he asked, fisting his hands tightly

at his sides.

I considered lying, but the look in his eyes stopped me. He smiled darkly, sitting on the couch with his knee between my thighs, forcing my legs to lift and spread apart to accommodate him between them. It pushed my back against the cushion in a resting position, which was awkward. My chest heaved and fell with fear, which I was confident he could see, smell, and taste in the air as he loomed over me. It was leaking from my pores. I wasn't scared; I was terrified and yet excited, which made me the biggest idiot alive.

His hand touched my center, and I paused, no longer afraid and more uncertain of where Knox was going with his actions. A single brow lifted, and I was pretty sure my *what-the-fuck* face was on full display in all its glory. He applied more pressure, and I moaned softly through trembling lips, staring down between our bodies at the single finger that touched me, running slowly over my center. My nipples hardened, and my entire body became supple, like I was bending to his will. My knees moved inward, blocking his body from mine before my foot connected to his chest, and I held him back, looking awkward as fuck with my foot on his chest and his hand still on my pussy. It was almost like the most messed up version of—*Twister* —without playing the game that I'd ever seen.

"I'm going to pass," I swallowed breathlessly.

He landed on me hard, pushing my leg up to my shoulder, which knocked the wind out of my lungs. His growl sounded from deep in his chest, and he held me there. He didn't caress me, didn't touch me other than to apply all his weight onto my frame, locking me in place.

"I should snap you in half," he uttered hoarsely.

"I'm actually not that bendable," I informed through my mouth being smothered by his shoulder, which smelled enticingly of male. "Besides, then you would have two of me to deal with."

"You wouldn't be a fucking problem dead, Aria Primrose."

"Ew, don't call me that. So, is this where you smother me to death?" I inquired huskily, having felt the appendage that had grown while he had been holding me pinned to the couch.

He lifted his head, staring down at me through dark eyes that sent my pulse racing. He didn't speak as something in his chest rattled, and his hips moved against mine. My mouth opened, and my tongue slipped over my dry lips. He looked as if he was about to consume me, or worse, kiss me. I'd be lying if I said I didn't want to taste his lips. I'd never had a real kiss in my entire life, so I wasn't sure he should be my first since he was a prick.

He snorted, slowly moving toward my mouth as I closed my eyes, preparing to be kissed. Only he didn't kiss me. Knox's hot breath fanned against the shell of my ear before he whispered into it.

"Go to fucking bed before I forget what you are, and who you are."

"What happens if you forget?" I whispered through the embarrassment that I'd been dumb enough to think he'd lower himself to kiss me, who he thought was beneath him.

"Run, Aria," he said, pulling away from me as he

stood up, staring at me. "You have five seconds before I give chase, and if I catch you, you won't like what happens. Go." I was up instantly, hauling ass through the darkness to reach the room they had given me.

I didn't stop running until I was inside the room and sliding down the wall as an inhuman snarl sounded on the other side. Nails tapped on the wall, and I crawled away from it, staring at it while everything within me silently screamed as a dark laugh echoed through the hallway, slithering down my spine.

Whatever the fuck Knox was, he was moving up the animal guide to the biggest monster I'd ever confronted. But he hadn't caught me. I jumped as something pounded through the wall, my eyes following the noise until it stopped. My breathing was ragged, and my legs trembled and burned from running as I got up, standing to face whatever was on the other side of that wall. I shivered violently, noting my body had responded with a need for Knox that excited me more than it terrified me at the moment.

Crawling into bed, I pulled the covers over my head and closed my eyes, even though I knew sleep wouldn't happen after tonight. Knox had rare things here, things that didn't belong in this realm.

He had an entire library that not only grew, the entire library also expanded and changed. It was not the same room I had entered earlier; it was shorter, and there were no books, no ice, no...Just nothing. Like it had all vanished without a trace, just as Amara had.

It boggled the mind, but if he'd somehow opened into another dimension, as some of the biggest, scariest monsters could, he could easily have done it here, and it would make perfect sense why my sister had vanished, and I couldn't trace her. Especially if she wasn't even in this realm anymore.

CHAPTER
14

Seated in the breakfast room, I fidgeted in the silence. I'd tried to explore more of the house, but Greer seemed to have been instructed to prevent it. Every time I'd started down a hallway, he'd been there, glaring at me. Greer didn't like me, but I wasn't offended by it. He was only the butler who served Knox. It stood to reason he'd be a prick like him.

I smelled Knox before he entered the room; his pheromones released, and my ovaries were all over it. Ovaries didn't have brains, and Knox was about to have thirteen witches with PMS in his house, and I wasn't thrilled about being one of them. My fingers drummed on the table as my chin rested in my hand, exhaustion washing over me with the added uneasiness of being surrounded by males with my body on high alert.

Witches ovulated like normal humans, usually. Not our line; no, because that would be too easy. Hecate had taken steps to force her line to procreate, and it made any of us in ovulation mimic a bitch in heat. We, of course, weren't in heat, but our bodies emitted pheromones sensitive to males that drove their need to fuck us— *thanks*, Grandma.

My sisters got incredibly antsy and would vanish for twenty-four hours, or until the end of their cycle depending on if the guy was worth it, or not. I, on the other hand, would read romance and self-soothe because nothing else worked, and it just wasn't worth it.

"Self-soothing…" he started, and I jumped, spinning around as I shook my head.

"Were you in my head?" I demanded while he frowned, crossing his arms over the white cotton shirt he wore.

"Were you thinking about touching yourself?"

"Absolutely not," I returned suspiciously.

"Then why the fuck would you think I was in your head?" he pointed out.

"Whatever," I said like a petulant child and sat back down, staring at the white wall in front of me. I'd been shown to this room, and it held nothing. There was nothing to look at and nothing to check out. Everywhere I looked was white, including the teapot and the coffee carafe. "I should grab my sisters," I announced, uncomfortable with the direction of the conversation and the current level of heat blooming in my cheeks.

"They will eat elsewhere this morning," he informed, making his way to the coffee and pouring some into an espresso cup that looked ridiculous in his grip. "Get coffee," he snapped.

"No, thank you," I replied, staring at the wall once

more as if it held the secrets to the universe.

He stared at me before he spoke again. "Get a fucking cup of coffee."

"I don't drink it black," I hissed, lifting a brow. "And I'm not your bitch. You don't get to order me around."

He grabbed the entire carafe and set it in front of me, slamming a cup down and pouring it. I opened my mouth to tell him where he could shove it when a woman entered with a large tray balanced on her palms. Placing it in front of me, I chewed my lip before watching her vanish just as quickly as she had shown up.

"I bet you're used to women serving you, aren't you?" I snapped irritably. "Bet they just lie down and do whatever you tell them to do." I reached for the cream, pouring it into the cup before adding sugar. "Why am I here, and why are we alone?" I asked, sipping the hot coffee. It tasted of heaven, and I much needed caffeine after having slept very little, if at all, last night.

"So I can bend you over the table and fuck you," he said as I took a sip, inhaling it into my lungs as his words echoed in my ears.

I choked, sputtering as I stood. My hand covered my mouth as coffee came out of my nose until everything burned.

"Pass," I choked out, moving to grab napkins.

"If I wanted to fuck you, you'd be fucked."

"Then it's a good thing you hate me," I reminded, wiping my chest down as people came into the room, moving to clean the mess without having to be told. One woman walked toward me with her hand out, but her eyes were vacant as she reached to assist cleaning my chest off.

"Get away from her, Katlin, now." Knox stood up as if he intended to assist me, but I turned away from him, cleaning the coffee out of my cleavage and off my sundress without his help. "Turn around," he demanded.

"I can clean myself off, jerk. That wasn't funny, not even a little."

"Sit down, then," he snapped. "Katlin, serve us the meal at five."

I passed him, bumping into his shoulder as I did. Once I was assured that the chair was clean, I retook my place, ignoring the coffee over the bodice of the sundress. I continued cleaning off the spot and the sticky coffee between my boobs as he took his seat, watching me.

"You could remove it," he offered.

"You could fuck off." I hated that heat was perpetually in my cheeks with his slick sexual innuendos. Normally what men said slid right off me, but Knox, he had a way of catching me off guard, and worse, the jerk made me blush. "So, why am I really here, since I have no intention of letting you bend me over the table? Also, I am very aware of what self-soothing is, so if you intend to give me a pep talk about that, save it. I also know that you can do it silently, without screaming to the rafters or waking up the entire house to achieve the end goal. I'm a virgin, not a fucking saint."

"Why are you still a virgin?" he asked, noting the way my head turned slowly to his.

"That's none of your business."

"No witch has ever made it past eighteen with her virginity, and yet you're what, Aria? Twenty-four years old and still have it, I know because I can smell it."

"You can *smell* it?" I frowned and then began fidgeting under the scrutiny of his gaze before he finally answered me.

"There's a pureness to a woman when she is untouched or untainted by a male."

"Awesome," I grumbled.

"Why keep it?"

"Look, my vagina is not up for discussion. I'd also prefer your lips not to drip nonsense about my lady parts, Knox."

"You're missing the magnitude of what I am asking. You're a Hecate witch, cursed to breed once a month, and yet you've never parted those thighs and allowed a man between them."

Looking away, I picked at my finger as I absently bit my lip, considering how much to tell him. My head tilted before I stared at the wall to ignore the heat of his eyes, burning the side of my head.

"Have you ever felt physically sick when someone touched you?" I asked softly, not meeting his stare.

"No," he said abruptly, without hesitation.

"I do," I snorted. "My first try was when I was seventeen. His name was Tommy Mason, and he was a sweetheart, but he tried to kiss me, and I barfed all over him. We made good friends, but his touch made me sick. The next boy was just some boy I'd met at a dance. My sisters were there, and they'd had dates. I chose a guy at random to give my virginity because I was sick and tired of hearing my sisters talk about it. He took me deep into the woods and stripped naked. He started removing my clothes, but I felt sick, so I tried to stop it. He got forceful and mean, so I made him choke to death slowly. He wouldn't take no for an answer, and there was a sickness in him. Next time, I was older. I had been dating Jared for weeks, but when he touched me, I felt nothing, like literally nothing. His hand would slip into my shirt, and he could touch me, but I couldn't feel him. We tried spells, tried to create a male from clay, which was actually a terrible idea. Either way, nothing worked. I'm a dud," I snorted, turning in his direction.

"You felt me," he said, after a moment of silence.

"Yeah, lucky me," I said sarcastically. "Also, hard pass. I don't like you."

"I don't like you either, but I don't have to like you to fuck you."

"I'm not interested, Knox. I prefer to sleep with a man I like."

"Sex with people you like is messy. All you need to fuck is basic chemistry. Your pussy needs to be wet, and a dick needs to be hard enough to fill it. That is what chemistry does. Your body knows what to do without your feelings, making it a fucking mess."

"Do you want to fuck me, Knox?" My voice came out sultry, and I winced inwardly.

"No," he clipped. "I like my women fast and hard, and to have more experience than rubbing her clit in a dark room as she bites her fucking lip, so no one else knows she's self-soothing her cunt," he snorted, pouring himself more coffee as if he hadn't just torn me down in one fluid sentence.

"Okay," I muttered, using my finger to pull on my lip to keep myself from rebuking his statement, not that he was wrong. He'd pegged me so hard I'd felt it in my ass. Brutal but honest.

"You're not my type," he stated.

"Got it the first time," I growled, and my stomach agreed. On cue, servers entered the room, clearing the cream and sugar before placing platters of meats and fruit along with other delicious-smelling food onto the table. My eyes widened at the amount of food before us, it was enough to feed an entire room of children. Once the room cleared out, Knox began using his fork to grab meat he then piled onto his plate.

I watched silently as he pushed a large chunk of meat into his mouth and chewed it soundlessly. Slowly, my eyes went back to the mountain of food, and I sucked my lip between my teeth, holding it there before he spoke, causing me to turn in his direction.

"Eat, you're too skinny."

"I am not," I muttered.

"Eat," he continued.

"I don't even know where to start." The thing with having a large family is that you normally ended up with scraps. Aurora had done her best with us, but there were a lot of mouths to feed, and my mother was great at draining the account for months before she put the money back, like she got off on showing us who held power over us. "That's enough food to feed an entire school of starving kids."

I stood up since I couldn't reach most of the dishes from a sitting position and grabbed toast, strawberries, and mixed fruit before sitting back down. I pushed a large piece of pineapple into my mouth and barely caught the juice as it drove past my lips and ran down my chin. Grabbing a napkin, I dabbed at my lips and sat back, chewing it in silence.

"Eat, or I'll take it as an invitation to bend you over the table and do what we both really want to be doing right now."

"No, that's pretty much just you. I don't want to bend over anything," I squeaked as I pushed food into my mouth, stalling the conversation. Knox smiled devilishly, watching my mouth as I licked my lips around the fruit.

CHAPTER
15

I hoped the others had as much food as we did to chow down on. Picking up a giant strawberry, I broke it in half, plopping one piece into my mouth before sucking my thumb clean. Turning, I looked at Knox, who watched my mouth with a dark look in his eyes.

"If the portals are weakening, why aren't more people here to enforce the covenant?" I asked, trying to get him to stop looking at me as if I was part of the meal.

"I'm here," he stated as if that was the end of the discussion. "You like the pineapple?" He studied me as I picked up another piece without caring that he watched me pushing it into my mouth. I nodded, and he continued. "They say it makes your pussy taste sweeter."

I coughed, and he moved as if he would save me from choking. I held my hand up, watching him through narrowed eyes. Once I'd swallowed it, I licked the juices from my fingers on purpose, noting the way he locked onto the action.

"Who says it?" I asked, knowing he wanted a reaction to his words.

"Scientists do, along with studies they've run."

"Do you think they actually run studies on it? Like, have women eat a ton of pineapple and then spread their thighs, parting their petals so that scientists can lick them to discern the difference? I mean, pussy before pineapple, and pussy after pineapple, and the men who tasted them for science?" I pushed another piece into my mouth before turning away from him. I stood, grabbing the orange juice, and poured a glass before sitting back down to peer innocently at him over the rim as I drank.

"I've tasted a lot of pussy, and I prefer the taste when she's a fan of fruit."

"Maybe you should just stick some fruit in her pussy, and then you'd have a fruit snack for later," I offered, shrugging before I took a long swig of orange juice. "Anyway, back to the problem. I'm certain you didn't have the others eat elsewhere just to bend me over the table and fuck me or bore me with your sexual prowess while filling me full of fruit." One delicate brow lifted as I waited for him to speak.

"Maybe I will," he shrugged, shoving food into his mouth without breathing before eating more. "Amara showed up to town with a purpose. What was it?" Knox set his fork down, apparently done with eating.

"She came to sit on the council since Freya vacated it without warning. There's also the store we own that has to be run by someone in our line, and Freya vanishing put a kibosh on us, ignoring this place. Amara volunteered to come back, and when I offered begrudgingly to join her, she said no."

"And you didn't think it was strange that she didn't want you here?"

"No, because lately, she'd been putting more and more distance between us," I admitted with a soft shrug as a pang filled my heart. "I just figured maybe she needed space, but then I called, and she didn't answer. I sent her messages, and they went unread until they disconnected her number. Now we're here."

"Amara showed up in town with an agenda, Aria. She vanished seven days ago."

"You're lying. Amara's phone has been shut off for two weeks. If she vanished one week ago, that would mean she turned off her own phone. I scried, trying to locate her, and she wasn't in Haven Falls. If she was, I'd have found her. I have never missed a target I have scried for in my entire life. Not to mention, I didn't feel her here. Why wait until now to tell me this?" I asked carefully.

"Because there are things that aren't adding up," he said, observing me. "The day Amara showed up, she took down the magic that protected your home. She disabled the House of Magic. Why? It would have protected her. She fucked anyone who would let her and even tried to fuck me. The thing is, every male she fucked is dead. They're not just dead, Aria, they were put onto their knees and executed and then arranged on an altar to make it look as if they were sacrificed. That isn't something creatures in this realm do. That's something someone from the Nine Realms would do to someone who had trespassed or stolen something from them.

"Then the attack on the portals happened, three places at once. To weaken it as it has been, those wanting to get inside this realm would have needed an outsider to help them. The thing is, Aria, they'd have needed a Hecate witch to weaken the portals to the Human Realm because they were erected by the goddess. The creatures that went after you while you bathed your virgin pussy in the creek? They came out of a tear in a portal on your property. Someone helped create that hole from your bloodline. Then there was the sacrificed alpha we found on your altar, in your backyard. Her scent was all over it, all over him. Amara isn't missing, Aria. She's committed treason against the Nine Realms."

"You're lying," I whispered through trembling lips.

"Am I? Or do you just not want to believe she was capable of it? Because it's the only thing that makes sense," he said, dabbing his mouth with a napkin and chugging the milk he'd poured. "Amara had a lover in the Nine Realms, did she not?"

"Fuck you," I snapped, standing up to leave the table. I didn't make it more than a few steps before he picked me up and slammed me on the chair, jolting my teeth as he leaned over and stared into my eyes. "I won't condemn my sister."

"You don't fucking have to, she is already condemned, Aria. Did she have a fucking lover in the Nine Realms? Answer me, because your fucking life depends on it."

I swallowed and gave myself an internal shake. What the hell had she done? This wasn't something I could save her from, not if it was true. I didn't believe it in a million years, but I also couldn't let the entire bloodline take the fall if she had. I could prove her innocence or figure out the truth, but if he had the council's ear, I couldn't lie.

He growled, and I nodded. "Yes," I admitted closing my eyes briefly with guilt.

He straightened and nodded. "Fucking figures," he muttered. "You guys can't keep your legs closed no matter what the laws are, can you?" My eyes held his, and a delicate brow lifted. "Nah, Aria. You are something else entirely."

"Excuse me?"

"You're a witch, but that's only part of what you are. Your other half is more dominant. If it wasn't, you wouldn't have that pesky little hymen in the way of your ovaries."

"Can you keep my ovaries out of your mouth?"

"That's anatomically impossible, Aria." He shot my words back at me, and I rolled my eyes at his effort to point it out. "Or it is as long as they remain within you."

I exhaled, turning as the servers entered the room to clear the dishes. They had removed one plate before a male stepped in behind me and growled. I spun in my chair, looking up as he lunged. My arms went up to cover my head, but an arm reached over me and yanked the man around the chair I sat in before he could reach me, tossing him out the door. Standing, I looked at Knox, who sniffed the air and turned to watch as another male moved toward me.

"Bloody hell," Knox hissed, catching the man mid-leap and wrapping his hand around his throat, snapping it until the room echoed from the kill. "Out!" he snapped, and I moved to obey, but his arm caught me before I reached the door, shoving me into the chair before he slammed the exit closed—along with any chance I had of escaping. "Your *ovaries* just dropped an egg."

I stared at him blankly before peering at the motionless body on the floor in utter horror. Slowly, I looked up at Knox, whose nostrils flared, and the moment he moved to step closer, I grabbed the chair holding it in front of me like a shield.

"What the fuck are you doing, woman?" he demanded.

"Not dying today," I warned.

"Cover your scent," he snapped, grabbing the body and tossing it aside like the man's life meant nothing. "I don't care how you fucking do it, just do it now."

I turned, staring at the food before frowning. "With what?" I asked, jumping as something clawed at the door.

"I don't care what you do, just do it now. I won't fight my men for you; I'll toss your untouched ass out that door and watch them fight for scraps of you before I do that."

Swallowing hard, I shook my head to clear my thoughts and grabbed the pineapple, pushing into my panties before scrunching my face up.

"Did you just push pineapple into your pussy?" he asked, leaning against the door, studying me through heated eyes.

"Did it work?" I demanded not bothering to deliberate at *where* I'd placed it, which wasn't inside of my body—because that would be *nasty*.

"No, not at all," he confirmed huskily.

"Think, Aria," I whispered softly. "There's no spell that will magically erase my scent. If I'm ovulating, so are my sisters."

"The difference between them and you is that yours is a virgin pussy, and the need to mount you will bypass most men's moral compass. You are a rarity, and in the Nine Realms, men would track your scent and take what they want from you whether you wanted them to or not. Fix it, or I will."

"How?" I whispered, ignoring the growls and fights that were unfolding outside the door.

"You won't like it," he warned.

"If it doesn't end with your cock in me, I'm game," I replied without hesitation. He chuckled darkly, smirking as he left the door to grab my hand. "What are you doing?"

"Fixing it without bending you over," he snarled, stopping and then turning as the door creaked and bowed.

He moved me in front of him, and I felt his pulsing cock rub against my back. Yelping, I leaned forward, arching my back to get distance between us, but he pulled me back even while fingering the code into a hidden panel that had blended in with the white wall. The moment it opened, he pushed me inside, following behind me.

"Careful, little lamb," he warned huskily. "Not even I am immune to your scent right now." Knox held me in place as the rattling in his chest sounded, and my body went pliant in his grip.

I stared down the pitch dark hallway, or what I assumed was one, and waited for whatever was happening to him to pass. I didn't breathe, let alone move.

"Walk," he ordered, and I bolted at the sound of his voice, only to be yanked back. "You run, this ends with you mounted and screaming my name, Aria. Do not fucking tempt me right now."

CHAPTER
16

Knox followed me, issuing directions in the dark and preventing me from slamming into walls as we made our way through the labyrinth of secret passageways in his mansion. We passed walls with holes that allowed a little light into the darkness, and I hadn't missed that they looked into bedrooms. I also hadn't missed that my vagina was covered in pineapple and that I'd left it in my panties due to the room being in danger of being breached.

We approached a glowing doorway, and I slowly turned, watching his head nod as I pointed at the room. Once through it, I took in the library, staring at the changes that had occurred since I was in it last night. We ended up in the room where I'd found him last, but the fireplace was gone and had been replaced with a chair if you could call it that. It was large, plush, and looked as if it could fit several people. The couch was missing, along with the entire length of the passageway that led out of the room.

"Uh," I whispered as my eyes focused on anything but him as he watched me through a hooded stare. "So, is there a garbage can in here by chance?" I asked carefully.

"For?"

"I have a pineapple issue." I watched his lips curling into a wolfish smile that set every nerve ending on high alert.

"So you do," he chuckled, stepping closer, watching me for any sign of movement.

It wasn't his usual predatory gaze. It was feral. It was the look a wolf had as he watched his prey for any sign of weakness, and once shown, he'd exploit it to get an easy kill. He stopped in front of me, holding my gaze as one hand lifted my dress while the other slipped between my legs. I gasped and then sucked air into my lungs to hold the moan in as his fingers collided with my clit and then slid through the slick, sticky mess the pineapple had made.

The entire time, he watched me, trembling lips and all. My body shivered, reacting to his touch as if he was the match that lit the fire within me. He pulled the pineapple out, smelling it, and I opened my mouth, snapping it closed as his smile formed the closest thing to an actual smile he'd had since I'd met him. His teeth were no longer blunt, which I wasn't sure he noticed as he plopped the chunk of pineapple between his lips, devouring the fruit that had been in my panties.

"That was... Oh *my* God," I uttered, watching as Knox licked his lips clean.

"It does make it taste sweeter," he rasped, sending

every nerve in my body to high alert with need.

"Gross!" I cried, taking a step away from him, noting he moved forward with me. "Remember, you don't like me."

"I don't need to like you to fuck you. It's better for you if I don't."

"Knox," I whispered, licking my lips to wet them. "I'm a witch, remember?"

"I'm not planning to fuck you." He watched as my legs buckled, and I slammed down on the chair ungracefully. "Do not fucking move. I mean it, Aria. You move, and they'll smell you. They smell you, and I'll bend you over and breed your cunt myself, woman. You get me?" he snapped harshly. "I'll take you first, but they won't care as long as they can have whatever scraps are left of you when I am finished taking what I want."

"Understood." I swallowed hard, folding my hands in my lap as I sucked my lip between my teeth and waited. Staring up at him, I watched his eyes narrowing as his nostrils flared, even while his tongue slipped over his bottom lip seductively.

"So, you *can* listen," he snorted, taking a step away from me. "Good girl."

I watched his eyes darkening before he turned, taking long, angry strides toward the wall that opened up and expanded a moment before he would have walked into it. His footsteps receded down the hallway, and I watched as he turned back, looking at me over his shoulder, smirking before he spoke softly.

"Do not let anyone get near her unless she moves.

Do not hurt my men if they come, just stop them from reaching her, understood?"

My eyes lifted and my jaw dropped open as the gargoyles I'd assumed were statues crafted by an artist *moved*, watching me as they grew in size and dropped from the perch they'd been sitting on to stand around me, one resting gray eyes on me as he took in my naked legs.

"Are we still beautiful, mistress?" he asked, his tone eerie and foreign, and yet he spoke English flawlessly, as if he'd been doing it his entire life.

"Very," I whispered through the dryness of my throat. Gargoyles were freaking extinct, and yet here they were, hiding and very much alive in Knox's freaking library! "So very beautiful," I swallowed thickly.

"Move for me, little one." He watched me with a wicked grin as he shivered, inhaling deeply.

"No," I countered. "Where are you from?"

"Not here, nor will I spill his secrets to his enemies."

"I'm not his enemy."

"You most assuredly are, as you are the granddaughter of Hecate." He stood up taller, his wings unfurling but no longer stone. He was all man and sexually charged with enough power that it slithered over my flesh. "You are pretty and clean. You are not pure witch, are you?"

"No, my father was other, but it is unknown."

He leaned closer, sniffing me, which almost caused me to retreat, but growling sounded, and they cleared out quickly. My gaze moved to Knox walking with Lacey and another woman. Lacey looked different, her eyes were vacant, and there were marks over her flesh, including red handprints on her throat. I studied her before moving my stare to the new lady who marched beside Knox with her hand touching him. The man had women falling all over him, and I found it pathetic.

"Examine her, Regina."

"Hell no," I stated.

"Option A, or option B, Aria?" His face tightened, and his eyes slanted as he smiled coldly. He looked like he was hoping I would choose option B. Option B was violent, it was apparent in the way he'd spoken of it.

"Tell me what option A is."

"I will put blood into a vial and add ink into it, mixing the two together. Then I'm going to use the ink to place my personal runes on your flesh as well as my name, at which time every male will know you are mine. Ovulation isn't a one day process, and the mark should outlast it."

"How long will your name be on me?" I asked carefully, knowing that what he was planning to do was something men did to their untouched brides in the Nine Realms. It was taught to every child in the academy we'd attended. It was also the only way to prevent my scent from luring men to me in mass, but there was more to it, a lot more to it.

"Three weeks, since my blood is pure, and my scent is rather potent."

"For this to work…" I lowered my gaze as I exhaled, slowly lifting it back to watch him as I spoke. "You have to be the strongest male in this realm. They could challenge you for me if you're not, and the cost would be your life."

"I am, and they won't." He didn't hesitate before assuring me he was the strongest, most dominant creature in town.

"You'll feel me on a deeper level than you probably are willing to." I paused, tilting my head as I considered what it would mean. If I touched myself, he'd feel my need. If anyone else touched me without gaining his permission, he could claim their life in payment. I would literally be his property until it wore off. "Why are you helping me?"

"It's not by choice. As I have said before, someone very powerful wants you alive. If it was up to me, I would just take what I wanted and snap your pretty fucking neck and remove the problem. You are a problem. I fix problems."

"Okay." Swallowing hard, I watched as the female glared at me before moving closer.

Regina grabbed my arm, holding it out so she could smell my wrist. Her sharp silverish-blue eyes narrowed as her soft black hair fell over my arm, seconds before her tongue slipped over my flesh then she pulled back, staring down at me with intrigue in her icy stare.

"You're right. She smells different. Almost like roses, or some other delicate flower." Her tone softened for him, and I relaxed until her hands lifted, grabbing the dress I wore and ripping it apart at the bodice. "Remove it, or I will."

"Fine," I growled, hating that I was about to be half-naked and exposed to the people in the room. I was magically muted, alone, and naked. What could possibly go wrong?

CHAPTER
17

I stood up, wishing I'd worn anything other than the sundress I'd taken from Amara's room. Letting it slide down my body, I covered my breasts and sat back down, fully aware of how exposed and vulnerable I was. I needed my magic, needed it to fight off anything that tried to harm me. Here, in his house, I was vulnerable around him without my magic to protect me.

"She's very beautiful. Why spare her? The men would leave such lovely marks on her delicate flesh for me to heal."

"Do your fucking job, Regina."

My eyes remained on the floor, unwilling to look up and see either heat or disgust in Knox's eyes at my too skinny body, or revulsion at the scars covering my ribs where my mother had tried to catch me in the water to drown me by weakening me with her blade covered in poisonous hemlock.

"What are these from?" Regina asked coldly.

"Knives," I answered, knowing what she meant without having to see where her eyes looked. I sucked my lip between my teeth and worried it as I swallowed down the memories of how I'd gotten them.

"You're a witch. Why didn't they heal correctly?"

"It was a blade covered in hemlock." The cuts had mostly healed, leaving tiny silver-colored scars long after the wounds had sealed. Aurora had spent weeks healing them to save my life, casting spell after spell to draw out the infection that tried to take me to the grave.

Hemlock was poison to witches like wolfsbane was to werewolves. It weakened us, targeting the blood until infection grabbed hold of the victim and fought hard to end their lives, even in immortals.

"She meant to end your life," she whistled, grabbing my arms, which caused my gaze to flutter to hers. "I need to see all of them."

I let her hold my arms out, turning my head to stare at the gargoyles' backs that ignored us as if we didn't exist. Her eyes took in my breasts, noting the three deeper marks below the rib cage on the left side, where Freya had barely missed ending my life as a child. Once she'd examined them, she stepped back, letting her gaze drop to my stomach and lower yet.

"Do you want me to check everywhere, my love?" she asked, and my head turned, watching Knox, who stared at my breasts before I covered them up, praying silently that he said no.

"Is she strong enough?" he countered.

"She's strong enough, but her scent... I cannot place it. It is as you said, she is unknown. Her scars are minimal, and while disfigured, it doesn't take from her genetic makeup. She's strong enough to survive your blood and the marking you will place."

"Good, get out," he snapped gutturally. "You as well, creatures. Go guard the entrances. No one gets into this room tonight, no one."

I frowned, turning to look at Lacey, who had yet to speak or flap her lips. Her eyes had remained vacant. Knox even spoke to her, yet her eyes remained empty even though she replied. Knox whispered in a foreign language, and she moved, grabbing a bowl. He moved a table with candles on it, along with onyx crystals placed in a pattern I didn't recognize right offhand. He produced a dagger as the candles ignited, and silently I watched as he slit his wrist wide open.

Knox didn't flinch or acknowledge the pain even though it had to have hurt. Next, he held his wrist over the bowl, lifting his heated stare to mine as Lacey chanted, causing the candles to leap higher with her spell.

The crystals hummed with power, and my arms dropped from where they protected my naked breasts. I watched it with curiosity as erotic magic filled the air until it was suffocating.

I'd done thousands of spells, but never with the amount of blood he was using, and never in foreign words such as the ones coming out of Lacey's lips. Power dripped from her words, and it slithered over me, making my eyes grow heavy as I watched her lips moving. A sliver of fear rushed down my spine, but I ignored it as my nipples hardened, and my throat became tight with a moan fighting to escape.

Magic exploded into the room as she finished chanting. It wasn't light or dark magic, it was something else entirely. It felt ancient and caused my pulse to race as my insides burned with the call to join them in the spell.

My mouth opened to moan, but the heat from Knox's gaze and the sinful curve of his lips stopped it, forcing the moan back down into my lungs. I shook my head, trying to dispel the lust and power that rushed through me. My body fell backward, and my hands dropped, revealing hardened nipples, to hold onto the chair as I arched my spine, even as I fought it. It was raw, untainted magic that begged to be tasted and touched. It drugged me without permission, filling the entire room with a dark, erotic state that I couldn't escape.

I was still lying on the chair lost in the magic when Knox touched me, causing my hypersensitive skin to tremble before goosebumps spread over it. He chuckled, fully aware that I was in a magic-drugged state.

Knox studied the way my body moved through heated eyes, the way I arched my spine as the magic continued to slither through me as if it was within me and slowly touching me in the most deliciously sinful way it could. He missed nothing as I rocked to the magic, needing release more than I needed to be saved right now.

"It's powerful, isn't it?" he rasped, moving his fingertips over the thin scars on my ribcage. My flesh begged for his touch, even though my mind struggled to remember who I was and who I was with. His fingers continued to leisurely explore as I realized where he touched me. The dark, black ravens that sat beneath or beside each slash. The unkindness. "You hide them well," he stated, pulling up a chair while my head turned to watch him.

"Where are you putting it?" I asked huskily.

"I was going to place it on your pretty naked cunt," he stated crudely. "But I decided the inside of your thigh, right here," he said, touching me where my leg met my covered flesh. "Every time you self-soothe, you'll remember me there," he chuckled darkly.

"You're a dick."

"I am okay with that," he announced, pushing my legs apart, staring between them as his nostrils flared, and the tick in his jaw began hammering slowly.

I leaned up, watching him where he'd moved the chair to sit between my thighs, and he rearranged me until I was spread-eagle, with him at my most vulnerable position. His mouth lowered, and I shivered as his heated breath fanned the flesh on my thigh.

His tongue snaked out, dragging over the flesh where he said he planned to place the ink, and my eyes widened as pleasure ripped through me, unfurling something within me that rattled while I watched him. Ocean-blue eyes locked to the turquoise of mine, and I smiled seductively, uncertain why I smiled like an idiot, and yet I was.

He pulled away, and I fought the urge to demand he continue, to demand he go with option B, but that terrified me. My head dropped back, and my hands covered my naked breast, fear rushing back to the front of my mind as he chuckled before pain ripped through my leg, pushing deeper as a humming noise began.

"Ouch."

"It's a sensitive spot. Since I'm saving your ass, you'll fucking deal with it. I'm not immune to your need, either. I have to suffer right beside you, ignoring every male instinct inside of me that wants to push that sweet flesh apart and bury my cock balls deep in that tight cunt, Aria. You'll learn to like the pain I intend to give you, at least for now. Either that, or we go back to option B, and I enjoy every fucking moment of it."

"This is fine, pain is good."

My gaze moved around the room, searching for Lacey and then going back to the pain of the tattoo I was getting in the worst possible location… Okay, so there were a few more tender spots, but this one still was high up there. His thumb grazed my flesh, and I moaned, lifting my head to glare at him.

"Suffer," he snapped. "You're not the only one in pain here," he announced. It took almost an hour of the gun's painful bite, mixed with Knox's fingers touching or skimming my flesh. At the same time, I was seconds away from coming undone before the pain was finally bearable. He chuckled darkly, and his head lowered, sniffing the area where his knuckles continued skimming over.

I watched him carefully as he set the tattoo gun aside and stared at me. "What are you doing?" I whispered through heavy lust that dripped with every word I uttered.

Before I could stop him, Knox pushed my panties aside and trailed his tongue through the mess he'd made before his tongue slid in a circle over my clit and sucked softly. I moaned loudly as I arched into his mouth, grasping the edge of the chair as everything within me sprang to life. One simple lick and he lifted his dark head, smiling wolfishly as he licked his lips clean.

"What the hell, why would you do that?" My breathing caught in my throat as I shivered from the heat of his mouth. My entire body was taut, ready to unfurl explosively.

"Now I have your scent and your taste, Aria. You run, I'll follow you. You fuck me, I'll destroy you. You taste sweet, almost like a pineapple."

"You're fucking disturbed." The magic was still making my head spin, but I was slowly starting to feel somewhat normal, or I had been until he'd tasted me.

"Yeah, but you fucking felt me, didn't you?" His voice was raspy, filled with lust that rocketed through my system violently. Knox smiled, but he was all predator, watching me as I shivered against the feel of him against my sex.

"That matters little, Knox. You seem to forget that I don't like you, and it may not matter to you, but it does to me," I said, observing him as he began to move from his chair.

He stood up, staring down at his work before I struggled to sit up. I stared down at the long-ass word that went from the front of my leg to the back in the crease of my junction. On the bright side, no one else would see it, but I was pretty sure it wasn't his name.

"You do know how to spell your name, right?"

His brow lifted, and then a dark smile played on his lips. "It's my last name, in my language, Aria."

"Which is?" I asked pointedly.

"You can figure that out on your own. Go to sleep. Until the ink is sunk into your flesh and we're certain it worked, you sleep here."

I looked beyond him, finding a bed with silver sheets and soft white pillows. I stood slowly, frowning. "Isn't it like…? Noon, didn't we just have breakfast?"

"It took twelve hours to place my name on you deeply enough that it stuck. Trust me, you're exhausted. The spell makes you think otherwise. Go to fucking bed, woman."

I slipped from the chair and winced as I walked to the bed, feeling the exhaustion hit me the moment I was upright. The aching throb between my thighs wasn't helping me. I still felt his touch. The sight of him chewing the pineapple couldn't even remove the need to reach between my legs and finish myself off. I turned, intending to thank him, but he was gone. Muscles ached in places I didn't even know they could hurt.

"Thanks, dick," I grumbled, sitting on the bed to stare at his name. I dropped back into the softest bed I'd ever lain on and groaned in bliss. My body twisted with the tension between my thighs still aching from pent up need.

Sitting up, I peered around the room with a narrowed gaze before pulling the covers over my head. I pushed my hand between my legs and gasping at how swollen it was from a single touch of his traitorous tongue. Remembering the feel of it on me, I stroked the flames he had ignited, and the pleasure he'd given me by tasting where no man had tasted me before. Two strokes and I held my hand over my mouth, stifling the scream that built in my throat as my body jerked and color danced behind my eyes. Ocean-blue eyes filled my mind, and I paused, frowning as I sat up, pushing the covers off to sit up.

Knox was standing by the fireplace, which had once again returned to the room, staring right at me with heat filling his eyes. "You're welcome. You call me more dirty names tonight, and you'll do it choking on my cock to get the names out of your throat. Now, stop touching your pussy and go to sleep. You're loud, even if you think you're not. I'm trying to read," he growled, turning until his bulge was visible in the gray sweatpants he wore.

I leaned back, pulling the blankets up past my neck as I listened to the crackling fire along with the page-turning in the book he read, drifting into the phase right before dreams took hold of your mind. The man wasn't safe, not when he made my brain turn to mush, and all sense flew out the door.

"Knox," I whispered into the room, my voice husky with sleep and the orgasm still clinging to my throat. "Thank you."

"You're welcome, Aria." Dark laughter filled his tone, and he growled after a moment, closer to the bed, or I thought he was. I was probably hallucinating after everything that had happened today. "It was my pleasure."

CHAPTER
18

I awoke to something pressing firmly against me, groaning as every inch of my body ached. Turning, I silently took in the male sleeping soundly beside me, or I assumed Knox did. His chest didn't rise or fall with his breathing. He looked different in bed, unguarded, and less cold than when his eyes were open. Thick black lashes dusted his sharp, bronzed cheekbones. The five o'clock shadow was thicker, which I itched to touch to see if it would tickle or scratch my fingers as books often said they did.

He looked to be in his early thirties. The erotic scent of his pheromones filling the room made the sexual deviant within me perk up and want to drink the intensity they oozed. His body had come uncovered in sleep, and my gaze greedily took it in. His muscles were sharp, defined with masculinity that couldn't be denied, no matter how much I wished it was otherwise.

Knox's tattoos held words, ancient ones that no matter how many times I whispered them in my head,

I knew were wrong. Everything about Knox made it crystal clear that he wasn't from this realm, nor did he care to fit in here. Peering down farther, my mouth went dry with the sheer magnitude of the thing nestled between the dark bed of curls. Knox was hugely endowed, and everything within me said to get out of the bed and get the hell away from him.

I started to sit up but made it no farther than an inch before I was slammed against the bed, and that appendage was resting against my naked belly. I whimpered and stared into azure eyes that were hooded with lust and heavy with sleep. Knox's head lowered as his mouth brushed against mine. A growl rumbled from deep in his chest, exiting his lips to vibrate against mine.

"You talk in your sleep." His voice was sexy, filled with sleep, but he didn't appear to be moving from where he held me to the mattress with his weight. "It's annoying."

"And you're naked," I pointed out, which probably wasn't the smartest thing to do at the moment. "It's annoying, too."

"You can be naked, too, very easily."

"No thanks, I'm good." I blushed as he rocked his hips, pressing his thick cock against me.

He had lifted on his arms enough that when I looked between us, I could see his cock rested over my navel, which meant if he took me, it would bruise my lungs, or maybe even worse. Maybe that was being a little dramatic, but the man was seriously blessed in that department, and he knew it.

I swallowed and moved my stare to his, only to find

him studying me with an intensity that intrigued me. My hips lifted and then dropped, and yet he refused to budge. His hands sat beside my head, blocking off any thought of retreat.

He'd caged me in, and the mattress had sunk enough with our combined weight that I wasn't going anywhere unless he allowed it. Knox didn't speak, and I was pretty sure he knew how much his silence unnerved me.

My nipples hardened, and my spine lifted, arching with need, and those were things he, as a male hadn't missed. My knees lifted, and that only pushed him against my body more.

His lips curved into a devilish grin while he watched me plotting how best to escape him. My body didn't get the memo we didn't like this prick. Nope, instead, it responded to him. My pussy heated, signaling to the woman within me to let this jerk take what no one else had been able to.

The memory of how his mouth felt against my sex didn't help because my body was wet, dripping with the need to be taken as I recalled the details. He could smell it, which he made clear as his nostrils flared when he inhaled.

Knox wasn't even doing anything to me, and I was coming undone just from the intense burning in his stare. His shoulders bunched up as the muscles in his neck stretched. The sharp edges in his face became more defined, and the noise in his chest started, daring me to mimic it again. I knew that if I did, if that noise escaped from my lips, I was fucked. Literally and figuratively. The only sound within the room was our breathing, both rigid, leaving our lungs in short, shallow breaths.

I didn't dare move or make a single peep while he watched me. I lay there for what felt like hours peering into the depths that threatened to drown me. I inhaled the pheromones and shivered with need. My body tightened, clenching with an aching need I didn't comprehend or understand. I had little knowledge of males outside of books, and what little experience I had was an utter failure on my end.

Knox may not have liked me, but he wanted to rip the thin panties from my body and take what no one else had taken before. Power slithered over my naked flesh, and my skin pebbled in bumps of awareness. It spread over my entire body, knowing that this beast who watched me would rock my world, turning it inside out if I so much as whimpered.

His head lowered, and the heat of his mouth brushed over my throat, licking the pulse that beat wildly with both arousal and fear. The noise from whatever was within him filled the room the moment his tongue ran over my vein. His cock pushed against my belly rocking gently, and it took everything I had left within me not to moan from the heat he sent unfurling into a ball of pent up need that threatened to seep from my pores.

"Knox," I whispered breathlessly, no longer caring if he ripped the thin panties off and took me.

"Aria," he growled, but his voice didn't come out normal. It came out thickly, gravelly. Warmth spread through me at the sound of it. My nipples hardened more than I thought was possible as moisture banked between my thighs.

"This is really awkward," I continued wondering if I should point out that if we didn't stop soon, I'd make that noise and this would escalate to something neither of us wanted.

"Shut the fuck up, woman," he warned hoarsely.

"Okay," I hissed as teeth clamped down on my throat. A breathy sigh expelled from my lungs as I felt my body relaxing against his bite. It was as if his teeth had some magic power over my mind, and the moment they touched me, everything within me calmed to mush.

He chuckled against the flesh in his mouth, and yet his bite didn't hurt. My hands lifted, sliding over his sides until they rested against his chest. He held me there with his teeth, and I all but played dead for him. His hand moved, lowered to run over the side of one breast slowly.

I felt his need to learn every detail about my body. The need to bury himself so deep within me that I'd scream for him was violently exposed in his gaze. It was a raw, animalistic need that I shouldn't want, and yet I did. Worse than that, I felt my need to tell him to take me to end the slow torture that both of us were enduring slipping free.

I opened my mouth to speak, but he cut it off before the words could leave the tip of my tongue by tightening his bite and whispering through the flesh he still held between it.

"Don't. You do not understand what the fuck you are asking." His tongue slid over my flesh, lapping against my pulse as his teeth clamped against it painfully.

"Knox, I…" He lifted his mouth, flipping me onto my stomach as his fingers threaded through my hair. He ripped my head to the side, slamming my face into the mattress before his body dropped on me, pushing his thick cock against my drenched flesh. His hand grabbed an arm, bending it behind my back until I cried out in pain. Fear rushed through me, a healthy dose of it. His rattle filled the room, slipping over my heated skin as he chuckled wickedly while he rag-dolled my body.

"You are seconds away from me ripping you apart, do you fucking understand me, little girl? I won't be gentle, and I sure as fuck won't hold you when I'm finished. I would destroy you, and I wouldn't care what was left of you when I was finished with you. Do you understand me?" he asked, and when I didn't answer him past the swelling in my throat, he pulled my hair harder, pushing my arm up further, creating pain that ripped through me violently.

"Yes," I said through unshed tears that burned both my eyes and throat.

"Good." Snarling, he rubbed his cock between my thighs once more before he released me, climbing from the bed while leaving me trembling in fear and lust. "There're clothes on the chair; get dressed, and get the fuck out of my room now."

I tried to do as he said, but my body refused to move as tears built in my eyes. I struggled to get up, hating that he'd made me feel weak and exposed, which I was sure he'd done on purpose. A violent tremor rushed through me as I fought to control my emotions.

Sitting up slowly, I didn't bother to even try to cover myself as my soaked panties turned from heated to a cold reminder that I'd almost just begged Knox to take me. I slipped on the oversized black band tee, pulling my legs into the large gray sweatpants. At the same time, I continued trembling as the adrenaline abated and left me ice-cold.

Not bothering to look at him, I escaped the room with legs that shook. The door to his room led into a hallway I didn't recognize, and yet I knew without having to be told that I was on the top floor, where he'd forbidden us from entering. Finding the stairs, I made it down them and to the next floor before slipping into my room and entering the bathroom. I turned on the shower and stepped beneath the steaming water, dropping to my knees before the first tears escaped my eyes.

I hated him. I'd not liked him before, but now I hated the prick with an intensity that I couldn't understand. He had rejected me, and it had been obvious that he'd wanted me. It wasn't even the rejection that burned me the hottest. It was my reaction to him; to finally be able to feel another's touch and find pleasure within it, only to be rejected cruelly… It was like a slap in the face that hurt deeper and more painful than it should have.

It took an effort to stand, and the moment I did, I clawed my way out of his clothes and tossed them onto the floor. I scrubbed my flesh raw with the soap, needing to wash his scent from my flesh along with the touch of his mouth that I still felt burning there, taunting me. Using the shampoo I'd brought in my bag, I lathered my hair generously, washing it several times before adding conditioner, rinsing it off, then getting out right after.

It took three minutes to pack up everything I'd brought and exit the room as I'd found it, minus the wet clothes on the bathroom floor that no matter how much I'd wanted to clean the mess, I hadn't been able to touch again.

At the entrance, I paused hesitantly as Sabine and the others turned, studying me before noticing the bag. I wasn't staying here another night. If I did, I'd go insane. I could take care of myself and didn't need some cocky prick ordering me around. I also had to unravel the mess that surrounded Amara, because I wouldn't let them condemn her to the Void of Nothingness. She was my sister and my best friend. She deserved the truth to come out, and I couldn't do that here beneath the eyes of Knox, who watched every single thing we did through a microscope.

"You're not leaving," Sabine said. "It isn't safe."

"I'm not staying here another night, and neither should you guys."

"We're in heat," she frowned, watching me.

"Let her go," Knox said, entering the room, freshly showered with Regina at his side, staring at me coldly. "She thinks she can survive on her own, let's see how long she lasts out there."

"I don't need you to protect me."

"Yeah, that's why my name is on you, isn't it?" he chuckled darkly, staring me down with a bored look. He looked at me as if I was dirt he couldn't wipe off his shoe fast enough.

"Go to hell, Knox," I uttered through the tightening in my throat. Regina laughed coldly, her hand slipping up to wrap around Knox's wrist before her head rested against his shoulder while her stare burned through me.

"I need to ask you about Amara, and I can't leave everyone else here unprotected, Aria."

I looked Sabine in the eye and smiled sadly. "I know. She was sleeping with someone in the Nine Realms; I don't know who he is. I know nothing else, but I intended to figure it out. Let me know when you're prepared for the blessing. I will go prepare the house. Be safe, sisters."

"I don't like separating," she insisted.

"I'm the strongest one here. I don't need you or anyone else to pull magic from. I'll be okay, Sabine. I'm always okay. It's my thing, remember? I am fine on my own," I assured her, turning and walking out the door as Greer rushed to hold it open for me.

"Good riddance, Aria."

"Bye, Greer," I chuckled, flipping him off as I left the house.

CHAPTER 19

I started in the front room, cleaning every inch of the house while I searched for any clue that would prove Amara hadn't betrayed the covenant of immortals. It was mindless, numbing work, so I'd turned the music up, locking the world out. I'd cast a novice spell that, should any of my sisters be so inclined to come home, they could get through. It would, however, keep everyone and everything else out.

I changed into my joggers and a soft baby blue camisole before pulling my hair into a bun that was more mess than an actual bun. I cracked my neck as I stared at the kitchen floor, still covered in blood. Frowning, I moved deeper into the kitchen, grabbing the bucket we kept beneath the sink before heading outside.

Outside, the sun was already setting and creating a backsplash of vibrant colors that drew the eyes to it. Pausing, I wiped my brow and exhaled while letting nature refresh me. After a moment, I started again, eyeing the large black tourmaline rock that sat in the creek. It wasn't as large as it had been when we were kids, but then everything had been larger than life when I was a child. Memories had a way of making everything seem smaller, more insignificant as you got older. I dipped the bucket into the creek, hefting it back up before a voice caused me to drop it.

"Jasper?" I grabbed the bucket once more before looking up to find my childhood friend sniffing me. "What are you doing here?" I studied him, noting the way he held himself poised to pounce if I moved wrong.

Jasper was the son of the high alpha wolf. One of the elite pack of werewolves that had come to this realm to settle when the covenant was created among immortals of the Nine Realms. He'd also been my classmate and my first crush, but he only had eyes for Amara.

We'd been forced through endless hours of learning about the realm we had come from and preparing us for the journey we would eventually take back into it. Jasper had been my first and only crush in this town, but he'd also been one of the boys who followed us around, vowing to protect us.

The Nine Realms were created and powered by the original bloodlines. These families began to spread throughout the many realms outside the nine. Therefore, a council was formed from the bloodlines to select and govern a High King who would rule over the lower king and queens in each of the Nine Realms, also chosen by the council.

In order to preserve the Nine Realms, a pact was made between the original bloodlines stating those originals living outside the Nine Realms would be required to send a member of their family back once a year to perform their duties on the council. During that time, each of those representing their bloodline would go to their home realm within the nine, gathering at a secret location to perform a ritual that would reinforce and feed power to the Nine Realms, replenishing their respective magical properties to the realms.

"We used to be good friends, Aria."

"We also used to be stupid kids," I muttered, refilling the bucket before I set it down and turned back to study the changes in him since we'd last seen each other.

He'd filled out nicely and grown into an alpha his father could be proud of. Thick black hair clung in gentle waves to his shoulders, while his striking blue eyes watched me with interest. His arms were both covered in muscles and tattoos. The *A* on his lower forearm marked him as an alpha from the original bloodline. He wore a blue cotton shirt with rough, faded jeans and white shoes.

"Yeah." Chuckling uncomfortably, he scratched the back of his neck as he watched me. "We did a lot of stupid shit, didn't we?"

"We were twelve." I didn't trust him entirely, but then I didn't trust anyone nowadays. Call me cold or jaded, either worked for me. I had sisters I knew would go to war for me, and they meant the world to me. Outsiders couldn't be trusted, a lesson most had learned the hard way.

"You didn't have tits back then, and you sure as shit wasn't this hot." His voice broke as his eyes lowered to my breasts with heat banking in his electric-blue gaze. "But you do now."

AMELIA HUTCHINS

"My eyes are up here." I snapped my fingers, frowning while I watched his eyes lifting to mine.

"I always knew you'd be pretty, never this, though."

"Thanks. Did you see Amara before she vanished?" I asked, knowing he would have noted my sister more than the others. He had slept with her once or twice, after all.

"Aria," he warned, studying me before he shook his head. "You know I can't help you. Knox will figure out where she is."

"Before or after he condemns her to the Void?" I watched him close off to me while his posture became defensive.

"You need to be careful with him, Aria. I know you can feel him, and I know you can sense that he is different from what we are. He's… *more* than we are. You need to tread carefully with him."

"Someone murdered alphas in my backyard. My sister is missing, along with others, Jasper. If it's true what he says, I need to hear it from our people. I don't know Knox from a hole in the ground, and I don't really want to either. Tell me what happened here, please. You cared for Amara at one time. I can believe you, not him. Hell, his bloody house wasn't here the last time I was, and yet it takes up an entire freaking block, and expands for miles behind the house from what I could see. He has everyone on their knees, and yet no one seems to care or speak against him. Why? Since when do original bloodlines bow to others from the Nine Realms?"

"They can't speak against him, and neither can you. Amara came home, Aria. She came home, and she shut the blinds and did nothing normal. You guys used to dance beneath the full moon, hold harvest ceremonies, or chant together. She stayed in your house or inside the shop. She came to meetings, sure. She came to argue against everything we put to the vote. She wanted us to put some guy into a speed vote to be allowed in this realm, and when the others wouldn't agree, she got angry. She slept with husbands of prominent women, and everyone knew she did it to sway their votes, and when she put it up to a vote again and got the same answer, she changed. She wasn't just angry; she was colder, calculated, and furious at all of us. Men still came to her, though, because what was the slogan your mother used? Once you go witch, you'll never switch?" His head tilted, and he watched me carefully.

"Something like that." My brow creased, and I frowned, absorbing what he said. I rubbed my eyes before groaning. "I don't understand why she would want that creature here. She knew he used her, she bitched about him and yet she continued to request to be sent back to the Nine Realms every time. She broke my leg so that when my turn came, I couldn't go. I'd dreamt of going since before I could remember. The thing is, Jasper, she wasn't powerful enough to bring down an alpha, not even during the weakest moon phase. Amara refused to learn to fight, and she lacked the concentration and conviction to cast alone. Unlike me, she needed the others to cast magic other than minor spells. How the hell could she have brought an alpha to his knees and executed him?"

"What if she didn't do it alone?"

"No one else would be stupid enough to help her

break through a portal, no one. It's treason against all immortals, not to mention against the Nine Realms."

"Aria, someone from your line helped creatures into this realm. Someone executed an alpha on your family's altar, draining their blood into the family crypt below it. If it was not Amara, then who else would be able to do it? You and your sisters were all elsewhere, and she was the only one here."

"Yeah, but she wasn't strong enough to cast a spell that would break through a portal. It looks bad, I know, but Amara was kind, and she wanted a family, one who wasn't controlled by this place. She was dating and kept serious relationships for long periods of time. That's unheard of for our kind, you know that. She, out of everyone else, wanted to marry and settle down somewhere quiet."

"My mother betrayed the Nine Realms, did you know that?" he asked softly, his hands pushing into his pockets. "She abandoned us and found a lover within the Nine Realms. He promised her a kingdom, and all she had to do was bring him two children from each bloodline that lived outside the Nine Realms. She agreed to his terms and started a mother's-day-out program for immortals living in this realm. My mother took those children to her lover in the Nine Realms, where he murdered them. He drained them of blood and made her bring their bodies back into this realm.

"Eventually, Knox came, and he ended it. He told us of what she had done and who she had been with. Knox took her head, Aria. To repay the lives she'd taken, he took her head. I stood there as her blood splattered my face as his sword severed her head from her body.

I didn't believe she could be so evil, but he presented her lover to us, and all the evidence that proved what she had done. He won't murder your sister until he is sure she committed treason. If she is guilty, she won't go to the Void. The alphas have requested the same punishment for her. A life for the life she took." His head bowed, and he rested his hands on his hips while a frown marred his lips.

I listened to him tell me what he knew and replay all the events that had occurred since we left this town twelve years ago. He didn't tell me everything, and I could tell he was holding back important information. He also kept Knox out of it mostly, but every once in a while, his story would shift, and a detail would cause the hair on my neck to lift with unease.

He'd been the first man here to sleep with Amara after she'd returned to town, and he kept it from me. I could hear the jealousy in his tone as he listed the names of her lovers and noted which ones had been murdered shortly after.

It wasn't black and white. He filled in the grays I'd wanted to know and informed me that Amara spent endless hours locked within the store we owned. She'd fired the witches who had been hired to run it immediately after returning and spent most of her time there. It explained why the house had shown little evidence of her being there.

Long after he'd left, I stood there staring at the house. The information hadn't helped, but then it hadn't been what I'd wanted to hear, which made it a tough pill to swallow. Eventually, I picked up the bucket and entered the house silently, working to scrub the blood that covered the floors. It gave me an escape from focusing on Knox, and the feel of his hands on my body, which had yet to dissipate.

I worked until it had exhausted me, and eventually, I hiked up the stairs, and entered Amara's room instead of mine, staring at the empty bed. Beside it was a picture of her and me sitting on the altar outside.

I picked up the picture, staring at the eyes that smiled at whoever had taken the picture. In it, Amara's eyes had dark shadows, while mine reflected the light. It wasn't a reflection or result of the lighting, it was something else. I also noted something standing in the backyard—no, not something, *someone*. A man stood on the far border of the property, covered in shadows that made him seem as if he belonged to them. He watched us, but even in the distance where he stood, I could see the smile that curved his lips. *Weird.*

I set the photo down and moved out of the bedroom, closing the door behind me before entering my room and changing into a thin nightgown. It was the hottest month of summer and having no power sucked.

CHAPTER
20

I awoke in the middle of the night to a sound downstairs. Standing from the bed, I wiped the sleep from my eyes. Something smashed against the wall, and I frowned. The noise came again, and I started moving without grabbing my robe as I took the stairs two at a time, coming down the back staircase.

I noted the candlelight illuminating the grimoire room, and I slowed my breathing, stepping closer to the crashing sounds and staring at the back of a woman. She turned, screaming out a spell. I thrust my left hand forward, deflecting her spell from hitting me, as my right hand lifted, forcing her to hover in the air.

"What are we looking for?" I lifted a brow as I stood in the doorway, watching her while she flailed in the air. "You know that you're in the House of Magic, and Hecate witches have no mercy, right?" I dropped my finger, slamming her against the floor before lifting it, causing her to hover in the air again.

"You're one of them, traitor! You don't deserve to

hold the grimoires of the Nine Realms; they belong to all witches, not just the Hecate bloodline! You will all suffer painful deaths for your betrayal."

"I have betrayed no one." I shrugged, watching her bounce off the floor again before lifting my finger to hold her with my magic. "Who sent you here?"

"Freya has disowned you as her daughters. She told me where to find her family's home, so I could take the grimoires and restore them to their rightful owners. She told us it was unprotected, and that you're all worthless sluts who can't cast to save your hinnies."

"*Hinnies*?" I scoffed, laughing at her as she waved her arms helplessly in the air. "What the hell is a hinnie?"

"You little bitch, you will pay!" Her screaming cracked as she bounced off the floor again, hitting the desk, which unseated a few books and sent papers across the floor.

"You know, it actually sounds like something my evil bitch mother would do. Sending some wannabe witch into our home to take grimoires she's very aware cannot be removed. The book you're holding, it can't leave the house. Period. Not even if the House of Magic is down and exposed. Here, let me show you," I stated, turning with my finger in the air, forcing her to follow as she continued to hover, waving her arms while holding on to the grimoire for dear life.

The moment we reached the front door, I used my other hand to open it with magic and sent her sailing through the opening. She exploded, and yet the grimoire fell to the ground without a single drop of blood marring the leather-bound cover. I whispered a spell, cleaning up the blood before it even touched the wood and grinned wickedly.

I exhaled, lifting my stare to glare at Knox, who watched me from the porch where he leaned against a column, his arms folded over his chest and his slut at his side. I smiled coldly, lifting my fingers to slam the door closed in their faces.

Trekking into the kitchen, I fixed my mess of a hairdo and grabbed the dirty pail of water before heading back to the front room to find Knox and Regina inside the house. Regina held the grimoire, turning the pages as her hand glowed blue. I dropped the pail of water and grabbed her with magic, holding her against the wall while I held my hand out for the book, catching it without releasing my hold on her.

"That isn't yours," I hissed, holding the powerful grimoire. I watched her for several satisfying moments until the hold I had on my magic vanished, and a smile curved Knox's lips.

"Play nice, ladies."

"Get out of my house." Dismissing them both, I moved back toward the room, housing held the ancient books of spells and magic. Inside, I touched the grimoires the other witch had piled on the desk, looking around it before I whispered a spell to stack the books back in their places, only for nothing to happen. I exhaled as sweat dripped down my neck.

Bending down, I picked up the pages that had been strewn about and set them in a pile, standing to put them back into the drawer when I was grabbed and pushed toward the desk. My leg hit it, and I cried out, grasping my leg while angry eyes locked with mine. My chest rose and fell slowly with anger, and yet Knox didn't speak while he hungrily took in the tight nightgown clinging to every curve from the sweat that coated my skin.

"What the fuck do you think you're doing, little girl?" He released me, standing back to take the mess in.

"I believe I dismissed you," I stated, turning around to open the drawer while dropping the papers back into it.

"Pouting?"

"What would I have to pout about?" I ignored him, continuing to take my frustration out on the mess while doing my best to ignore his overpowering presence.

"How about the fact that you were about to ask me to fuck you this morning, and then I scared you off?"

"No, you didn't scare me. You saved me from making a huge mistake, probably the worst mistake of my life. I should be thanking you, but I just don't like you enough to be that civil. You need to leave, though. Take your whore with you, Knox, and get out."

"As of now, Aria, nothing in this house is off-limits to me, or anyone I bring into it. That includes you," he snapped, forcing me to turn toward him.

"These are Hecate bloodline grimoires, and no witch may take them out of this house, or even look at them unless we say so. You want to peek through them, fine. She touches one, and I will make her explode, slowly, so she feels every fucking moment of it before she detonates. And, Knox, thanks again for stopping me from the biggest mistake of my life." I exited the room and slammed the door behind Knox the moment he was out of it. It sealed shut behind me, and I smiled victoriously.

Even without the power of the house, the power of a goddess sealed the door once it was closed by one of our bloodlines. It had been sloppy to forget to close it earlier, but then I'd been tired and searching through grimoires for the blessing. It took a lot out of me since I was still drained from scrubbing every inch of the main level of the mansion.

"Night, jerk." Chuckling softly, I took in his glare when it landed on the door as gold and silver magic locked the bolt into place. The sound of deadbolts sliding home within the door was comforting as the tick in his jaw began hammering.

"Where the fuck do you think you are going?"

"To bed, alone," I said, not bothering to stop as I climbed the steps for the ninth time today. By all rights, I should have a banging ass by morning.

My feet touched the floor and moved through the hallway until I reached my room. I turned to close the door only to be shoved into the room hard. I hadn't even heard him walking behind me, assuming he'd remained on the first level with his whore. Knox didn't speak; his cold, hard eyes told me all I needed to know. He strolled in, staring me down with heat and anger building within him.

"I guess you need it spelled out for you?"

Knox didn't respond, or maybe he just didn't like women speaking down to him. Instead, he paced around me, walking in a circle, glaring at me like he thought it would intimidate me, so I turned with him, never giving him my back. I followed him in the tight circle until my head began to get dizzy.

"Look, I'm exhausted and just committed a murder, which takes a toll when it's done with magic, in case you are unaware of that fact. But you're Knox, and you know things. I'm going to bed." He still moved in a circle around me, but where he was walking around me, I was spinning, which was fucking with my head. "Hey, it has been fun playing spin the witches with you, but some of us are tired." He stopped, grabbing me by the throat, walking me to the bed slowly.

I trembled, staring at him as he gave a wolfish grin, trailing heated eyes down my body as he spoke. The moment he did, everything inside of me snapped tautly and hung on his every word. *Oh shit.* This was bad, this was really bad.

CHAPTER
21

He didn't hurt me, but he let me know that doing so would be an easy feat. He pushed me onto the bed, and I stared up at him, hating him even more than I had this morning if it was at all possible. He watched me sitting back up as his head tilted to the side, staring at the thin, sheer panties I wore that hid nothing from his heated deep-sea-colored depths.

"Touch your pussy for me, Aria."

"Like I'm going to...What the hell?" My hand moved while my eyes rounded with the movement of my hand. *"The fuck?"* I snapped in shock, watching my hand run down my stomach, inching toward the sheer fabric.

"You think I would put my name on you just to protect you?" He watched my hand vanish into my panties as my finger slid through the wetness his presence created. "Fuck with me, and I'll fuck you without even having to touch you."

My fingers slipped through my sex as heat filled my cheeks. A moan tightened my throat and fought to escape.

"Slower," he ordered, never taking his oceanic depths from where they'd locked with mine. "Fuck your tight flesh. Slower, Aria. Don't want you to come now, do we?"

"No," I hissed through clenched teeth, but my finger entered my body while it clamped around the digit, and I arched off of the bed, crying out with the need for something more. "Knox!"

"Taste yourself."

My finger pushed into my mouth, and I sank my teeth into it, smiling around it as his eyes watched the trail of blood that dripped down my chin, defiance lit in my eyes.

He smiled wolfishly, kneeling before the bed. His hands parted my thighs, inhaling deeply before he rose, licking the blood from my chin before his mouth hovered against mine. His hand lifted, pulling on my finger.

"Release it." His tongue trailed over my lips, and I moaned as I did what he'd instructed.

Holding my hand, he sucked my finger clean before running his tongue over the wound I'd inflicted. Dropping my hand, he lowered his mouth, kissing a spot on my exposed cleavage where a drop of blood had landed.

"You won't hurt yourself again, ever," he whispered huskily, backing up to glare at me. "Now, since I have you here alone, where the fuck is Amara?"

"What?" Confusion entered my stare, and I shook my head as he watched me.

His eyes searched mine before he repeated his question again, causing the skin to burn where his name had been placed. I hissed, opening my mouth to tell him where to stick it, but nothing came out. Instead, my body responded to the pain, and I moaned before I jerked in pleasure. He narrowed his gaze, dropping it between my thighs before moving it slowly back to my face.

"I don't know where she is, Knox." I'd answered honestly, but then I was confident with his name on my flesh, I wouldn't be able to lie, anyway.

"Who was her lover?"

"Kevin Kline, but he wasn't like Calvin Klein. There was also Harry, but they didn't last long…"

"Who was her lover in the Nine Realms?"

"I don't know," I replied, closing my eyes. "I don't fucking know who he was. Only that Amara kept going to the Nine Realms because of him."

"Do you think she helped him escape into this realm?" He stood up, peering around my tidy room before slowly dragging his penetrative stare back to mine.

"No, Amara is too weak to do that."

"Hecate witches are never weak." Knox picked up a picture of Amara and me that Aurora took shortly after my mother had tried to drown and murder me. In it, I didn't smile. I wouldn't make eye contact with anyone for a very long time after it had happened. Amara was hugging me like she could save me from the pain the infection of the hemlock-covered blade had caused if she only loved me enough. "Did you enjoy last night?" he asked, and the self-assurance in his tone tore at my nerves, which he was pulling on.

"Not at all, asshole," I smirked, watching him turn around slowly. I punched him in the nose, smiling as the satisfying crunch of it filled the room.

He picked me up swiftly, dropping me to the floor while his hand wrapped around my throat, watching me coldly as he stopped air from reaching my lungs. He held me there, staring down at me as his blood dripped onto my face. His smile was icy, and my hands did little to budge his from my throat.

"What the fuck was that about?" He lessened his hold to allow me enough air to speak. He didn't remove his hand altogether, but then his weight alone left me crushed beneath it.

"Don't you ever make me touch myself just to prove you can, asshole," I choked out. Knox smirked, watching me struggle beneath his substantial frame. "I'm no one's bitch, Knox. Not even yours. I'll cut your fucking name off my flesh and take my chances with the others before I allow you to use me in that way, ever again."

His thumb brushed over my wildly beating pulse while he watched me glaring murderously at him. His mouth lowered, and I turned away, staring at the box beneath my bed, and felt his head moving to look in that direction. I turned back, claiming his lips softly, nipping his plump bottom lip as a resounding growl filled my throat before I released it and narrowed my eyes on his lips.

The simple action sent a shock wave crashing through me, causing my eyes to round in horror. His grip tightened on my throat, and he smiled. I hated that I was drawn to him on a physical level, but worse, there was something deeper, something that drew the part of me that wasn't a witch to him. It was as if he was drawing me in without trying to, and yet both of us were denying it. Or maybe it was just one-sided, but his cock seemed to grow around me, which I thought was like when a dog humped your leg, assuming it meant he liked me a little.

"Nice try, Aria. What did you see?" His nose brushed against my cheek as he watched me struggling to fight his influence.

"Go to the devil... A secret box of letters." I glared at him as I let my tongue trail over my lip while he watched me through a heated stare.

His head lowered to brush against mine softly, pushing his ear against my mouth as he peered beneath my bed. My lips touched his ear, and the hair tickled my nose.

"I fucking hate you," I whispered, barely audible, and yet he caught it.

"Good," he uttered, moving off of me to retrieve the box. He opened it, and I watched as he pulled out a note. I struggled to my feet, staring at the letter he held.

Aria, my sweetest, prickly twin, you are officially given. I know you came to find me, and I know right now you're confused and hurt by what they will tell you. Don't believe them; there's so much more happening, and soon you will know it all intimately. He will come to collect you soon. I wish there was another way, but I couldn't find it in time to save you. I know you want me to be happy, and are willing to do whatever it takes to make it so. Forgive me, there was no other way. ~A

"What the hell does that even mean?" I took the letter I'd read from over his shoulder, rereading it before it caught fire. "Son of a bitch," I snapped, sucking my finger where the flesh had been seared.

"You are given, huh?" he asked, hiking a dark brow while watching my finger where it sat between my lips.

"You don't know she wrote that."

"Did she?" he asked, and I nodded, hating the weight that sat on my chest with the idea that she would sign me over to anyone. "Who is he?"

"I don't know. I have no idea." I sat on the bed, pulling my knees up to my chest while my heart ached with the betrayal only Amara could deliver. My shoulders slumped, and I dropped my head into my hands.

"Don't worry, I won't let them get you." He knelt down with his arms resting on his knees as a wolfish grin covered his sinful mouth. "If anyone gets to break your pretty little neck, it's me."

"You say the sweetest shit to me, jerk." I frowned, exhaling deeply as I tried to make sense of my sister's letter, not bothering to lift my head to look at him. "Someone could have placed it for us to find."

"I don't imagine they'd have added prickly, which only someone close to you would say. I think Amara made the same deal with Jasper's mother, Kianna, made, but instead of bringing children to the Nine Realms to murder, your sister chose you."

"Way to sugarcoat it." I lifted my glare, exhaling through the tightening in my throat. That's exactly where my mind had gone too. The question was, did she realize that some creatures in the Nine Realms wanted us dead, or to impregnate us to gain entry into this realm? If she was aware of that, then why me? Why offer me to them? I hadn't been that difficult to live with.

"Get your shit, ward the house, and let's go. I can't protect you if you're being reckless here alone."

I hated that he was right, that if someone was really after me, I couldn't be alone. It was reckless. It also meant I had a target on me, more than the one Knox had painted. I stood, turning to the closet and frowned.

"The creature in the woods, maybe it was him? He said my name, and that he'd come for me."

"The creature in the wood was a woodland fae, and he can't come after you, I ripped his fucking throat out the moment I knew he wasn't in on anything with your sister. He heard you say your name and thought to scare you. His death sent a message to the others that you're off-limits."

"How the hell am I going to live out my dream of being fucked by fairy cock now?" I scoffed, smirking at the narrowing of his eyes. He didn't find it funny; oh well, I did.

"A woman like you, she needs someone who isn't afraid to push her fucking buttons. One who can handle that mouth of yours and give it back to you. You need someone who isn't afraid to hurt you, because, Aria, you fucking enjoy being manhandled, and it gets you fucking wet when I do it."

Lowering my stare, I wanted to ignore his words, but honestly, I responded to the way he grabbed me. The way he'd thrown me down on the floor, holding my throat. I hated that he was right; it had actually turned me on. Not the painful hold, but just hard enough that he took control, if even for a moment. I was officially fucked up.

"Pass," I muttered at my own thoughts.

"Didn't offer." His stare was dark as he watched me, smiling while I imagined us doing nasty things together. I was going to need brain bleach to rid the dirty images from my head. "You're the one who imagined it being me. Don't get me confused with someone who wants you; I don't. You're messy from the inside out. It's why you clean rooms the way you do. Not because you have OCD, but because inside, you are nothing but a mess, so you fix the messes you can since you can't reach the one you really want to be cleaned."

"You got me all figured out, don't you?"

"No, not even close." He exited the room, not waiting for me to pack. Downstairs, men stood with my sisters, watching as we made our way to them.

"Problem?" Knox asked.

"You could say that," Brander snorted. "There was an alpha just discovered on the altar outside. Fresh, dead within the last half an hour," he explained, staring at me.

"Don't look at me. I was in the bedroom getting thrown around by your *brother*. Ask him." I waited for

Knox to agree, and when he didn't, I looked at him.

"You need to come back to the other house for now," Kinvara muttered. "We can't lose you too. It's not safe here without the house being blessed and active to protect us."

"I'm uncertain we lost Amara," I admitted begrudgingly. "I think she may have left on her own. She left me a note in the message box we used as children to hide messages we didn't want anyone to find, it was spelled to keep you guys from finding it. The note said she was sorry, but that I was given, whatever that means. I think she made a deal with the man she was with in the Nine Realms, and I think she bartered me instead of herself." I told them of what the rest of the note said and watched their eyes fill with pity as I finished.

"You're certain she wrote it?" Aine questioned, her lip sucked between her teeth with anger at hearing what Amara had written.

"She called me her prickly sister." I watched as Sabine covered her mouth to stifle the volley of cuss words she wished to unleash, but held back for me.

"Oh, Aria," she said, stepping toward me only to pause as Knox started to issue orders.

"Take the witches to the house, and don't let them out of your sight, Brander. I don't care if you have to tape them to the fucking wall, they don't leave. The alphas will want answers, and they'll be demanding them from the witches."

"We didn't do it. I was with you," I stated, lifting a brow at him.

"Now, Brander," he said, ignoring me altogether.

"Regina, with me, lovely." At his endearment, she lit up, smiling as she pushed past me to get to his side.

I stared after them until Brander grabbed my arm, pulling my body against his, sending a shock wave up my spine. He smirked, lowering his mouth to my ear. "Come on, little witch. You've been dismissed."

"Holy fuck, I felt you!" I gawked at him, not because he was being an asshole, because I'd felt him against my breasts, and it hadn't repulsed me. In fact, they'd responded to the electricity of his touch the same as they had for Knox.

"Keep gawking at me with an open mouth, and I'll use that tight throat of yours."

"I just might let you," I laughed, smirking before my eyes held Knox's briefly, dismissing him while Brander stared at me as if I was off my rocker. "Come on, big boy. Don't keep ladies waiting, it's rude."

CHAPTER
22

Inside Knox's house, they had set drinks out. We were being watched by the men who had been instructed to do so, yet they didn't seem to mind us getting drunk. Music played quietly in the background while my sisters spoke in soft voices, discussing the issue and what to do about it.

The blessing had to be done on the house, that was a given. The real problem was Amara, and what she'd done—*if* she had really done it. Right now, everything pointed to her, which seemed a little too convenient.

Then there were the words Amara used in her note, which confirmed she had written it. She always told me how prickly I was, and how blocked off I was from the world. I had shields I'd placed, but they were more to protect the damage within me, rather than to keep people out. I was standoffish with strangers, not quick to trust people or their motives. I protected my family, which I didn't think was a bad thing.

"You need this." Kinvara sat beside me, offering a

bottle of tequila. "You think she did this, don't you?"

"I think everything points to it, yes. It makes little sense, though. Nothing makes sense right now. What the hell did she even mean? You are given? I mean, it feels like we stepped into a mess, and she lured us into it. Then there's the fact that everything is way too conveniently pointing to her. Amara isn't stupid. She's borderline genius, so if she did this, why didn't she cover her tracks?"

"Maybe she didn't care if it did? She's gone, and we're left to deal with the aftermath. Amara could be anywhere by now, hell, even on a beach in Fiji with her lover, sucking down mojitos and laughing in the sun for all we know." Kinvara shrugged, watching me.

"It's still way too expedient to just brush it under the rug," I replied, unscrewing the lid on the tequila and taking a shot before passing it back to her. I rested my head against her shoulder, watching as the others drank and began to loosen up. Aine was talking to one of the men, her hand brushing seductively over his chest.

"I bet she has him naked within the hour, riding that pony," Kinvara chuckled, tipping back the bottle.

"Knox forbids it. He loathes witches, y'know."

"Oh, he took that back. We're free to fuck whoever we want now." She smiled while I narrowed my gaze on her, watching her chugging the agave nectar down.

"When?" I asked carefully.

"After you left to go to the house," she explained, telling me what he'd said and what the rules were. "No breeding though, apparently. Not that any of us want to ruin our hips soon. Guess he assumes we're all the same, in search of a baby daddy."

"Oh," I frowned, accepting the bottle to watch Aine. "I can feel him, Kin. When he touches me, I don't get sick."

"Shut the fuck up," she laughed, leveling me with a serious look. "Please tell me you're joking."

"No, unfortunately, he seems to have some invisible pull on my string, and he can unravel me. Tonight though, Brander pulled me against him, and I felt him too," I said, watching the male in question who sat away from the group, glaring at them all.

"Aria, this means you can finally get dick," she stated loudly, which caused the others to turn in our direction.

"Shut up, asshole," I laughed, taking another drink. I hadn't eaten today, which probably meant I shouldn't be drinking, but I missed this part of being away from the house we'd lived in before coming back here.

When we moved away from Haven Falls, we'd become closer than we'd been here. Instead of being separated to learn magic, we'd started practicing it together. We'd gone to an ordinary high school and lived normal lives with actual jobs to hone our crafts. We got drunk together, got into fights like normal kids, and while we lived in a house together, we gave each other room when we felt the others needed to have it.

It also allowed us to grow and mature in a way that Haven Falls had been preventing. I almost felt the need to thank Freya for being such a bitch, and for being so harsh on us that Aurora had taken us away from her, sheltering us while also letting us flourish.

The last time Freya had tried to murder me, we'd fled with nothing. No spellbooks, no grimoires, or anything, so we'd begun making our own. We used the internet to pull spells from the dark web, utilizing connotations to perfect them.

I started buying crystals, infusing them with magic, and selling them online until the money in my account had vanished, being added to the trust. I'd been living, though, surviving on my own with no need for this place or my mother.

It's what made this so confusing for me since Amara had been the one to point out how much happier we were away from Haven Falls. Yet she'd volunteered to come back, which I'd figured was due to our fighting. I was tired of her talking about the guy she'd been meeting in the Nine Realms, and upset she kept that secret from everyone else. I had also been angry that she'd hurt us to make sure she was the one that got to go back.

Amara had broken my leg the day before I was scheduled to take my turn, traveling to the Nine Realms, and while I'd known she'd done it on purpose, I hidden it from the others. I also told her if she did it again, after physically hurting Reign, I'd tell the others. It drove a wedge between us I'd ignored, assuming she'd get over it.

To maintain the pact between the original bloodlines, once a year, one descendant of our bloodline had to go to the court we silently ruled. It had become a massive thing once we hit the age we could begin visiting our lands. Sabine had been the first, and when she'd come back to tell us about it, we'd all craved the adventure to visit the land whence we'd come.

Amara, though, when she went for her first time had been terrified, and cried on my shoulder about leaving me alone for the few months she'd be gone. It was our first time being separated since I'd been quarantined due to infection and sepsis the hemlock had caused in my system.

She'd been inconsolable and demanded she stay. It wasn't possible to miss the rotation, and so she'd been forced to go by Aurora. She returned and told me about the man she'd met and what he'd been like. She never mentioned his name or where he was from within the Nine Realms, only that she couldn't wait to go back.

I was next, but she took my place when she cast a minor spell that had broken my leg. It happened again after that, and again until I'd warned her of what would happen should she continue to cast magic on us. She'd almost killed Reign with a spell she had no business casting, and if I hadn't been there to reverse it, she would have. She'd cast magic on Aurora to be chosen to enter the Nine Realms in our places, and I knew our aunt had figured it out but held her tongue.

Guilt ate at me for not telling the others, and yet I'd kept her secrets because she was my sister, my twin—my best friend. During the weeks before she'd come back to Haven Falls, she wasn't the same. She'd changed, and that was a hard thing to admit. Gone was the docile sister I'd had who would brush my hair and tell me stories of the Nine Realms, and in her place was someone I hardly recognized.

"Are you going to take a drink and pass it back?"

I took a long pull from the bottle before handing it to her again. "Does Aine ever keep things from you,

Kinny?"

"Like who she fucks?" she asked, drinking.

"Things like that, I guess," I frowned and took the bottle back. I was already feeling a little tipsier than I liked to be, and yet I didn't stop drinking.

"Never, we're twins. We have no secrets, not that we could keep them from the other if we tried. We'd know if the other was trying," she chuckled and then stared at me. "I don't imagine it feels good, Aria, but you have us."

"Amara broke my leg with a spell to take my place in the rotation," I admitted, feeling a weight lift from my chest.

"We knew she did that," she shrugged when my mouth dropped open. "Aria, she was a selfish prick, and whoever she hooked up with inside the Nine Realms, he had to be packing one hell of a dick to get her that worked up. Aurora knew too, but she followed her." She shrugged. "She never figured out who it was, or why he was so important for her to go, but hell if she wasn't trying to find out."

"Does everybody know?" I winced when she nodded. "I kept her secrets, but I threatened to tell if she continued."

"We knew that too," she snorted, handing me the bottle as the door to the room opened abruptly.

I tipped the bottle back, chugging it to numb the pain of what her note meant. Knox entered with Regina at his side, her eyes immediately seeking me out. She said something, and he laughed, turning his ocean eyes to lock with mine before dismissing me to lean down, whispering in her ear as Regina tipped her head back, laughing at whatever it was he'd said.

I chugged more succulent blue agave down my throat and leaned my head against Kinvara as she patted it.

"He's nice to look at, Aria, but you don't want someone like that for your first time. Pick someone safe."

Knox moved to Brander, and then they both looked at me, speaking in another tongue, one that I couldn't understand. They moved into a group, and I shook my head. My eyes moved to Brander's backside, noting the way he filled out the jeans he wore. His legs were muscular enough that you could see the power of his thighs through them. Every once in a while, one would turn and look at me before spinning back around to say something else.

Lifting the bottle to my lips, I felt my stomach churning and complaining about being empty. I needed some food to absorb the alcohol, but there was nothing here, at least not anything that had been offered.

"I'm going to bed," I said begrudgingly, knowing that I wouldn't be getting food before morning, and I couldn't stomach any more tequila without it. Standing, I moved toward the door, only to be stopped in my tracks as Knox's voice sounded, my name on his lips.

"Where the fuck do you think you're going, Aria?"

"I'm going to bed before I ruin your perfectly good couch by vomiting on it," I explained before I hiccupped, and covered my mouth, staring at him.

"Are you drunk?" He glared at me as a look of

annoyance covered his face.

My gaze slid to where Regina watched me with a smirk on her full red lips. Enjoying the show at my cost, bitch.

"Absolutely," I said, flipping him a one-finger salute using my middle finger before opening the door and slipping out.

I didn't make it three steps out the door before he was in front of me, pushing me back inside carefully. I fell back as I lost my balance, landing on my ass upon the floor. I glared up at him, and my chest rattled in warning.

"Don't fucking touch me again."

"What the fuck is wrong with you?" Sabine demanded, rushing over with the others to pick me up off the floor.

The alcohol had altered my balance and made it impossible for me to stand. I shoved my sisters away as I climbed to my feet and looked him dead in the eyes, growling. "Keep your fucking hands off of me, Knox."

"Did you kill the alpha?" he hissed.

"What? I was with *you*, asshole."

"Did you kill Jasper?" he asked, his tone turning cold and lethal.

"Jasper?" I whispered, and my heart thudded in my chest. Tears burned my eyes for the childhood friend who had played with me on the playground. My head shook as denial burned my tongue. "Jasper isn't dead. I just talked to him, not even eight hours ago. He was fine when he left." My throat tightened as my eyes pricked with unshed tears.

"He isn't fine now. We found him sacrificed on your altar, and you're the only Hecate witch that was home when it happened."

It was as if he physically slapped me. I blinked and frowned, tilting my head as I replayed the day's events.

"Jasper was alive when I saw him, and I sure as hell wouldn't have killed him. He was a friend."

"When you were a child, he was. He voted for Amara to be executed if I found her guilty."

"I know that, and I agreed with him. You think *I* killed him?" I asked.

"I think you're a self-serving little bitch who would do anything to be certain her sister isn't executed. I don't think you'd bat a pretty little eyelash at murdering someone, not after what you did tonight."

"Well then, get out your sword and kill me, executioner. Let's do this."

"You have not been found guilty yet, Aria Primrose Hecate, but you're under investigation as of now. You don't leave this house. You don't breathe without me knowing your every move. Understood?"

"Yes, master. I'm going to bed now. Did you wish to assign an escort? I may escape in my drunken state from the 'oh, so powerful male' who likes to throw me around lately." I snorted loudly before heading toward the door again. "Can I go, or do you want to throw me around a little more?"

"Brander, walk the drunken little witch to her room, and tuck her in," he called to the male who watched us silently. I turned, assuring my sisters I was fine and that I had not sacrificed an alpha this week before I started down the hall with my silent, broody guard beside me.

"You don't strike me as an idiot," Brander stated beside me as we entered the hallway. "So why the fuck are you goading him?"

"He's a dick."

"You're not a fluffy fucking bunny either, witch."

"Thanks," I stated.

"It wasn't a compliment."

"I know," I chuckled as I tilted sideways and held on to the wall for a moment to catch my balance.

"Walk," he ordered.

"I need a moment," I stated, pressing my hand against my mouth. My eyes closed, and the world began to spin around me. I opened them and started again, only to sway on my feet. "I drank way too much."

He opened the door after we'd finally made it to my room, and I entered it. Everything had been removed but the bed. No couch sat beside it, no vanity with the large oval mirror, just the large bed with one blanket and a single pillow. Great, I was in jail.

CHAPTER
23

Sitting on the bed, I frowned while gazing around the empty room. All of my personal things had been removed from the room, which meant I had nothing to change into. I turned, staring at the male who watched me with pretty blue eyes. He leaned against the door, frowning as he took in the room. Huffing, I lifted a brow.

"He took my clothes, really?" I stood up, kicking off my shoes while struggling to keep my balance. "What am I supposed to wear to bed?"

"Sleep naked, I don't mind." Brander chuckled darkly, watching me as I struggled to remove my shoes.

"Are you to be my jailer?"

"No, your room now only locks from the outside."

"Peachy," I snorted, pulling my shirt over my head, which took several times of trying before I was able to remove it. His gaze dipped to the white bra I'd changed into when we had been sent back here for Knox to investigate the murder.

Had I known I would be accused, I may have escaped and hid food and liquor in my room. If I was going to be in jail or locked up in Knox's house, it would take a lot of both to survive it. I undid the jeans I wore, pushing them down and stepping out of them.

"Are you planning to watch me get naked?" I asked, noting the smolder in his eyes while he did just that. "Want to help me get naked?" I didn't want to die a virgin, and I'd felt him, which made him one of two men I could enjoy sleeping with.

"You want me to?" he countered, and then turned, staring down the hall. "Hold that thought, my replacement is coming. He can assist you."

Knox entered the doorway, and I scoffed. "Pass," I muttered, turning around to unclasp my bra. Once the girls were free, I climbed onto the bed and pulled the shitty blanket over my head, listening as they spoke in that strange, hypnotic language.

The door closed, and still, I refused to remove the blanket, my eyes growing heavy with the need to sleep. I had almost succumbed to sleep when something sat on the bed, ripping the blanket from my head and body. I started to sit up, but the world spun around me, so I lay there, staring up at Knox, who watched me through mere slits.

"Just plan to fuck anyone willing now?"

"Well, anyone but you," I snorted, dropping my eyes from the look of disgust I read in his. "Don't take it personally, Knox, you're just a dick."

I turned onto my side, ignoring him or the fact that

I could feel his heated stare as he took in the ravens that moved up my spine and around the side of my waist to slip beneath my breastbone. He didn't speak, at least not until I was almost asleep again.

"Did you kill Jasper?" he asked, and when I didn't answer him fast enough, he asked again, the place where his name was began burning.

"You know I didn't," I hissed angrily.

"Answer the question."

"No," I whispered sleepily.

"Did you help Amara murder Jasper?"

"No."

"Have you seen her since you've been back to Haven Falls?"

"No," I replied impatiently.

"Do you want to fuck Brander?" His eyes smiled with the question, burning in them as he awaited my answering reply.

Dick.

"No." I turned to stare at him through sleep-filled eyes. "Dick move, jerk."

"Do you want to fuck me?"

"No," I stated, turning to stare at the wall as burning started in my thigh until I screamed from the pain of lying. "I hate you!"

"You hate me enough to fuck me, though," he chuckled darkly, turning me back over until he was staring down at me. "Are you still drunk?"

"Yes, very much so, Knox. Can you go now?"

"I'm debating on that now."

"Let me make this easy for you, get out. I don't like you sober, and getting drunk didn't help either. So run back to Regen, or whatever her name is, and get fucked." I turned away again, giving him my back.

"Regina is a generous lover," he divulged, and I frowned, hating him more.

"Cool story, bro. Go get it then," I muttered hoarsely.

"You chose battle ravens, why?"

I ignored him until he repeated it and forced me to answer. "Because they've been wounded, but they still fly fearlessly."

"Did you know they say the gods used them to be their eyes and ears in this realm at one time?"

"Greek or Norse, because both are believed to have used them to carry messages or warnings with their presence?" I questioned.

"It's said the Tower of London will fall if the ravens leave."

"So they clipped their wings to keep them from flying, guaranteeing it never fell. They cheated, ensuring the raven couldn't fly was mean. Apollo considered them bad luck, and Odin used them for his eyes and ears. Apollo also used them to spy on his lover because he was an insecure prat. Why are you still in my room?"

He chuckled, turning me over and moving so smoothly that my brain didn't register he'd trapped me to the bed. He stared at me, watching me carefully before I glared up at him with a loathing I couldn't fake.

"You kissed me today," he announced.

"Yeah, but it didn't work."

"You've never been properly kissed before, have you?"

"Does it matter? And so what, I wasn't trying to make out with you. I was trying to keep you from looking under the bed."

He leaned down, and my mouth opened and closed while he lowered his head, brushing his mouth against mine. I held my mouth shut, watching him until the room began spinning, and I closed them to keep from being swallowed up by the ocean swimming within his gaze. His tongue prodded my mouth to open, and I did, letting him taste the alcohol I'd drank earlier.

His hand slid beneath my head, and before I could argue, he had me sitting up without ever breaking the kiss. Knox deepened the kiss the moment my tongue slipped against his, it began pulling at something within me.

Knox didn't just kiss me.

He sent electricity rushing through me, opening something untapped within me. It was all-consuming, earthshattering, and I felt him everywhere all at once. As if by kissing me, this man had slipped into my soul and was leaving his name written in permanent ink. Knox took the air from my lungs, slowly giving it back to me with his kiss. I inhaled every inch of him into my lungs hungrily.

He deepened the kiss, making it primal as something snapped within me, and I couldn't get close enough to him. I couldn't get *enough* of him. His hand slipped to

189

the back of my neck, holding me as if he feared I would escape his hungry kiss, but thought wasn't something I could achieve with his mouth against mine. His other hand lifted, tilting my chin to gain further depth, which I wasn't sure I should allow. He wasn't asking; he took, and I gave. The heat that shot through me wasn't pleasant, it was fucking delicious, and I craved burning to ashes from the intensity of it.

Knox pulled away slowly with his forehead still resting against mine, breathing hard as he glared at me as if I'd been the one to kiss him instead of it being the other way around. There were storm clouds in his eyes, shadows of the sweetest darkness I'd ever witnessed danced within them, and I craved to taste it on my flesh. We fought to gain control of our breathing, and the moment before I had mine under control, he stood, leaving the room and slamming the door behind him, jolting me back to reality with the cool aloofness of who I'd just kissed, and what I'd allowed to happen.

"What the fuck just happened?" I whispered, touching my swollen lips.

The man kissed like he was going to war, and my mouth was an enemy he wanted to destroy. It was brutal and yet beautiful. I wanted to feel it again, to see if it happened again. I'd had boys touch my lips, but never anyone as terrifying or like Knox.

The man didn't just kiss; he fucking dominated you, and you went with it or got destroyed in the wake. My lips tingled, rejoicing with having been given my first taste of real passion, and yet it was Knox who had given it to me. No, Knox hadn't given it, he'd demanded it, and then he'd glared at me as if I was the one who had started it.

Had it scared him as much as it had terrified me? No, he was Knox, and I was just some wishy-washy witch to him. But damn, it had been like making out with a power line, the electrical sizzle that still rushed through me was everything I'd ever wanted, and yet I hated that it was him. The one prick who treated me like I was nothing, and now I'd remember him for the rest of my life and compare everyone else to him and his stupid, superb, really fucking sexy mouth.

I hated him! I loathed him more than I ever had hated another human being, and yet I craved him. I desired the connection I felt from him, which was all wrong and twisted.

Lying back, I stared at the ceiling, unable to take my fingers away from my swollen lips. I should have stopped him. I should have slapped the conceited, condescending asshole who liked to toss me about like I was something he could break and be completely okay with breaking. I was stupid to think the kiss meant anything, but then why kiss me at all? To be my first? Probably.

He'd known I'd never tasted the kiss of another, and wouldn't he be a smug prick out telling his men he'd just claimed it? He sucked. I needed to act cool tomorrow when I saw him, ignore him, and pretend he hadn't just delivered the perfect first kiss.

I could do that, right? Right.

Fuck him.

CHAPTER
24

I woke up with someone's hand touching my leg. Turning over, I stared into the amber eyes of the male I'd punched in the throat the first time I came to Knox's house, carrying a bottle of whiskey. He grabbed the blankets and pulled them back, moving onto the bed as I winced at the pain in my head. He watched me before reaching up to push his platinum-colored hair behind his pointed ear, which I strained to see through bloodshot eyes. I couldn't have awoken any faster had the ceiling been caving in on my head.

"You wear his name on you well, don't you sweetie," he chuckled huskily, tilting his head while studying me. "That explains his decree."

"Who the hell are you?" I demanded, turning to face him, uncaring that it exposed my back to the open door, but then I was wearing a thong, and it covered more than most swimsuits did this year. Soon, they were just going to be putting up stickers for your asshole and charging out the ying-yang just to cover them. "I asked you a question."

"Calm your pretty tits, girl. I'm here to wake you up and deliver you to the dining room. Clothes are in the bathroom. I suggest you start by washing that unsated flesh before you start a fucking riot." He lay back, dismissing me while folding his arms behind his head. "Go, because if there's no food, you will be my breakfast, witch, and I'm fucking ravenous right now."

I pulled the blanket around me and rushed into the bathroom, glaring at the lack of a lock or a way to bar the door from the entrance. Inside the room lay a pile of clothes, but they weren't mine. A white dress created in lace unfolded the moment I touched it, and beneath it was a garter, along with nylons and high heels that looked more like fuck-me heels than anything else.

They had brought in my makeup bag as I'd slept, along with my shampoo and conditioner. I sniffed the dress, noting that it hadn't been laundered in our laundry soap but smelled clean, and not like anyone else.

It took me less than thirty minutes to dress, and when all that remained on the counter were the nylons and garter, I slipped into the stiff shoes and realized it wasn't something I could forget. Swallowing down frustration, I grabbed the items, staring at them and the small straps that appeared to connect to the thigh-high nylons.

"Need help?" he called from the other room.

"No."

The dress itself was a white maxi spaghetti-strap dress, which meant no bra could be worn with it— which, whatever, not a problem. It would expose the thigh-highs when walking or sitting by the single slit that stopped just below the top of my thigh.

That part didn't impress me, which I wasn't so sure was an oversight by whoever had picked out the dress. Once I slipped the nylons and garter on, and looked at my reflection, I smiled. My lips were cherry red, and my eyes looked larger, more striking with the thin line of eyeliner and mascara.

Exiting the bathroom, I stared at the male who opened his mouth and then clamped it shut. He stood up, staring at where the slit in the dress rose higher than it should, and his smile twisted into something sinister.

"After you, beautiful," he stated, holding his hand out toward the door.

I moved toward the door, ignoring him as best as I could even though he made a strangled noise behind me. I barely contained a snort when Brander exited a room beside mine, watching me as his gaze dropped to the deep V-neck of the bodice, allowing him to see the raven that flew toward my heart in the middle of my breasts.

"Morning," he uttered, wiping his hand over his mouth as I passed by him.

"Good morning, Brander," I said dismissively, feeling like a doll who'd been dressed up to show off.

The moment we entered the dining room, I paused. It was full of alphas, and I had no magic in my arsenal to defend myself. The male behind me paused and waited silently. The table was covered in meats, with a single dish of pineapple on it. My heart slammed against my chest at the sheer amount of raw, unguarded power and testosterone in the small room. It was a formula for disaster.

"Aria." Knox's voice pulled me from the need to bolt. "On my right, sweetheart," he said huskily.

Frowning at his endearment, I glared at him while making my way to him. He stood the moment I approached and moved to kiss me, but I pulled back, narrowing my eyes on his. Had he bumped his ever-loving head this morning?

"Sit, you've not had your breakfast and are looking peckish, my love."

I frowned, watching as his eyes warned me silently not to argue with him. My mouth wanted to; in fact, it had a lot to say, and yet I bit my tongue and smiled demurely, or I gave it my best try for one. My head pounded, and the noise of the room intensified the headache. Maybe tequila hadn't been such a good idea last night.

I pushed my unbound hair away from my shoulders as he held my chair out for me. Taking a seat, I stared down the line of alphas surrounding the table, all looking like they'd rather be eating my heart instead of the impressive spread of food. I couldn't calm the increasing rate of my heart, and the fact that his bitch, Regina, was eating with us on his left didn't help me either.

"What is this?"

"It's breakfast with the alpha council, sweet girl."

"Stunning, considering what a whore her mother is," an alpha stated icily, cutting in on our whispered words.

"We should bend her over and fuck the grief out on her," another said.

"If you wish to keep your fucking tongue, Landon, you will keep it in your mouth and not speak about bending any bitch over my table. Especially one who now carries my scent on her and is under my protection," Knox said offhandedly, as if he'd just announced it looked as if it might rain today.

I turned, staring at Knox as he piled meat onto his plate before picking up a piece of pineapple and pushed it between his lips, drawing his gaze back to mine as he made a noise indicating it was delicious. I blushed to the white-silver roots of my hairline and swallowed the groan before tearing my eyes from his back to the meat.

"She is accused of murdering my son and heir. Yet you would claim her and offer her your protection?" Fallon, the head alpha, asked in outright disgust.

"She is merely accused, not condemned. She had nothing to do with your son's death, and the investigation is ongoing. Eat, woman. You're too thin as is." His eyes watched the rise and fall of my breasts before he pushed the entire plate of pineapple in front of me. "Eat now."

I picked up a piece, shoving it into my mouth without waiting to see if he said anything else.

"She didn't murder your son because she was with me," he said, and I exhaled, grabbing another piece as relief washed through me.

"Doing what exactly?" Fallon asked coldly.

"She was riding my dick," Knox stated, pushing meat into his mouth. I coughed, covering my mouth while my eyes widened in horror. "Smell her pretty pussy, she carries my scent, but more than that, gentlemen, she carries my name next to her flesh, and has to speak the truth when I command it. You will cease demanding her head be brought to you, and will immediately cancel the bounties you placed for it. If you murder an innocent witch, well, you become no better than the one who murdered your son. I understand your grief, better than most of you. She belongs to me now, unless anyone wishes to challenge that claim?" He waited, pushing more meat between lips while I watched him chewing it silently as his eyes smiled at me.

"No challenges will be forthcoming, but I would like to know what Aria had to say about your claim on her since she is royalty by the laws of the Nine Realms."

I turned to Fallon with genuine grief, smiling sadly with tears in my eyes. "I am so sorry for your loss, Fallon. Jasper was one of the few children—ever—who showed kindness to me outside of my sisters. I am so sorry that he was taken, and I hope you find who is responsible and get justice for him. You are owed it by the law of the Nine Realms."

"And if it is your twin? Your flesh and blood who murdered my son?" He waited, watching me for any sign of guilt or weakness.

"If it was Amara, then I'll take her head myself. If she is behind this, whatever befalls her...Well, she would be beyond our protection, now wouldn't she? The law states that we cannot offer her sanction or sanctuary if it interferes with those investigating the case. If she is guilty, then by the laws of the Nine Realms, she will be punished accordingly, or a representative from there will help decide her fate."

"And your family's name?" he continued, sitting back as he inhaled.

"My mother has already besmirched it enough, Fallon. We can withstand the charges, as whatever is happening does not involve us. We may be guilty of claiming the evil bitch that created us, but I assure you, we can stand on our own without worry. As you know, Hecate witches are resourceful and favored within the Nine Realms by men from all nine.

"Our bloodline is the reason you sit here today, having created the portal that discovered every realm. We helped unite them, did we not? We broke down the walls that separated the realms between each one of them. Hecate herself brokered the peace between the realms, showing that trade from each would ensure prosperity and power for each race that lived there and followed the pact.

"I may be young, but I have studied our homeland and know what each race and land provides in exchange for peace. I also know which creatures are where, and which of them are favored to win a war should it come to pass. I am very accustomed to the laws of treason, as well as the cause and consequences of them. If the accusations are true, then Amara will pay for what she has done. Neither my sisters nor I would think to protect her past the laws of the Nine Realms, should they be followed and proof is provided. Do not think you can threaten me with ruining my family's name, as we have survived much worse than this."

"Of all the women Jasper could have chased around, you, Aria, were the one I hoped caught his eye for a fruitful union between our bloodlines. Your mind is beautiful, and not many women come with the full package. Yet you never showed interest in the royal heirs, even when your sisters began showing interest to some races. You were well-studied, and loved learning of our home realms, and would have made a great queen to the alphas when Jasper took his throne. Now you claim this creature instead of a match among one of the Nine Realms original bloodlines, why?"

Creature?

Knox placed his hand on my leg beneath the table, squeezing it. I didn't flinch or jolt, even though I wanted to from the heat of his touch. He was offering me an out by confronting the alphas, and while I was glad for it, I wasn't his anything.

"Because he makes me shiver, and gives me the most delicious feelings when he fucks me," I informed huskily, playing the part. Knox's hold tightened on my leg, and I shivered. "It may change later, but for now, his cock suffices to fill my needs. I have agreed to give him a spin around the block to see where this thing goes. If he can continue to sate my rather large appetite, I may allow him to continue doing so. You know how we witches are, never satisfied and always on the lookout for someone with more power."

."Aria, there is no one more powerful than Knox Karnavious."

I blinked and smothered my surprise by covering my mouth with the napkin, dotting at the invisible juice. Looking to Knox, I narrowed them ever so slightly. "We'll see; the world is large and vast, and there are plenty of men within the Nine Realms to choose from. We are immortals, are we not?"

"Even in the Nine Realms, Aria, you'd be hard-pressed to find something bigger or stronger than the man sitting beside you."

My heart stopped, restarted, and then sped up. I fully knew of the monsters within the Nine Realms because I'd made it my purpose in life to know everything bigger than me if I had to visit that realm. His fingers pinched my thigh, and I nodded on cue, turning to stare at him. I couldn't very well come out and ask what he was since I was supposed to be *riding* him already.

There were rules about crossbreeding species, and it was against the covenant to even sleep with another creature before asking details about the creature they could create from a union. Not that it was enforced, but still, people wanted to know what would show up during the birth of their offspring.

"Indeed," I stated through clenched teeth. "I'm very aware of that, but I am hopeful all the same. A girl can always dream, can she not?"

"You got a wild one there, Knox. I hope you realize what she is." He was fishing for what I was, which no one knew. Freya had royally fucked me on that one.

"No one knows what Aria's other half is, nor has she experienced the changes necessary to figure it out. I can tell you that when she went into heat, it was deliciously erotic, and sent even my men into a state of frenzied need. Had I not intervened and slipped my cock into that weeping slit of hers, you and your men would have been at my gates, declaring war to be the first to fuck her. It doesn't matter what she is, because the laws of your realm and the Nine Realms doesn't apply to my men or me."

FLAMES of CHAOS

I winced at the crudeness of his words, but he wasn't wrong. I hadn't even stopped to think of that fact when I'd rushed back to find my twin. The alphas and whoever claimed me could have bred my womb, could have hunted me, sealing their own fate.

It could have even gone worse than that, since alphas shared unclaimed women among themselves, breeding a womb until anyone who fucked her found entrance and created a child. I knew that because Luna and Aine would endure that fate if they didn't choose a mate to protect them from it.

The room grew tense with Knox's words, or rather his declaration of what I'd been doing, and how he'd protected the wolves present from fighting them. Like he knew it would make their egos kick into gear, and he craved a fight with him.

This wasn't where I wanted to be, between a male who oozed lethal from his pores, and the heads of the alphas who sat on the council. The tension was so thick it could have been cut with a knife. If this went bad, it would do so quickly. Knox's arm brushed against mine as if he sensed my unease and sought to calm me.

CHAPTER
25

The entire room held its breath as we waited for Knox or Fallon to speak. When Fallon finally spoke, after hearing Knox's rather crude description of what I'd been doing, I exhaled. Knox's fingers skimmed the inside of my thigh until it brushed over his name, causing my body to tighten with need. My gaze swung to his in warning, but a devilish smirk was the only indication he was aware of what he was doing to me.

"I stand corrected," Fallon uttered, inhaling deeply, watching Knox as he stood, causing the rest of the alphas to rise. I stood, nodding to them as they started to leave the room. "Aria, I am ashamed of myself, and that I jumped to a conclusion so hastily. Forgive me?" he asked, holding his hand out. I placed my hand in his, and his lips touched my palm gently, causing a shiver of disgust. "I may not be a king yet, but if you ever find yourself in need, I will welcome you into my bed, covenant or not, Aria."

"Pass," I blurted unexpectedly, then winced at my bluntness while Knox chuckled against my shoulder, staring at Fallon. "I mean, I'm good with Knox. And there's nothing to forgive. You are grieving and acting out of pain. I'd like to say that I would have done it differently, but I don't know what I would have done to make any difference. I'm kind of hot-headed when those I love are hurt, and I can't imagine what I would do if they were taken from me as brutally as Jasper was taken from you."

"I wish your mother had confided in me when she returned so heavily pregnant with you from the Nine Realms."

"You can stop fishing, Fallon. I have no idea who fathered me. All I know is that my power is strong, and when I need it, it is there without hesitation. That is all that matters to me."

"I had to try, but you should know that your mother was in the Nine Realms during your conception. She didn't speak when she returned. Aurora tried to get her to tell her what had happened, and the only words she would speak were darkness, flames, and monster. They woke Hecate from her slumber and her advice to Freya? Abort the monstrosity that grew within her womb, or end its life before it reached adulthood." I stared at him as he stepped around me, moving to the door and exiting. "I hope you find out what you are and if you belong here, sweet Aria." His smile was tight and not friendly. His tone had held a warning, one created from my outright rejection of his offer for protection.

"Leave us," Knox stated to Regina, and I moved to do as he said in my state of confusion. "Not you, Aria," he growled, grabbing my shoulder to stop me.

I watched Regina pausing as she stood, her angry gaze locking on to where Knox touched me. She huffed and made an unladylike noise before she spoke. She pushed her hair away from her face, leveling a nasty look at me as if she wanted to shred my face apart. It was so violent that I felt it slithering over my flesh.

"Don't let the little slut ruin my dress, Knox," she said demurely. "It's one of your favorites on me."

My eyes couldn't have rolled harder if I had taken them out and bowled with them. I smirked, turning to look at Knox, who hadn't taken his eyes off me.

"Make this fast. I have spellbooks to retrieve. Seems I have a tattoo dilemma as well and need to find the blessing spell needed for the House of Magic, *lover* boy," I snapped, crossing my arms to glare at him once the room had cleared.

"I just saved your pretty head from my blade, and this is how you act?"

"I didn't kill Jasper. I was beneath your stupid body, and you used that voice thing on me. Whatever it is when you question me, and I answered you honestly, if you recall? I sure in the hell would never have told you half of that shit unless you'd forced me."

"But it appears someone wishes you dead. I found this beside Jasper before we allowed the alpha over to see the body." He held up my hair tie, which appeared to be snapped in half. "You have enemies, and I want to know who they are."

My gaze lifted from the hair tie to him, and my heart sputtered while denial burned on the tip of my tongue.

I didn't have enemies. I was an asshole, that much was a given. I said everything that popped into my head before thinking it through, but that didn't make people hate me. In fact, most people appreciated the truth, no matter how brutal I was about it. Now, humans, they didn't share that sentiment, and yet they were quicker than I was to blurt shit out.

"Someone wanted me to find it, lamb. They snuck into the house and took it from where I had left it and pushed it beneath Jasper's corpse this morning for us to find when we moved his body. It was the only thing in the house with your DNA on it, which I was aware of since I planted it to see if whoever murdered Jasper would take it."

"I don't understand," I whispered. "My mother is the only one who has ever wanted me dead, Knox. Amara was not the sweetest, but she wasn't a cold-hearted bitch either. Now, she's writing me notes speaking gibberish—I mean, who says you are given? What the hell does it even mean?" I sat in the chair before my brow creased with frustration, then folded my hands in my lap.

"In the Nine Realms, when someone is given, it means they've been given as a trophy, or as a wife." He sat down in his chair, watching me. "You said your sister loved you. My guess is that some creature inside the Nine Realms is coming to collect his pretty innocent bride from this realm to parade her virginity around like a trophy catch. It leaves you in quite the predicament, Aria."

"Yeah," I frowned as I picked at my fingernail, unwilling to hold his stare for any longer. "I'm getting the feeling something bad is about to happen, and I'm about to be right beside Jasper in an unmarked grave in a realm I don't even belong."

"Nothing is getting past me. You aren't dying unless it's by my hand. I found the spellbook for the blessing." Knox rose from his chair to retrieve an ancient piece of vellum. "Your sisters will enter the Nine Realms together, but you will stay behind with me. I won't take the chance of you entering and wiping my scent from your flesh. The scent of my blood warns off males, but it won't keep monsters away if you enter a realm, and I am not with you. I'm guessing since you're still alive, you've never entered the Nine Realms at all, have you?"

"I wasn't well enough at first because of the hemlock ravaging my system. The Court of Witches only needs one witch from the Hecate line to be present. While they send us in to learn the land and show our support and strength as we refuel the power of the realm, it has never been me who has gone to do so. Not because I didn't want to go, but because you have to be in perfect health to enter the portals between realms."

"Go fucking figure," he snorted, barely loud enough to be heard. "You're also sure you have no idea what your heritage is other than a witch?"

I held his gaze as I whispered, "I know it is strong. I know that whatever I am when I reach for the land in this realm, I pull power to me from my homeland inside the Nine Realms. I can feel the power when it brushes through my fingertips and the rush of it through my blood. The call to come home is like a siren going off, pulsing through my entire body. I told Aurora one time what it felt like, and she cried for hours, but never said why. Days afterward, she would burst into tears every time she looked at me, like I was something bad. I don't feel bad, or evil, it's quite the opposite, really. I want to see the land where we were created, to know what happens in our absence. I want to know what the people really think of us for abandoning them for a realm we have no business being in. I don't think we belong here, and I have a feeling eating at me that we won't be here for much longer."

"That's blunt, Aria. Considering your grandmother was the one who decided we did belong in this realm."

"Just because she's a goddess doesn't make her opinion right. Our realms run on magic, and we are the ones who feed them magic. We're here, in a foreign realm that doesn't need magic. The books I have read say, if the magic is removed from the Nine Realms, it will cease to exist. So why are the creatures who feed magic to the Nine Realms, here and not where we are needed? It seems wrong to me. I get that Hecate wanted this realm to be one of ours, but we've been here long enough to create magic in this one, and yet it rejects us.

"We've created magic within humans, sure, but they are not like us. They're not immortal. Witches are Wiccan's, our human counterpart. That in itself shows we are failing to do as she wished, but then we are not her; we cannot make immortals without her presence. So, in conclusion to those findings, we should take our ass's home where we belong and power the realms as we are supposed to be doing."

Knox narrowed his eyes on my lips and then shook his head slowly, as if he didn't agree with my findings. "And which realm calls to you the most?"

"It's actually crazy," I laughed, staring at him with mirth as a smile slipped over my lips.

"Which realm, Aria?" he repeated, his eyes watching me carefully.

"Norvalla," I admitted softly. "It's rumored to hold the most magnificent beasts in all of creation. The land is ripe for growing food, and the forest is filled with wild animals to provide meat. It also never gets cold, and I don't like the cold. I crave heat to kiss my flesh and sun to warm it."

"Something as wild and untamed as you would crave a realm that matches," he breathed, gazing at me for a moment before he frowned. He handed me the spell, and I glanced at it and then glanced again.

"The blood of a hymen from a Hecate bloodline witch?" My mouth went dry as I frowned deeper, scrunching up my forehead as I read it several more times to be sure I'd read it correctly.

"Lucky for us, we have a witch who is a virgin right in our hands." He stood, staring at me with a dark look in his eyes. "I'm leaving for a few days. I expect your hymen to be properly punctured when I get back; if not, I'll do it my-fucking-self. Do you understand me?"

"But… I don't have anyone I want to sleep with. I can just do it myself," I nodded as my hands trembled with the vellum in it. Of all the shit luck to have, why the hell would it require that?

"Do you honestly think that will work?" he asked indifferently, narrowing his eyes at my trembling hands.

"No," I sighed, studying the spell. "That explains why it needs to be blessed every fifty years. It might also explain why I ended up stuck with my virginity until mere days before my twenty-fifth birthday. On the plus side, I won't die a virgin."

"You won't die, not unless…"

"I know, Knox. I won't die unless you end my life. What if I can't do it, what if I end up getting sick? What if I'm bad at it?" I asked carefully, wincing at the thought.

"Then you'll be mine the moment I return and not a second later. I want my fucking house back."

"And the creatures or people hunting me?"

"I'll know the second you're in mortal danger, or in your case, immortal," he said, nodding toward the door. "Out, I have shit to get done before I can leave."

"Who do I choose?" I asked, and he slammed his hands on the table, sending the dishes clattering to the floor.

"I don't fucking care who you choose," he snarled, but his voice echoed as if he struggled to contain something. "You're not my problem, witch. The only reason I haven't snapped that neck of yours is that someone powerful wants you alive. If it was my choice, I'd have run my blade through your throat and watched your fucking head bounce off the ground as it left your neck."

"Understood," I whispered softly, walking away. At the door, I paused, turning to look at him, where he watched me with darkness in his eyes. "I hope you choke on a pineapple, prick."

I left the room before he could see the tears shining

in my eyes or the pain his words had inflicted. Ignoring the looks of the others, I entered the room and shed the dress the moment I did. Staring at the door, I let the tears fall as anger and pain collided.

My hands lifted to my hair, and I pushed it away from my face, gasping as Knox entered, staring into my eyes. I spun around, shielding him from my naked breasts and presented him with my scantily garter-covered backside. I wiped at my eyes, hating that he'd seen the tears before I'd been able to prevent it.

"Get the fuck out," I whispered through the closing in my throat as I wrapped my arms around myself, waiting for him to leave. "Please?" I needed to keep whatever pieces of my dignity were left, and then I had to go ask a stranger to take what no one else had been given. Even worse than that, I'd have to ask him to collect the blood and preserve it. As if it wouldn't be embarrassing enough to sleep with a total stranger and have to face him afterward.

"Brander, pick him," he said, leaving the room silently.

CHAPTER
26

KNOX

Everything inside of me wanted to claim, fuck, and destroy that little witch. I'd craved nothing else as much as I did the need to wreck Aria Hecate. Her full mouth taunted me, begging for a cock to push between her pouty lips and fuck that sass out of her fast and hard, ending her taunts violently.

The scent of her pheromones had me in a perpetual state of need to take her innocent flesh brutally. No fucking mercy needed or granted. She'd beg me for mercy, but I didn't have any to give her. Didn't fucking matter, because once I started, she wouldn't need it or care for it anymore. She would take what I gave, and I'd watch her come unraveled on my cock until there was nothing left of her.

She'd break apart. I'd enjoy watching the end result of what she became when she shattered. I wanted to watch those pretty eyes turn colors as she rode my cock, discovering the pleasure of it as she watched herself coming undone around me, clenching me tightly.

Aria was delicate. I wasn't.

She was all soft curves and smooth flesh. I was jagged edges; sharply defined sinewy, hard muscles.

Aria was created of lace and innocence. I was all brutality and ancient.

She was innocent smiles and beauty. I was violence and ageless death.

Aria smirked; I bared my teeth. She didn't shy away, but she knew damn well that she should, yet didn't. She baited me, and fuck if I didn't want to bite down hard.

Braver men had died for taunting me. Aria tilted her head, taunting me with the delicate curve of her throat, and she was very aware that I could end her life easily. Did it stop her from tempting me? No, she pushed back, waiting, watching to see if I would come unhinged.

I wanted to go toe-to-toe with her just fucking once in the bedroom. I wanted to know if she'd be barebones or if, when I let the mask of humanity slip, she'd run from me. Would she run away with whatever I'd left of her that was still undamaged? I'd make her fucking roar for me, showing her exactly what it felt like to be fucked to nothing more than a trembling mess. She'd fucking tremble for me, and I'd watch her, doing so with no regret.

Aria was pure innocence and I wanted to corrupt her in the most delicious, basic way. I wanted to debase everything pure within her and see what she did with it. See if she unraveled and liked the end result. I wanted to feel her as she changed, wanted to watch her eyes widen as she realized she could never go back to before I fucked her. And I would fuck her; I'd wreak havoc on her senses, destroying her thoughts of what gentle and sweet was, replacing them with new thoughts. She'd know what being owned felt like, being brutally fucked and savaged until she no longer craved gentleness and sweetness from a man.

I wanted to set the little bitch on fire and watch as she burned; to see what the fuck stepped out of the ashes when she rose still covered in the dust. I wanted to set her world on fire and fuck her in the ashes of it, watching as she realized just how ruined she was when I was finished with her.

I had no trouble ignoring the scent of breeding bitches, but Aria, her scent had me rock hard with the need to fuck her since the moment I smelled her in my domain. I'd driven outside of the town barrier to figure out what that delicious scent was. Then she'd fucking challenged me, then dropped her name, and I'd felt the punch of it in my balls.

I hated her the moment that name slipped off her pretty pink lips. Still, I craved her. I craved the need to make the little bitch feel all of me in the worst imaginable way. I craved to know how she screamed when I was buried deep within her cunt, stretching it so fucking hard that it made her whimper in pain.

Her screams filled my dreams; to hear her pain mixing with pleasure as I pushed through that pesky barrier and slammed into her hard enough that she'd always feel me there. Yeah, I fucking wanted that more than I wanted air to fill my lungs.

Women were like exotic cars. You needed to drive

them hard, fast, and often. See what the limits were and push the fuck out of them until you knew everything about them, down the smallest detail. Details fucking mattered when fucking, and learning a woman was half the fun.

Whiskey, that little bitch smelled like the finest whiskey ever aged into perfection. You didn't drink that kind of whiskey and not crave it again. You got addicted, needed to taste it until you were drunk from it. You didn't sip it; you fucking swallow it down until you take every drop that is offered.

I wanted to throw her down and be what creatures like us became without the skin we wore to hide the monsters. A dirty little witch and the beast that wanted to fucking devour her whole. I wanted to spread her legs and watch as her eyes filled with wonder while I pounded into her with unrestricted anger.

The pain she'd feel excited me and kept my dick hard for her. My hand on her throat, watching as fear slipped into that brilliantly clever mind she kept hidden from others. She can't hide it from me. I've seen moments of her brilliance, the way she observed me as if she knew her clock was ticking down slowly. I was pacing outside the cage that protected her, counting down every second until I got the order to destroy her, and fuck, would I enjoy doing precisely that.

Someone powerful within the Nine Realms wanted her alive, protected. I wanted to destroy her, to wrap my hands around her throat and watch as the realization sunk into those pretty turquoise eyes that her fate was sealed. I wanted to fist the soft silk of her silver hair as I ruined her pretty naked cunt, watching my length vanish into the depths of her while destroying everything she thought was normal and safe. She didn't need safe. She needed a man who wasn't afraid to push her limits, rip her world apart, and toss her to the wolves, because Aria Primrose Hecate was the type of woman who would return, leading that rabid pack with a fire in her eyes that would belong to me. I'd be the one who had placed it there. The man who brought her into our realm without an ounce of mercy and pissed on everything she assumed she needed or wanted.

She demanded to know what I was. She thought something was hiding within me, but there isn't. I was more than she could see on the surface, and she knew that the monster inside of her craved me. I didn't hide it when we were alone. I let her hear the rattle from deep inside my chest. The noise my kind made when it wanted its next victim, and she'd be the perfect fucking victim. Her pouty lips excited me. The flame dancing within the shadows of her eyes ignited the fire inside me.

I'd fucking destroy her. Leave her in so many broken pieces that she'd spend her days trying to rearrange them into what they had been before I'd fucked her perception of who she was.

There would be another version of her created in my bed; the Aria before I fucked her and the Aria after I had fucked her.

I waited.

Counting down until her destruction would be complete.

Devouring her without even touching her flesh, and

yet she didn't understand that it was happening. I craved her mind, her pain, and fuck if I didn't want more than that.

As a basic rule, I didn't fuck witches, not unless I had hidden motives. Still, whatever Aria was hiding within her called to me viscerally. It watched me, learning me without her even knowing it had awoken. She looked sweet, innocent, but she's a monster like me. That creature which was peering back at me when I looked at her? It was fucking feral, untrained, and unkind.

It was a ticking time bomb within her, set to detonate in a realm it doesn't belong to, in a realm it would seek to destroy.

She was pink lace, it was black leather.

Aria was innocent nibbles, it was fucking starving.

She was curious, it was fucking interested.

They couldn't be more different if they tried.

The monster smelled me and wanted what it had scented. It had terrified Aria. *It* was excited because it had finally found a male strong enough to take it on without destroying him. Aria hated me, and I fucking loved that she did. Fucking someone you hated was hard, raw, painful, and so fucking beautiful. It was going barebones with something that you're not afraid to break, and fuck, did I crave the need to snap her in half.

Aria fucking rattled, which was rare and even more so considering her tender age. The noises drove me insane, and fuck if I didn't answer the call to her creature willingly. I wanted to see it, to discover if it would be primal, unbreakable, and so much fucking more.

I hadn't heard a female creature rattle in over six hundred years, and those who could have lost their ability. Yet Aria answered my beast, and fuck if it hadn't made my dick hard to respond to a female's call.

The issue was, I had no fucking idea what she was or how she could do it. Mimics could make the sound, but it never demanded a response. Her noises excited, aroused, and elicited a visceral response that couldn't be ignored—and that pissed me off.

The monster within her—wanted me in a primal manner its host couldn't comprehend or would ever understand. It was why when she looked at me, her back arched and her hips parted, demanding I fucking mount her regardless of where we were or who was watching us. Her pupils dilated to allow the monster inside to peer out, see, and learn who it was craving with wild hunger. Her pussy gushed for me, inviting me by scent, telling me it was ripe and needed me to fuck it hard and fast. My balls fucking ached when I walked away without satisfying my need deep in her belly.

The little bitch host… *She* was too fucking soft for that. Break the host before it prepares the monster to enter the world, you kill the monster also. I wanted to play with that monster in the worst way, and it knew it. It could sense the alpha that was prowling around it and refused to give me its back. I took it by force, proving I could, and it purred for me.

The monster would roar for me when I made it come, and come it would, repeatedly until I let it go. Aria had no idea what wanted her or why she wanted it too. Didn't fucking matter, she was now on my radar, and mine until I decide otherwise.

Her mother knew what she'd done and tried to rectify it, but she couldn't have even if she'd tried wholeheartedly to abort the monsters she grew within her womb. Once planted, they held on, refusing to let go until they sucked air into their lungs and came to life. By the time they drew their first breath, it was too fucking late to rectify the mistake.

It was unclear which king of the Nine Realms she fucked, but I'd narrowed it down to the worst ones who craved to create forbidden life, and Aria was the final result of what they created. Bloodlines be damned, she took after the monsters they feared. The ones the families fled from when they left the Nine Realms behind claiming to need another one, but we didn't. They just wanted out before they were victims to the beasts who hunted them.

The problem was, they forgot to close the fucking door on their way out. They sought to control us, to tell who could and who couldn't leave the Nine Realms. Conceited fucks thought they were strong enough to prevent our kind from escaping their cages, but we cracked those cages the moment we entered this realm. We just waited for the time to strike against them, and that time was now.

The other leaders of the rebellion sent me here to deal with this realm. Me; the beast they pretend didn't exist, the darkest, deadliest monster within their arsenal, and now they wanted me to protect some little witch? I was the one asshole who wouldn't protect her, not when everything male inside of me craved the woman she would become. Not when I helped make the problems start to begin with.

The one thing I never expected to find was Aria, with a monster from the Nine Realms hidden in pretty pink flesh, right in front of their fucking noses. I'd assumed she was pliant, an easy fuck, but then her monster rattled to mine, and I felt it.

I'd gazed into her eyes and knew she was different. Everything within me said to destroy her now before she ended up in my way. She would be messy, and I wanted to see her unfold, but I couldn't afford to get sidetracked right now. Not when all my plans were coming into play.

If it was one of the council members within the Nine Realms who wanted her safe, I'd have already wrapped my hands around her throat and fucked her until the life drained from her pretty turquoise eyes, but it wasn't them who wanted her alive.

The monsters of the Nine Realms decreed she live, that she survived and be brought back with me. That's a bad fucking day for her, but not for me. In my realm, I can claim her. I can mount her to the wall and leave her there, destroying everything she was and building her into what I wanted her to be.

My smile lifted, the picture my mind painted of her naked on my wall like a prized trophy made my dick rock hard. Her body pliable, fuckable at my whim, and that naughty little mouth of hers parted on a silent scream as she realized where she was, and who owned her in every fucking way. Would she still talk back then? Would she still fucking fight me? I fucking hoped so. Aria Primrose was mine, that much was a given. She had my name on her thigh, and that wasn't something that could ever be undone. No one could erase that mark except for me, and I liked it there.

I'd set the stage, unhinged the staff. My men fought to get through the door, scaring her until she did what I had wanted her to do, letting me write my name on her flesh. I tagged her cunt, her body, her pleasure. I wrote my name on her flesh, watching as it pushed through her flesh, marking her immortal soul forever. The only way out of that marking is through death, and I wouldn't allow that to happen. Not after tasting her passion or seeing those eyes igniting with need. I may hate that I fucking wanted her, but that didn't change the fact that I still did.

I'd tasted her delicious pussy, licking it greedily when the magic took hold and held her within a state of need neither of us could fight. She'd dripped down my chin as I fucked that heated slit with my mouth, knowing damn well they both watched me taking them over the edge. I'd felt her body shivering, shaking, and the sweet noises she'd made as she rode my face, making my cock explode without even being buried in her untried flesh. That shit never happened to me until Aria, but her pleas had fucked me harder than any woman had ever managed before her. I'd made her hurt from coming so hard and so fast that she'd whimpered, crying my name, pleading for me to stop giving her pleasure.

I'd punished her for making me come like some little fucking boy finding his first wet hole and playing with his cock in it. I didn't grant her wish for mercy, devouring her until tears streamed down her cheeks. Hours had passed by in a blur, hours of nothing but tasting the sweetness of her body as she came apart for me beautifully as her inhibition shed, and the glimpse of the woman she was becoming was uncaged.

I'd never wanted to fuck anyone as hard as I wanted to fuck her with her thighs dropped wide open with invitation, and her pussy glistening with cum as I'd eaten that pineapple-flavored flesh, and fuck if I didn't crave pineapple after tasting it on her. It had taken everything I had not to fuck that pussy, which dripped so wantonly against my lips. I still tasted it, and fuck if I didn't still crave more.

She had no idea that she'd held my mouth to her pussy, begging me to fuck her sweet flesh to ease the ache that I'd left. Aria had pleaded for me to batter past her innocence and take what she offered, but I wouldn't. Not like that. Not with the magic drugging her mind and her reaction to me while under its influence.

I wanted her very aware when I fucked her, and I wanted her to need it because her body responded to mine, not the magic that rushed through us as the mark seared us together. It was ancient, dark magic, enhancing everything as it connected us on a deeper level.

I saw the moment she realized what she'd allowed me to do to her cunt. The regret and hate that sank in as her mind returned from the pleasure I'd given her. She'd have hated me for making her body respond in the way it had. It wouldn't have been the hate I desired, but a painful hurt that women got after the body cooled, and the mind told it things.

She'd have blamed me for forcing it, unable to take responsibility for asking me to make her come undone. I'd watched her pretty eyes filling with self-loathing, and I'd hated watching the change in her. I didn't want her to feel guilty about fucking my mouth, not when we'd both been under the influence of the ancient magic.

It had taken everything I had in me not to rip those thin lace panties apart and drive my thick, hard cock into her as the magic fucked us both. Had I? No. I'd behaved, and I'd let her find release without taking what she certainly would have regretted later. I fucking gave the little bitch mercy, and that pissed me off more than wanting her.

I'd taken her memories to stop it from happening and gave her my name on her flesh. I'd told her she could not lie to me if I used the perfect tone and sent subliminal messages into her subconscious to enforce them. My name on her flesh claimed her as mine.

It ensured that if anything thought to hurt her, I could find her quickly and know she was in danger before she realized it. No one was breaking her but me. I shouldn't want to protect her, but I fucking did. It was a primal need, something so possessive that I didn't even fully understand it. I should want the little bitch dead, but even thinking of a world where she didn't exist pissed me off. It was a fucking complication that I hated, and yet she wasn't fucking dying unless I decided she could.

I didn't even like her, but I wanted her. I hated everything about her, down to her pretty painted toes. I loathed that she fought against me, and she did it with a fire smoldering in her eyes. Her pretty pink lips parted with a 'pass' on them anytime her mind showed her us fucking. It wasn't because she didn't want it. I could smell the need to rip her clothes off and mount me pouring through her flesh. No, she knew that when it happened, she'd never be the same. She'd be a broken, destroyed thing that no amount of magic could fix, and it terrified her—and worse, it excited her. Good. It should.

"Knox, can I ease your mind?" Regina asked, her eyes studying me with fear and hope.

"Get on your fucking knees and open your worthless fucking mouth."

"I thought we could do more this time?" she whispered, and I turned, staring at the brainless bitch who thought she was more than warm flesh. Regina was ancient, useful at the moment, but still, she would die here. It was written in the lore that her life would end here and now before we ever finished in this worthless realm of humans.

She thought she could play me, yet she didn't even know the rules of my game. Aria was fire and passion. Regina was ice and lackluster. She was here because she served a purpose in my plans, but she was easily replaceable. Aria wasn't. She was different, more than just warm flesh to sate a need, and I fucking hated it.

"Get on your fucking knees or get the fuck out, hag."

"It's Aria, isn't it? You want her. I watched you with her; you were crazed with need. She will be the death of you if you do not end her life now."

I didn't answer because it wasn't a question and I didn't answer this bitch; she answered to me for crimes against my kind. She was pathetic and worthless, her body used by all, and yet she wanted me because I had no care if I broke her. She smelled of my men, and it disgusted me.

Aria wouldn't be like that when she got fucked. She wouldn't need to part her cunt and beg men to fuck it. What we were, we didn't beg; we took and wrecked them for any other man or creature alive. We didn't fuck worthless creatures unless we were playing a part. I was playing it, but the thought of fucking Regina made my dick go limp.

"Get out."

"Knox, baby," she uttered, and I let her hear the monster's call, let the power within me brush over her, causing fear to ignite in her eyes.

Aria got excited without knowing what it was. She fucking rattled back, and everything within me went silent, craving to hear it. Most women would run, but she faltered, studied, and wanted to examine it deeper. Aria was beyond intelligent, and that fucking excited me more than her pretty pink flesh could ever achieve. She wasn't just three holes to destroy; she was brains and beauty.

Her need to know our land made her a step better than the other useless originals in this strange realm they craved to become a part of, yet hide within the shadows like weak-minded bitches. They hid, Aria didn't.

She watched, learning, studying, and knew every way to bring this place down upon their heads should the need arise, and she didn't even know she was doing it. She even did it with me, learning me as I abused her to bring out the beast within her, and fuck if I wasn't pushing her around just to watch that fire burning inside her.

I was a bastard, but I didn't enjoy hurting women. I hurt her to push her, to drive that thing inside of her to the limit and watch as it raised its head, baring its teeth in warning.

CHAPTER
27

Knox

I had purposely pinned Aria to my bed, my cock on her stomach showing her exactly how deep I'd be in her pretty cunt the moment I took her. I'd fucking wreck that innocent flesh, and she knew it. She had a healthy dose of fear for a moment, but in her eyes, there was excitement.

Aria knew there would be pain, yet she still wanted it. If she'd have asked, I'd have fucking went to war on her cunt in a way that she wouldn't have understood. I'd spared her because I couldn't stand the idea of hurting her, why? She was my fucking enemy, and I should have wanted to destroy her, which I did, just not beyond repair. Not yet.

It had taken every ounce of willpower I had not to rip her thin panties off and let loose on her just to show her what I would feel like buried in her pussy. Her scent drew me to her, but the fire that burned in her soul and eyes? It brought me to my knees like some fucking child who had just discovered his dick. I hated it, hated the need I felt for her, marring the memory of my mate.

I had never wanted my mate as much as I wanted Aria. That fucking made me hate her more than I already did. That made her a target for rage she didn't understand and never could. I shouldn't feel shit with Aria. I hadn't ever kissed anyone except for my mate, but I'd wanted to kiss Aria. I wanted to be her first, and I'd fucking made sure the bar was set so high she'd find anyone else lacking.

Liliana had been gentle and everything soft. Aria, she called to the beast and sensed his need to consume her. I'd had to be careful with my mate, but they had created Aria to be savagely fucked, and she craved it. Liliana had never argued or complained, but Aria was quick to. She would go toe-to-toe in and out of the bedroom regardless of what I was.

I'd been a heartless prick to Aria, but she fucked my mind in the worst way. She made me want her, made me crave to taste those pouty lips, and know the feel of them against mine. I betrayed the memory of my mate every time I tasted Aria's fire. It made me need to snap her pretty neck and fuck her throat to show my dead, murdered mate that I hadn't forgotten my promise to avenge her. Destroy the Hecate bloodline and make them all pay.

Yet I'd had Aria in my bed, needing to know how she felt from the inside as I wrote my name upon her womb. I'd wanted her so badly that it scared me, and I was never afraid of anything. I was the creature who murdered those who wreaked havoc on our realms, and yet that little bitch had terrified me. It pissed me off. So I'd been a prick, scaring the hell out of her, but my monster? He'd fought me. He'd fought me until I'd won, and she knew it wasn't me and yet had been about to whisper the words that would have sealed her fate.

One wrong move she'd have been mine. One single noise, and it would have snapped the thin thread of control I'd held. I almost lost it, and I never lose control, ever. She may not want me, but that beast within her? It would have been primal, visceral, and I'd have fed that bitch until she purred like a kitten pinned on my cock. My teeth in her shoulder made the beast within her calm to a subdued mess, and that had scared Aria. Pliant, submissiveness came to mind when my mouth touched her shoulder, and even the hint of teeth made whatever is hiding within her submit to me.

I fucking craved her submission. I also craved the fight I watched burning in her eyes.

Then I'd gone and fucking kissed the little bitch.

I kissed her, me, the monster that didn't fucking kiss anyone because that shit insinuated feelings, and that shit made it messy. Still, I'd needed to taste her passion, feel it firsthand and know what it looked like. It knocked me back, me, the bastard who fucked women and watched them vanish into oblivion as their souls left through their eyes to the realm within the Void of Nothingness.

Her kiss had knocked me on my ass, creating a storm within me that threatened to snap what little control I had. No one had ever fucking kissed me like that, nor had my body ever responded to a simple kiss. Aria, though, that girl kissed me back like I was the air needed to fill her lungs.

I took what I want, and I fucked hard. I didn't take her, which pissed me off.

I enjoyed breaking pretty things and leaving shells of what they'd been in my wake. If that girl fucked like she kissed, I was in trouble. That's the kind of girl you got attached to, needed to keep around to get fucked by, and fucked by often.

Aria was all fire and about to set the world ablaze in her wake.

I sensed her the moment she stood on that hill. I hadn't even stopped to think as we'd raced to her location, prepared to claim her. My dick had gotten hard by her scent, but the moment I took in her pretty stare, I fucking ached. My balls ached to release within her, marking that pussy as mine by adding my scent to hers. I never placed my scent on pussy, so why her?

I felt something lethal watching me from within her, and I had been pissed when I figured out that she was fucking clueless. Her pussy begged to be fucked, it got wet around me. Those pretty pink nipples responded to my voice and fuck if I didn't want to suck on them. She didn't understand why or how it could respond to me, but I sure in the fuck did.

That creature within her needed something more powerful than it was, and my men had stepped back, sensing the fight it would give them. They weren't willing to take her on, but I was.

She was a challenge, and it was one I wanted to take.

Aria *was* an alpha in her own right. She was fast-witted, and her mind worked overtime when she was working together pieces she shouldn't be able to see. She refused to back down. She dug her heels in and watched as she waited for any sign of weakness. The best part about that was, she didn't even know she was waiting for that one subtle sign of weakness to slaughter the victim.

I'd smelled the likeness, but then I'd pushed the pieces together to force the witches to come back to this town. Amara, worthless and self-absorbed as she was, was an easy fucking target to get to in the Nine Realms. She'd already been moving in that direction on her own, grasping on to things to hold her there, so I'd given her a little push. She'd been unclean, tainted by magic she craved and could never reach. Fueled by greed and anger that Aria was stronger, but then Aria was the whole package deal. Amara was a basic bitch who craved things she couldn't have. Only one monster was born that day, one child created from Freya lying in a bed of monsters, unable to deny their need as her cunt wept to be fucked by the kings of the Nine Realms, all of them. Magic was a bitch when thought you were invincible to it.

The question was which king had planted the seed into her poisonous womb, and grown the beautiful prickly rose? I intended to find out and see what emerged from the cocoon that housed it.

Regina's sobs filled the room, and slowly, I turned to glare at her pathetic attempt for sympathy, watching her walk out of the library with defeat oozing from her pores, I smiled coldly. Stupid bitch. She thought I wanted her when the only thing I wanted was for her to do her job. She could either help me get the witches back into the Nine Realms, or she could die. She was useful, but the moment that ended, her life would too.

Lacey tried to warn Aria, and Brander fucked her into a state of nothingness, and yet she clung on tightly within her mind. Didn't fucking matter. She'd lost the ability to communicate without us controlling what slipped from her tongue.

I was here to destroy them all for what they did, and while I wanted to keep Aria around, I doubted I could achieve it without starting a fucking war. Wars didn't scare me; I'd fought thousands of them and bathed in the blood of the fallen creatures who had thought to rise above their rank. I didn't have time to wage one when everything I'd planned for over five hundred years was finally coming together.

She was in my way.

Unexpected, but a fun distraction, nonetheless.

Unfortunately, it was one I didn't need right now. I'd fuck her and be done with it, and the moment that monster rose, I'd fuck it too, and if it fought me, I'd kill it to protect my plans. It would be a waste of what I assumed would be some very good pussy, but waste it, I would. I'd deal with the consequences—and those who demanded she was returned to the Nine Realms alive—afterward.

These assholes had murdered my child, cursing him to die one thousand times at his tender age of seven. I'd held him through them all, weeping as I begged the witches to spare his life, but they had refused.

I would show them what pain felt like, let them feel it on a level so profound and deep that none of them got back off their knees. My mate took her life after his death, seeking a witch to end her immortality. She found one of Hecate's daughters and achieved the one thing our kind could never have: death.

Now…now, I would destroy them all and send their realms into an eternal darkness that they'd never forget. I was about to start the war against them, and I wasn't planning to give them an ounce of mercy. I'd been planning this since the day I'd returned to find Liliana dead in our bed. I'd lost my family, and in return, I would destroy theirs.

Hecate's daughter had laughed, smiling at me as I'd wept while begging her to bring my family back, but she refused. Now I would end her entire line for what she had done to mine.

I'd give it back to them tit for fucking tat. The only problem I could foresee? Aria Primrose Hecate—but she was only a problem if I let her become one.

Every time Aria smiled at me, it made me feel shit. Her sweet smile made me want her on a deeper level than just fucking. I hated it. I hated her for marring the memories of my wife and mate. Wanting her shouldn't happen. I hadn't wanted another woman for anything other than rutting since the first moment I'd met Liliana, until Aria, and that was a fucking problem. She was a problem.

I'd been mated, truly mated, and in love, which our kind only got once in a lifetime. Yet, I had never felt the raw need to fuck with Liliana. I'd never felt her kiss me as Aria had, nor the need to continue kissing her regardless of the air we needed to breathe to sustain life. Aria had made my heartbeat thump for the first time in five hundred years. It had raced with her lips against mine, both fucking sets. Her pussy had made it erratic, but her lips? Her lips had brought it back from the grave where it had remained since I'd buried my wife. It made the need to hurt her deeper, to punish her for making me feel anything and betraying the love of my life.

I'd died that day my mate had gone to her grave, and yet Aria was bringing me back, but with Aria, I couldn't remember what Liliana had looked like, or the sound of her voice when she spoke. I forgot the woman I had loved since my youth, wiping her image away as Aria fucking Hecate erased it from my mind. She dulled the fucking pain that fueled me with a simple smirk, and that was a big fucking problem.

When I closed my eyes at night, I no longer saw my wife's face or heard my son's laughter as he discovered something new. Instead, I saw beautiful turquoise eyes that smiled when they lit up and curves that I wanted to know on the deepest level a man could know a woman. It made me crave the need to murder her to get the memories back. I couldn't forget them now, not when everything I'd done had been for them.

Aria was a fire within me that needed to be extinguished and smothered. I would fuck her and end this obsession quickly. She wasn't mine, and yet I'd placed my name right beside her pussy so I would know if anyone touched it or tried to hurt her. I'd done that because I'd wanted to.

I wanted her to survive, but I also wanted to hurt her. Aria was one of *them*. She was one of the enemies who had taken my family from me, and I would stop at nothing to get revenge against them. Not even chaining her to my wall and keeping her there to play with could prevent what I'd set into motion. She'd hate me when she learned the truth and even more the moment I started murdering witches. Neither fucking mattered to me since she was my enemy.

CHAPTER
28

ARIA

I silently drummed my fingers on the table that held the feast of all feasts on it. I watched my sisters shoveling food on their plates, while the men joined them eagerly. The only sound in the room was the silverware scraping the expensive china they'd pulled out. Today everyone was leaving me, going into the Nine Realms to get the items we needed to bless the house and fix the spell which would activate it.

Pushing food over my plate, I watched Brander from beneath my lashes as he sat silently brooding. At the same time, he consumed enough meat to feed a village on an undiscovered coastline, or maybe the entire coastline of Fiji. It reminded me of how Knox ate; consuming mainly meat, while gulping down milk by the gallon.

He was pleasant enough to look at and used a napkin to dab his mouth, which was more than some men were doing. Still, I didn't feel a connection to him. I felt lust, and that was easy enough to achieve, but there wasn't the sizzle I felt with Knox. Every once in a while, he'd move his stare to me and hold mine, but the moment Aine spoke, it would go right back to her with intrigue.

He seemed safe enough, but it made me wonder why Knox would say to pick him. From what I'd seen since coming here, he had a different woman in his room every day. I wasn't worried about STDs since it was one perk of being immortal. Even if he was a slut, I didn't have to worry about getting the last woman's residue on me.

"Aria," Kinvara whispered, interrupting my thoughts and placing her hand on my shoulder as she spoke.

"Yeah?"

I turned to look at her, and she smiled. "Are you going to devour poor Brander?" She looked between us and tilted her head, and my stare slid to Brander, who smiled before covering his mouth as heat banked in his pretty blue eyes.

"No," I said in a high-pitched tone. "No, I was just lost in thought."

"You look as if you're trying to decide to either fuck him or fight him. I'm not sure which thought is winning." She dropped a large piece of meat back onto her plate and then wiggled her brows at me. "I'm stuffed, but I bet Brander would stuff you in an entirely different way." The men chuckled at her words, and I groaned, hating that my cheeks heated with color.

"Knox has been kind enough to prepare packs for us to take and sent word to the Witchery that we're coming,"

Sabine informed the room, causing me to slouch at the thought of being left behind. "Aria will remain here, protected and safeguarded by his men. We can't chance her entering the Nine Realms and anything catching her scent. I have tasked Brander with protecting her during the time Knox is gone."

"Yay me," I muttered as I sat back in my chair, folding my hands in my lap to keep them from fidgeting.

"Aria, you know if we weren't counting on you being our virgin sacrifice, we'd take you with us. Knox is right, his mark only works here or wherever he is, if he is telling the truth. We cannot take the chance of you losing your virginity before we gather the other materials we need. I have sent word to Aunt Aurora that we could use her and the others. She's been keeping up to date with the situation here and is selling off the house to move here."

At the last part of her words, the chatter started up. Aurora was selling our home to come to Haven Falls, which meant we wouldn't be leaving here again. I frowned and listened to what everyone's chattering was about. Normally, I'd be doing the same thing with my twin, but she wasn't here.

"That means your communication to the friends you made, the men you fucked, ends now. Do whatever you need to do, call, or email them, whatever. Just break any connection to that world off because they're not able to come here or discover this place for any reason. You can do it once you return from your trip." I frowned as they groaned at my words.

I was the sister in charge of ex-communication and communication. I served as the representative of the family since I'd studied communication and diplomatic relationships. We each had taken a major to increase our place here or in the Nine Realms once the time came to play our part.

"But they're our friends," Aine said as she shook her head.

"No, Aine. They were, but once the house is sold, we are again residents of Haven Falls, and by being so, we can't have outside relationships. There are over twenty-thousand people here in this town. You will make friends here."

"My friends were witches," Luna interjected into the conversation.

I smiled sadly while she frowned. "Outside witches are not witches of the Nine Realms, nor can you tell them anything other than what I have stated. Cut all ties, end all communication. Be glad you have your twin, Luna. Some of us do not even get that." I pushed away from the table to leave the room, offering her a tight smile as I went.

I made it most the way down the hall before Brander called my name. I turned, dropping my eyes to the package in his hand.

"Knox left this for you. It's for your birthday. Happy birthday, Aria." He handed me the package and pushed his hand through his hair, studying me.

I watched him a moment before speaking. "Thank you," I frowned, noting how heavy the package was. "He didn't have to do this."

"Take it, Aria. Knox doesn't do gifts. Whatever the hell is happening between the two of you, I'm about to be thrown in the middle of it."

"He told you? I haven't decided on you yet, to be honest."

"You haven't?" He cocked a brow before rubbing his finger over his lip, exhaling slowly. "Knox said you would pick me and told me to be gentle with you."

"This is awkward," I muttered, adjusting my hold on the box. "Honestly, I have no idea what to do. I mean, it should be easy, but it isn't."

"If you do pick me, I will be gentle with you. I can handle plucking your cherry, as Kinvara referred to it. I'll respect you in the bedroom, but I will dominate you. I accept nothing less in the bedroom. Knox won't be back before your sisters' return, and if all goes to plan, you must choose someone by tomorrow night. Happy birthday, Aria," he said, leaning over to kiss my cheek. I was about to turn away from him and make my way to the bedroom, but his hand lifted, cupping my chin. "Maybe this will help you choose." His mouth lowered, brushing his lips against mine softly.

He smirked, watching me as my eyes widened, knowing that there was a wow factor from the touch of his lips. I didn't feel like throwing up all over him, either. I set the box on the floor, and his gaze narrowed.

Stepping on my toes, I brushed my lips against his, pleading to feel something or even a fraction of what I'd felt with Knox. His hand slipped to my back, and his mouth opened against mine, forcing my tongue to duel with his slowly in an erotic dance as old as time.

Brander walked me toward the wall, the gift forgotten on the floor as he took control, directing my tongue with his as they dueled. His hands grabbed mine, capturing them over my head as he broke apart the kiss, slipping his heated mouth to my throat, to kiss my pulse before slowly moving up to my ear.

"You're fucking delicious-smelling. Can you feel that?" He pressed his hardened cock against me, and I gasped. "Feel that wetness between your thighs? That's our bodies working to help this happen, Aria. Choose me because I want to spend hours bringing you into womanhood and cherish every inch of your flesh while giving as much pleasure as possible as I do it. You won't be sorry, little witch." His lips brushed against mine softly, barely touching them. "Plus, it would piss Knox off that I had you first, and I'm getting the feeling you enjoy doing that."

"He told me to pick you."

"Yeah, because anyone else would be in such a rush, and they'd forget that we need your blood for the blessing. You're rare, Aria. In a realm of immortals, the women have one first time to give their purity to a male of their choosing. Some men spend an eternity trying to find that first time for a woman, but normally it ends up being lost to some man who can't be bothered to prepare her cunt to take him. It shouldn't hurt more than it has to. Not if you find someone who knows how precious it really is."

"You make it sound like it is something bigger than it really is."

"I'm over a thousand years old, and I've never been blessed with deflowering a maiden. Think about that, Aria. In a thousand years, I've never found a maiden who still hadn't known the touch of a man. I pick up broken females because, through me, they heal. Others come to me because they want to be controlled, and I give it to them. I'm a kinky prick, but for you, and considering what I am getting from it, I'll play nice, I promise."

He kissed my cheek before heading down the hallway with a purpose. I turned to leave and remembered the gift, lifting it up. I frowned at how heavy it was. Inside the bedroom, I set it on the bed and then gasped at what sat on the pillow. A single long-stemmed midnight rose.

I lifted it up, grabbing the note beside it and read.

Happy birthday, Aria Primrose.

I inhaled it, sitting on the bed in silence while smelling the rose and the rare beauty of the flower. I'd never seen one before, let alone held something still alive from the Nine Realms. Setting it down on the nightstand, I turned to glare at the box.

The man was an enigma. My own sisters had forgotten my birthday, but he hadn't? The man didn't even like me, and yet he'd sent me gifts? Rare, once-in-a-lifetime gifts in the shape of a rose from a land he knew I craved. I lunged for the package, tearing it open until it revealed a box. I frowned, opening the blood-red box to brush my finger over the gown.

He'd bought a deflowering dress. Of course, he had.

I picked it up, noting the expensive design as another note fell from the package.

I thought it would look beautiful on you, and it's new. Inside the box are pictures and things from the realm you so wish to see. Sorry, you missed out on being able to go home with your sisters; someday, you will see the Nine Realms. ~Knox Karnavious.

I set the note down and picked up the smaller box, staring at the picture of a castle that had cascading waterfalls in the background. The castle had massive spiraling pillars and towers, with an actual battlement that surrounded the top of it. Masculine handwriting was beside the photo, and it matched the note in the box, with the description 'Norvalla Stronghold, Castle Karnavious' on the back.

There were several pictures, most from Norvalla, with images of creatures all around it. Smiling, I looked through them all before pulling out the crystals that were filled with rainbow hues inside them. They resembled high-quality quartz, but the rainbow coloring that moved as if filled with water told me they were something else. The moment they touched my hand, power leapt into my body, and I closed my eyes. I wondered if everything from the Nine Realms would feel so exotic and pure once I got to experience it firsthand. Someday I would go home, and I'd spend weeks there learning the realm I'd originally come from.

I lay back against the pillows, staring at the ceiling before exhaling. Knox had given me things I'd never touched before, things from our homeland that, to him, probably weren't such a big deal. To me, it was everything. I looked at the clock, realizing I'd lost track of time with the gifts and staring at the pictures, and would miss seeing my sisters off. Pushing everything back into the box and eyeing the flower, I left the room in a hurry.

CHAPTER
29

I returned to the mansion shortly after my sisters stepped through the portal, leaving me with an army of men at my back and Brander between me and the portal. The moment it closed, they whisked me back in a dark SUV with sinisterly tinted windows.

Changing into my pajamas, I scooped up the pictures and began studying each one again. I knew I should protect the rose or drain the essence, but I had nothing to pour it into. It would be a loss since the essence wouldn't be collected within the first few hours of harvest.

Bringing it to my nose, I inhaled the scent greedily. It smelled like I imagined heaven would smell. It had an aroma that seeped from the flower onto my fingers. I smiled to myself, running my fingers against my neck to keep the exotic scent on my flesh. Getting back up, I headed into the shower silently, picking out a sheer white nightgown that hugged my frame and yet left a little to the imagination instead of giving everything away.

Showered and ready for bed, I entered the room to find Regina sitting on the bed with the rose in her hand. Her eyes turned to me and slid over my body with mirth like I wasn't even worth looking at.

"You won't keep his attention long, you know."

"Whose?" I asked, staring at the rose.

"Don't play coy with me, bitch. You know who I speak of."

"If you're speaking of Knox, I'm relieved that I won't."

"He ate your pussy, and you fucked his face while he did."

I scoffed, shaking my head. "He licked it once."

"No, you stupid girl, he ate it, and you came on his tongue for hours, you just don't remember. Knox isn't from this realm—he doesn't play by the rules either. You're cute, but that only lasts until he fucks you, then his interest will wane, and he'll come back to me. It's just that innocent pussy he wants from you. The moment you lose your virginity, you will lose his interest and just be another discarded whore. Hundreds of them pine for him. You'll just be another one of the sad, pitiful bitches discarded into the trash bin."

"He isn't taking my virginity, Brander is." I crossed my arms, studying her as she lifted the notes I'd placed together and then gazed at the dress. "You should go now."

"You think he will allow his brother to take your innocence? Don't be stupid, girl. He is a virile male, all hunter, and you are marked as prey." Her anger erupted, slithering through the room, and for a moment, her face changed into that of a hag.

I stepped back, noting the smirk that lifted her lips while she fingered the red chiffon cocktail dress. She tossed it aside, standing to stare at me.

"Doesn't matter, I chose Brander. Knox didn't want it and left."

"You're not even pretty." She ignored my statement as she let her gaze slide down me with disdain. "Why do you get gifts when everyone else gets bent over whatever is closest and pounded into it like a piece of fucking meat?"

"Because you allow him to do it," I mocked, watching her as her cheeks heated with anger. "Look, you don't want to be treated like a whore? Stop allowing him to treat you like one. Stand up for yourself, or shut the fuck up, sit down, and continue to take it. You are allowing him to treat you as he does. If you allow him to do it, he will continue to treat you the same way. Bottom line, Regina? Close your legs until he respects you. You have the pussy, he wants it. Use that, and if you don't, you have no one but yourself to blame."

"You think you get a choice? Knox is the type of man you want to be owned by. When he fucks, he fucks you with every part of him. It's so fucking brutal that you spend the rest of your life searching for it again, and never find it. Being owned by him means you are his to use when he sees fit. Why do you think his household is mostly run by women? There isn't one who wouldn't slit your throat to take his bed for one night to feel him again. He offers protection and his body. You'll fucking take it if you're smart."

"I'd rather not know what it feels like to be owned. I am a Hecate witch. I'm royalty by birth. Neither Knox nor any other man will ever own me. I choose my fate and my chaos, and what I allow to happen to me is on me, no one else. You won't find me bitching about you sleeping with my man, because the moment he betrays me, I'm done. I'm worth more than that, Regina. So you want to be owned? Fine, but not me," I snorted, shaking my head as she frowned, and her power filled the room again.

She snorted and shook her head. "You already are, Aria. The moment you laid down in that chair and allowed him to place his name on you, you became his. The moment you parted your thighs and came for him, you sealed the fucking deal. You parted your flesh, touching it while he placed his name on your thigh, and when you started coming with your clumsy attempt to fuck your own flesh, he did it for you. You screamed his name, riding his face until your screams turned painful because he wouldn't let you stop coming. He drank your essence, slurping it clean before he covered it back up. I listened to him as he erased your memories, and you woke up talking as if it had never even happened, but I know otherwise because I watched it happen. He needed one last taste, so you knew he'd tasted your sloppy cunt first. It was so sloppy, glistening with come from that glorious tongue of his."

"He never did that for you, has he?" I noted the longing in her tone and the betrayal in her eyes. "He never pleasured you with his mouth? Don't come in here telling me fucking lies. Get out!" I trembled with anger as her lies slammed against my head, feeding me false images.

Brander filled the doorway, staring between us before he hiked his finger over his shoulder. "Get the fuck out, Regina. You were told to keep your distance."

"Why? Because Knox is planning to fuck her?"

"I won't ask you again," he stated coldly.

She stared between us, smashing the rose in her hand before she exited the room with it. I swallowed past the anger. Looking to Brander, I watched as he followed her down the hallway with his eyes before turning back to look at me.

"Does Knox have the power to erase memories?" I whispered through trembling lips.

"Go to bed, sugar. Don't listen to displaced hags, they live to hurt pretty little things with their lies." He reached in, grabbing the door to pull it shut.

I heard the lock sliding into place, and my eyes closed, replaying the morning Knox had tasted me. Opening them, I frowned, knowing that he said hours had passed, and yet it hadn't felt like any time had passed at all. Moving to the bed, I took a seat and hugged my legs against my chest. I could do a memory spell, but that would alert the house I'd wielded magic, and lord knew what it would do to me.

I reached over, grabbed the pictures, and set them on the nightstand before pushing the dress away from me, lying back on the bed to sleep as the day weighed on my mind. I said a silent prayer for my sisters, and prayed that Amara was safe; even if she wasn't who she used to be, she was still my sister and my womb mate.

My eyes grew heavy as I picked up one small shard of the crystal, holding it as a smile slipped over my lips. Regina was bitter, and she was a hag. I'd caught a glimpse of her, and it had been something I wouldn't forget soon.

Tomorrow I would lose my virginity to a stranger, one I hadn't felt fire for when I kissed. Maybe it was my mood, or perhaps I was cursed like Regina to always crave more than I knew I should reach for. I slept, oblivious to what was happening around me, uncaring that tomorrow was coming faster than I wanted it to—with the wrong man.

I woke up to something in the bedroom and turned on the light beside the bed. Knox stood in the corner, his eyes dark with something primal banked in them. His shirt was covered in blood; his hands were covered in black ooze that dripped onto the floor.

"Knox, what the fuck happened?" I whispered, moving from the bed to where he stood.

"Worried about me, lamb?" he asked huskily.

"No, I'm worried for whoever pissed you off," I muttered, holding Knox's stare as his lips curled into a devilish smirk.

"Smart girl. I heard your rose got stolen, so I brought a couple in vials to replace it. Would you like to see them?" he asked carefully as I moved back to the bed, sitting down to stare at him.

I studied at him silently, frowning as I chewed my lip. "Now?"

"You'll lose the essence if you wait."

"Okay," I stated quickly, standing up and righting the nightgown I wore as he watched me.

"The fuck is that?"

"It's a nightgown?" I replied, watching him.

"It's ugly."

"Good, wasn't trying to impress you, anyway."

He snorted, pushing off the walls as he moved toward me. I frowned, watching as he lifted his hand, ripping the nightgown from my body before smirking coldly. Knox lifted his hands, holding me against him as his mouth crushed against mine. I tasted blood on his tongue and pulled back, but he didn't allow it.

His hands wrapped around my throat, sealing off my airway as I struggled to bring air into my lungs. The moment he released my neck, I inhaled and felt something slithering down my throat with the air I sucked in greedily.

"What a waste of pretty lips, Aria." He chuckled against my mouth before something pushed into my throat, diving deeper and deeper until I felt it searching within me, tasting me from the inside as if devouring me.

I screamed and screamed until something shook me. I attacked, punching and moving to claw out his eyes.

"What the fuck, woman," Brander screamed, backing up to stare down at me where my nightgown was ripped, and blood dripped from my face. "*Fuck*!" He scooped down, lifting me up and ran with me in his arms. "Lore, clear the fucking table, and grab a witch."

"What the hell happened to her?" Lore asked,

pushing platinum hair away from his face as his amber eyes stared down at me.

"Dream demon," Brander hissed, nodding at Regina, who stepped from the shadows with crystals in her hands. "My guess, someone planted ears in the house."

One man entered the room with sweat dripping down his face. "That explains the shadows that just tried to lock me in the gym." He was shirtless, with thick black tribal tattoos covering the sides of his waist up to just beneath his arms. Obsidian-colored hair dripped water down his chest, while midnight-blue eyes sparkled with the light of a thousand stars in their depths.

"Send word to Knox, now, Fade. They probably slipped into the house the moment he left tonight, and just waited for us to let our guard down. You," he said to me. "Lay the fuck back because this will hurt."

"What was it?"

"Pretty sure he placed something inside of you, and I'm about to get it out."

I stared at him and then tilted my head. "It was a demon named Knox."

"Nah, he just showed up in the skin you wanted him to appear in, probably slipped into your mind through the water in the shower. That's what the slimy pricks do."

"What exactly is it they plant, Brander?" I asked carefully.

"You don't want to know."

"What the fuck is inside of me?"

"Larva, it takes control of the body and the mind of

249

the creature who houses it."

I gagged violently.

"She's going to throw up," Lore stated, stepping back.

I did, violently. My body twitched, and I leaned over, gagging even more than before as I tried to expel whatever had been planted inside of me. Something inside of me wasn't having it, and I cried as I forced it up. I threw up water until something substantial exploded from my mouth and got stuck.

"Fucking hell, that's nasty."

I reached up, ripping it out of my throat and throwing up even more the moment it hit the floor, screeching and wailing while they tried to stomp on whatever the hell the alien-looking squid was. It was the shit of nightmares, flailing squid-like arms as it tried to find a place to hide.

The room ignited with power, and Knox materialized from thin air, stomping the creature beneath his thick boots. He turned, staring at me as I held my hand over my mouth while tears slid from my eyes.

A squid had *violated* me!

I gagged again, holding my hand against my stomach.

Knox wore a crown that looked like bones. His eyes were turbulent, as if a hurricane played in his ocean depths. He had on armor, like honest-to-God armor that was covered in ravens. He turned away from me, staring at the few men inside the room. He took a step forward, and the armor clinked. I peered down, looking at the metal that covered his boots and the knight spurs that were attached to his heels as if he'd just returned from riding a warhorse. His mantle was black, and yet it shimmered with his movement. Everything about the man screamed God of War.

"How the fuck did it get to her?" he snarled, but his voice echoed through the room, like it wasn't big enough to contain him like this.

"I'm guessing it showed up the moment you left tonight."

"I had Regina add wards and war runes. Pretty hag, did you get jealous because I refused to fuck you?" he snapped, but there was none of his usual tone; it was cold, lifeless. "If I find out you did, you're done here. You will never see your home again, Regina. You know I will find out who altered the wards, I always do."

"You were replacing me! You wouldn't fuck me because that little whore has your mind under her control! You ate her cunt, and ever since, you have not looked at or used any of us again. You gave that stupid bitch gifts!"

"Take Regina away now." He turned, staring at me. *"Sleep, Aria."*

CHAPTER
30

The next morning was rough. Nightmares of the thing that had been inside of me had made sleep elusive. However, through the night, I'd felt Knox close to me, and it had comforted me, disturbingly enough. I would have assumed it would have made sleeping more difficult, but it hadn't. I woke up redressed in a soft blue nightgown, my hair damp from sweat and nightmares. Knox sat beside the bed in a chair, watching me as I sat up slowly, touching my mouth as nausea pushed at the back of my throat. He'd promised that nothing would reach me, but he'd failed in that department. I'd been attacked in my sleep by a fucking demon!

"Demons like the one who planted the larva inside of you; they're slippery fuckers, Aria." His tone was cold, but the heat in his gaze said otherwise, letting it drift down the sheer material of the gown. "It came through the plumbing, and it was searching for you. Something powerful is hunting you. It's reaching for you inside my house, so if you have any idea what or who it is, I need to know now."

"I told you, I don't know what is happening. I have no enemies that I know of. I don't see why a demon would want me, or who would even have enough power to send one after me."

"Let me make this as clear as I can for you, little witch. Had it planted within you and taken root, you'd have been in the backseat while it drove your body. You would have done whatever it wanted, with whoever it wanted. If it had wanted you to stand in front of a bus going down the interstate, you would have. You'd have watched it happen and then dealt with whatever backlash it had left you with. I can't protect you if you don't talk to me."

"I don't have enemies, and you've even used your strange tone of voice to ask this question before, Knox. I told you everything. I'm nobody. I'm definitely not worth the effort this person or creature is going through to reach me—and were you wearing a crown last night?" I asked offhandedly as my mind replayed the image of him, which was hot as fuck.

His lips curved into a dark smile before he sat back, brushing his hand over his mouth. He watched me, his eyes slowly roaming over my face as he considered his reply. The hair on my nape rose from the look in his intense, smoldering gaze.

"You're still a virgin. You were told to remedy that. You didn't. Should I take it as an invitation, Aria?"

"Absolutely not," I scoffed as the smile dropped, and I frowned, the answer I'd wanted to say heavy on my tongue. I snorted before rolling my eyes so he could see my response.

The timbre of his voice filled with rough gravel when he spoke after a moment. "You've decided on Brander?"

"You said to choose him, so I did. You said he was safe, and safe is what I need." My body heated with the way he continued staring, letting his head tilt to the side before he stood.

"It's your choice, Aria. He is safe, and he'll be gentle with you."

I wanted to ask him to do it, to be the one that took my virginity, and yet my tongue wouldn't move. There was nothing gentle about Knox, and yet, surprisingly, I didn't crave gentle. I may have needed it for the first time, but I wanted the electricity that erupted when Knox touched me. Brander sent butterflies fluttering; Knox sent ravens into flight violently inside my belly. It was night and day between the twos' touches, and I craved the sexual predator that lurked right beneath the surface of Knox. Brander had a beast too, but where his was silent and content to pace, Knox's monster wanted to destroy and conquer—and I wanted that from him.

Knox watched silently, waiting for one wrong move to claim and destroy me. His lips curved into a conceited grin, as if he felt my choice on a cellular level. As if every cell in my body knew it should be him, and yet my mouth didn't open to tell him. Nodding, he moved to the door where he stopped and stared out into the hallway.

"Your outfit for tonight is in the bathroom. Brander

picked it himself for the occasion. Dinner won't be served tonight; they will bring a small meal to your room instead. I'll be heading out again tonight." He turned, smirking wolfishly. "At six, someone will retrieve you; they'll deliver you to Brander's room on the third floor." He waited, and when I failed to say what refused to come out, he left, silently closing the door behind him.

I stared at the door for too long. My sigh exploded while I groaned, dropping back onto the bed. It had been less than a week since we'd returned to this town, and already everything that could go wrong *had* or was doing so now.

Tonight I'd be sleeping with a male I didn't even know well. I knew he had unlimited women trailing through his revolving bedroom door. Now I'd learned it wasn't even his bedroom; if what Knox said was true, Brander's bedroom was on the third floor.

Dinner showed up at five, and it wasn't a small meal by any means. There was roasted lamb marinated in a light rosemary sauce that melted in my mouth. The red baby potatoes soaked in butter with a light rosemary base was to die for. The wine was red and delicious, and by 5:30 PM, I'd drunk half the bottle to numb the nerves that grew more intense with every minute the clock ticked down to six o'clock.

At 6:00 PM, I was dressed in a ruby red dress with a deep V-neck that had a matching back. The belt was a bow, and it sat right beneath the bodice. It had a unique skirt that spiraled around and reached for the bust line. It was cute, while still maintaining a hint of class and sexiness. High heels adorned my feet, with wraparound ribbons that went past my ankles, stopping just below my calves. My hair was up, exposing the delicate lines of my throat, and the bra and panties that had been sent with the dress revealed no lines and matched in color.

I had to give it to Knox. He'd chosen an outfit that positively screamed sex while allowing the woman to feel not entirely exposed at the same time. The dress Brander had chosen remained hanging in the bathroom.

I felt sexy in the one Knox had purchased for me for my birthday, whereas the one Brander chose was more revealing. I checked the pins in my hair and used my finger to rub on some lipstick to lighten my natural lip color. Stepping back, I frowned, wondering what Knox would think if he saw me right now. Probably not a lot, since he had women who literally did whatever it took to sleep with him.

Giving myself a mental shake, I turned as a knuckled knock sounded against the door.

Opening the door, Greer stood outside of it.

"Hey, Greer," I said, watching as his lip curled up with disdain even though his gaze slid over my dress, heating before lifting back to my eyes.

"I am here to escort you to the third floor. If you could refrain from speaking to me through the duration of that time, I'd be eternally grateful."

He waited as if he expected me to rebuke his words, and yet my heart was fluttering with what I was preparing to do and where he was taking me, so I just stared at him. His smile was predatory when it finally came, and I tilted my head, noting the fangs that clicked into place when he smiled.

"Greer, the vampire, huh?" I tightened my lips to

the side as my nose scrunched up. "Who would have thought it?" I chuckled, stepping into the hallway with him.

"Apparently, not you," he sighed dramatically for effect. "Hopefully, Brander isn't gentle tonight, mistress."

"I mean with the name Greer, I'd be thinking demon or something that was created. It's more like a human name in a case where your mother didn't entirely like you."

"Must you speak?" he grunted as we continued walking.

"I knew you were old. To get to your level of cankerous, that takes time and work to achieve with the perfection you have mastered, Greer the Vampire."

"Mistress Aria," he muttered beneath his breath, pushing a code into the wall before the elevator doors opened. "Get in, please. I'm not getting any younger, and neither are you."

CHAPTER
31

I stepped inside the elevator, watching as he shielded the code box and added a badge to it to make us move. My stomach churned with the need to say this was a mistake, or that I had changed my mind, and yet I didn't. It stopped on the third floor and opened into an apartment. Stepping off the elevator, I turned to wait for Greer but watched the doors close quickly with him still in the elevator.

I took in the candles that burned through the apartment, and the expensive white cashmere couch and chair that sat in the entrance. Exhaling, I struggled to get my nerves under control while my hands trembled at the mistake I was making.

My hands rubbed down my arms as I inhaled the familiar scent of a male. Not just any male, the room reeked of Knox, but then Brander had a similar smell. Power exuded from within the room, and it sent a ripple of apprehension shooting down my spine. I was moments away from bolting.

"Greer, dick move," I mumbled under my breath, fighting for calm as I started into the apartment, only for my jaw drop.

Books lined the shelves on one wall, while the other held weapons behind glowing glass. Crystals sat on a large desk that faced into the room, and a large bed sat against a wall. The entire bedroom was huge, filled with interesting items that made it feel like a library, office, and bedroom all pushed into one overly large room. One I itched to explore leisurely.

"Fuck me," a masculine timbre erupted behind me, forcing me to turn in the direction it had come. Brander scrubbed his hand down his face, letting his eyes move from mine to the red heels I wore, and back up. He opened his mouth before closing it.

"Excuse me?"

"We should drink," he muttered beneath his breath, holding his hand out to indicate that I should follow him toward the large settee that sat next to the bed. On the table, there was an aged bottle of scotch, and my lips jerked in the corners as I noted it was the same type that had been shattered on the floor in this very house earlier in the week.

"How did you manage that?" I asked curiously, feeling a little calmer with knowing he'd noticed the age and brand of scotch, and had cared enough to pay attention to the details.

"Knox brought it back with him when he returned from Scotland last night."

My heart stopped and then restarted with a flutter. Of course, it had been Knox who had thought of it. For an absolute prick, he had a knack for noting fine details. I didn't sit down, not with the nervousness that flooded my system the moment my brain registered the cut of his suit, and that he was dressed for seduction. I exploded with anxiety until I thought I would pass out from the blood running to my head at the decision I was making.

I was about to give this man a piece of myself that I'd never been able to give to another man. It was supposed to be something that happened, not something planned or done because a spell called for it.

Brander watched me moving around the large room, studying certain items as he poured two glasses of scotch then stood there in silence. His room was larger than the main floor of our mansion. It stretched down long, dark hallways that appeared to extend further into other rooms, and yet from my vantage point, I couldn't make them out.

My fingers hovered over a crystal, sensing the power that pushed through it before I finally turned, looking at him, trembling nervously while fidgeting and biting my lip to find peace in pain.

"So, how do we do this?" I asked, hating the shiver in my voice that made my words seem weak, forced.

I wasn't afraid of many things, but forking out the missing ingredient for the blessing spell? It had my insides churning with anxious energy. My hands shook as they rose, brushing over my naked arms as he trailed his vision over my dress and frowned. My heart raced at a rapid beat, which I was sure Brander could hear even at the distance from where I stood, quaking.

"Why me, Aria?" he asked softly, countering my

question with a look in his eyes that tugged at something deeper within me than I cared to acknowledge at this moment.

I took in the wide stance of his legs and the fold of his arms as they crossed over his heavily built chest. He stared me down without looking away as I debated my answer.

"Because I don't like you," I admitted, shrugging my shoulders as my hands dropped to my sides. "It's messy if we tie emotions to the act, and I'm not looking for messy. I'm looking for someone who won't hurt me, and will also walk away after we're done."

"You don't like Knox, so you could have chosen him."

"Knox is a predator. He looks at me as if I am something he can easily devour. I loathe him, and you, well, you, I just don't like. Knox is intense, the way he looks at me makes my insides quiver. He awakens something within me, and honestly, it terrifies me. He's also the most arrogant, self-assured, conceited prick on this planet. Knox wouldn't be safe or easy with me, and you will. He'd also enjoy taking my virginity entirely too much to allow him to have it."

His smile curved into a dark, sinful smirk. "I'm a predator, too."

"Yes, you are. But you, Brander, don't terrify me, and Knox does. Knox is intensely dangerous, and he doesn't care who he hurts or who knows he can murder them with a mere thought, and the deed would be done. He's very secure in playing the prick, and not even you can argue that fact. Besides, I don't care that you're about to take my virginity, really. It's a nuisance at this point."

"Then why haven't you given it away yet? Not that I'm complaining, but it is curious why you still have it."

"I had my reasons." I wasn't willing to divulge that I was a dud and couldn't manage to give it away, considering what we were about to do. "It wasn't so much that I didn't want to have sex as much as I couldn't." I offered, knowing he deserved some explanation to know that there wasn't something wrong with me. I opened my mouth to say more, but his dark brow rose as the smile twisted a little more.

"Drink," he offered, nodding his dark head at the glass that sat untouched on the table in front of the settee. "You're nervous, and it's starting to mess with my vibe, woman."

I made my way to the settee and sat, lifting the amber-colored scotch to my nose, inhaling it deeply before I drank it down in one gulp. It burned its way down my throat. I silently watched him reaching to refill the glass I held. He sat across from me, placing his feet on the table before tipping back his drink, studying me over the rim.

"You're a nervous little thing, aren't you?" he asked huskily before taking a long swig from the glass.

"I'm not that nervous." It was a lie, one that hung heavy on my tongue. He'd noted the shiver that etched my tone, and the way the glass trembled even though I held it with both hands to prevent it from being too obvious.

The tattletale heartbeat that raced against my ribs

was audible to my ears, which meant his inhuman ones had noted the erratic rhythm. It didn't help that it raced like nitrogen gasses had fueled it, either.

"Fine, then strip out of that dress for me, and prove how not nervous you are, Aria. After that, finish the scotch, and we'll start this thing so I can show you how it's done instead of telling you."

Placing the glass on the table, I stood. My hands vibrated with tense energy, and yet I wouldn't stop. I couldn't afford to. My sisters depended on me to play my part, to get the blood of an untouched witch, one of purity. Spells like the one we were preparing to perform were ancient, written by witches who used the carotid artery when it called for the blood of a virgin.

Pure witches were rare—mixed with the fact it had to be from my bloodline made it more unique, meaning there was no way to do this myself. Ancient spells were more detailed, fine-tuned, and precise. If it called for a sacrifice, it wasn't talking about animals. They didn't mess around in the old days and, of course, didn't think twice about slitting someone's throat to make sure the gods knew they meant business.

Slowly, I untied the thin ribbon around my waist. My hands reached around, unzipping the dress, pushing the thin straps from my shoulders as it pooled to the floor at my feet. His breathing hitched in his lungs as I bent down, lifting the dress to fold it and place it onto the arm of the settee. Gradually, my eyes rose to his, watching them smolder as they moved down my long frame.

"Damn, woman," he groaned, covering his face with his hand before he sat up, pouring more scotch into my glass. "Finish that, and when you're done, stand by the bed, and we'll begin with binding your hands."

"What?" I asked in a high pitch squeal. "You're fucking with me, right?" I probed, worried I'd heard him right.

"No, not at all." His voice was husky, filled with enough gravel to refill an entire driveway. His gaze slid over my body when I stood, turning to follow him as he moved through the room. "You asked me to do this, and I'm pretty sure Knox is still here, so I can go get him if you'd like to change your mind in that pretty little head of yours. I have rules that I play by, and I won't break them, not even for you. You will be bound and blindfolded before I fuck you. If you can't do it, you can find someone else to pluck that cherry. I'm a kinky prick, but I plan to be gentle with you, and I won't hurt you, Aria. Now come to me and give me your hands."

I downed the remnants left in my glass and set it down. Pulling on the strength I had left in the reserve I kept stored in my mental bank, I took the first step toward him. I told myself that once I finished this, once I played my part, we could go home.

Brander was safe, I told myself. So what if he was a kinky prick, but who wasn't these days? I talked myself into continuing this path by the time I reached him and stood before him.

"Give me your hands. Hold your wrists together." Once I had done what he instructed, he held my wrists together, tying them with a length of black silk, then lifted his eyes to hold mine as a smirk spread over his lips. My breathing hitched, struggling to calm my reaction to his touch. I watched in utter silence as he finished binding my wrists and lifted his eyes to mine. "Is that too tight?"

"A little," I admitted, moving my hands as far as they would go.

"Good, then it's perfect."

"Now, what happens?" I asked through quivering lips, watching him closely as he moved across the room, grabbing a blindfold.

"Walk backward toward the bed and take a seat," he ordered in a strained tone, running his finger over his top lip as his eyes turned to slits.

"You do know that you were supposed to be the easy one." I fidgeted nervously as I stepped back carefully. The nerves within me were on edge, and the moment my legs touched the bed, I turned, staring into a giant mirror before sitting down.

The entire room smelled of Knox the longer I was in here, causing everything within me to struggle with the decision I was making. It was too late now to change my mind; by now, Knox had left the house to do whatever the hell he did when he vanished—supposedly, though, Brander had said he was still here. It both comforted and unnerved me.

"Oh, I'm easy, sweetheart. Easy like a Sunday morning."

I chuckled at his attempt at humor. "Heels left on or off?" I asked, uncertain which I should do.

"On for now," he said, watching me as I studied him from where he stood in front of me.

"When do you strip?" I asked, and his jaw tensed. "I

just meant that I'm feeling a little undressed here."

"Are you in a hurry, sweet one? I sure hope not," he chuckled darkly, stepping between my legs. "This isn't ending quickly." He pushed a stray strand of hair from my temple, and shocks ignited from his touch. He placed the blindfold over my eyes and leaned down, brushing his mouth against mine and sent a flurry of heat and emotions pulsing through me. "Stand up." I trembled at the tone of his voice as it changed, becoming darker.

Standing, I held my hands out in front of me, and as I did, a whisper of power erupted through the room, causing my hair to disturb from the pins that held it up. My flesh heated, and when hands reached for mine, I allowed it. Brander placed them above my head, using his foot to part my legs until I was standing with them slightly parted. Then, he secured my hands to what I assumed was a hook I hadn't noticed earlier.

"Doing okay?"

"Yes," I answered as apprehension slithered up my spine, and my mind focused on oceanic blue eyes that had swells within their murky depths. The memory of Knox against my flesh, the way he'd kissed me as if I was the air that filled his lungs and he was starving for oxygen. It calmed me from within.

"Good," he growled, and more wind stirred within the room, rustling papers from the end tables.

The room filled with the promise of power as it brushed over my naked flesh. I inhaled, drinking in the faint scent of Knox that clung to the air as if he had been in here in the last few hours. I waited with my hands above my head, and my legs spread apart for

Brander to begin. Only he never started, or he watched me squirming as I tried to trail his footsteps as I used my senses. It sounded as if he was across the room, but then his thumb trailed over my lips, making me jump.

"Be gentle with me," I pleaded, swallowing hard as dark laughter echoed in my ears.

CHAPTER
32

I waited with bated breath, listening to the room as music started playing softly across from where I stood. Breaking Benjamin's *Dance with the Devil* began, and for a moment, I was lost in the sound of the lead singer's voice and the instruments that caused my blood to spike, rushing through me in tune with the tempo of the song. Fingers touched my spine slowly, and I arched, feeling the sparks it created, igniting a smoldering candle within me.

They continued to trail down my back, settling on my ass before they squeezed one cheek. I felt his heat as he moved closer, standing behind me as his mouth touched my shoulder, fanning heated breath over it. Hard, sinewy muscled flesh touched against my back while his hand slipped around my front, pulling me back as teeth grazed my shoulder. I felt his fingers as they pushed my bra aside, exposing one nipple, pinching it hard enough to expel a gasp from the delicious pain it created.

Throaty laughter whispered over my skin as his hand moved up, touching my throat as his mouth skimmed against my neck, kissing it softly, barely touching it with the softest butterfly wings which forced heat to soak my core, clenching with need. The simplest touch sent a wealth of need pooling in my sex until I felt it dripping down my leg embarrassingly so.

The growl that sounded from deep within him created a need that I couldn't explain, as if my mind had replaced Brander with Knox, and my body was reacting to him because of it. A foot spread my legs further apart, while the other hand that held my throat released it, slipping down my stomach to touch beneath my panties, skimming over the delicate nub briefly before pushing through my sex, finding it wet with need.

"Not sure we need the foreplay, do we?" I whispered as an angry growl answered.

I felt him withdrawing his hand from my panties, ripping them off in a swift movement that pulled a cry from my parted lips. I opened my mouth to speak, and he pushed my panties between my lips, stilling my words as my brows furrowed. I could take a hint. His knees forced my legs apart. I felt him skimming my entrance from behind, while his other arm slipped around the front, brushing his thumb over the nub that connected to every erogenous nerve in my body.

A single finger entered my core, creating a moan that built deep in my chest and escaped through a muffled cry. Another finger pushed into me, and I whimpered at the fullness it created in my body. Slowly, torturously slow, he drove them deeper, only to withdraw them, turning them while his thumb worked circles against my clitoris.

Heat unfurled violently from my middle and moans exploded from my mouth. He slowly increased the speed kissing the curve of my neck as his hot breath fanned against it. My legs threatened to give out. He laughed hoarsely, watching as my body bent over with my arms twisting painfully above me, preventing me from falling to the floor. I began moving with his motion, helping him as he fucked me with two fingers until I gasped, screaming as everything exploded.

Bass pounded in my ears, or maybe it was my heartbeat. Lights filled my vision, replacing the darkness the blindfold created. He didn't stop, not even after the orgasm began to abate and another one threatened to take hold. My breathing was labored. Spitting my panties out of my mouth, I gasped air in, fighting to regain control.

His fingers withdrew, and I listened to the sound of bare feet as they padded around me. One hand grasped me around the neck lifting me up as he pushed his fingers between my lips, forcing me to taste myself until his tongue joined in, brushing against mine. It was erotic, tasting myself with him as he growled against my mouth, noting the eagerness of my tongue.

Withdrawing his fingers, he let his mouth brush against mine as his hands snaked up, unhooking the pins that held my hair in the updo. I felt it falling down my back, but his fingers slipped through it, gripping it as he exposed my neck to his mouth. He kissed me slowly, letting his tongue escape his mouth as it brushed over my flesh, working around my throat as he controlled my head with his fingers threaded through my hair.

He slipped his mouth against my ear, nipping the earlobe playfully, and I moaned loudly, feeling everything he did viscerally. The man knew how to use every part of a woman's body explicitly. No wonder he had a new woman in his room every night. There was probably a line all the way out of town to fuck him.

He didn't stick his tongue into my ear, which was a relief. Instead, he used it against the bottom of my lobe, flicking it like it was my pussy instead of my ear. My breathing was shallow, coming in gasped breaths as he continued using every inch of me to ignite a raging inferno that threatened to leave me in ashes.

He stepped away, and I whimpered, rocking my hips in search of his touch. I shouldn't be this excited for him, but I wasn't imagining Brander—I was imagining it was Knox slowly unraveling me, sending me into a frenzied state of need. Oceanic eyes would stare at my naked flesh, touching it and bringing me into the state of womanhood.

Something touched against my ass, and I turned my head, listening. Hands positioned me, lifting my legs, causing me to cry out in surprise as I left the floor. My ass was placed onto something hard, and yet he didn't release my thighs. Instead, he rested them over his shoulders, and then his mouth brushed against the inside of my thigh before fanning my pussy with his heated breath, yet never touching it.

I could feel the arousal that dripped with need from my needy pussy. It was embarrassing, and I started to realize just how vulnerable and exposed I truly was. Teeth skimmed my flesh, and I gasped, letting his tongue which was slowly running up my thigh, ease my embarrassment at being this excited for him. It did little to calm the panic that was blossoming within me as I realized that I was literally helpless, bound and blindfolded in a room with a man I knew nothing about.

His fingers tightened on my legs, as if he sensed my unease, reassuring me I was safe. That was why I settled on him right. He was safe? Yet here I was, blindfolded and tied to the ceiling like something that waited to be sacrificed. Nothing about this was safe. This was insanity in all its damn glory!

His mouth brushed against my flesh, and a deep growl escaped his lips, whispering against my pussy as he let his tongue lick through it greedily. I wailed, calling out the name that was on the tip of my tongue, and then muttered an apology as dark laughter filled the room, echoing in my ears before his mouth descended on my flesh.

He didn't lick, he devoured. His mouth sucked, tasted, and rocked through me like a bomb detonating slowly, each stick of dynamite placed strategically to impact the most damage possible. He wrote the alphabet with his tongue, not the human one, but the long, endless one of the Nine Realms. He didn't stop until I was shaking, crying out as the orgasm exploded, causing my body to jerk and spasm with the sheer force of it. I pleaded for mercy, begging for him to stop and let me catch my breath, but his laughter was the only noise other than my pleas that filled the room, echoing through it loudly.

He abruptly stopped devouring me, lifting my legs from his shoulders. He undid the heels from my feet slowly, methodically, making it sensual instead of a task. His mouth brushed over my calves, kissing my leg before he set it down on the floor, then did the same with the other. His hands grabbed my wrist, pulling me down from the hook he'd placed them in.

My legs wouldn't support me, which he found amusing as he slowly helped me to the bed, ripping the bra straps off to remove it before he followed me down, capturing my nipple between his lips biting the delicate peak teasingly. He grabbed both breasts, squeezing them without taking his tongue away. He slowly flicked his tongue over the swollen peak, slowly, as he applied pressure, learning them thoroughly.

One hand released the globe of my breast, slipping down my belly until his fingers trailed through the mess he'd created. He pushed them into my body as my spine arched, and my legs dropped open for him while my hips rocked forward. His mouth moved away from my breasts, and I knew without having to see, he was staring at my flesh, where I took what he gave me wantonly.

He claimed my nipple again, using his tongue to trace a circle around the raised peak. His mouth tightened against my nipple as his thumb once more began to play with the swollen nub between my thighs. His fingers pushed apart inside my body, spreading me before forcing a whimpered cry to explode from my lips as he stretched me, readying my body to take him. He made a noise against my breast, half-pain and half-excitement as my body clenched against his fingers, trying to dispel them.

He continued stretching me slowly, adding another finger into my pussy. It created a painful burn as muscles clenched tightly against him from the foreign fullness he created in my pussy. I moaned and trembled with the need of the unknown, feeling every thrust as he created wetness to be able to accommodate his cock. This was an ache I'd never felt before, a need for more to fill me.

Lips unclasped from my breast, and I whimpered, needing the distraction of his teeth to hold my focus from the sensation of his fingers readying my body to take him. He withdrew them, and I groaned, missing the burning fullness they had been creating as they'd been building pressure in my core.

The bed moved, and the sound of pants sliding over flesh sent ravens fighting against my insides. My knees lifted, and I waited in silence as he stripped and sat on the bed again. He carefully turned me onto my stomach. I frowned, wondering what the hell he was doing until his mouth touched the globe of my cheek, nipping at it before his tongue tasted my core once more. I moaned as pleasure erupted through me, sliding my legs further apart as my ass lifted into the air, giving him unhindered access to my center.

He repositioned me the moment he pulled away. He lifted my knees before his hands spanned over my hips, holding them until I was resting on my knees with my top half balanced on my elbows against the bed. Something velvety soft and yet hard as steel pushed against my opening, pushing into my body a mere inch before it stopped. I clamped down around it like I was trying to hold it there, but his deep, guttural growl forced me to peer over my shoulder, only to remember I had been blindfolded and couldn't see him. He tortured me slowly, rubbing it against my opening until I thought I would go insane.

I pushed back, but he went back at the same moment, as if he knew it was a game. He made a low tsking noise with his tongue. I rocked my hips invitingly, letting him see how wet and ready my body was for him.

"I need it," I admitted with lust hanging on each word.

I had never been so sexually charged or in need of sex in my entire life. He chuckled against my shoulder, nipping it as my body grew pliant. My brain itched as I expelled a sigh, as if his teeth had direct access to the storm brewing within me, holding it at bay.

He pulled me up on my knees, bringing my body flush against his chest, testing the weight of my breasts in his hands before he adjusted himself behind me. He placed me on the tip of his cock, causing me to lift even higher on my knees as the erotic thought of being impaled made reason slip into my mind. It was awkward with my hands tied, but then he did the last thing I expected him to do. He placed my bound hands over his head, forcing our bodies even closer together with his chest against my back.

I moved to glide down his cock, but he stopped me, pushing his body back, which only allowed me to accept the thick tip of it within my needy pussy. I rocked against it, needing it more than I needed the air that filled my lungs. Fuck breathing, I need to feel him pushing into my body hard and fast.

"Not yet," he hissed in a deep, husky voice that made something inside of me stop and pause.

His fingers moved against my clit, and I dismissed it, marking it up to the fact that I'd imagined it was

Knox with me all this time. Was it possible to manifest him by sheer willpower alone?

I swallowed and moaned, past the point of thinking with the most basic, carnal need forcing my body to react. He righted us again, lifting his fingers to remove the blindfold, and I blinked, refocusing my vision.

Staring into the mirror as his mouth grazed my shoulder, smiling. Oceanic eyes captured and held mine in the reflection, and the smile fell from my lips, tugging into a frown. His hands held my breasts while he watched me slowly taking in how I looked naked against him. His devilish grin pressed against my shoulder as his predatory stare smiled at the confusion on my face.

CHAPTER
33

Knox laughed wickedly, watching me as my eyes widened as the realization of who had been with me this entire time fully sank in. It hadn't been me imagining it was him, because it had actually been him. I wanted to scream at him, to rant about playing tricks, and yet I wasn't upset it was him. I was relieved. He smiled as I rubbed against him, trembling with need from the way he'd wound my body up tightly. I licked my dry lips, smirking at the vision of us together that reflected in the mirror.

"Did you think I'd allow anyone else to fuck you, Aria?" His gaze held mine as he pushed into my body without warning.

I screamed and whimpered, shivering as tremors rushed through me, and pain pierced my core as he stretched me entirely too full. It didn't hurt; it fucking burned and ached as muscles never used before clamped down, trying to expel the overly large member that had just battered past my innocence and ripped through my body to fill every inch full.

"I'm entirely too self-centered, too conceited, and too assured of myself to allow anyone else to fuck you, sweet girl."

"Knox," I moaned hoarsely through chattering teeth, unable to get words out of the tightening in my throat as a deep burning pain hummed through my core. "It aches."

He didn't move, didn't ease the pain as it ripped me apart from the inside out. He hadn't been gentle; he'd pushed into my body with one swift thrust that stretched me beyond my limits, carving his way through it until he was buried within me, leaving nothing untouched. I was fully seated to the base of his enormous cock, clenching hungrily against it as I rocked to ease the pain.

"That's my name. It's also what you'll be screaming all night. Look at you, so fucking exquisite taking my cock, and you took all of it, little one. Look at that pretty cunt stretched to fit me like a glove, so fucking tight." His hand slipped around to my front, watching my eyes as he rubbed my clit, forcing another whimper to expel from my lips. "You feel me now, don't you, Aria? You feel all of me filling that tight, needy cunt that's clenching against me hungrily, sucking my cock off. Look at that greedy cunt fucking my cock, milking me so fucking perfectly." His hand moved to my hip, using them to lift me slowly before he pushed me back down slowly, watching as his thick cock disappeared into my body. "Fucking hell, woman, you're perfect."

"It hurts," I uttered through trembling lips.

"I wanted it to," he whispered against my ear. "I

wanted you to hurt for me, to feel every fucking inch of me in this tight, dripping cunt until you never forget how I feel in it, or what it felt like when I made you mine."

"You're a dick," I whispered huskily.

"You wanted me; don't even pretend like you didn't. You screamed my name when this sweet pussy came on my lips, dripping so fucking gloriously down my throat as I drank your pretty cunt dry. You fucking roared for me, pretty little lamb. You want to hate me for playing tricks to become the first man in this tight cunt? Fine with me, but this isn't over, not by a long shot. I'm going to fuck you until anytime this pussy needs to be filled, it is me you crave satisfying it. When you leave here, you'll be ruined for any other male alive, because my cock will be the one you worship. You shouldn't have expected a wolf to hand the kill to anyone else. Predators don't share their prey, and make no mistake, Aria, you are my prey, and now you're claimed until I decide otherwise. My scent is painted on this sweet pussy and about to be buried so fucking deep that no man will dare to touch it again."

"Why the ploy, why not just tell me I'd be with you?"

"What the fuck is the fun in telling you? You hated that it wasn't me, and I got to witness you through the eyes of another. You wanted him to be me. I saw it in your eyes, the tremble in your voice when you spoke, all of it. It's okay, I want you too, little one."

"And Brander, what about him, or was he in on it from the start too?"

"Brander would never be the one who made you into a woman, Aria. I'd have never allowed anyone else to have this from you, not when I craved it this much. Now, are you ready to get fucked? This pussy is clenching for me, and I'm so fucking ready to wreck you."

He pushed me down until my ass was in the air, causing his cock to go deeper into my body as a scream ripped from my lips. His deep, husky laughter filled the room as he withdrew from my flesh, using a cloth to collect the blood before the sound of the plastic bag crinkled. My cheeks heated with the knowledge of what he was doing, and I watched him in the mirror as he tossed it aside, staring down where my ass was lifted for him.

Once that was finished, he flipped me over onto my back, untying my hands. Knox watched me; the storm gathering in his eyes was dark and delicious, and suddenly I didn't feel like such a dick for accidently screaming his name as he'd fucked me with his mouth when I had assumed it was Brander.

"Get on your knees and face me," he ordered thickly. Knox settled on the bed on his knees, sitting back while he watched me crawl toward him slowly. I got to my knees, and he smirked roguishly. "Stand up and straddle me, Aria."

I did, standing until my flesh was in front of his face. He pulled me down, positioning me until I was sitting on his lap with my legs around his waist. His head leaned against my shoulder as he used one hand to lift my ass, pushing his cock into my body with the other, before lifting his head to stare into my eyes.

"You break eye contact, and I'll bend you over and destroy this cunt until you're begging me to stop, and I assure you, I won't, understand me?" He growled as my body clenched against his, causing his voice to become as strained as I was seated on his thick cock.

"I understand, Knox," I uttered breathlessly as he used my hips to rock them, causing my muscles to tense against him.

"Relax for me, sweet girl." He spoke roughly, staring between us where our bodies were joined together. "You keep clamping down on my cock like that, and this will end before either of us is ready for that to happen."

"It aches, Knox."

"Good," he uttered with a sinful smile on his lips.

His lips brushed mine, claiming them hungrily as he started to move me faster against him. It changed, the pain turned to something more intense, something that sat just beyond my reach and out of my grasp. His mouth fucked me as hard as his cock was, delving deeper to claim my tongue as he growled against my mouth hungrily while devouring it.

It wasn't fucking; it was something deeper than either of us knew or cared to examine. Knox went slower, trying his best to be gentle when I knew he wanted to unleash on me, to pin me to the bed and demand I take what he gave, and yet he didn't. His eyes studied me, consuming me as if he was trying to remember every detail of my face as he slowly moved in my core erotically.

My hands threaded through his hair, devouring him as much as he destroyed me. I rocked against him, no longer needing him to control the pace as I took control of it, using him to reach the whisper of pleasure that beckoned me closer hauntingly. My mouth opened on a cry as he pulled back, watching me coming undone for him.

"Good girl, take what you need." He gazed at me through heavily hooded eyes as his hand slipped between our bodies, rubbing my clit to increase the pleasure as I toppled over the edge crying his name repeatedly. "Bloody hell, you're so beautiful, Aria." He pushed me back onto the bed as he followed me down.

Knox settled between my thighs, slowly withdrawing from my body until only the tip remained buried, only to lunge forward, causing a scream to escape past the lump in my throat. Tears escaped my eyes as he watched me continuing to come undone for him as the most intense and beautiful sensation filled my emotions. He leaned over, placing his forehead against mine and peered into my soul as he rocked his hips, pushing deeper into my body before his mouth touched mine, pulling at my bottom lip with his teeth, seductively.

"You make the most beautiful noises when I'm fucking you, sweet girl," he whispered gutturally. His tone was laced with hunger, filled with a huskiness that slithered around me, pulling me into the debauchery he delivered.

He sat back, pushing my legs apart to gain further depth as his hands held the back of my knees. I watched him as he began moving slowly, staring at where he stretched me full. The man knew right where to push me and where to pull to hit every nerve ending perfectly. He'd lied; he was being gentle, and yet there was a darkness that lurked right beneath the surface that wanted to let loose of the tight reins he held on them.

His body moved, leaning over mine as he placed his hands onto the bed, trapping my head between them, watching me carefully. He stared into my eyes as he started moving faster, harder, his body dominating mine in every way imaginable. I moved against him, wanting to reach the precipice he took me to so effortlessly. His lips curled into a smile, and he leaned over, kissing my forehead.

"Use me, Aria. Take what you need from me."

It was unlike him to show affection. He pulled away as if showing me tenderness had jarred him as much as it had me. Gazing down at me, he stopped moving, and then abruptly flipped me onto my stomach without warning and stared at me through the reflection of the mirror. His hands adjusted my hips, sliding down my spine as he lifted my ass up into the air. Something dark and dangerous filled the oceanic depths, threatening to drown me with the storm brewing within them.

"Now, Aria, I will fuck you so hard that anytime you arc with another man, you remember me, and find him pathetically lacking. Tomorrow, when the flesh has cooled, and you ache where I used you, you'll know who destroyed your pretty, naked pussy. You had to know that I would leave my mark on you. One way another, you knew you'd be mine." His eyes lowered to my ass, and he smiled, running his hand over it before he pushed deeper into my body.

My hands dug into the blankets, grasping for a hold as he began to move slowly. The intensity in his eyes darkened as something deliciously carnal peered down at me. His hands lifted my hips up further, adjusting my body until my ass was in the air, and I whimpered against the pain and fullness he created. My core clenched around him, burning with endless pain that I stifled until he began moving. He was giving me everything he'd held back. He moved faster until all I could do was grasp the blankets and feel him owning me as he fucked me savagely hard, yet deliciously glorious.

My grip tightened against the blanket, and I lifted my head so a scream could escape from my throat as I met his hooded stare in the mirror. He slammed into my body harder, and I repeatedly whimpered until it changed from pain, turning to pleasure. I moaned huskily, watching him and my own reflection, noting the way my breasts moved with every thrust of his body against mine. He gave no mercy and I didn't ask for it. I took what he gave, spreading my hips to allow him to go deeper yet, growling and moaning until my body clenched against his cock, milking him hungrily.

Knox watched me coming undone for him, watched me breaking apart and shattering into a million pieces. Pieces he picked up and held together while I scrambled to rearrange who I was before him and who I would become after him.

He didn't stop, not after I'd come and resorted to holding on to his thighs behind me as he used me to wreck any sense of gentleness I had thought I wanted. I wanted *this*. The rawness that was Knox, destroying my perception of safe, nice, and sweet. He replaced them with words like raw, brutal, and visceral. He then defined every one of them in a singular form until I was whimpering and writhing beneath him, pleading for mercy, which he gave not a single ounce of as he destroyed me.

He threaded his fingers through my hair, pulling me back against his chest again and slipping his fingers through the swollen mess of my pussy while he continued to fuck me, staring at my naked flesh that cradled him.

"This belongs to me now. Do you understand me, Aria? Nobody else touches you, or they fucking die. You belong to me now until I say otherwise."

"Knox," I whispered huskily.

He growled against my ear, watching me as the rattling began deep from his chest. My chest echoed his, and he smirked against my ear, pulling on it gently with his teeth. "Good girl, Aria."

His body jerked, tightening with his release as he growled, slamming his hips against mine until he slowed and dropped his hold on me. He stared down at me as his eyes narrowed, and he slowly closed off. Something akin to anger flashed in his eyes, and I blinked, shaking my head as confusion took root in my stomach.

He backed off the bed, moving away from me as if he needed distance. His hand scrubbed down his face as he stared at my naked body, watching as I sat up to watch him. I chewed my lip nervously, trying to figure what to say without sounding needy since I was naked and in his bed. Something had just happened, and I wasn't sure what I had done to make him angry.

Knox continued backing away from the bed, staring at me as I whispered his name with swollen lips, pushing messed up hair away from my face. I smiled, staring at him before my hand lifted to him, ready for more. His hand moved over his face again, and emptiness and anger entered his gaze.

His fingers pushed through his hair, which caused his stomach muscles to tighten as my gaze dipped to the monstrous thing I'd just had inside of me. Even sated, it was huge and intimidating.

"Knox?" I viewed his face closing down as his body tensed. The tick in his jawline began hammering while staring at me coldly. The temperature in the room dropped, and I became fully aware of my reaction to him and, worse, that I'd just parted with a piece of my soul that I couldn't ever get back. My stomach twisted with the look in his eyes, and I wanted to flee the room.

He didn't answer me. Instead, he walked into the bathroom, and I watched his perfect ass moving with absolute precision as the muscles bunched with every step he took. He exited the bathroom and threw a cloth at me. I caught it and stared at him, watching as he grabbed sweatpants and shoved his legs through them angrily.

"Wash your cunt off, it's bleeding all over my bed."

I blinked slowly, noting the anger that now filled his tone. I frowned in confusion, shaking my head as my heart stuttered, and then beat faster. "Did I do something wrong?"

"You're breathing, isn't it enough, *witch*?"

"You're un-*fucking*-believable." I wrapped the sheet around me as unshed tears burned my eyes and threatened to choke my words off as my throat tightened with them.

"Am I? Good," he snapped harshly. "Get the fuck out of my room, woman."

"I didn't ask for you, Knox. You had no fucking right to take someone else's place if you didn't want me, and yet I didn't scream about it. You are the one who is in the wrong, not me. I came here to do a task, and it's done, so what's the fucking problem? What did I do to piss you off now?"

"You are. You are the fucking problem, Aria. Get the fuck out of my room—I'm done with you. I got what I wanted, now leave."

He stared at me as tears glistened in my eyes, and pain shot through me. "You're a bastard."

"I can live with that."

My mouth opened and closed as I shook my head, turning around before I decided to attack him. That was one fight I wouldn't win. I was done with him, finished. You didn't do that to a woman; you didn't take something special and throw it back at her as if it was trash. I was going to find a spell and curse the asshole to be impotent for eternity.

I stepped to grab my panties, glaring at the shambles he'd made of them, and turned to stare at my bra. They were both ruined, just as I was from his cold, dismissive demeanor. I grabbed the dress and slipped it on before I left the room in bare feet, passing the sitting room to slam my hand against the elevator button.

Knox walked toward me with a bag in his hand, smirking as he took in the angry glare that filled my eyes.

"You forgot this," he stated, tossing it at me.

"I don't fucking need it, prick. There's enough left to do the blessing."

His gaze lowered to where the blood was dripping down my legs, mixed with his cum. I felt disgusting, used, and discarded like trash, which I was certain had been his point. He opened his mouth, but I beat him to it.

"You can stay the fuck away from me, Knox. Don't speak to me, don't look at me, and if you see me on fire, don't bother getting water. Let me fucking burn, because I want nothing from you. I'd rather burn to ashes than see you ever again," I whispered thickly. I touched the button, and he dropped his gaze to my bare feet, shaking his head.

"Aria," he uttered.

"Fuck you, Knox, just fuck you!" Tears slipped down my cheeks, while anger ignited.

"You deserve better, but I'm a selfish prick, remember? Get smarter, little lamb. Get smarter faster, or you'll get eaten."

I smiled coldly through emotionless eyes. "As long as I'm being eaten by anyone *but* you, then I'm okay with that." I turned away from him, pushing the button repeatedly to escape him. When I turned back, he slammed me against the wall and stared into my eyes as his head pressed against mine. His chest rose and fell with his labored breathing while his nostrils flared as if he was fighting something internally. His hand held my throat just hard enough to keep me there, and I swallowed harshly. "Do it, Knox. Do it or get the fuck off of me."

He dropped his hold, stepping back before he turned, pushing in a code and stepping out of the elevator. "We're done here. Your sisters are outside, and they have the items to bless the house. Get the fuck out and don't ever come back. Understand me? You have ten minutes, and then I hunt you and any of your sisters that remain in my domain. Your time starts now. Tick tock, little girl."

The elevator door closed, and when it reopened, I took off through the hallway, not bothering to stop and grab my things. I'd get new things. Fuck him.

At the entrance to the house, Brander turned, dropping his gaze to my blood-covered thighs as I moved past him, flipping him off without saying a word.

"Open the door," I demanded of Greer, who turned, doing the same thing Brander had done. It was as if the assholes couldn't give a woman any sense of dignity.

"I can't," he stated, and I hissed, moving him with magic as I opened the doors myself and marched out of the house.

"It's not safe," Greer called to my back. "Fine, end up dead, and I will animate your corpse to torture it!"

"Fine!" I screamed over my shoulder, watching the dark SUV as it pulled up to the curb outside the gates. My eyes followed it as it came to a full stop. The moment Sabine exited the SUV, she smiled.

Power ignited around us, and I turned, staring briefly at Knox for a moment before dismissing him outright, coldly. I moved toward Sabine, waiting for the rest of them to exit the car.

"Look who's a woman now," she giggled until she

noticed the look on my face. "What's wrong, Aria?"

"Who plucked it?" Kinvara asked as she landed on the curb. "Was it Knox? I had fifty dollars on him intervening to tap that cherry pie first."

"You won, we need to go home, now," I stated, not bothering with further details as I moved past them into the street.

"Aria, what is wrong?" Callista asked. "If it was painful, it's normal. Did he hurt you?"

"Let's just say it was educational, and I never want to do it again, ever," I muttered, tossing the bag at her. Hearing a car speeding up the road, I turned, staring at it. "That's Amara's car." I watched the car as it accelerated toward us. My eyes noted the driver was male, and I swallowed. "Fuck," I hissed, turning to look at where my sisters stood huddled together and then back at the car that raced up the road.

Without thinking twice, I held my hand up, stopping the car as I rushed toward it, intending to throw it back away from my sisters, but the driver continued applying pressure on the gas.

My sisters cried my name as I approached it, slowly pushing more magic against it, staring at the driver who lifted his hand and clamped his thumb down on something. The car exploded, and pain shot through me. It was violent, brutal, and debilitating pain, and everything tried to shut down as it consumed my mind.

My body absorbed the blast, and I was thrown against the concrete to stare up at the stars. Echoes of the explosion continued inside my head as I frowned, realizing what I had done. I'd fucked up this time. There were moments in your life where you realized mid-step that you had fucked up. This was one of those moments. I was on *fire*.

I could hear the screams of my sisters. I could hear Knox, as well as his men, trying to calm them. I stared at the mangled car where the man should have been, but he wasn't in it. The entire top of the vehicle had imploded, and he'd been ejected or consumed in the blast. My ears rang as I lay on the ground. I could see everything. I could feel the flames as they licked my flesh, but that wasn't what hurt. My bones hurt, probably percussion from the blast.

Of course, I was on fire, because that was just what I'd told Knox, wasn't it? I was inside the carnage, with flames licking my flesh, and yet it didn't hurt, not even a little. Only my bones ached and cracked as if something was within me, fighting to get out.

Slowly, I rose to my feet as my vision grew sharper. The ringing in my ears stopped, and over the sound of the screams, I heard insects buzzing in the yard beside us. I cracked my neck, whimpering as pain rushed through me before darkness consumed me.

CHAPTER
34

The Creature Within

I stared curiously at the people who watched me emerging from the flames. They smelled familiar, and yet I didn't know them by sight. I lifted my nose, inhaling them into my lungs to see if they were prey I could devour, only to grimace at their combined odor. The screams irritated my ears, making me itch to end their constant cries.

My presence gave them pause as they watched me closing the distance between us. Once I stood in front of them, cries turned to gasps of shock, and I paused, peering past the females to a large male who narrowed his eyes on me, lifting his nose to the air as he watched me carefully. He was the largest, and definitely the biggest one I'd have to worry about if I chose to fight them. Something whizzed past my head, causing me to turn in the direction it had come. Another male stood in the distance with metal in his hands, pointing it back it in my direction.

"You're on fire!" one of the women screamed, and I turned back, staring at her as the familiarity of her voice touched my mind.

"Aria, roll, or something," another one shouted, and I turned in the direction of the man who continued sending metal flying in our direction.

Dismissing the women and men, I started toward him as he lowered the metal and stared at me in horror. His mouth dropped open as I caught his scent on the breeze and smiled for him. Lifting my hand, I fixed my hair as I walked in his direction. He started to run, and I laughed as I followed, using my muscles to rush toward him as he dropped the metal to the ground. He was slow, not fast enough to escape me. The moment I reached him, hunger pangs ignited, and I lunged, sinking my teeth into his throat as everything within me craved the meat of his flesh. My mind shut down on everything, but hunger and a red haze took over.

Something moved beside me, and I hissed. Growling, I turned with my kill still struggling in my hold, staring at the man with oceanic eyes, watching me holding my dinner with a curious look. I snarled in warning, baring my teeth around the man's throat. Another male approached and stopped short, noticing that I'd made a kill. His gaze lowered and slowly slid down my body.

"What the fuck are you doing, Aria?"

I snarled around the mouthful of meat, warning him as my body tensed to fight for the food I held. I peered into pretty eyes that held ancient knowledge banked within them. Familiar eyes that were like mine, hiding something within them. I didn't look away while following his movements.

"Aren't you pretty, fangs and all? What are you, my naked little firebug?" the largest male asked, and I hissed, knowing that whatever I did, I should never give him my back. His power filled the area, and whatever he was, he was dominant and lethal.

He also wasn't touching my kill. He could get his own damn dinner. He was all male, his scent oozing off of him in waves that created a new ache deep within me. Blood dripped out of my mouth as I watched him, knowing that he was big enough to take my dinner, but that didn't mean I planned to let it go without a fight.

"She's on fire," another male uttered softly, "yet there's not a single inch of her touched by it, she's fucking immune."

Another male moved in close to where I stood as well, staring at me as he sidled up next to the other male. His amber eyes slid down my body, narrowing as they came back up. I ripped a piece of meat from my dinner, shoving my kill to the ground at their feet. Stepping back, still holding the meat against my mouth, I took another bite before swallowing it down ravenously. Blood dripped down my chin as I gripped the flesh tightly, chewing it while they observed me carefully.

"Fangs and flames," the large, masculine one with sea-blue eyes, uttered. "What are you, Aria?"

"No hair, though," the one with sapphire eyes muttered. "Nothing else has changed, but she smells different. You smell that, right? Tell me she doesn't smell like…"

"I smell it, but that's fucking impossible, and you know it."

"My money had been on a hybrid wolf or lion shifter," the amber-eyed male said as he chuckled. "Naked little pussy, all hairless and shit, it's perfect. Fucking hell, you beat that shit up real nice, Knox."

"Stop looking at her pussy, asshole," the leader snapped angrily. His hands drifted lower at his sides, and I watched them, inhaling the leader's scent and smelling his mixed with my own. "That's right, you smell yourself on me, don't you?"

"What the fuck is happening to her?" A female demanded. I turned my stare toward her, never giving the males access to my back.

"Sabine, I suggest you back the fuck up, now," the second guy demanded.

"She's on fucking *fire*!"

"The fire isn't hurting her. It is coming *from* her; do you understand me? Whatever the fuck your mother mated with, it controlled flames, and now Aria can as well, which is very dangerous and precarious considering she doesn't know how to control them."

"Then it should be easy to figure out what she is, right?"

They continued arguing back and forth, and my eyes slid back to the male that held my scent mixed with his. He smirked roguishly, watching me through narrowed slits while his chest rattled loudly. My stare narrowed as the sound called to me, making my spine arch with an intensity I wanted to explore deeper, more carnally. I opened my mouth, answering his call, letting the rattle build before it escaped. It was loud, husky, and violent. It vibrated through me until his eyes lowered to my chest before once again locking with mine.

"That's new," the female stated. "Why is she rattling like a snake?"

"Yeah, you're about to find out a lot of new things, if you fucking live long enough to and get the fuck back, woman. Listen to me and back the fuck up, now, Sabine. For all we know, she could be a fire elemental and level the entire fucking town if she's set off."

Dismissing them altogether, the moment I grew bored with their bickering, I tilted my head toward the male. He discarded his shirt, exposing ropes of solid muscle. His scent filled the air, and I lifted my nose, inhaling it deeply. A noise sounded behind me, and his hands went up as I turned, watching another male who stepped too close to me, and I hissed. I crouched down, letting my teeth grow, and claws extend from my fingertips.

"Back the fuck off her, now. She's about to attack," the shirtless male hissed.

"That's not an element. She's got fucking razor-sharp fangs *and* claws," said another male.

I made myself small close to the ground to jump if I needed to, turning to take on the people who were boxing me in. They seemed and sounded familiar, but my ears pulsed as blood echoed in them. I was starving, my body ached with pain, and everything was too sharp, too bright, and just too much.

"Brander, get Sabine the fuck out of here, now," the leader with ocean-colored eyes warned.

I pulled power to me as my chest rattled while fear of being trapped ripped through my mind, focusing my power on a goal: taking them all down to escape before they tried to capture me, or breed me.

"You do that, and you will hurt your sisters, Aria. Remember them? You love them and don't want to hurt them, do you?"

My head tilted as the rattle vibrated from deep in his chest, and the other men joined him. Idiots, I wasn't stupid. I wouldn't give him my back in order to subdue me. I stood up, judging the distance between me and the woods, knowing there would be creatures to hunt within them. I stepped back, watching as the shirtless male took a step forward, crouching as if he intended to catch me the moment I moved—right, like he could.

"Can't let you do that, little lamb."

I took off running with a burst of speed, knowing that I was smaller, faster, and as long as my fire burned, he couldn't touch me. My feet slammed against the pavement as the freeing sensation of running in the wide open hit me. My arms extended, and I started to leap into the air as something moved in front of me.

Skidding to a stop to prevent colliding, I slammed against the larger male. He fell to the ground with me, smoothly rolling back onto his feet, watching me as I began to circle him. My arms went out, extending talons as I followed him closely, intending to take him down quickly and claim him. Once he was subdued, I'd take him with me into the woods and mate with him after I'd sated my hunger for meat.

"Fuck me sideways. She's trying to dominate you,

Knox," someone chuckled. "She's fucking wickedly delicious."

I didn't take my eyes from the male I circled, knowing out of them all, he was the largest and most dominant male here. Take him down, and the others would leave, sensing the predator in me. He smiled as if he thought it was cute. He put his arms out wide like mine, and I shivered at the scent of him as he showed his sleek build that bunched his muscular abdomen with every step he took as we danced in a circle. I lunged, swiping across his bare chest before I ducked and jumped back, not allowing him to capture me.

"Fucking hell, little monster!" He peered down at his chest at where my nail marks had gone deep, drawing blood. I'd marked him, drawing first blood. I smiled victoriously as I started hunting him again, watching as he moved with me.

Everyone went silent around us, finally understanding that I wasn't playing. A bitch needed to eat, and I was hungry. I didn't want to play anymore, I had needs. I needed substance badly, and he'd interrupted my feeding. He could either feed me or get the hell out of my way so I could do it myself.

My mouth opened, and I released a loud, angry rattle in warning. His teeth pulled back, revealing wicked fangs, and I paused, watching him with intrigue, shivering with desire as I tried to sense what he was. He sounded like me, but his scent was different, more primal and masculine. It created a hum within my core, causing my muscles to clench with excitement. I opened my mouth, showing him my teeth before growling again loudly. He smirked, letting his tongue run over his teeth to hold my attention, lowering his head as he crouched down.

"Go for her back, Brander."

My heart slammed against my chest, beating wildly with fear as the males fanned out to circle me. I added flames to my flesh, protecting myself from their fangs. I let them hear my warning again, loudly letting the noise rise from my lungs to explode into the night air. Seven masculine rattles mimicked mine, sounding all around me. I spun in a tight circle, realizing I was once more being surrounded, and there were too many to fight alone. I jumped over them without much effort, rushing toward the woods without looking back.

"What the fucking-fuckity, fuck is she? An Ifrit?" someone asked, but I didn't care.

I was running free!

Adrenaline rushed through me as I felt the call to move faster, to expand my lungs as I released myself into the wild. I felt invincible!

Running felt amazing! My legs pumped faster as I felt the wind against my face, excitement rushing through me. *Zoom, I was free…*until I slammed into something hard again and went to the ground in frustration. I rolled on the ground, coming up on my feet, staring into dark sapphire eyes, opening my mouth to move in for the kill. Something touched against my shoulder, and I turned to attack, but the mouth of the large male brushed against the soft hollow place between my neck and shoulder, and I moaned loudly.

"Mmm," I purred from deep in my chest.

Teeth sank into my shoulder deeply, and I sagged

against him. My head turned to the scent of blood mixing with male, and more purring erupted from my lungs at the delicious feel of his claiming bite. His hand wrapped around my belly, pulling my body against his. I nuzzled him invitingly, letting the fire extinguish as a new kind of warmth erupted in me, dripping from my pores as my scent exploded, signaling my sexual need.

"Fucking hell, she smells…delicious," the sapphire-eyed male in front of us whispered and scrubbed his hand down his face. "What the hell is she?"

Growling started against my shoulder, and I nuzzled him more, adoring him for wanting to protect me with his claim. He laughed wickedly, and my eyes grew heavy from the sound of it. Silence filled the area, and I whimpered, rubbing my ass against him with the need to let him claim me, dominate me, and breed me.

"So fucking hot," someone else said, and my male snarled with his mouth full of my flesh, baring his teeth at them. "She's all yours, my king." He put his hands in the air and nodded at something behind us. "The alphas are incoming from the east, Knox."

"Handle them, she's mine. If they don't listen, kill them all."

I purred huskily in agreement, bringing my hand up to his cheek as my claws retracted. I rubbed my ass against him again, showing him what I wanted, and he growled deliciously, but he still didn't give me what I needed. I had to figure out how to make my voice work to tell him quickly.

His hand lowered, skimming my sex, and I purred louder until it filled the area, in case he was slow to pick up my cues. He seemed to lack smarts, which I hoped he made up for in other ways. If not, I could always find another male and eat this one; he'd provide a good meal.

"Are you drenched for me, little creature?"

"Mmm," I moaned, or tried to. I grabbed his hand, pushing it against my aching sex, mewling as words failed to leave my throat.

"You can't speak, can you?" He loosened his bite enough to be understood around my flesh he held in his mouth. I rubbed against the thick cock in his pants, sending my scent out to lure him to me. "Bloody hell, woman," he growled huskily as his fingers slipped through the mess of my core. "Stop that shit, or I promise I will bend you over and fuck you right here without caring who watches me wrecking that tight, delicious scented cunt."

I bucked against him as I made strangled noises of frustration, needing him to do what he promised. Gods, males were so thick. What did a bitch have to do to get dick around here? He rattled from deep in his chest as he started to lift my body, not removing his teeth from my shoulder.

He knew the moment he did, I was gone. Maybe he had some brains, after all? Probably a very tiny brain, but hopefully he could sate other needs.

The large male walked me past the other males and females, all who stared at his bite and how he held me. I didn't care. I needed his dick, a place to use him, and tons of meat to sate the hunger that burned within me, growing more painful by the moment.

I growled, and he bit down harder as my body continued to lure him by scent. "Impatient little thing, aren't you? You just got off my dick, and you already crave it again?" As I purred loudly, he smiled around the flesh his teeth held. Blood dripped down my shoulder, and I turned, licking it clean as he watched. "What the hell are you? You're obviously not a lamb. Not with how you feed off humans and raw meat."

"Mmm," I moaned, bucking against his hold.

"You could have died; you're not done changing, Aria."

I snorted impatiently, recalling how Aria articulated words when she spoke. "Fuck me." I smiled in victory as it came out perfectly.

"Plan to," he growled gutturally and then groaned as my sex drenched with more need. "You keep fucking doing that, we won't make it to the house, Aria. I'll be fighting every fucking shifter in this town to keep you and your pretty pussy to myself." I smiled and did it again until it was dripping down my thigh for him.

He snarled loudly, letting the rattle in his chest warn the others to keep their distance. He veered away from them, moving with long angry steps as he took us into the shadows. The male pushed me down hard against the side of a wooden structure. His teeth never left my shoulder as he parted my thighs and entered me painfully.

I cried out as he filled me full, hurting me deliciously as he entered my body even though I'd prepared it for him. He was very large and stretched my body to accommodate his. I bucked against him on instinct, slamming my ass against him as he snarled against my shoulder. Rattling with need, he grunted, fucking me mercilessly with his massive cock. Basic instincts took over, and my body shivered with the mixture of pain and primal, carnal need while he dominated me by force and strength until I was purring loudly as my body sang with praise for his.

He was virile, masculinity in its truest form. He pounded into my body like a starving beast. He took, controlled, and conquered until I was screaming, and we purred together. My orgasm clamped my body against his, milking his cock as he jerked once, then twice, before slowly withdrawing to shove his fingers into the core of my flesh. He rubbed the scent of our coupling over me, using it to cover the scent I used to show him what I wanted and needed. He was all male, and I was his prey. I purred as he fought to control his breathing from the violence of our mating.

I lifted my hips again, turning to nudge him as he watched me through black slits. "More."

He was like me, starving and needing to shed this flesh and fuck like animals. His need was burning in his dark eyes. I purred, and he purred low, deep from in his chest, which slithered over me and calmed my fears. I smiled with pride, knowing I'd made this masculine creature purr with the heat of my body and the scent it was creating for him from our mating.

"Try not to leak your fucking pheromones again until we're in your new room."

"More," I growled, even though it came out hardly a word.

"You will get so much fucking more, woman. I plan to make you beg me to stop fucking you."

"Knox, she's breeding."

"She's mine," he snarled to the male—Brander, he was Brander, and the one holding me was called Knox.

"You don't want her no matter her scent tells you," he countered. "Whatever she is, she's also a Hecate witch."

My male, Knox, seemed to go tense behind me, and I frowned, turning my nose to him, rattling my chest as his grip tightened on my hips, holding me closer to him as he watched me.

"So, she is. Tell Greer to open the elevator to the basement. She's unsafe to be outside until she learns to control what she is and stops leaking her scent everywhere. And, Brander, it doesn't fucking matter, our kind doesn't breed anymore."

"She was on fire. She has sharp teeth that mimicked ours almost identically but a hell of a lot more feminine. Her hands formed into claws, and she wanted to *run*, Knox. She's also a carnivore, one who wanted to fight you over the kill she made. *She* tried to dominate *you*."

"And she fucking lost; she'll always lose against me, you know that. I cannot be dominated, no matter what the fuck she is. It doesn't matter how much I come in her tight pussy, we can't breed together. Or did you fucking forget that issue? Get the basement opened before she has every male in the city itching to breed her dripping cunt."

Knox lifted me, and I preened, not worried about anyone else trying to breed me since I had the ultimate alpha craving me. His scent was in me and all over my flesh, and my scent was on him. His teeth held me subdued, but I'd fight him once I was released. If he wanted me, then he could prove he could handle me. He held me through the door, and the annoying females were there. One touched his shoulder, and I snarled in warning, letting my claws extend to remove her hand by force. I bet they would taste crunchy and tasty. I was hungry enough to eat them all.

"What the hell is happening to her?" the female demanded.

"She's in some form of transition, to what, we have no idea."

"Yeah, but she has fangs, claws, and your come is dripping out of her pussy, Knox," the female retorted. "She's my sister first, no matter what the hell she is. Where are you taking her?"

"Get the fuck out of my way."

"He is taking her to the basement because she is unstable." The one called Brander pinched the bridge of his nose. "She isn't your fucking sister right now; she's merging with whatever is inside of her. She isn't safe to be outside the fireproof room. We have no idea what the fuck she is, but right now, she's exhibiting similarities to an Ifrit, which, if pissed off, goes fucking nuclear. No one in this town would live through it, understand me? She isn't going for just your protection, but for her own. If she killed you, she'd never recover from it, Sabine. Let him help her, and when she gets her shit together, she can go home with you."

Knox snorted, turning to move toward a large wall.

An older male pushed some bumps on the wall, and a large opening was revealed as we approached a box within the wall. Knox stepped inside, turning with me in his arms, they opened and then closed as we stepped inside. I wiggled wantonly against him, and he set me down carefully, releasing his bite unhurriedly before his tongue trailed through the blood, tasting me.

I didn't move, waiting for him to finish cleaning the mark he'd made. His eyes peered down, taking in the damage he'd done while I watched him. Knox didn't heal the damage he'd done to me. Turning my head, I ran my tongue over the part of the wound I could reach as he watched me closely. We stopped moving, and I peered out as the box opened, noting the room built of metal and colored glass.

He shoved me, and I smirked, entering the room to inspect it. There was nothing soft here, just hard, shiny metal. I turned, frowning as he watched me from the box. He reached in front of him, closing it, causing my heart to race.

I moved closer, touching my hands against the glass, looking at him as blood dripped from my shoulder. He hadn't healed me with his tongue, and I had needs that had yet to be met. I was ravenous, starving so badly that it ached on a painful level. He looked away, and I pounded on the glass, watching him turn to leave as I erupted, exploding in flames as my hands beat against the glass.

He didn't care; he left me alone as a fire of need blossomed within my chest. I needed substance. Instead, I was alone. I turned, taking in the bed that didn't melt, and the glass that didn't crack as the fire got hotter.

If that dick didn't feed me, I'd burn all of this to the fucking ground.

I smiled coldly, closing my eyes as I dug into my mind that I shared with Aria. I knew words were within it, words I needed to know to speak to him. He obviously needed instructions on what I needed from him, and without having the means to know what to say, I'd never get it from him. He lacked intelligence, and my tummy rumbled with unsated hunger. Frowning, I turned as noise sounded from within the room as a small black thing turned, following me as I moved closer to it. A tiny red thing blinked on it, and I hissed, digging through my mind for the word. *Light.* Knox. *Stupid male. Dicker.*

I rattled while staring up at it, slowly dropping my gaze to the sterile, sex scented room. It reeked of other bitches here, other bitches and *him.*

Moving to the glass, I slammed my hands against it, watching as it refused to give or break. The box he'd gotten into had yet to come back, and the wall in front of it wouldn't budge. I bared my teeth to the red-dot, turning to stare at a metal square that sat in the middle of the room. He wasn't a good provider, nor bright. I hoped he tasted good because that was his only redeemable factor right now. I slid down the wall in the corner as lights blinded me. I hummed a warning, staring directly into them as my eyes focused as magic rushed to the nearest one, shooting sparks down the moment it touched it. I preened at my control and focus, learning everything within Aria's mind along with her magic as I used the time to prepare for my dinner's return.

I was so going to eat him. Who locked a female in

need into a glass box and left her starving? Idiotic males who couldn't take a female's scent dripping down her legs with invitation, that's who. I hoped another male returned with him or maybe more, so I could try them out and see which one was compatible since the one named Knox had no working brains whatsoever.

CHAPTER
35

THE CREATURE WITHIN

Pacing inside the room, I wailed when the hunger became too much to handle and rocked against the wall when it abated. It was never-ending; the need to feed that ripped through me was all-consuming. I couldn't escape the glass room, and couldn't find food within it. The ocean-eyed male called Knox had abandoned me, leaving me in a pit of despair.

Something moved above me, and I watched as meat hit the floor. Moving to it, I sniffed, frowning at the scent of death. It wasn't fresh, proving once again he was stupid. He obviously sucked at hunting since there was an entire house full of things to hunt outside the elevator. I picked up a small piece and went to my corner, digging in with fervor to stave off the hunger pangs clenching in my belly.

Once most of the pile was gone, I paced, noting the stench of the male that was all over me. I looked for

water, touching a metal sink and watching as the water
began flowing when I hit a button. Standing back, water
shot up at a weird angle. I lowered my nose, sniffing it
before I frowned. There was no way I was fitting into
that thing to bathe. Turning, I looked around the room
until I found a large bathtub. Smiling, I moved to it,
grabbed the edge, and dragged it to me, uncaring that it
left large rivets on his floor.

I eyed the sink and then the tub, using Aria's magic
to direct water to the tub. Pain itched in my hands, and
noise sounded from above me. My eyes rolled, and I
continued using her magic until I had filled the tub.
I pushed my hands into the water, boiling it before I
climbed in, washing Knox's scent from me.

He may be the strongest male, but he sucked at
everything a female needed. Who left a bitch in heat
unattended and on her own? Who fed them dead food?
He would not be on my list of males as potential mates,
or I'd end up stuck doing everything alone when we
created our little ones.

I dipped into the water, using my hands to wash my
flesh, and smiled at the soreness between my thighs. He
may suck, but he left something to remember him by.
My fingers continued brushing against my opening until
need became a concern. I rose from the water, staring at
the door as if I could will him back into the room with
my mind. No such luck, not that he'd notice since he
was so dense.

Rising from the water after I'd bathed, I pushed the
tub with my foot, sending it directly at the glass wall
that caged me in. It didn't shatter or even crack, but the
water splashing everywhere was satisfying. Moving to

the metal rack, I sat, placing my hands into my lap and humming a song I didn't recognize, and yet I knew every word from Aria's mind, which was slowly opening to me. He'd aroused me, rutting me once, and then he'd ditched me. The song changed in my head, and I sang it, learning to speak as I waited for him to return.

The elevator doors opened, and I stood, still dripping with need. Knox walked into the room, and the doors sealed closed behind him. He paused, listening to me.

"Aria?" he uttered huskily, sniffing. "You're singing," he grinned, tilting his head. "Puddle of Mudd *She Hates Me*… That's almost…sweet."

I sat back down and spread my legs, watching his gaze lower to where I was soaked, waiting for him. My eyes narrowed, nostrils flaring as I once more caught my scent still on him. He just stood there, staring at me as he inhaled and exhaled, almost as if I was too much for him to handle. I puffed out a frustrated sigh and shook my head as I stood up.

He was defective.

"You're a naughty little one, aren't you? Did I fuck you into becoming a little monster, woman?" I perked up at his words, hoping he wasn't as defective as I'd assumed.

I purred, and he watched me, slowly lifting his gaze from where my need ran down my leg to lock with mine. He rubbed his hand over his face, and I frowned. My head tilted while I watched his response to my scent, the arch of my spine should have been enough to indicate what I wanted, but he wasn't picking up on the scent of subtle signs. Maybe he would understand if I bent over and pointed at it? This male was too dimwitted to understand basic needs, apparently. It was really too bad because he had a nice dick.

"You are not good at this," I whispered huskily.

His brow lifted. "You fucking hate me. I pushed you away, and you almost fucking died because of it, and then you changed. What are you?"

"I'm me." I watched as he pushed down his pants, and I smiled at how large and erect he was. "Oh, it's nice. It's a good thing it is large since you are too stupid and probably will not live much longer."

His head lifted, and he stared at me as his mouth opened and closed several times. Yup, he had no brains and all dick, but it was a very nice dick. He could not even speak well. I sort of felt bad for him, but he'd be okay, or he'd get eaten. Either choice would be okay with me. Maybe after I'd sated my need for mating, I'd eat him for dessert. Yes, he'd make a good meal, considering how big he was.

I moved toward him as he studied me. Music started in the room, and I paused, frowning as Pop Evil's *Monster You Made* started through a speaker in the corner. Aria played this song, loving the music. I listened within, preening that she loved me without knowing she had a monster inside of her, and I was such a good monster. One day, we'd become one.

This male needed help figuring out what I needed from him. My eyes slipped to his cock, erect and dripping for me, and yet still, he couldn't figure out that my desire was literally dripping down my legs. He needed help.

Dismissing the music after a moment, I continued walking to him, dropping to my knees and touching my tongue against the scent of him I craved. My hand wrapped around it, but my fingertips wouldn't fully meet around the massive appendage. He really was well-endowed, made for fucking. It explained his lack of brains. His hand lowered, lifting to my mouth to brush across my lips before he let it drop, pushing the other one through my hair while he studied me on my knees.

"Eyes are slanted with silver specks in them; ears are slightly pointed as well."

I licked my tongue over the velvet-soft head, tasting the bead of cum that held his unique scent before purring. His hands pushed the hair away from my face as he swallowed audibly. I smiled, wrapping my lips around the tip of him before pushing him into my mouth, not bothering to stop until I had all of him buried deep in my throat. He cried out, staring down at me with wide eyes as I used my mouth to pleasure him. I smiled around him, watching his mouth open and close as my tongue darted out, licking him more, trying to get him to purr for me.

He didn't purr. He was such a disappointment. I pulled back and then took him again, staring at the confusion in his eyes. My tongue licked his balls, and I moaned to get him to respond to what I was doing for him. Man, didn't he like getting his cock sucked? Maybe he was more into men than women? I glared up at him, wondering if he would respond if I let my fangs out to shred his dick. Instead, I swallowed him several times, trying to force him to give me what I wanted from him.

"Bloody hell, woman." He brushed both thumbs over my cheeks, staring at my lips around the base of his cock. "Jaw extends, *fully*."

"Did she just swallow your entire cock?" A male's voice echoed through the room, and I pulled away from him, standing to look around the room for the voice, dismissing him. "Knox, please tell me she did what I think she did."

Hands cupped my breasts, pulling my attention back to him as he smirked. "The entire thing, which hasn't *ever* happened before," he said to the air. "Her body is defined, harder than it was earlier today. Her skin is the same color, but muscles are more taut, and firmer. She looks feral, yet the same. Her features are sharper, more distinct."

I dismissed him again, rolling my eyes as I moved away from his hands. He followed me, watching me as if he expected me to pleasure him more. As *if*, not with him talking to the male as I'd gotten down on my knees for the prick on his dirty floor.

"That's it for now; turn off the camera and the microphones."

"You're just getting to the fun part," the voice said.

"Turn the fucking camera off, Lore, or I'll rip your heart out, and you can regrow it."

I moved around the room slowly, letting him follow me with my back to him. He stopped, sensing I was playing with him. Males hated being played with, but so did females. At the water, I bent over, taking a long pull from it before turning around, gazing at him as it dripped from my chin, reminding him he could have been dripping from it if he wasn't so dense.

"You taught yourself how to speak, didn't you? You adapt to your surroundings."

"Mmm, so I do. Too bad you don't. You are not smart enough to pick up on my needs. You are a horrible provider for a female. You also speak to the air, and strangely enough, it speaks back to you, which is rather disturbing. You made it only a few moments in my flesh before you succumbed to the pleasure, which was a letdown. I'm looking for a mate strong enough to provide me what I need, but you lack brains, strength, and you're too weak to handle me. You don't even hunt for your female, do you?" I asked, carefully studying the anger that burned in his gaze at my overall assessment of him. "Are you looking for a female strong enough to maintain your life expectancy because you are too weak and should have been eaten before you drew air and sustained life?"

"You're not mine, Aria." Growling, he turned dark, his eyes narrowing to mere slits, and something akin to regret mingled with sadness tainted the air as I inhaled it deeply.

"You mounted me indicating that you were interested in mating," I countered as my finger tapped my chin, noting he wasn't pleased with me. "You wanted to be inside of me, and it was a primal need, yet you lacked the stamina to continue. You enjoyed it and purred your approval for my flesh."

"You released pheromones to lure me in."

"Before I came out to play, you took us then too. I

leaked nothing for you, yet you still fucked Aria. You called us yours," I pointed out, studying him.

He frowned, reading me with a sharp gaze, showing me he did house some intelligence, but maybe he didn't know how to use it correctly. "You're awake within her, aren't you?"

"Aria and I are the same person, silly beast. She's in pain, so I am here to protect her as she protects me as I grow stronger within her. When she is ready, we will meld together and be one."

"You don't know what you are, do you?"

"Does it matter? There are no creatures here like you and me. They're like she is, and she protects me as I rest."

"You're not a part of this realm, but you know that. You are from my realm, which is why you crave knowledge of Norvalla."

"Your mouth bores me, male. I prefer it to be busy elsewhere."

"It didn't bore you earlier when you screamed my name as I ate that drenched pussy, now did it?"

"No, it made me scream loudly. You enjoyed the screams, didn't you?"

"Immensely," he acknowledged.

His head turned from side to side as it made a cracking noise. He knew that I planned to fight him, which lost the element of surprise. I started walking again, needing to exercise my cramped limbs. My arms stretched behind me as I gave him my back, a ploy as old as time. Turning around, I discovered him directly behind me close enough to touch his nose against mine, his eyes heavy with lust. He hadn't made a single noise when he moved, which was a sign of a good predator.

"Are you planning to fight me, or fuck me, little monster?"

"Both, and then I will eat you." I shrugged nonchalantly. "It matters little in which order the events occur."

CHAPTER
36

THE CREATURE WITHIN

He smiled wolfishly, which exposed a dimple in his cheek. "You washed my scent off your pretty cunt. I should spank it for doing so without my permission. I placed it there to mark you as mine, creature."

"You suck at providing; I had to be ready if another male entered the room. I need a male who is up to provide for my needs and will hunt fresh meat. I need someone strong enough to satisfy my urges, but you leave me when I am in need, proving you are not the male for me."

"You think I'd let anyone else in here to fuck you, little girl?"

"It isn't your choice. *I* choose my mate, not you."

His eyes dipped to my mouth and back up. "Mates are messy. You get attached, and then they fucking die on you like some fucking martyr."

"If they're weak, yes, they eventually die, or a bad provider, such as you, and needs to be taken down so a new male can service and provide for the female," I stated casually, shrugging to be sure he got the message since his skull was very thick. "A female needs very few things in her life. She needs a strong mate who can provide her substance, dick, and a home for the babes she will eventually give him to fill it. You locked me in a room when I was dripping my scent for you, indicating my immense painful need for your cock. You still chose to abandon me. Even scenting the need I had, you couldn't pick up the hint. You fed me old, dead meat, which is lazy. A beast needs to hunt for his bitch, giving her enough sustenance to be able to be bred roughly and often. This room is cold, sterile, and reeks of other bitches you've fucked, which I do not care for or wish to smell while I fuck you. It proves you are a horrible choice in a mate, and that I need to be ready to find a new one."

"I had shit to tend to, such as your sisters upstairs causing a shit-storm because you caught fire and freaked them the fuck out. I didn't have time to hunt for you because you were starving and needed to be fed immediately before your dainty little ass tried to devour me instead of fuck me. The room is sterile because it is fireproofed since you're a fucking newborn...whatever the fuck you are, and you more than likely have no fucking control over those flames. I have provided for an entire kingdom, and they have never said I wasn't a good provider to them. You don't even know what the fuck you are, and you think I'm not good enough? Fuck you, creature."

"Did your kingdom consist of only your needs? Because it seems to me that is only what you wish to soothe. I am also not a newborn anything. I was born in Aria the moment she inhaled her first breath, and therefore I am not new. I am twenty-five years old. I have slept so she can grow in power, and I can grow in strength."

"Oh, my bad," he chuckled, narrowing his gaze on me. "You're practically a fucking antique."

"You are mocking me. How old are you?"

"Over one thousand years old, give or take a few centuries," he replied, carefully studying me and noting the way I sucked my lip between my teeth as I thought within her.

"Your dick works awfully well for someone so ancient. Do you often swallow little blue pills? I saw an ad in a magazine that Aria read one time that said you could get erect at even ninety-four years of age, but they did give a few warnings and precautions for someone as old as you. As long as you do not suffer a heart condition or drink nitroglycerin gas, you should be okay. I guess your balls weren't too bad; they were firm to the touch with my tongue. You could still produce offspring, but one would assume your age could be an issue. You're ancient as fuck."

His lips twitched, and I grew angry as he continued to question my intelligence. "I am very virile and can handle you, creature. You absorb everything Aria sees or reads, don't you?"

"Aria is brilliant on everything but males."

"Is that so?" he asked, stepping closer to touch my

unhealed shoulder and brushed his fingertips across his bite.

I shivered with the reminder of how his teeth felt buried in my flesh. I danced out of his reach as he watched me, smirking devilishly as he once more closed the distance between us, prowling toward me and letting the sheer masculinity of his body lure me in. Idiot, I was a needy bitch, and it took more than just strength to get me.

"She chose weak men, and I made her sick, so we didn't mate with one. It would be a waste to find a lame mate who couldn't satisfy our needs; they're ravenous as we will become once we are one being. I'd have to eat him, and that's just messy and not worth the trouble. Plus, they'd have left weak creatures in our womb, and I'm not much for eating my own offspring. I also don't think Aria would be okay with that before the merge is completed. She loves little ones, mostly. Not so much when they stink."

He smiled, and it touched his eyes, watching me as he bent over, kissing my shoulder. "But you let me fuck her."

"You smelled powerful and of equal strength. You and I held a mutual connection, or it was until you hurt her. Witches are sexual creatures, but her bloodline more so than usual because of the curse placed on them. Normally, presenting their virginity to a male is a significant thing, a gift they can only part with once. In her mind, she chose you, but you made her hesitate, and so she chose another. You then played a trick on her when she was already upset that it would not be you. Then when she was happily surprised it was you who would receive her gift, you made her feel as if it was garbage, and not a gift at all. You made her cry, and Aria does not often cry, if ever. Not even at the memories of her mother trying to murder her. She compartmentalizes it and pushes it deep within her soul to use as fire and fuel. You've made her cry more than you know, which also makes you, as she says, a dicker."

"Aria will survive. She's tougher than she looks. Dicker?"

"It's just another example of why you won't be our mate."

I lunged, slapping him across the face with my claws extended. He was faster than I assumed he would be, pulling my arm behind my back as he slammed me down on the bed, growling in anger. Blood dripped down from his face, and I moaned as he rubbed against my core. Too bad he'd have to prove his worth first. I was needy and shit.

I bucked against his head, turning to use my legs to kick him across the room. He hit the glass and shook his head at the velocity of the impact, staring at me as his teeth grew, and his eyes turned to mere slits. His hands balled into fists at his side as I swayed my hips, walking toward him slowly. He moved, and it was faster than I could detect. I was thrown across the room, landing against the glass to slide down it to the floor. Knox's bare feet padded across the floor as he kneeled down, rattling from deep in his chest.

My foot came up, moving with speed and brute force to send him to the ground, but he deflected it, pulling me up by my hair to slam me against the glass. His mouth lowered to my shoulder, and I dropped my weight, raking my nails down his chest before I rolled, coming up on my feet at his back. I lunged, but his elbow connected to my face, pulling a gasp from my lungs as he added his brutal strength to the blow. I danced back, dazed as I shook it off. I watched his body moving, lowering to lunge, and at the last moment, I jumped and flung his body mid-air, watching as he slid down the glass, and I snarled.

Standing up, he tilted his head, watching me prowl slowly around him as I tried to cage him in against the glass. His smile was cold as he moved against it and watched as I leapt toward him, only for his hand to catch my throat, slamming me against the glass until it trembled and groaned from the pressure. My knee lifted, landing against his balls before I grabbed his hair and slammed his face into my knee, laughing as I danced away from the anger in his stare. I made it a few feet before he moved with unnatural speed, lifting me up to throw me against the glass, watching as I slid down it to my knees.

I winced, wiping blood away from my nose to stand again. I crouched, and he smiled darkly, mimicking the movement with the sleek muscles of a predator. Standing back up, I narrowed my gaze at the way he stalked me, sensing my movements with ease. Leaning against the glass, I watched him, letting his gaze slide slowly down to where my naked flesh was red and swollen with a need for him.

"You want to fucking play with me, creature?" Lust dripped from his lips, and my body arched before I smiled, nodding my answer.

I didn't need to vocalize my reply as I moved around

him, intending to get to his back to subdue him. Every time I got close, he'd easily dodge my attempt. He was faster, stronger, and outdid me in every maneuver I tried, as if he sensed it coming before I had even moved.

"You're not even on my level, little monster."

I danced around his lunge only to realize he was playing with me. He was wearing me down, but he had no idea what he was playing with. Not that I knew what I was since I'd been born in the Human Realm. Aria didn't even realize I was a part of her yet, or that we were meant to combine into one being. Claws pushed out of his fingertips, and I paused, knowing that Aria didn't heal fast. She hadn't fused our souls, and if he used them, we'd be scarred forever.

"She will not heal," I whispered.

"Then concede defeat to me," he demanded coldly, and yet lust was dripping in his words, aching for my submission. He was all male, and his power ignited a flame within me that wanted to burn.

Still, denial entered my mind and slipped to the tip of my tongue as he prowled closer, his claws extending to large black talons. I was an alpha female, and he would be a good fight. I wouldn't care about scars, but Aria's needs surpassed mine. I turned around, moving my hair as my nails retracted, and his breath fanned my shoulder.

"Good girl," he muttered.

He sank his teeth into my shoulder, deep enough that my body sagged as everything within me stilled to absolute silence. He'd done this to Aria without her understanding what it did to us. He licked it slowly, healing the bite with his saliva once he knew I wouldn't fight him. Backing me up, he pushed me against the glass wall, staring into my eyes with my blood dripping from his lips.

"You're more durable than she is, right?" he asked huskily, his fingers slipping to my pussy to slide through the heat of it. He pushed them into my body, and I purred as he watched me, knowing I craved this from him.

"Aria is durable because she and I share the body and strengthen each other. Are you fireproofed like this room?"

"I wouldn't be here if I wasn't, Aria." He dropped to his knees as he lifted my leg over his shoulder and ran his tongue through the need that covered my cunt for him. He growled, and I dripped even more, unable to stop my response to the noises he made as he devoured me.

His mouth licked through my core, and I moaned, slipping my hands through his hair as he lapped greedily against my pussy. Knox was voracious in his need to fuck me. He didn't play with my sex. He pushed me up, forcing me to hold on to his hair as he lifted me against the wall. My legs were around his neck as he pushed his tongue deep into my body. Everything within me unfurled, my hands ignited, and he smiled against my sex as the fire burning in my eyes reflected in his.

He gave no mercy, not even when the orgasm exploded through me violently, causing me to scream. He ignored me, continuing to fuck me with his mouth, uncaring that I'd finished several times. Instead, Knox's tongue grew within my body, and I whimpered his name, shocked at the way it licked my insides, hitting nerve endings that had never been touched before. He fucking destroyed me until my hands tightened on his shoulders, releasing his hair. Everything within me was firing into an inferno as I pushed my core against his heated kiss, coming undone for him.

Knox chuckled darkly against my sex as he sucked it clean before letting my body slide down, and then pushed his swollen cock into me. His hips moved relentlessly, slamming against mine hard as my ass pounded against the glass painfully, his gaze never leaving mine. He didn't stop, not until I was rocking against him, whimpering his name as my body clenched tightly against his.

He set me down and turned me around, pushing my head against the glass. I leaned against its coolness as his hands slid around the inside of my thighs, lifting my ass as he stretched me apart painfully. My head rested against the glass wall as he began hammering into my body in a forceful thrust that had me whimpering and uttering his name as if he was salvation, and I desperately needed saving.

I came, repeatedly, as he hit the spot within me that created a dangerous storm that erupted, sending tears running down my face. He paused, turning me over to look at him before he shoved me to my knees. His cock rubbed against my lips, and I peered up, knowing he craved eye contact, and then I took him deep into my throat, all the way. I worked his cock, noting every single article Aria had read in her magazines. I used every tongue swivel and twirl it said men loved until he was leaning against the glass for support, watching me as I fucked his world, turning it upside down. His hands pulled on my hair, and he forced me backward on my knees toward the rack until he pulled me up, running his thumb over my lip with heat banked in his fiery depths.

"Get on the bed, and give me that pretty ass, little girl."

"I wasn't done sucking your cock."

"You are for now. Don't worry, little one. You can suck me off as often as you want, with how pretty you look when those lips are around me as I fuck that tight throat, I'll let you do it often."

He flipped me over, touching me without hesitation as he lifted my hips, pushing into my body in a swift thrust. I bounced forward, my hips slammed against the metal, and I cried out as he adjusted me until only my hands touched the bed, forcing me to hold myself upright against it in the air. He held my hips as I dangled, using my body to maneuver me as he fucked me. He didn't hold back. Instead, he went fast and hard until he roared when he came, and I smirked, using my body to drain him until he sagged and purred loudly.

Knox set me down, and I purred, turning around as he watched me through narrowed eyes. I moved over the metal frame, rolling onto my side, sated and exhausted.

"Maybe you'd be an okay mate; you know how to calm my mind. Maybe someday you'll let me calm your demons."

"You don't want to play with my demons, Aria. Sleep; tomorrow, you learn how to shield the world from that fire you wield. The sooner you learn to control it, the sooner you can get the fuck out of my house and away from me, so I don't fucking hurt you."

CHAPTER
37

ARIA

My eyes opened slowly, gaining focus after clearing the sleep from them. I was inside a room made of glass. There were char marks on the glass, and other stuff I didn't want to even take a guess at what it was or had been. I sniffed the air, noting the room smelled like Knox. My body ached, but the worst of the pain seemed to be centered between my thighs, ass, and throat. My hand lifted, touching my swollen lips. I lowered my hand, lifting my head as I took in the red marks that covered my hips, breasts, and naked flesh. How the hell was I alive? I'd been blown up with a bomb, hadn't I?

Turning over, I stared at the smug look on Knox's face, lowering my gaze to the thick cock he leisurely stroked. Frowning deeply, I brought my gaze back to his and opened my mouth, but the swelling in my throat was too much, and nothing other than a groan escaped.

I sat up, looking around the room that held metal…well, everything. The water fountain caught my eye, and I stood, whimpering as the swollen flesh between my legs screamed with the movement.

I waddled to the fountain, moving my hair away from my face before bending down to drink the blessed water. Exhaling, I wiped my mouth off with the back of my hand, turning to glare at Knox; he'd rolled onto his back, continuing to stroke the monstrosity between his legs, as if he expected something.

"Climb on, it won't fuck itself," he growled huskily, closing his eyes and leaning his head back as his thumb rubbed a bead of come over the rounded top.

"What the fuck, Knox? Why are you naked? Why am *I* naked? Stop touching that thing, for fuck's sake, Jesus. Put it away, asshole." I looked around for somewhere to sit that didn't have a naked Knox on it but found nothing. "What the hell happened?"

His head lifted, and he watched me as I moved back to the bed slowly. "Aria?"

"Who the fuck else would it be?"

"Climb on my dick," he demanded huskily, letting his gaze drift down my naked body.

"Fuck you, asshole. Fuck it yourself! I told you to stay the fuck away from me!" I sat on the edge of the bed carefully, giving him my back as I groaned as every part of me screamed in pain.

"Fucking hell," he grumbled, staring at me as I took in my war wounds.

My hand lifted to my shoulder, which burned in red-hot pain. "Did you fucking bite me?" I whimpered as my fingers skimmed over raw flesh. "Dick move."

He sat up, turning to look at me as he stretched like a lion waking up from feasting on a kill. He stood slowly, moving around the bed until he was in front of me, smirking as his dick pointed right at my face.

"Sore?"

"*Why* am I so sore?"

"Because I fucked you every which way but the right way, Aria." His dark rumble made me frown as I wiped the sleep from my vision.

"As if, prick, you kicked me out of here, so why the fuck am I here with you? How am I alive?" I lifted my gaze to hold his, watching as his mouth curved into a smile. "I deflected a bomb, and should be dead." I felt like he'd fucked me, and worse, I felt like he'd been in me enough to imprint his name on my insides. I didn't remember it, luckily. Deniability was everything if you couldn't remember it, right? Heat infused in my cheeks as I groaned.

"You survived." He watched me as he knelt down, reaching for my face.

"You keep your penis flavored hands to yourself, asshole. Why does my throat hurt?"

"Because I fucked it," he chuckled darkly as his thumb brushed over my lip.

"Pretty sure that thing wouldn't fit past my lips."

"Oh, trust me, it did, and you took all of it like a bitch in heat down that tight, greedy throat." His eyes burned with heat as he studied me, smiling like he had jokes. "It has been an entire week since you stood in front of the bomb. You've been recovering here."

"Recovering on what, your dick?"

"You don't remember?" he asked, studying me through narrowed eyes.

"I remember you being a fucking bastard to me after you fucked me, and then threatening to hunt us down. I also remember the bomb, and then I remember hearing screaming, but after that, everything goes dark. Everything just vanishes, which I'm guessing is because I got blown up. I remember pain, like I was fusing together with the concrete. Then everything disappears until I wake up here, with you telling me to ride your worthless cock, which isn't fucking happening, prick."

"You remember nothing after that?" he asked cautiously, as if he didn't like the answers I was giving him. His hands moved before I could deflect them, cradling my face as he examined me.

"Let me go, Knox."

His hands dropped, and I watched as he moved across the room, his perfect ass flexed with every step he took. We were both naked, and I was swollen. No, swollen didn't cut it. It hurt to sit, and worse, every single part of me ached.

"Knox, why does my ass hurt?" I asked, and he replied by chuckling. "You are a bastard. Was I even awake when you fucked me?"

"You were more than willing to take me anywhere I wanted to go, Aria."

My scalp ached as if he'd tried ripping my hair out

from my head. My shoulder burned, and the raw skin was angry and red. I had bruises on my wrist and thighs, and my sex was bright red, swollen, and leaking his come, as if we'd had sex not too long ago. Tears filled my eyes, and my chest burned with denial.

"I'm losing my mind, right? I'm going crazy." My head dropped into my hands, and I exhaled slowly.

"Your other half made an appearance, and she's rather…wild and primal."

"Then you know what the hell I am?" I asked carefully, standing up as he pushed his legs into gray sweatpants and turned around, throwing me a smaller pair.

"We don't know, only that your mind changed along with a few other tiny details." He stared at my battered body with masculine pride burning in his gaze, which only pissed me off more.

"Did you maybe stop to think you should cease fucking me? That maybe I wasn't a willing participant after what you did to me?"

"You begged me to fuck you. You taunted me, pushing your dripping cunt in my face, and you screamed for me, Aria. You fucking roared your approval as I fucked every single inch of your perfect fucking body."

"Not me, Knox. I hate you."

"Yeah, but that naughty little creature inside of you likes what I do to her. She purrs for me, Aria. She comes on my cock and fucking roars in the most visceral, unabashed way that a woman can. Whatever is within you, she's wild and doesn't live by your rules."

I snorted before crossing my arms over the teeth marks that marred my nipples. "I thought that was why you didn't like witches, because we fuck with wild abandonment?"

His eyes darkened at my words, but I didn't back down. "I'd be careful with the next words to leave your pretty fuckable lips, Aria. You won't like pissing me off."

"What else can you do to me, Knox? You've taken everything I've done and thrown it in my face. You threw me out of your room after you fucked me like I'm nothing but a whore who you wanted gone the moment you had finished. Then you fuck me while I don't even realize it is happening? Throw me around? Treat me like I'm fucking dirt that you can't scrape off your boot fast enough? What? What the fuck can you possibly do me that you haven't already done?" Tears slipped from my eyes, and I hugged myself, turning away from him.

Power erupted in the room, lethal power that promised death. My head turned, staring at Knox as he moved toward me. I was picked up and slammed on the bed, gasping as the air whooshed from my lungs. He didn't speak right away, and when he did, it wasn't right.

"I can twist your fucking head off your shoulders, witch. I can destroy you in ways you can't even begin to imagine. You think I raped you? I wasn't the one sticking my gushing cunt up and begging to be mounted like a bitch in heat. You sucked my dick, not because I wanted you to, but because that thing asleep inside of you decided she wanted it. You don't get to make me into the villain here, Aria. You want to fucking hate me?

Good, I fucking hate you too. You think I care? I don't. Your kind are murderous whores who take what they want, and when they don't get it? They fucking murder anyone not strong enough to survive their magic. You, you can get the fuck out of my sight, you needy little bitch."

I stared at him, shaking my head. "Fuck you, Knox," I whispered brokenly.

"No, Aria, I've had enough of you in this last week that I won't need to fuck you again. You're just like the other witches, weak, needy, and miserable right down to your corruptible black heart. Cover your tits, and get the fuck out my sight, little girl." His gaze slid over me with disdain, and something inside of me closed down, feeling as if he thought me nothing but a whore because of what had happened without my knowledge.

I stared at him, shaking my head. "I'm not a whore, Knox."

His eyes widened, and he shook his head, snorting before he placed his hands on his tapered hips and smiled coldly. "Not yet, you're not, but give it time, Aria."

"I wish I had never met you."

"The feeling is mutual, I assure you," he said, retrieving a shirt and throwing it at me.

I slipped it over my head and then was slammed against the wall before I'd finished getting it on. His mouth pushed against mine through the shirt, holding me by the throat as he growled loudly. I didn't make a sound. He pushed against my throat harder, shoving his fingers against my sore flesh to steal a cry from my lips before he chuckled.

"You should have left town when I gave you the chance, Aria Primrose," he hissed, pushing harder until the air refused to enter my throat. His head rested against mine, and his chest rattled, but mine didn't answer him in return. His hand released me, and I slid down the wall, gasping for air past the pressure he'd placed on my already swollen throat. I trembled, not bothering to fix the shirt as it hid the tears from the fear that had flooded me.

His feet padded across the floor, and something beeped, and the sound of glass doors sliding opening and closing filled the room. I didn't move, couldn't move as a violent tremor rushed through me. I felt boneless, and worse, I felt him in my body and knew he'd left more than a mark on my flesh. He'd written his name within me, marking me on a visceral level that wouldn't ever be erased, no matter how much I wished it otherwise.

Slowly, I pushed myself up the wall and slipped the shirt over my head. Wiping the tears away, I looked at the open elevator and started toward it at a run, slamming my hands on the buttons until the doors closed, and I exhaled a shuddered breath. The moment they opened, I was heading toward the front door, the same as I had after he'd taken my virginity.

Greer watched me approaching as Brander moved to the door, holding it open before Greer could react. His eyes took in the tears and what I was sure were red marks covering my throat before he stepped back and watched me escape as if the devil himself were on my heels. The House of Magic was lit up, and in the dark of night, I cried as I barreled toward the protection it would offer me.

CHAPTER
38

When I burst through the door, Aurora turned, staring at me with wide eyes. The moment I saw her, my silent tears became giant sobs as she rushed to where I stood, pulling me into her arms. Her soothing noises offered comfort as she patted my head, holding me even as I dropped to the floor. I felt other hands touching me; my sisters moved in close, dropping to their knees as they tried to soothe the ache in my soul. It wasn't pain; it was something deeper. He'd broken something within me, and it hurt on a different level than I could comprehend.

"You're home now," Aurora whispered, running her fingers through my silver hair. "You're safe, Aria. Nothing can hurt you here."

"I'm losing my mind. There's something inside of me; I can feel it."

"We know, but we don't know what it is yet; no one does." She cradled my face between her hands to wipe away my tears. "My sweet Aria, we have always known you carried something else inside of you. It's a part of you, and whatever it is, we will deal with it."

"When did you get here?" I asked, pulling back as a smile curved her full lips.

Aurora looked to be in her early thirties, but then she'd looked that age ever since I could remember. Witches from the Hecate line stopped aging at twenty-five, and while it was a blessing, it also made it hard to judge our ages. No one wanted to listen to a younger woman for advice, especially on the council.

Soft turquoise eyes watched me, frowning as she took in the mark on my throat, touching it as her magic pushed through me. She healed my neck, but there was concern marring her face. Her blond hair was held in a braid and pinned in a bun to the top of her head, while fine strands framed her ageless face. This woman had been my mother. Unlike the others, who had Freya's undivided attention when she was here, I'd had Aurora's.

"I used magic to sell the house to a gentleman who could afford it but tried to argue the price. He offered me ten times what it was worth. How could I refuse him? I had everything packed, and when Sabine told me what had happened to you, we came."

"I'm glad you're here. We need you," I admitted, exhaling.

"The house is blessed once more, and the skeletal remains of my father are in the correct order. It appears someone moved one of the smaller bones, making it hard to determine which bone had been removed. The house itself is still acting peculiar, but working."

"Amara?"

"It appears so, since the bone wasn't taken from the altar, and instead placed elsewhere. Anyone else wouldn't have cared if it was ever replaced."

"Do you think she did this? These crimes are bad," I swallowed, hating the tightening in my throat that burned with the words. I hadn't wanted to believe it, but everything stacked together looked really bad.

"I think it doesn't matter right now, you need to come first." She clapped her hands together once and shooed me. "You need a bath, you smell of his creature and sex. Then you need to be examined for new changes since I can see a difference in your eyes, and your hair is now black on the tips," she concluded, sending me off to shower.

In the bathroom, I stared at my reflection. I had changed; my face was more defined. My silver hair had obsidian-colored tips as if it had been scorched. Naked, I looked like I'd been abused, but a closer look showed he'd had a lot of fun with my bits and pieces.

My nipples were swollen. Knox's teeth marks sat around the pink, swollen tips. There were bruises on my hips, probably used to control my body since the fingerprints were on the front. My thighs held the same marks just above my knees, and more around my ankles. My flesh was purple, covered in a substantial bruise from days of fucking, or so he'd said. If it was causing me pain, why hadn't the thing inside of me realized it?

I'd never considered it being a separate being, but I carried the proof of sex I hadn't been a part of all over my flesh.

Most of my sisters had been aware of what they

would become or shift into once they reached a certain age. Freya hadn't been forthcoming with the names of the creatures she'd been with when Amara and I were conceived. Aurora had begged her to tell her so that we could prepare for it when the time came, and she'd laughed in her sister's face. My sisters had either shifted into a creature while holding the mental link to their mind or had been born with abilities. If I shared the same body and mind, then I wouldn't remember taking Knox every which way from Sunday? Obviously, I'd been willing and fully participated. Admitting that sucked, but my bruises were from being used, not held down or forced.

I felt a deep connection to what lived within me. So why the hell would she sleep with Knox? What if she was like a split personality, and I started waking up in strange places with strange men? What if she told Knox we liked his dick? Or worse, I continued waking up naked and sore without a single memory of what had happened?

I turned around and peered over my shoulder, staring at my ass, which still ached painfully. That one should have been off-limits, especially since we didn't like the prick. Glaring at my hands, I looked at the tips of my fingers, noting the red swelling there. Opening my mouth, I gazed at my tongue and then at the back of my throat. At least he hadn't pushed through the back of my skull, I guess. I still hadn't figured out how he could hurt my throat, considering there was no way he'd fit into my mouth.

My eyes looked different, turquoise with tiny flecks of silver. It was hardly noticeable unless you were looking for it.

"If you're in there, no more fucking Knox, understood? He's a dick." Nothing happened. Scrunching up my nose, I sucked my lip between my teeth. "If you are in there, I'd like to meet you. I'd like to know what is inside of me. I also think we should have a sit down about whom we fuck, and what we allow them to do to our body. You got to hide, but *my* ass hurts." And this was what life had resulted to now: speaking to myself in the mirror as if something else was inside of me. I mean, I knew I had something within me. I knew I was powerful, but that was me, not her. Whatever was inside of me, she rattled and matched the sound Knox made deep in his chest.

She loomed within me but didn't expose herself. I could feel her, but I couldn't grasp her. What the fuck made a rattling noise? There were no snake shifters, thank fuck. I hated snakes and all scaly creatures. Anything that sheds its own skin was eerie and not something I wanted to be. There were a few creatures that weren't allowed outside of the Nine Realms. A few who were so terrifying that they'd never learned to take human form, or had outright refused to do so. What if I lost myself when I changed? What if I could never come back from fully forming like those monsters that couldn't hold a human form? I'd lose everyone I loved because those monsters didn't have human emotions.

I leaned against the counter, closing my eyes. "I hope you're not a snake or something with scales. Please don't have scales."

Opening my eyes, I moved away from the mirror, crawling into the bath filled with healing oils and sprinkled with dried rose petals. It was like a balm over my soul, and I moaned as it eased the pain from my body. My hands reached for the soap, lifting one leg to scrub it before following with the other. Sitting up, I grabbed my shampoo, pouring a generous amount into my hand, and purred. My eyes widened, and I stiffened.

"The fuck?"

I listened, tilting my head as if it would help me hear the sound better. I held the shampoo to my nose again. The noise came from deep within me, and I shivered as my heart accelerated, I dropped my hand into the water, washing the shampoo off. I fucking *purred*? Great, I was a fucking cat.

Sitting in the bath, I waited for something to happen. I waited for *anything* to freaking happen. Nothing did, and when I poured more shampoo into my hand, still nothing happened. Frowning, I washed my hair and used the conditioner before leaning back. I couldn't be a cat, I enjoyed bathing. I didn't like yarn and was lactose intolerant. I would be the worst cat ever. There were cat shifters, but they were rather large and were usually thicker. I had coveted their beautiful eyes and thick hips, which would be a plus, rather than my small curves. If I was, I would be pissed that I'd been ripped off in the bubble butt and hip area.

Thinking about it more, it wouldn't be so horrible to be a cat shifter. They were beautiful and sleek, able to jump high, and had massive claws to rip assholes' faces off. I mean, that was a bonus. I closed my eyes and leaned my head back, soaking in the tub.

I jolted from the tub and realized I'd dozed off. I stared around the room, frowning as I replayed the dream. Knox had been in front of me, the rattling sound vibrating from his chest as I sucked his dick, and by suck it, I mean I was taking it all as he pushed the hair away from my face. He'd made noises that I'd craved, wanting to hear them. I'd done whatever he wanted me to. Not that Knox asked me to get on my knees; I'd fucking done it even though he'd tried to pull back, not wanting to hurt me. His eyes were black, flecked with fiery embers within them as he watched me, and any time I took him all, *he* fucking purred.

Knox was a pussy! I snorted, smirking as I stood up, letting the water drip from my body as I left the tub. I guess it took a pussycat to know one, but if he thought he was getting any more of this cream, he was wrong. I would do everything in my power to stay away from him, avoiding him at all costs. He could do the same because even if we were cat shifters, he wasn't sniffing my ass anymore.

CHAPTER
39

THREE MONTHS LATER

Days turned into weeks and weeks into months as we dug into the events that led to Amara's vanishing act. Every time we began to make headway, it would end up being a dead end. It had gotten so exhausting that I'd started offering to work a shift in the store, even though I barely left the house to avoid running into Knox, who apparently had become chummy with Aurora. She'd gushed about his perfect etiquette and manners, spouting ballads in his name while I stared at her, stunned, like she'd bonked her head. Obviously, we hadn't encountered the same version of Knox.

The man had her eating out of his palm, and Aurora couldn't shut up about it, which was why I was at Wickedly Rocked, currently slinging crystals like they were crack. Because I couldn't stand that she liked the pompous, self-assured prick.

A male in his early thirties approached me as I stacked rainbow-hued quartz stones above a lighted counter. He had gray eyes and a smirk that made me hesitant to acknowledge him. Pushing the silver hair away from my face, I smiled in a manner as friendly as I could muster, or what I hoped looked friendly. I wasn't a people person, even if I did have a master's degree in communications.

"Do you have any carnelian?" he asked, staring at my breasts.

My shirt said *Come and Hex it, Baby,* and was hot pink. "My eyes are up here," I snapped, watching as his lifted with a deep glow of azure. "Wolf, you're in the wrong store. There's wolfsbane within this building, and it bites. Let's show you the carnelian, and you can get out with your fur still pretty."

I turned and made my way to the small case of carnelian tumblers. Once I'd set them out, he stared at them and back at me.

"Is it true they can help with confidence?"

"It is," I watched as he touched one, and then another. "Do they call to you?"

"They're rocks," he muttered, as if he couldn't believe he was buying one.

"It's a powerful crystal, blessed and charged by Hecate witches. You won't find any better ones than here. Take it or leave it, but you can't stay in the store too long. They're brewing tonics below using wolfsbane. There's a sign on the door giving warning."

"Listen, I need to impress my mate. She's been acting strange. She keeps growling at me when I get close to the bed, and she bitches about everything. I need her to accept me into our bed, but she won't."

"Was she breeding before her behavior changed?"

"Yes."

"Congratulations, you're going to be a father. Your mate won't let you back into the bed until your child is securely planted. She's nesting, per se. She doesn't want to lose your child. You don't need carnelian. You need some massive patience. Give her a week and try again."

"How the hell would you know that?" he asked, dumbfounded.

"Because my sister, Luna, is pregnant, and she's a massive bitch right now. She bares her teeth if we even get close to her door. She's part witch and part alpha wolf. The guy she rutted with isn't interested in the babes, so it falls on us to help her through the pregnancy."

"Wolves don't nest."

"Same shit, different breed. You get my point. Your mate is pregnant and defending the unborn babe she grows within her. My guess is that it's her first, and she's afraid you will unseat it within her womb. Give her a week and then see what happens."

"You are no fucking help, witch," he snorted and exited the store.

Turning toward the counter, I placed the carnelian back beneath the cupboard while pulling out mixed tumblers to make into an assorted arrangement of rainbow colors on the counter. I leaned over further, grabbing the citrine and a few others before backing out and turning around. My gaze slid up the fancy suit to the delicious ocean-blue eyes of Knox, and I growled.

"Get out, we don't serve dicks."

"Your aunt sent me here for some things I needed," he announced, picking up a set of rainbow aura points. "You've been hiding from me." He stared at me as his finger slowly trailed over the sharp tip of the crystal.

"No, it's called *avoiding* you like the plague. Remember, you threw me out after assuring me I'd become a whore, or is your memory as fucked up as you are?" I set the rocks out on the counter and pushed them into order before a customer stepped up.

"I need an amethyst sphere, highest quality you have."

"They're on the back wall, top shelf. They're untainted, so if you touch it, you buy it," I said, spinning around to move through the store to the herbs.

"You don't leave the house, woman." Knox watched me, following as I moved through the store. He chose to ignore my words and I rolled my eyes, laughing soundlessly.

"Nope, rarely these days, and when I do, I sneak out to avoid certain pricks I don't wish to encounter ever again in this lifetime, and by pricks, I mean you."

Dismissing him outright, I moved to the herbs, pulling the older bags from behind the new ones, placing them in the front so they would sell before their potency expired. Knox stood mere feet away from me, and I watched from the corner of my eye as he picked up random items, studying them before setting them back onto the shelves.

"Do you have any potions to increase libido?" an imp asked.

I guessed her species based on the way her nose stuck out further than the rest of her. "Do you have a willing partner?" I asked curtly.

"Does it matter if they're willing?"

"People don't enjoy waking up naked with someone they didn't want to end up in bed with in the first place, so yes, it actually does matter."

"Uh," the imp stammered.

"People begged to be fucked, and got pissy when they got what they asked for," Knox pointed out.

The imp's head moved between us and then snapped back to Knox, letting her gaze linger over his crotch. I glared at him as he smiled at the imp, giving her a wiggle of his brow that made my blood boil. I dismissed them both and retrieved the potion.

"Here, if I find out you use it on an unwilling partner, I will personally make it my mission in life to fucking destroy you—but have a nice day and shit. Get the fuck out of my store."

I dismissed them both as my sister, Valeria, hooted from the register. She was pushing popcorn into her mouth, watching me as I methodically moved through the store, cleaning it, and stacking everything where it needed to go. I bent over a shelf, and he crowded behind me. Sweat beaded on my brow, and I turned, glaring at him.

"Stay away from me."

"You're not in heat."

"No, I'm not. When it happens, I'll find someone to assist me who actually *likes* me. I have no intention of ever slipping up and landing on that dick again."

"You should be in heat by now," he muttered.

"Nope, didn't happen once in the last three months, but thanks for coming in to sniff my pussy. You can go now," I stated, folding my arms over my chest.

He stared at me, dropping his gaze to my breasts, and then sniffed the air. I snorted, turning back to polish off the crystals from people coming in all day and touching them, smudging them with their fingers. I pulled the cloth from my pocket and cleaned one gently, placing it back down before I lowered my head to check the glow. Perfect.

I spun around, and Knox was flush against me. My nostrils flared with his scent, and a deep purr erupted from my chest as I took him in. His smile turned cocky, his eyes narrowing to slits. I stepped back, watching him as he stepped forward, placing his hands on the glass shelf behind me, locking me into place.

"You're not pregnant."

"Thank fuck for that. Wouldn't want a reminder for eternity that I'd been stupid enough to be with you, now would I?" I snapped icily, ducking under his arm.

He turned cold, and I paused, watching the brief flash of pain that entered his eyes, dismissing it as an optical illusion, since everyone knew that asshole didn't have any emotion. I stopped in front of the spheres and made sure each was placed to lure the eye. Once I'd ensured each was perfect, I turned, finding him leaning against the glass counter, watching me silently.

"You're still here?" I let my gaze drink in the sight of him quickly before exhaling. It would be a lot easier to ignore the prick if he didn't look like sex incarnate and smell like it too.

"Indeed, I am," he answered, bringing his finger up to run over his lip. "You purred."

"So do you," I smirked saucily, licking my lips slowly, so he didn't miss the action. I watched as his eyes mirrored mine, turning to slits. His lips turned up in the corners as he continued studying me.

"What else do you remember?"

"That you fit down my throat, and that you tasted magically fucking delicious when you came. The noises you made, they soothed me and made me feel exhilarated, protected., and that I'd have done anything you wanted me to just so you would make them. Obviously, whatever is within me is bipolar and has horrible taste in men."

"You chose me too," he pointed out.

"Hey." I held my hands up in mock surrender. "I didn't say I was any smarter. I just pointed out the obvious. Do you intend to buy anything? We're closing."

"Twenty more minutes, Aria." Valeria smiled as I turned to glare at her.

"We're closing early, there's a gathering with the alphas Aurora agreed to be at tonight."

"The gathering? You're going alone?" he asked.

"No, I have men lined up to mount my cunt," I lied crudely, turning to close the counters with the rare crystals inside.

"I'll see you there, little lamb. Careful not to taunt the wolves, they share territory and pussy."

His lips brushed across my shoulder, and I shivered, hating that my body responded to his. It was basic logic, I told myself. He was a man; I was a woman. Shit tended to get twisted, and panties ended up in a bunch on the floor. I just had to fight it. I'd spent three months hiding inside of my house to do just that. I'd been mixing potions to sell, purifying crystals, and endlessly working only to fall into bed exhausted, no longer haunted by the oceanic eyes that had controlled my dreams. No more, he could kiss my ass.

"Maybe I'd like it since I'm *such* a slut," I offered, moving away from him to let him mull it over.

His chest rattled, and I closed my eyes, ignoring the need to answer him. My body arched, and my spine curved for him. My hands held onto the wood, and I screamed before it split, sending an entire shelf of herbs crashing onto the floor. I turned, glaring at him as a cocky smile crossed his lips.

"The alphas wouldn't be enough to satisfy you, Aria."

He turned, walking out of the shop as Valeria moved closer, staring at me. I shook my head, unable to open my mouth as my gums ached, and my spine shifted.

"That can't be good," she uttered, bending down to pick up the herbs. "You hurt yourself, didn't you? You were trying to ignore the noise he made, and oh my God, Aria, he makes the same sound as you do."

"It's not good, it's really not good," I whispered

through the pain in my mouth. "Something isn't right."

"Yeah, you got a dental problem. Aurora said it was best not to tell you because you thought you were going insane, but Aria, you've got a mouth full of razor-sharp teeth. I saw them when Sabine touched you while Knox held you with his; they matched. It was intense and scary as shit, Aria. You also had a little pyro problem."

"Why didn't anyone say anything?"

"Duh, you weren't handling it very well. You were shutting down, and telling you wouldn't make it better. In fact, I'm not even sure why I am telling you now!" she cried, staring down at the vial of potion that had shattered when it hit the floor. "Damn, truth potion." She sat back and looked up at me sadly. "You are my sister, and I don't care if you're…whatever you are. We all have some major issues, y'know? You're just more like us now, not different."

"I love you, too. I know you guys are trying to protect me, but you can't protect me from something that is literally *inside* of me."

"Yeah, I mentioned that to them. Not everyone agreed to hide it from you. When I turned into a teenager, my other half was already a part of me. Aine and Luna, they transformed at sixteen. You're twenty-five and just now starting your transformation. The rest of us have lived our entire lives knowing what we would become. We've had time to adjust, to realize that changing was normal. You've never known, and you have no idea what to expect. It is a part of you, but it's more."

"I thought I might have been a cat shifter."

"You made fire, so unless you're like some mythical

cat, I doubt it."

"Yeah, and fangs," I groaned.

"I'm not so sure I'd qualify those as fangs. You have an entire row of razor-sharp teeth on the top, and I wasn't getting close enough to give you an exam. I'm the fun one, not the crazy one. Ask Reign to do that, she's the crazy one."

"Great. I'm a monster."

CHAPTER
40

I entered the alpha mansion in a crimson red dress with slits that stopped just below my hips. It was vivid, exposing the curve of my hips and accentuating my cleavage by showing off the rounded tops of my breasts with a small V-line, without revealing too much. The entire back of the dress was decorated in thin, crisscrossed laces to keep it secured. My hair was up, exposing the curve of my throat, forcing me to add concealer to the light scar from Knox's teeth adorning my shoulder, which still hadn't healed enough to vanish. I'd forgone any other makeup, settling on just a touch of lipstick to match the dress, and mascara to make my eyes pop.

"Well, ladies, shall we move?" Valeria clapped her hands together, smiling at the men who turned as we entered. "I'm getting laid, how about you?" she chuckled, staring down the stairs.

My eyes searched the crowd, not entirely happy with the amount of attention we'd drawn with our entrance.

Our names were called, and, one by one, someone came to escort us down the stairs to the ballroom floor. I started down the stairs slowly, since I was wearing higher heels than I was used to. They were a perfect match to the dress, tied around my calves into delicate bows, adding to the sex appeal.

I reached the landing in the middle of the stairs and lifted my gaze, finding Lore studying me as he walked forward, extending his elbow to escort me down the stairs with a naughty grin on his full lips.

"Red suits you, Aria. A primal color for a primal beauty, my lady," he said, bowing at the waist before he rose, offering me his hand.

"Thank you, Lore." I smiled at his attempt at humor, or what I assumed was him jesting at my expense. Slipping my arm through his, he walked me to the bottom of the stairs, and then leaned closer, kissing my cheek.

"Be careful tonight. Don't wake the beast, little one," he offered cryptically before starting through the crowd.

I frowned, uncertain what to do with myself once I stood alone. I was already awkward enough, but alone I felt even more so. My sisters were already on the dancefloor, dancing. My gaze slowly slid through the crowd, finally finding and settling on the male I'd searched for. He watched me with his arm around a small, petite Asian woman's waist. I rolled my eyes, starting toward the bar to grab a drink. I should have stayed home and played sick tonight.

At the bar, I leaned over and smiled at the bartender,

who whistled beneath his breath as he approached me. "Scotch, neat." I turned around with my elbows leaning back against the bar, watching the people decked out in their finery.

It was insane how many immortals had come to the gathering, but then, like us, most had been ordered to attend. The crowd was filled with happy couples dancing to the slow beats of Motown jazz that soothed my soul and made me wish I had someone with which to dance. Not that I felt left out, but sometimes I did wish I had one person who would hold me and dance with me like I meant something to them.

The bartender returned with my drink. Accepting it politely, I brought it close to my nose, staring over the rim as I watched Knox lean against his date, whispering into her ear, which caused her to throw her head back and laugh like an idiot.

"Dick," I muttered before taking a sip and dismissing him.

"Aria Hecate, is that you, trouble?"

I turned to the voice, narrowing my eyes on the man with dark hair bound behind his head. A pair of striking alpha blue eyes studied me, never dipping below my face, which was refreshing. I sucked my lip between my teeth and tilted my head, trying to remember who he was, and then smiled wide as it hit me.

"Dimitri?" I asked cautiously, watching as his lips curved into a smile. "Oh my word, it is you!" I stood, hugging him as he let his hands settle on my hips, inhaling my scent before I pulled away. "Look at you, you grew up from that puny little kid into…oh, wow, you're buff." My hand tested his arms, smiling wider as he chuckled at my response.

"I was a child the last time I saw you, Aria. So were you, for that matter, but that is far from the case now." He settled in the seat beside me as I went back to crowd-gazing with an idiotic smile on my face as he watched me.

"You've been here this entire time and didn't say hello?" I asked, pretending to pout as he shook his head.

"No, I just got back not too long ago, a couple of months now, maybe four. My father called the pack home. He didn't give me much of an option on whether I had a choice in the matter."

"You're away from home and still an alpha? I'm impressed." I studied his face as he smirked broadly and took in the dancing couples. "If I remember correctly, you used to chase me, and you also pulled my hair once or twice on the monkey bars."

"You never saw me, Aria. You were oblivious to the boys who fawned over you and your pretty wide eyes at school. Poor bastards anyway," he finished speaking and lifted his drink in the air. "To being stupid kids and thinking we ruled the playground."

"Oh, Dimitri, I did rule that playground. If I remember correctly, you followed right behind me with your wide, puppy eyes, and I did notice you. You annoyed the hell out of me."

"I may have annoyed you, but someone had to have your back. You didn't care to make friends, nor did you care if anyone liked you. I liked you well enough," he announced, noting I hadn't looked away from him.

"You're much more beautiful than the awkward little girl you were back then. Not that I ever thought you were awkward, as much as I thought you were the most beautiful girl in the entire Nine Realms."

"I was an awkward kid. You had a crush on me back then?"

"No, you weren't that awkward, I was fucking awkward. Do you remember my feet? And Aria, the entire male population of that school thought you were cute, but for me, you hung the fucking stars and created the moon."

"I do remember your feet. I swore one day you'd become a giant, and your dad would be so angry at your mother for sleeping with one." I ignored the last part of his words as a pink hue tinged my cheeks.

He choked on his drink, looking at me as he grabbed a napkin, covering his mouth before he spoke. "You thought that?"

"Well, Dimitri, did you see the size of your feet?" I asked, holding my hands out as I embellished the size.

"You're incorrigible, woman. You were always so vivacious until the accident. Then you just vanished, and I thought you died. No one would speak about it. I came to your house, you know? I came every day, and they wouldn't let me in to see you. I remember your mother cuffing me on the back of my head, telling me you weren't good enough for me."

"I guess it changed me, my own mother trying to murder me. No one else spoke about it either, since no one else even cared that she had tried to kill her own daughter. I'm pretty sure after all that happened, no one wanted to speak about the incident—or me. It was easier to hide from the pitying stares or the whispers of the people in this town."

I turned away from Dimitri's stare to find Knox watching me from across the room. Sadness wrapped around my heart, clenching it tightly as my mother's hate-filled eyes entered my mind before I shook it off. That was one of the memories that still haunted me, knowing that everyone had been aware of what she'd done to me, yet not one single person had tried to protect me as a child. It had left me colder than I'd been, reserved about who I allowed into my life from that point forward.

"I'm sorry if I brought up old wounds."

"It happened a long time ago, wolf. I'm not that scared little girl anymore, nor do I give a shit what others think of me. Life is a bitch, and you can let it destroy you, or you can face it head-on and show that it doesn't define who you choose to become in life."

"You were twelve years old, Aria. You were a fucking child, who should have been protected, but everyone ignored what was happening, and that bothered me the most."

"I remember it very clearly." I tore my eyes from Knox to studying Dimitri.

Dimitri hailed from Wintermane, one of the larger realms of our homeland. His hair was the darkest black I'd ever seen that caught and held the light as if it was absorbing it. He wore a midnight-colored tux that hugged his muscular form seductively. Beneath the crisp white undershirt, I could see tattoos that he'd gotten since the last time I'd seen him peeking from his wrists and forearms. He was striking and definitely fit the alpha mode. He bespoke power, but unlike Knox's, Dimitri's was silent and lethal and didn't explode into a room, announcing his presence. His electric-blue eyes studied me back, and I frowned, finding him lacking compared to Knox, which pissed me off.

"Your parents must be proud of you. Few dare to set out into the States to find a pack and become their alpha."

"I'm a second-born son, and with the covenant in place, I have more room to move out there. They sent my brother back to be molded into a king for our tribe. As much as I wanted to sit around and do nothing, I wanted to get out and take control of my future more."

"Makes sense, those of us with several siblings understand that all too well." I nodded, exhaling as I drank the rest of the scotch in my glass, catching the eye of the bartender for a refill.

"Scotch, huh? A woman after my own heart," he smiled tightly with a wink before turning to watch the crowd dancing to the fast-moving beat of the song.

I followed his stare, watching the people who moved on the floor, and spotted my sisters all dancing together. My gaze turned, finding Lore speaking to Knox as Dimitri's lips touched my ear.

"You should be out there dancing. A pretty girl like you shouldn't be sitting here drinking with some asshole like me." His words caused my lips to curve into a smile. Knox glared murderously at us, and I shivered as Dimitri's lips touched the shell of my ear.

AMELIA HUTCHINS

"I'm waiting for you to ask me." I brushed my lips against his cheek as he started to pull away, letting his hand settle against my side when he stood.

"You're trying to get me killed, aren't you?"

"Why would you think that?" I asked as my nose scrunched up.

"You have every alpha in this room watching to see if you make a move on one of them, and deciding if you could be easily subdued. You are something strong; even I can smell it on your flesh. You are the talk of the town. Apparently, the male they sent to save us is smitten with you. His scent clings to you in warning, sweet girl. You've been with him, and he wants everyone to know it."

"Smitten? No. Knox is anything but smitten with me. It's more like I made a mistake and let him have something he didn't deserve. He's an asshole, one who likes to puff his chest and pound it for any bitch in need to hear his masculine war cry. *His?* Absolutely not," I snorted as I finished my drink, holding it up for the bartender to see that I needed another refill. "Knox is here to investigate Amara, but the investigation doesn't appear to be going anywhere. I agree that she looks guilty, but she isn't stupid."

"Unless she never intended to be here when it was discovered what she had done," he pointed out.

"Amara needs the coven to use magic. She isn't like me at all. I pull from our homeland, she pulls from us. She is helpless without us, so why would she leave? A witch without magic becomes mortal, and she knows that. Every day she is without magic rushing through her veins, she becomes more mortal. Witches need magic to remain immortal. Our line is no different, we need it."

"What if her lover led her to believe that he could turn her into something else? What if he's a wolf or something that can turn a witch into another creature? Vampires have accomplished it, as have wolves."

"Maybe, but she's always hated the idea of changing into anything other than what we were born to be. So, not going to dance with me?" I changed the conversation, enjoying the heat from the alcohol that slid down my throat, warming my body deliciously. He shook his head, studying me.

"Depends, do you accept his claim?"

"No, I don't. I am not ready to be claimed. Besides, Knox doesn't even like me, so he doesn't get to claim me."

"You never played fair, either. If I remember correctly, it was how you ruled the monkey bars."

"Hey, they were mine. No one else wanted to sit on them, they wanted to be like little monkeys and go across them. I used them to watch my sisters to make sure they weren't being bullied."

"Let's dance, pretty witch," he chuckled, taking the drink from my hand and placing the glass on the bar before he held out his hand to me. "I can't be held responsible for what happens on the dancefloor."

"And what would happen?" I placed my hand into his much larger one, watching him as he walked backward, pulling me onto the dance floor.

"The possibilities are endless with the way you

look tonight. I always knew you'd be pretty, but you exceeded my expectations." He slipped his arms around my back as I wrapped mine around his neck, peering into his heady gaze.

Lewis Capaldi's *Hold Me While You Wait* was playing, the beat slow and yet methodical to sway to. His deep blue eyes watched me as I did the same to him. The feel of his hands on my back was pleasant, but I didn't feel the electricity that sparked when Knox touched me. Still, it was nice, and he moved us slowly, letting his fingers skim over my back.

"You're pretty hot, too, Dimitri, but I think you're aware that you are."

His mouth lowered without warning, brushing against mine softly. His kiss was searching, asking permission. I opened to it, letting him delve deeper, and he growled against my lips, bringing his hand up to the back of my neck to hold me there as the room continued moving around us. His kiss was sensual, sending a wave of heat washing through me. He didn't end it right away, but when he did, his nose continued to touch mine. He exhaled, staring into my gaze as his hands slowly slid down my spine to the arch of my ass.

"I shouldn't kiss you like that," he whispered, staring into my eyes as he pulled back.

I stared up at him, unable to get words to leave my tongue as heat pooled in my apex from the seductive kiss. Dimitri's kiss had been gentle, something I hadn't ever felt before. Knox kissed like he was going to war against your senses. Dimitri asked permission, and then slowly took control. I sucked my bottom lip between my teeth as he turned me around on the dance floor. I found

Knox with his mouth against his date's ear, whispering into it as he watched me. His date turned her mouth, brushing her lips against his as a sensual smile lifted his generous mouth, igniting a fire in his eyes.

"Will you excuse me for a moment?" Dimitri asked as he frowned. I nodded, stepping back from him so he could pass by me, watching him as he moved toward Fallon, who stared at me across the room with an angry glare.

I watched him moving away from us through the crowd and lowered my lashes, watching Knox through them. His fingers skimmed over the hip of the woman beside him, touching her as if she was familiar and not a last-minute date. I mentally gave myself a shake and turned to go back to my drink.

Lore leaned against the bar the moment I stopped to pick up my glass. He didn't speak, just stood there watching the people dance. Bringing the drink to my lips, I watched as Knox walked past where I stood. Smiling, he settled beside me with his date, which stood in front of him, leaning back against him as her hands slipped around his muscular thighs.

Downing my drink, I turned around, brushing against his shoulder to get the bartender's attention. It sent shocks racing through my system, and I swallowed hard. I could smell the scent he oozed, and it wrapped around me, enveloping me with need. From the corner of my eye, I could see his date rubbing her ass against him in a pathetic attempt to get his attention. His hands moved to hold her hips, assisting her as she ground against him, moaning loudly.

Once my glass was refilled, I downed it in one drink

and set it on the bar, heading out onto the dance floor where my sisters were dancing.

"We need a better song," I announced as they turned.

"Yeah? You planning on actually dancing? Or do you intend to drink them out of scotch tonight?" Kinvara asked, smirking as she watched me narrowing my eyes on her pointedly.

"I am planning to dance, make sure it is sexy and sensual. This slow shit is for the couples, and we don't need it. Let's liven it up, shall we?"

"*Pussy Liquor* work for you?"

"Fuck, yes. Let's show them how witches do things."

"On it." Kinvara didn't sit around. She booked it to the booth where the DJ stood watching the party with a bored look on his face.

I stood there among the couples, awkwardly alone, turning to look at where Knox watched me with Lore at his side with a heated glare. Knox wanted me to see his date grinding against him, hoping it would piss me off. He'd wanted me to be jealous, and maybe I was a little, but I was about to remind him who the fuck I was and how much better I looked alone. He could keep his whore, and I'd stay by myself because I wasn't afraid of being on my own.

CHAPTER
41

The music started, and I smirked as Kinvara, and the others stepped closer while the couples cleared off the dance floor. It wasn't our song, though; it was Pop Evil's *Be Legendary*. It was, however, an excellent warm-up song. My body swayed to the song, moving with my sisters as we found the beat and danced to it as if no one else watched. It fit us. In fact, it fit perfectly since we were here to learn how to take the places of our parents or those who had ruled the covenant before us. We were here to be a part of it and voice our opinions on how to make the covenant more efficient.

Kinvara and Callista were laughing while the crowd watched us, moving as the song ended. She screamed over the music, and I reached up, letting my hair down to stop the ache the pins had caused in my head. It was perfectly timed as Rob Zombie's *Pussy Liquor* started. Howls erupted in the crowd as men hollered and howled loudly, knowing that we were about to give them a show.

Witches were notorious at parties for letting loose. It didn't matter who watched; it wasn't for them. It was a sensual thing we did, swaying to the music that drove us. My body swayed slowly, turning and twisting seductively to the beat. I felt sexy; I felt compelled by a deeper need by the music's sexy beat. I was a woman, sexual, and fierce.

My sexuality showed in every sway of my hips and every move I made as I gave in to the music and closed out the world. Men watched us as we all moved, dancing as our hands lifted, and our asses lowered slowly to the floor. My hands pushed through my hair as I slowly twisted back up, moving them into the air before I let them drop to my side as sweat beaded on my brow.

My eyes slid open, locking with Knox's possessive stare, I noticed the mere slits that followed every sway my hips took. He was tracking me, watching every subtle move I made as I rocked my curves, holding his gaze. My hands lifted above my head, exposing more cleavage with the V-line, and then dropped them down to run over my thighs, exposing them with the movement. I brushed my fingers over his name on my thigh before slowly twisting back up.

He didn't look away, and neither did I as I reminded him of what he could have had, but lost. I fucked him hard without touching him, rocking my hips, trailing the tips of my fingers over his name to be sure he was receiving the message I was sending him.

The heat in his eyes made sweat run down my neck, and my body responded to it. I danced slower, erotically, as I imagined I was with him, moving as I needed to against his hard muscles. My eyes invited, beckoning him to me with the siren's song that sang within my soul. My hands pushed against my breasts, heat banked in my core, and I closed my eyes against the intense stare that consumed my mind.

Everything and everyone else faded from the room, and I parted my lips, imagining him, touching me slowly, and learning me intimately. Opening my gaze, I found him smirking at me as if he knew exactly what I'd been picturing. I sucked my bottom lip between my teeth, stopping the tremble of it as need rushed through me violently causing my core to clench achingly.

I danced for several songs, using my body as a weapon against him, pushing myself to remain there, even though my legs burned, and sweat dripped down my spine. When the next song ended, I moved to the bar, leaning over it to grab my glass, bringing it to my nose, frowning as I caught a whiff of something in it other than scotch.

Knox was a few seats over now; Lore was in the opposite direction, talking to a nymph. I held the glass in my hands, watching my sisters who continued to dance, now with men who had decided it was time to pick one for the night. No one approached me, and I had a feeling it was because of what Dimitri had said: Knox's scent still lingered on my flesh, even though it should have expired by now.

I brought the glass to my lips, turning and pouring it out beside me before I set it back on the counter. Lore noticed and frowned, staring at me before he walked over, lifting the glass to his nose, before placing it back down.

"Someone wants you badly enough to dose you with

narcotics, but after watching you dance and knowing damn well you didn't leave one single dick limp in the place. I don't blame them for resulting to petty tricks," he uttered, dismissing me to move back to the nymph who gyrated and touched her breasts, unable to stop herself as sensual music filled the room.

I turned, silently taking in the bartender before staring at the cup that still held the narcotic's toxic scent. Knox's date was still grinding against him, yet his eyes didn't move from the dancefloor. The tick in his jaw beat slowly, yet it was visibly ticking away as his eyes remained on the spot I'd been dancing in. I wondered which sister he was watching since, apparently, it hadn't been me, after all. Either that, or he had been so stunned by my moves, he'd yet to be released from the trance. I wanted to go with the second option, but with my luck, it was the first.

Dismissing the dancers, I sat on the barstool until a growl erupted behind me. The hair on my neck rose, and I shivered at the sound. Slowly, I turned to find Fallon standing behind me; his teeth were bared while a loud growl reverberated from his chest in a challenge. Claws had extended from his hands, and the entire room had gone silent at the growling alpha and what it meant.

"I'm sorry, Aria, but I am the alpha, and you belong with me now."

"Don't do this, Fallon," I whispered as sweat trailed down my neck.

"You are mine!" Growling rose from his chest as he lunged at me without warning.

I dodged the attack, moving just barely in time to

escape his claws as I fell from the barstool and got back up to my feet while he prowled around me. My eyes slid to Knox, who smiled coldly, watching me without offering help.

Thanks, asshole.

The problem was, if I won this fight, Fallon would have to accept challenges from the other alphas in his pack. Losing a fight to a woman wasn't something they would look kindly on, and they would see it as a weakness.

"You can stop this still," I begged, knowing he wouldn't. He growled, lunging again, and I punched him hard. His head flew back as I moved around him, getting to the dance floor where I had more room to move. I was awkward in heels, but I also had no plans of going down to this bastard.

"You will give me strong sons, Aria. Every alpha here wants you, and you will be mine first before you are theirs."

"I was your son's friend, Fallon. Don't make me fight you."

"He's dead, and he is the reason why I am claiming you. I need strong heirs to hold my throne when I ascend. You will give them to me." He lunged again, and I backed up, skirting around him easily.

"I am a Hecate witch, I will only bare females," I reminded, but he hissed, showing his fangs in a move alpha wolves used to scare their females into submitting without a fight. A sane bitch would cave at the elongated teeth that could shred through flesh as easily as paper.

He attacked, and I once again moved out of the

way, hating that I wore heels, making it even more challenging to move as I dodged his attacks. Fallon's hand, sliced out, cutting through my arm, and I hissed as it burned, blood dripping down my shoulder until it slid off my fingers, hitting the floor. He smiled coldly, sensing he was winning.

I slowed my heartbeat, watching him through narrowed slits as he began to walk me in a wide circle, trying to get me to come closer so he could take another shot at me. He opened his arms, inviting me to make a move. I wasn't falling for it, but I could smell the other alphas closing in, waiting to see which of us prevailed.

It was a dance of dominance. If Fallon won, I'd be thrown onto the floor and raped by him, and after he'd finished mounting me, any alpha he found worthy could take me afterward, maybe even all the alphas. If I won, he'd be challenged for alpha and slaughtered by the ones who hadn't earned his throne outright; by his command, it was law.

He moved forward to grab me, and I lifted my foot, hiking it up into his nuts as hard as I could. When his face dropped, I threw an uppercut before dropping my body to a crouch, sweeping my leg out to dislodge his feet from beneath him. Fallon dropped to his stomach, and I launched myself onto him, landing on his back before I ripped the shirt away from his shoulder and sank my teeth into it as deep as I could, scraping against the bone. He bucked, refusing to submit even though he had to be in excruciating pain.

His howl filled the room, turning from angry to plaintive cries. My claws sank into his sides, demanding he submit to my bite as blood dripped from the wound around my mouth. I bit into his shoulder harder, pushing my razor-sharp claws deeper, snarling around the meat I had in my mouth. I rattled loudly, sensing the room as my power filled it while I held him down.

Fallon whined, whimpering as his hips started to pump against the floor violently. He succumbed to my demand to yield and submit. I smiled around the mouthful of flesh I had, relishing his submission as something within me preened and rattled loudly.

My eyes lifted from the floor, staring at the other alphas, who gazed at me in lust and something else. Intrigue? Intrigue that a female who wasn't an alpha wolf, because I'd taken theirs down, sealing his demise with the bite of one stronger than him. I rattled in warning against the other alphas testing me.

Watching them, Knox stood from his chair, pushing his date away as one of the alphas stepped toward me, pushing his hand into his pants, whining as he observed me. Fallon continued moving his hips against the floor, whining until the scent of semen filled the air, and I recoiled from what I had done, releasing his shoulder. I pushed away from him, staring at the mutilated shoulder that exposed the bone from where I'd ripped it apart.

CHAPTER
42

I stood up on shaky legs, watching as the other alpha wolves moved forward as a joined pack while Knox and his men moved to intervene. I rattled my chest violently, baring my bloodied mouth to them until they stepped back. Knox watched me, his gaze filling with something akin to dark lust as a smile curved his lips. His rattle echoed mine, and the pack turned, staring at him before sliding their gazes back to me. His eyes told me he'd known I wouldn't lose the fight, but he couldn't have known the outcome.

I stepped back, wiping the blood from my mouth as angry tears filled my eyes. I'd taken down the leader of the alpha pack, and I'd done it *easily*. I lifted my hands, staring at the claws that had pierced my fingers; they were razor-sharp and mirrored talons, and I had pushed them into Fallon's flesh like a hot blade cutting through butter. The rattle in my chest filled the room, echoing as Knox's sounded as if he sought to calm me.

Spinning around, I stared at my sisters, watching the

horror that played out on their faces as they took in my bloodied mouth and hands. I backed up slowly, staring at each one that gaped at me before stepping back as if they feared what I was. Mouths opened and closed as if they searched for something to say—but I didn't wait to hear the judgment or horror.

I started for the stairs, rushing from the room as the sound of alpha's tearing into Fallon filled the air. I felt on fire as if, at any moment, I'd erupt and implode. Wet screams tore through the room as I rushed out the doors into the cool evening air, not stopping until I was at the creek, diving into the water as everything within me erupted.

Beneath the water, I watched the bubbles rising as the water begun blistering around me. I didn't leave the depths until my lungs burned and forced me to the surface as a scream ripped from my lungs. My chest rattled with the screams, causing my entire body to tremble violently as if the thing within me felt my pain and cried out with me. I clapped my ears over the rattling noise that thumped up from my chest. It was violent, raw, and horrifying as it filled the night with my pain. I didn't stop until the trees felt the rattle from within me, staring at the moon as I shook in horror at what I was becoming. Steam rose around me, and a sob tore from my throat.

I was a monster.

I wasn't safe to be around my family.

I screamed until my lungs ached, and tears rolled down my face as sobs rocked through me. I slapped the water, hating everything that had happened since we'd come back to this town. My screaming ebbed, and I exhaled, sucking air into my burning lungs as tears slid down my cheeks.

My dress floated on the surface of the water that bubbled around me. I held my hair, closing my eyes as everything inside of me started to become too much to bear. I could still hear the alphas relishing the kill of one of their own. The howls of victory ignited, filling the night as they signaled Fallon had succumbed to another alpha who had claimed his position.

Rattling started around me, and I turned, finding Knox and his men watching as they set up a perimeter around me, and I wasn't sure if they did so for my protection, or for the safety of others. My sisters stood with my aunt, watching my mental breakdown playout.

Music started, and I turned, listening to Breaking Benjamin's *Ashes of Eden*. Luna stood on the balcony, staring down at me as she cradled her stomach with her hands. I shook my head as everyone remained silent. Water splashed, and I knew without looking that Knox had entered the creek and stood behind me, close enough that his power slid over my flesh.

If I moved, he would subdue me because he was something bigger than I was. I knew because I carried his mark on my flesh. I had felt it in the alphas' house, the beast within me had known right where he was through the entire fight. The entire night, I'd felt him on a deeper level than I could understand.

Someone rushed through the backyard, stopping at the edge of the water, and I lifted my gaze to Dimitri. His blue stare took in the sodden dress that clung to my curves, exposing the marking on my shoulder, where Knox had bitten me when I'd been incoherent, and a monster had been leading my body around.

"Are you okay?" Dimitri asked softly.

I didn't look away from him as he stood there, covered in blood and other body fluids from the wolf's celebration of their slaughtered alpha. It covered his mouth, along with his claws. My own claws had mirrored his, and yet I wasn't like him. I was something strong enough to subdue a high-born alpha.

The man who had dominated an entire pack of alphas violently had fallen to my fangs. I'd made him look weak like he was beneath me as he'd gyrated into the floor until he'd come on it from the intensity of my bite. My beast had made his submit in the most basic form. I'd violated him.

"Dimitri," I whispered through tears as I searched for the words I needed to say.

"He'd have raped you, Aria. He'd have thrown you down and taken you by force and then let us all have a turn when he'd finished with you. It's a tradition he ensured remained from the Nine Realms."

"I made him…" I couldn't say the words past the lump in my throat.

"You dominated him, and you saved yourself. No woman has ever dominated the head alpha, but you did tonight."

"You need to leave, little boy," Knox hissed behind me as his mouth brushed against my shoulder, touching his bite. Hatred dripping in his tone made a shiver race through me.

"I'll leave in a minute."

"You'll leave now. I am the King of Haven Falls and I just gave you a fucking order," Knox warned barely above a whisper, which was *definitely* a threat.

"You may be the king, but Aria isn't your queen, now is she?"

"Who is the new alpha?" I asked, interrupting them to end the argument.

"I am. You're not to be touched or hunted by the alpha pack, sweet girl. I have issued a warning for anyone stupid enough to try for you. Normally, you'd become a challenge we craved, but I forbid it tonight when I took the throne. I just wanted to be sure you were okay."

"I am," I said what he needed to hear, even though I was anything but okay.

"Leave, I won't ask again," Knox growled, and his men turned from their posts, waiting for the order to kill the new alpha.

I could see the intent in their posture. The way their heads tilted down, hiding the fangs I sensed had exploded from their gums. Knox grabbed me, pulling me against him as his lips brushed my shoulder, where his bite was no longer covered by the makeup I'd applied to conceal the mark.

"Aria," Dimitri whispered, watching me. "You know where to find me, and if you need me, just say it."

"She doesn't need you, mutt," Lore growled.

"I'm okay, Dimitri. Thank you for checking on me. I will be all right." He nodded his dark head, staring over my shoulder with a glare before he turned, moving through the yard.

No one moved, not until I turned and pushed Knox away from me. He hadn't prevented the fight from happening. He had known if Fallon had won, I'd have been legally his until he chose otherwise. Knox had let it play out and decided to place Fallon's death on my soul.

I glared at him, shaking my head. "Get away from me. I'm sure your date is waiting. Go enjoy her." I started back toward the bank.

"You wouldn't have lost to Fallon, Aria. You're stronger than he was."

"You don't know that!" I screamed, turning back toward him, and the water began to bubble around me.

His eyes dipped to the water before he turned to Aurora. "Take them inside now."

"No fucking way, she's our sister," Kinvara snapped.

"I concur, no fucking way," Sabine hissed.

"She's also experiencing an emotional overload, and we don't know what happens when it goes off. She'll be inside soon," he returned, watching me. "Aurora, please. Aria would never recover from murdering her sisters, even though it would be an accident. I won't hurt her."

"Like you could hurt her, she's fierce! Oh my God, Aria, you took down *the* alpha!" Kinvara cheered, and I swallowed down bile at the reminder.

"Yes, and now he's dead," I said in a deadpan tone.

She paused, staring at me with a deep furrow marring her forehead. "I'd see him dead a thousand times over before ever watching them throw you onto that floor and rape you. Do you understand me? He chose to fight you, and you gave him time to change his mind—he chose badly. That isn't on you."

"I know. But whatever I am becoming, I enjoyed emasculating Fallon for daring to think he could claim me without my permission, and I wanted to kill them all."

"You had fangs…or whatever they are, and your nails became claws. You kept your mind this time. You've got to see that's progress. But don't dare ask me to not celebrate you. You're my sister, and you just fucking mopped the floor with the alpha wolf, Aria. I don't care what you are because that doesn't change dick between us. We're here with you, always."

"I know," I repeated, and the water started to boil again. "But what if I *am* a monster? What if Amara realized what she was, and she left to protect us from what she was becoming?"

"Then she made a poor choice," Aurora stated. "We're Hecate witches, we don't fear our own. We don't reject them either. I have raised you from the moment you inhaled your first breath into your tiny lungs. I have raised you all to accept whatever comes, and whatever you become. You're my family, Aria. If Amara abandoned us, that's on her, not us. Now, everyone inside, right this minute. You don't hurt my girl, Knox."

"Wouldn't dream of it," he said, smiling as he watched her shake her head and move into the house.

I turned, staring at him, and he smirked devilishly,

shoving me beneath the water without warning, holding me down as I screamed and gasped for air. I scratched his hands, feeling my fingers transform into claws as I wrapped my hands around his wrists to remove them. I stared up at him, feeling the burn in my teeth, yet my fangs didn't come. The rattle within me grew, turning into a dangerous purr that sounded wrong.

"Come on, I'm right fucking here, Aria. Show me who you are. Fight me! You don't have the fucking balls to take me on, do you?" His gurgled words infuriated me.

Water began to boil faster, and he smiled, watching me closely. My mouth opened, and darkness blinked into my vision. My hands dropped from his, and he jerked me up.

"Bloody hell, breathe, woman! You're not fucking dying today."

"Bastard," I said, choking and spitting out copious amounts of water. Knox pulled me close, staring at my teeth, and then at my hands.

"Anger isn't the trigger to bring her beast out, nor is mortal danger."

"Oh, I assure you I am triggered, dick. Get your fucking hands off of me." I shoved him away from me, fixing my dress as he silently watched, soaked in his tux and expensive shoes.

"Leave us," he said over his shoulder, turning his eyes back to mine. He waited for the men to be out of hearing distance before he spoke again. "You kissed another male with my name on your flesh."

"And, so fucking what. I'm not yours, so what the

hell does it matter if I kiss someone else?" I demanded, watching him with a challenge burning in my depths.

"He'll be dead before the full moon next week."

"So…What? If I kiss someone else, they die? You don't even like me, remember? What was it you said I was…? Oh, yeah. I'm just a nasty whore who happens to be a *witch*. Or has that escaped your mind, Knox? I will fuck whoever the hell I want to fuck, and you can't say otherwise," I warned coldly, and he smirked, grabbing me and pushing me against the rock as his mouth brushed against mine, causing me to moan against him.

"I am the strongest asshole here, and my men and I are the only ones you cannot dominate, emasculate, or fucking devour. Do you understand that? I won't kill Dimitri, *you* will. That creature slumbering inside of you that terrifies you so much? It *should*. I went toe-to-toe with her, Aria. I didn't fucking lose, you did, but you fucking fought me so gloriously. That bite on your shoulder was me marking your creature, that way; your beast didn't forget who had been dominated between us, because it sure in the fuck wasn't me. That little boy wouldn't stand a chance against you. Your beast is bred to test men, and if she smells weakness in them, she will slaughter them without blinking or any hesitation. She chooses a mate based on three things. If he is strong enough to subdue her, the way he fucks her after he's managed to subdue, and his scent he oozes for her, marking him alpha enough to breed her needy cunt. You want that alpha puppy, little girl, go fucking get him." He released me, leaving the water as I watched him walking toward the shore.

I had to get out of here before I ended up killing everyone I loved. "Knox?" I whispered, following behind him as I hiked through the water in my ripped dress. My heels caught on a rock, and as I reached down to grab my shoe, I was yanked from the water and thrown back onto the ground. Knox grabbed the air, slicing through a creature effortlessly before he ripped the head from its body. I stared at it, slowly moving my eyes to the blackened claws that Knox's hands had become.

"Get inside, you're being hunted."

"What the hell was it?" I asked.

"A bounty hound from the Nine Realms," he said, crouching down to grab the note attached to the collar before standing back up. I struggled to my feet, fixing my gown again as he watched me. "They're given a scent to trace, and once they have it, they don't stop until they find it. Once they find it, they either attack to weaken their mark, leaving behind enough poison to render it too weak to hide, or they kill it."

"Which one would it have done to me?" I asked, and he stared at me crossly.

"I don't know. I didn't want to wait to see which one it chose before killing it."

I lifted my gaze to his and nodded slowly. I mean, I didn't want to be doggie chow either. I didn't move my gaze from his and still hadn't when he stepped closer, pinching my chin to lift my mouth to his. I pushed up on my toes, kissing him gently before he could change his mind. His mouth was soft, and yet he didn't kiss me back. He'd closed off, and now I looked needy.

"Thank you for not waiting to see if it killed me." I turned away, heading toward the house. He grabbed me, lifting me abruptly, threading his fingers through my hair to hold me still as his mouth crushed against mine. His tongue pushed against my lips, and I let him in, capturing his to duel against it. It was demanding, controlling, and all-consuming as he ravaged my mouth until my lungs burned for air.

He kissed me like he was waging war. A war neither of us would survive. His erection pushed against my apex, and I rocked my hips as my legs lifted to wrap around his waist. The purr started low in my chest, and he mirrored it, pulling away when it sounded from his chest in answer to mine. His eyes burned into mine and narrowed with confusion as he inhaled, fighting to get his breathing under control again.

"Don't piss me off again," he warned, letting me slide down his body slowly, feeling his erection, which started a need burning within me. "And the next time you dance like that, it better be for me, and you better not be wearing anything when you are. Go inside, Aria," he growled, pressing his forehead against mine briefly. "Stay the fuck away from the mutt, or he will die, either by your teeth or mine." He stepped back, turning on his heel as he left the property.

CHAPTER
43

It was days before I left the house, and when I did, it was only to the store and home. I would clean the store, polishing the crystals before decorating the shelves. I bundled sage, preparing smudge sticks and other herbs for use and spells. Everything was slowly moving on without Amara. She'd vanished without a trace, and there was nothing we could do to change it. I was walking back to my car when I noticed a note on my windshield, tucked beneath the wiper blade. I picked it up, looking around me before unfolding it.

I know you don't understand what is happening, Aria. The realms aren't what you think they are. You don't belong in the Human Realm; we're so much more than anything it could ever contain. I have taken steps to ensure your future is...fulfilled in every way you deserve it to be. Remember the old oak tree we used to pretend was white oak stolen from Norvalla? Meet me there on Sunday, and I will tell you everything. Time isn't something we have the luxury of waiting on, as your new life here awaits you. I promise it is everything you deserve in life, prickly twin. ~A

I folded the note and looked around, narrowing my gaze on the area. I exhaled, watching as Kinvara skipped toward the car while staring at her phone. One of these days, she'd end up hit by a car for not paying attention.

"Kinvara, look around before you walk into the parking lot. People actually want to hit you."

"It was one guy who said he was single. He lied about his situation." She shrugged. "She's better off without the cheating prick."

"Still, if you looked up, you may see her car coming before she hits you. I got a note," I announced, slipping behind the wheel before I checked the mirror while I waited for her to climb into the passenger seat.

"Love letter?"

I rolled my eyes. "Did you hear that? It's my eyeballs ringing that bell at the way back in my head, jerk. It's from Amara."

She gasped as I handed it to her and waited for her to read it. I waited and waited, and she had to have read the damn thing several times before she handed it back to me. I pushed the note into the center console and gazed into the mirror.

"That truck's been following us since we left the shop," I muttered, turning onto a random street, and watching as it turned with us.

I turned several more times, and Kinvara called the house to inform them of the situation as I started toward it with my foot on the gas. She chuckled, and I didn't look away from the road.

"What the hell is so funny?"

"It's Tamryn," she said, and I slowed down, peering at the driver before pulling off of the road. "That asshole, whose truck is she driving?" I questioned, watching my sister peel her tiny frame from the oversized truck.

Tamryn was ethereal and beautiful. She had platinum-colored hair that shined like diamonds in the sun's early morning light, and I wasn't jealous at all. Big, perky breasts bounced as she made her way to the car while her tiny hips swayed. Tamryn was full of fire, but it hid the pain she had been through. Losing the love of her life to cancer was brutal. We'd all watched his decline with sadness since he refused to allow us to help him.

He'd refused to be changed into an undead creature, or use the potions that would hold off the inevitable. He'd been brave and strong during his fight. Tamryn had been falling apart, but she never cried or broke down, not until he'd taken his last breath on this earth. Now she was reborn through the fire and pain she'd endured, and was still beautiful, maybe even more so because of what she'd been through.

"You trying to lose me?" She leaned against the window, glaring at us as her full lips twisted into a naughty grin.

"Are you trying to scare us to death?" Kinvara flipped her off before she leaned over me, squishing me to hug Tamryn over my lap.

"Get off of me, you asshat. Are you home for a while this time, or just passing through?" I watched as she stepped back and allowed me to open the door to exit the car to hug her properly.

"You bet your pretty titties I'm back. God damn, I have missed you girls something fierce, that and I heard we got trouble brewing. I also wouldn't miss being here for Luna and her new little ones for the world. Besides, I will be the best aunt they've ever known." Tamryn shrugged, smirking at me, and I stepped back.

"She has a lot of aunts, and most of us assume we will be the favorite." I shrugged as I held my hands up, leaning back against the car as she joined me. "I think that will be one fight where we will have to actually try to win. I'm glad you're home, Tamryn, you've been horribly missed around here."

"I missed you too, asshole."

"Try not to create too much of a scene, there's chaos playing out."

"Reign told me some badass bitch took down the alpha wolf this week. You wouldn't know where I could find her? I hear she's a beautiful badass who is about to set the world on fire, maybe even literally." She smiled, leaning against my shoulder before lifting her gaze to look at me with pride shining in her eyes.

"Fallon was slaughtered because of me."

"Fuck Fallon, he chose his death by choosing to hurt one of our bloodline. He tried to dominate you by force, he lost, and it is as simple as that. I'd say the prick got what he was asking for."

"Yeah, well, the entire House of Alpha is being rebuilt from the inside out. They'd been keeping us up all night while celebrating their crowning of a new king of the pack. Fallon's head has been placed on a spike outside the main house. There are screams that never end coming from within that mansion, and they don't ever seem to stop."

"Interesting, but it doesn't change the facts, sister mine, and you seem to think that if you hadn't taken him down, he'd still have that head on his shoulders? He grew sloppy, Aria. He was also very aware that you were an alpha by nature, which was apparent even before shit started getting twisted. He made a choice, and that choice cost him his head. That isn't something you can take the blame for. You want to feel guilty, fine, but even if it hadn't been you, he'd have died eventually. Now, I seem to be unable to remember the way home, so I'll follow you unless it's going to freak you out again."

I shook my head, uncertain I bought her reasoning. Fallon was brutal in his reign. He didn't fuck around, and if an alpha started acting out, he was sent back into the Nine Realms. He'd ruled for the last fifty years with an iron fist. While I shouldn't be upset about them murdering him for being taken down by me, I wasn't particularly normal. I'd enjoyed pinning him, the motion his hips made when I'd subdued him by force had something inside of me aching to do it again. It terrified me and left me numb. Knox had said that I could go get Dimitri if I wanted him, but the idea of doing that to him horrified me.

"Hey, you still with us, asshole?" Tamryn asked, snorting as she snapped her finger in front of my face.

"Get in the truck, Tamryn. I'll race you home."

"I don't know the way!"

"I'm aware and okay with cheating."

"Jerk."

"Bitch," I smirked.

"Fuckers, get in!" Kinvara snorted as her eyes rolled.

I watched her climb back into the truck before I slipped into the car and started toward home. The moment we got to the long winding hills that took us deep into the original family's mansions, I slowed as children became visible on the sidewalks. It was a rare sight to see the little ones outside, even when everything was right in the world, and right now, it wasn't right. It was all wrong.

"You know Tamryn came home because you need her, but also because Amara is missing. We gather when one of our own is in need, we always have since we were children."

"I know, and I love her for it, but she's also not fully healed from her husband dying."

"Technically, they were only married as humans and not mates."

"It's the same thing, Kinvara. The only difference is that our people wouldn't acknowledge the union. I don't think Tamryn cared since he was mortal. Love is love, and who are we to say differently? It broke her when he died, and she's finally coming back, and the end result is a new woman, born of chaos and remade from the ashes. Let's hope that if we ever live through that, we're half the woman she has become."

I pulled up into the driveway and moved to the trunk, pulling out a box of crystals that Aurora had asked me to bring home. Screaming sounded from across the block where Dimitri had been throwing one hell of a party for days now.

I hadn't seen more than a few glimpses of him since he'd checked on me. Knox had been radio silent. His house was dark, and little to no activity had come from it since the night of the party.

It had been days, and everyone had held their breath as the alphas returned some resemblance of normalcy to their house. I exhaled and moved to the front door, shutting the world out.

Later that night, I stood on the balcony, watching the House of Alphas as women were being escorted out. Car engines revved up as they'd pulled up to line the street. It was an endless stream of women, some in their early thirties, others younger. Each of them looked abused and exhausted. Some were half-naked, their bodies bearing claw marks or bite marks on their thighs and arms, still bleeding. I could smell the sex covering their flesh from the porch, and it made my stomach recoil with bile. Some hadn't even put more than a shirt on before being pushed out of the house.

Shinedown's *Monster* played quietly from inside my room while I watched the horror unfolding in front of our house. I'd turned it up to block out the endless screams that offered little relief to the debauchery coming from their house.

Women had screamed in pleasure or pain, sometimes both. Men had howled endlessly, sending chills racing down my spine as more had joined in as if it was one long orgy they shared in together. They celebrated in tradition, giving the alpha a sense of victory while they moved pieces around for the newly crowned king to take his throne.

I watched as Dimitri followed behind the women, hanging close to one of the cleaner females, shoving her to her knees in the dirty street. My heart raced as she looked up at Dimitri, watching him with hunger in her eyes. He moved his body until she became obscured by his larger frame. His hips pumped, and my body flushed with need. His hand rested against the car as he fucked her mouth, her moans loud enough that I could hear them from where I stood. It was horrifying, and yet my libido didn't seem to care, responding even though I was disgusted by the action.

"They're Fallon's women," Aine stated, settling next to me in her nightgown as she leaned over, watching Dimitri as he fucked the woman's mouth. "Tradition states they are fucked until it appeases the men, and all alphas are well sated. Had you not killed Fallon, it would have been you they fucked without care of your needs. As the alpha to the House of Alphas, Dimitri has to fuck each one of them first. They're then given to the others, who will rip them apart if the need strikes. It is brutal, and without a male claiming a female as his mate, it is still legal."

"There are over fifty women down there."

"Which is another sign of weakness for Fallon," she snorted, speaking softly. "An alpha will keep enough bitches on hand, so more than one is always in heat to carry his offspring. The alpha in charge fucks them for days, and if they don't breed his seed, they are then given to the others to see if her womb will accept another's child. If she cannot be bred, she is abandoned or murdered because she carries no use for them at that point. They're vile creatures, Aria. It's why I am here and not with them. They breed and feed, and don't always care what happens to the woman, nor are they treasured once they become pregnant. A true alpha will not collect a child, not until it becomes useful to him."

I studied the speed and motion of Dimitri's hips as he pumped his cock into her mouth. He growled and then grunted, slowing as he threw back his head and howled into the night. She slowly stood up, grasping his shirt as he pushed her into one of the vehicles, turning to stare up at me where I watched him. His hand came up to run over his mouth as he found me watching him with her.

A shadow moved in the street, and I followed it, watching as Knox stopped next to Dimitri, handing him a suitcase. Dimitri opened it, and I frowned, seeing stacks of cash.

"Well, that explains them leaving." Aine leaned against the rail, watching the shit unfolding before us.

Knox's eyes lifted to mine, holding them briefly before turning back to the girl who had jumped out of the car, holding on to Dimitri, creating a scene. Dimitri pushed her softly away from him, but she sobbed and spoke low, inaudibly.

"What do you mean?" I refused to take my eyes from Knox, who had dismissed me and was walking away from the chaotic scene in silence.

"As the top wolf, he is entitled to their lives. He can either slaughter them or breed them. It's unheard of for an alpha to release the breeding mates. I assume Knox paid Dimitri to release the women. Knox just saved their lives, yet he had no reason to do it since they are all wolves and cannot mate with him."

"Dimitri may have kept the women to mate with. Knox, though, why would he buy wolves? Not unless he is one, maybe a hybrid of some type?"

"It's worse when they do keep them to breed. The women go from being cherished to the lowest member within the household. They'd be nothing but a cunt to fuck, and a womb to fill. They'd be given scraps to eat, and more than likely, they'd waste away. It's brutal, but they knew there was a chance when they agreed to be with the alpha as his breeding mates. Also, I don't think Knox is any type of wolf, sweetie. I think he's something you and I have never seen or dealt with before."

A car door slammed, and I peered down, watching Dimitri as he started for our house. Swallowing hard, I watched until he stood at the protective barrier, staring up at me.

"You're being summoned," Aine said. "Guess that mouth didn't scratch his itch. If I was you, I'd keep my distance."

"It isn't like that."

"He kissed you on the dancefloor, Aria. He was adding his scent to you when Fallon called him over and demanded as alpha that he stay away from you. It wasn't by his choice he left you there. Dimitri found you the moment he'd removed the alpha's head. He had planned to fuck you, and he was denied in a big way. I assure you, as a wolf, we don't enjoy losing a mark. If he craved you, it hasn't lessened yet, and it won't until he has you beneath him. My suggestion? Don't get beneath him, because he intends to claim you and whatever you are. I don't think you can be claimed by one of our kind. I don't want to deal with another king being crowned in this lifetime. I miss sleep, do try not to kill him."

"That can't happen, and I miss sleep too." I left Aine standing on the balcony to head downstairs to meet Dimitri.

Stepping through the door, I made my way to where he stood, tracking me, watching the sway of my hips in the thin camisole top and tight boy-cut shorts I wore. I stopped in front of him, sucking my lip between my teeth as I noted the dilatation of his pupils. The pheromones he exuded slammed against my senses, but the stale stench of women did as well, and I recoiled physically. He smelled of sex with multiple partners; their scent still clung to him, which caused me to pause and step back further.

"You enjoy the show?"

"I was watching the women exiting the house in curiosity." I folded my arms over my chest and studied the way he walked impatiently in front of me.

"I imagined she was you on your knees, and then I smelled you, and there you were, watching me fuck her mouth."

"Ahh, well," I stammered. "That is…blunt and not awkward at all, Dimitri," I muttered uneasily, staring at the way he prowled. There was also the way his pupils were fully dilated. It wasn't a normal gaze; it was that of a predator, staring down something it wanted to devour.

"You don't play with words, so why the fuck should I?"

"Listen…" I started, but he grabbed me, pulling me against his body.

"No. You listen, Aria. I have thought of nothing else but you since I kissed you. As alpha, my duty is to my pack, yet I forbid any of them from hunting you down to claim you. You are what we call a trophy bitch. You're an alpha female with the capabilities to take down another alpha, which causes us excitement at the idea of claiming you and fighting you for your submission. The moment I gave that order, I slaughtered three alphas who argued it. I fucked every one of those females, and you were the woman I wished I was inside of the entire time. I crave you," he growled, brushing his mouth against mine as I turned my head to deflect the kiss.

I shoved him away and rattled in warning as anger spiked through me. I stepped back into the protective barrier, and he watched me silently as his nostrils flared with rage. He began pacing in front of me, clenching and unclenching his fists as he stared me down.

"Stop this shit—and you fucked them thinking about me? How fucking flattering. Go home, Dimitri."

"I am the alpha!"

"You're not *my* alpha!" I watched as he stopped, staring at me as his nostrils flared with his anger. "You don't own me, and I won't be one of your whores, Dimitri. I am worth more than that. You chose to claim the kill; you chose to become the alpha, fucking deal with it. You don't get to have me because you demand it. I'm not one of your fucking bitches that you can mount at will, remember that because it might save your fucking life."

"No, I am not your alpha *yet*. You reek of Knox. You let that monstrous beast fuck you, and yet you won't allow me to even kiss you? I can smell his claiming scent over every part of you, even those pretty red lips, Aria. He's tasted every part of you, and then he threw you away like last night's leftovers. I wouldn't do that to you."

"It isn't like that, Dimitri. I am unsafe. Do you understand me? Whatever sleeps within me wants to fight for dominance, not of me, but of anyone who tries to subdue me. You wouldn't win, and I cannot live with your death. I'm not a wolf. I couldn't be one of your breeders, and you will be forced to breed with many women they bring home to you. It is expected from you as the alpha to basically have an entire harem of bitches waiting to be bred. I couldn't accept that. I wouldn't, I am worth more. Your traditions are barbaric and unfair. I'd want you to myself."

"You'd have me, at least for now."

"I'm not the girl who does one-night stands, wolf. I won't just fuck because I have the itch to get fucked. I am not an average witch. I'm a forever girl, Dimitri. I'd want you, and to be the only one who you bred. You can't give that to me. It isn't something you can ever promise me, and it doesn't matter, because my beast would slaughter yours. The entire conversation is pointless, don't you see that?"

"I'm changing the laws for the pack. I'm working on it." He lifted his hand to cup my cheek, but I jerked away from him. "I have to sire sons, though."

"And I can only give you daughters."

He smiled sadly, staring at me before he exhaled. "Just because you're a Hecate witch doesn't mean your other half isn't more dominant. You could surprise us more than you already have and bring boys into your line." He stared at me for a moment longer before he moved away, heading back to the House of Alphas.

"Dimitri," I called, watching as he turned around. "Turn down the noise in your house. Some of us need rest."

His arms lifted in the air, and he howled, causing the men in the house to howl back. Dick. I would never get an entire eight uninterrupted hours of sleep. I turned, staring at Knox, who waited in the shadows, watching me through narrowed slits. I lifted my fingers to my lips, blowing him a kiss as he watched me. My heart raced at the sight of him, and then he melted into the shadows, and I frowned, wondering if he'd overheard anything we'd said. With my luck, he'd heard it all.

CHAPTER
44

Screaming woke me from a dead sleep. I stared at the alarm clock on my nightstand, sitting up in bed. I was covered in a subtle sheen of sweat as I slipped on the silk robe that stuck to my flesh and started toward the screaming. My sisters stood outside Luna's door, and I frowned as I pushed through, finding her bed covered in blood as she shrieked in pain, her legs red from the blood gushing out of her.

"We need a healer or a doctor. Aria, go to Knox and ask for his healer, now," Aurora cried, staring at me before Luna howled in pain again.

"Shouldn't we get the alpha's healer?"

"Get Knox's healer now, he is skilled in all breeds!" she snapped, and I turned, running through the house until my feet touched concrete as I barreled toward the dark mansion on the corner.

I pushed the intercom button on Knox's gate and waited, pushing it several more times before Greer hissed into the speaker in a strained voice.

"Yes?"

"Greer, I need Knox. We need help," I demanded, watching the gate slowly open as I slipped through, running toward the house. At the door, I paused until Greer opened it, fixing his robe to glare at me.

"Do you realize the time, peasant?"

"Not now, Greer. I need a healer." Power slithered over my flesh as the scent of a carnal male slammed against me. My gaze moved to the staircase as Knox slowly walked down, shirtless and covered in sweat that made his flesh glisten in the light of the chandelier. His hair was a mess. It was a mussed mess that my fingers itched to run through, and even though my brain reminded me of why I was here, my hormones or something deeper wanted him.

"I need a healer, please."

"For?"

"Luna, something is wrong with the babes, and she's bleeding out." He stared at me as if he was considering telling me to get out, and I shook my head as the plea left my lips. "Knox, please."

"Greer, go disturb Brander and his newest bed companion and tell him it's an emergency." Knox's voice was filled with sleep, raspy, and it slipped around every nerve in my body.

I closed my senses off and began pacing aimlessly in the entrance hallway. Knox vanished and then returned, pulling a shirt on as he made his way to where I stood. He stopped beside me, watching me as my hands balled into fists and then released them repeatedly. My feet tracked dirt over his pristine floor, and I didn't stop until he grabbed me, placing his hands on my shoulders as Brander came into the hall naked, swinging a massive sword between his legs. My eyebrows shot up in shock, and Knox growled from deep in his chest.

"Get your dick covered and grab your medical bag. Luna is experiencing difficulties in her pregnancy." Knox didn't ask for details, Brander did.

"How many months along is she?" he asked, uncaring that I was staring at his overly large weapon. "Aria, fucking focus, how many months along is Luna?" I shook my head, dispelling the raw need that was playing hell inside of me.

"I think four months or so, she got pregnant the first week we got back into town, or so we assume. She's part alpha wolf, and she took a male the first night we got here behind the store. I don't know for sure, but there is so much blood. It's all over the bed, and she's just screaming and howling. I don't know what to do to stop the bleeding."

He turned to Knox, staring at him as if he couldn't believe he was helping us. "I'll get my stuff."

"Calm down and shut your hormones off, woman." My eyes slipped to Knox's heated stare, and I shook my head while fighting the rattle that escaped my lips. His chest rattled, and my hands pushed through my hair as my head rolled, stretching to alleviate the heat it created.

"I feel like my skin is crawling, and everything is falling apart around me. My body is perpetually soaked from sweat, Knox. I can't shut it off, it's stifling. It's like I'm in heat, yet I know I'm not. So tell me, how do I fix it?"

"Listen to your body's needs before you end up burning the entire town down, Aria."

"That isn't happening, considering I would probably murder someone and end up fucking a corpse. Dead bodies are a huge no-no around here."

"You wouldn't kill me." He crossed his arms, staring me down.

"I'm fine."

"Keep telling yourself that."

"Let's fucking do this," Brander said, interrupting us.

My hands pushed through my hair as I internally screamed in frustration, following Brander out of the mansion, and started finally toward my house. I was acutely aware of Knox following us and didn't want to waste time arguing it. We entered the house to a room full of worried faces.

"Brander is the doctor? I thought he was the electrician?" Aine's hair was a mess from pulling it out as her twin screamed endlessly in pain. I shrugged, uncertain if he actually was. He seemed to be a jack of all trades.

A howl sounded from upstairs, and I moved toward it while Brander issued orders. I didn't stop running up the stairs until I reached the bedroom and threw the door open, gasping at the sheer volume of blood she was losing. I left the room, grabbing my phone to call the vampires to get blood to heal her.

Kerrigan Montgomery answered on the first ring and listened as I spoke. "Five spells for one bag," he negotiated. Greedy fucking bloodsuckers.

"Done—we need it now," I stated, hanging up before moving back to the room. "Vampires are sending blood." Brander looked up from where he stood beside Luna with a thankful look in his eyes.

"Good, we'll need it. Luna will lose the babes without it."

I nodded, stepping out of the room to lean against the wall, sliding down it silently while I pulled my knees against my chest and exhaled. Someone settled beside me, and I turned, staring into oceanic eyes.

"You cannot be running down the block half-naked, woman."

"This isn't about me."

"You have bounty hounds tracking you by scent, and you're covered in sweat; it *is* about you. You're not safe; next time, send someone else, Aria. Ignore my warning, and I will put you over my knee and spank your pretty little ass."

"Is that supposed to be an incentive or a deterrent?" I asked huskily, and his eyes dipped to my lips before they slowly rose, locking with mine. I frowned, realizing what I had said. "I can't believe I just said that." I shook off whatever the hell was happening to me.

Screaming erupted, and Aurora stepped out of the room, staring at us where we waited for her to speak. I wanted to clamp my hands over my ears and pretend my sister wasn't inside that room, screaming in pain as Luna lost her babies. I wasn't stupid; they were too tiny to live.

"I have to go get the blood." Aurora moved down the hallway with her shoulders slumped in defeat, and sadness washed over me with what she hadn't told us.

"Luna carries boys. Fuck." I wrapped my arms around my legs to lean my head against it.

"I need help in here!" At Brander's demand, I turned to look at Knox, who had a haunted look in his eyes as he stared at the wall opposite of us. I frowned, standing, and moving into the room. "You need to help me deliver the babes. If they're viable, they will need help breathing until the blood arrives."

"They won't be viable, save Luna."

"You don't fucking know that!" Luna cried.

"They're boys, Luna." I fought the tears that burned my eyes as she began to scream and wail against my words.

"No! No, they're not. We don't make boys!"

"No, Luna. We don't give birth to boys. We lose them before they can sustain life outside our bodies. Hecate witches don't birth boys; we lose them because of the curse which refuses to allow us to bring them into the world alive. I'm so sorry, honey." I ignored Brander, who glared at me as if I was being an insensitive asshole.

She pushed for what felt like hours, and I held her hand as she screamed and bore down with each contraction until the first son was born. I accepted his limp body, staring at the faceless creature as tears slipped free of the hold I'd held on them. Grabbing a blanket, I wrapped him in it as Brander stared at the lifeless boy.

"It doesn't have a face." Brander's tone held horror, and worse, accusation as if we had agreed to be cursed, when in fact, we were born with it.

"It's the curse. It ensures no male is born to the line, though I didn't realize this is what it meant."

He sat back down, delivering the second babe, and I took him too, placing him on the bed with his brother beside their mother. Once I'd wrapped both of them, I cradled them in my arms and lifted my gaze to their mother, finding Luna staring at the wall.

"Luna, they're here."

"Get them away from me now." She stared at the wall with tears in her eyes, shrugging me off as I held her stillborn sons.

"Luna, say goodbye to your sons," I encouraged.

"I said, get them away from me and get Aine in here, you stupid bitch!" I recoiled from her words, nodding my head as I moved out of the room and down the stairs.

I placed the babes in the kitchen on a towel that was freshly laundered and went to tell the others they'd been born male and dead. Once I'd made the sad announcement, I started to cleanse them for their burial.

Silently, I turned on the water as my shoulders shook with silent sobs. Checking that it was lukewarm, I grabbed the smallest of the smaller of the boys. Removing the cloth from his tiny body, I began washing the birthing matter and blood away from his skin. I was careful as I cleaned him, wrapping him in the shroud for burial once I'd finished. I repeated the action with the second child, listening as Luna sobbed above me.

Once they were both wrapped and ready for the altar to bless them into the next life, and hopefully not to be reborn into our line, I leaned over the counter, whispering a prayer for the strength to walk their tiny bodies to the altar alone.

Our bloodline buried our boys, but none of us had ever given birth until now. We'd heard it had happened before, especially to our mother. We'd never been witness to it, nor felt the emotional loss until now. After I'd moved the small bodies into the herb room where sage burned endlessly, I went back and leaned against the counter to clean the mess.

I felt him behind me, yet he said nothing as my shoulders rocked with silent sobs trembling through me. He didn't move, just stood there, offering me comfort as I prayed for strength. I exhaled, closing my eyes, and a sob pushed against my throat even as I swallowed it down.

"Breathe." Knox's mouth brushed against my shoulder, his teeth skimming over his mark, calming me instantly. "Just breathe, Aria."

"How do you do that to me, Knox? You touch me, and everything fades to black; even in the darkest of times, you can take it all away. How do you make everything fade to background noise?" I fought against the purr that built in my chest, but it exploded in a loud wave. I felt him smiling against my flesh, but he pulled away as a purr sounded from deep within him as well, as if his beast answered mine on a level I couldn't understand.

"It's not me; it's the bite that calms you. Whatever is within you, it's strong, and it has a profound reaction to what you feel. It's what a female wolf feels when the alpha touches her with his teeth. Anyone could do it for you, as long as they're strong enough to survive your beast."

"I'm not a wolf, though, so am I like you? What are you?" I spun around, looking up at him for answers.

"Are the boys always born dead?" he asked, swiftly changing the subject.

"From what I read, Hecate cursed us to only breed females. It was written in a strange language, and the spell I used to decipher it wasn't one hundred percent correct. It stated that boys will be delivered dead and then sent to the afterlife to be looked after by her. I had no idea that they were born with no facial features. It isn't fair to the babes or the mother," I uttered, watching as a tick began in his jaw.

"You just allow the curse to continue when Hecate isn't here to ensure it does?"

"It's not a curse that can be broken easily. It calls for the sacrifices of virgins, and the death of Hecate witches, whether watered down or not, it's still too many lives to take for one curse. That's not something we can just run out and collect, Knox."

He stared at the tiny shrouded bodies and then lifted dark eyes to me. "And you? You just wrap them up to throw them away?"

"Is that what you think I am doing?" I asked as he turned his head back to look at me, prowling toward me.

"I think your entire bloodline is a bunch of murderous

bitches that care little what they do to the innocent lives affected because of your actions." His fangs extended into rows of razor-sharp teeth, and I closed my eyes before opening them again as he boxed me in against the counter. "I think you are all alike and should pay for the innocent lives you and your kind extinguish as if it is your fucking right to do so."

I nodded, closing my eyes as my heart raced with fear. "I am wrapping them into a blessing cloth. It is also soaked with sacred oils to link them to another bloodline to ensure that they are never reborn to us or any females in our line. I will then place their tiny bodies on an altar and beg another god to take them from us. That is the only thing I can do for their little souls, Knox. I cannot break the curse, nor do I have the power of the goddess who cast it upon us to even try. Get out of my way so I can prepare them for when their grieving mother is ready, so that we may send them to their next life to be reborn to a mother who can carry their tiny souls to full-term and love them."

Opening my eyes, I started as he lowered his mouth against my throat. My hands lifted, pushing through his thick hair as I held him closer. If he was going to murder me, he needed to get it over with. Teeth touched my throat, and a single droplet of blood ran down my neck, and my mouth brushed against his ear as his hands wrapped around my waist to hold me there.

A cough sounded behind us, and Knox inched back, but he waited for his fangs to rescind before he turned, staring over his shoulder at Reign, who was trespassing against whatever was happening to him. There was a lethal look in his eyes, and the smell of overwhelming pain confused me as he slowly turned back, watching me before he slowly lowered his mouth to my throat, licking the blood he'd drawn.

"I'm all for taking it where you can get it, but this isn't the place or time to be fucking." Reign said, her voice thick with emotion. "Are the babes prepared?" I nodded. "If you just nodded, I can't see your head, asshole."

"I need a moment to finish."

"Finish what?"

"Reign, please. They're almost ready."

"Luna doesn't want to be present. She wants them gone. Brander said she is in shock and mixed with blood loss, she won't be out of the woods in time to bless them into the afterlife."

"Okay," I said, still being held in place by Knox, who breathed heavily against my throat, but it wasn't from lust, it was hatred. The moment she was away from us, I exhaled a shuddered breath and waited for him to move away from me. He didn't. Instead, he turned black eyes in my direction that were banked with flecks of red, as if a fire burned within him.

"I get that you hate us, Knox. I don't understand why or what we did to you, but you need to stay away from me. You confuse and disorientate me. I think you do it on purpose. I think you intend to hurt me, and you terrify me. I need you to stay away so that I can fight this need to be with you, please."

He smiled, threading his fingers through my hair before he pulled my ear to his lip. "I don't care what you want, Aria. You should be afraid. You should be very afraid of what I want from you." His nose brushed against the rapid pulse in my throat before he backed up, staring at me through black eyes that had filled with embers.

"You should go now." I entered the herb room and picked up the tiny bodies, moving out of the room to find him blocking my path. Silent tears slipped down my cheeks as he spoke.

"Aurora told me about the note. I want to know who put it on your car, and how the fuck you missed them doing so." His eyes dropped the swaddled bodies cradled in my arms, and he frowned. "This isn't finished."

"Oh, it's so finished," I countered, moving past him to take the bodies to the altar. Outside, the alphas lined the street, sensing the birth of a male wolf. I exhaled as my eyes captured Dimitri's, and he swallowed hard as he took in the tiny bodies I carried. His dark head bowed until Knox left the house behind me, following me to the altar.

I carefully placed the babes on the stone slab, igniting the candles the moment they touched it, lighting the crystals all around the yard. I felt the moment the connection to the afterlife opened, and stepped back, bumping into Knox.

"You need to get out of the yard," I whispered. "Leave, Knox."

"No," he growled, slipping arms around me as he pulled me against his chest. He didn't stop there; he continued backing up away from the altar as my sisters came out with sage and other things, each one playing a part to send the boys to a new mother. "What are they doing?"

"Blessing the babies, to give them strength for their journey to a new mother," I whispered softly. "The sage will cleanse the negative energy from the birth. The crystals keep anyone wishing to harm them away, or any sprits who think to intervene. Too bad it doesn't erase whatever you are too, or at the very least, repel you."

"It soaked your cunt at the idea of my teeth claiming your throat; that's dangerous, Aria."

"Knox?" I whispered huskily.

"Aria?"

"It's a funeral, behave."

He turned, and I didn't need to look to see he was staring at Dimitri with a triumphant glare. He purred, and I mirrored it, unable to stop it from escaping. I could feel both sets of eyes on me, and I stood silently, watching my family as they added herbs and flowers around the altar until rainbow-colored stones and flowers were laid out on the ground.

"What are they doing now?" Knox asked again, and I turned my head, whispering against his cheek.

"They're blessing the gods who we don't worship. It's the best chance the boys have at escaping our bloodline. Next, they will sing and then dance around the altar as they aim to please the gods to accept the male offspring, allowing them to escape the curse."

"You're not dancing," he pointed out.

"My magic isn't like theirs. Mine is something else, and we don't want it to influence blessing spells."

"I like to watch you dance," he rasped against my shoulder, and my chest rumbled with a purr. "How do they know if another god accepts the boys?"

"We don't, but we pray that they're never cursed to be carried in our deadly wombs again. You weren't even watching me dance, prick."

"The fuck I wasn't," he chuckled darkly.

"Oh."

"You danced to show me everything I couldn't have. You forgot one small thing, Aria. You're mine, whether you like it or not. I claimed you and that can't be undone unless I decide to allow it. Plus, your beast chose me too. I marked her too, which means you're both mine."

"We apparently have horrible taste in men," I whispered as candles burned in the wind while my sisters moved in a graceful dance that was raw with power. Tears slipped from my eyes, and his mouth kissed my shoulder, calming the struggle within me. Sweat beaded on my brow as my body sagged against his body with need. I'd been fighting my body's needs for days, and I was fully aware that I was losing the battle. Especially with close proximity and scent filling my senses, making the needs impossible to ignore.

"Careful, Aria," he warned thickly.

"I don't like what I am becoming." Admitting it was dangerous, considering I was sure the beast within me understood everything I said.

"That's because you're fighting the change. Stop fighting the inevitable and let it happen. It's evolution, and it's beautiful. You're beautiful in both forms, and you're not a monster. You're a queen among beasts since most women in the Nine Realms cannot even take their beast form and show no physical attributes of what they truly are. You, Aria, you have fangs and claws. Most females are created to be bred, but you, you were created for war. Embrace it, little lamb."

"It's easy for you to say. I don't even know what I am, so how am I supposed to accept it? What if what I am doesn't belong in this realm? What if I hurt someone?"

"What if suppressing it does more damage?" he countered, kissing my shoulder.

"If you keep kissing me, I'm going to end up needing to go change."

"Change what?" he chuckled huskily, but the vibration of his lips against my flesh made my back arch, and my core released molten need.

"My panties."

"Behave, woman. We're at a funeral," he swallowed a growl as his chest trembled. His hands yanked me back, holding me against his cock, which was resting on my lower back. "Fucking hell."

"I agree, we're being very inappropriate right now."

"You need to go inside, because in a moment, I'm going to leave, and you will be exposed, with the scent of your arousal thick in the air. Walk, Aria." He moved me toward the house without releasing me. I could feel the eyes of the alphas on me as we passed them and stopped on the porch. "Go bathe now."

"Knox," I whispered. "Whatever happened to you, I hope you find peace from the demons that haunt you."

"Don't talk to me about fucking demons, woman.

You can't even imagine the ones I house." I watched as he moved into the street, pushing his shoulder into Dimitri as he walked past him on his way home, itching for a fight.

CHAPTER
45

It was a tense week before Luna finally started to recover, and no matter what we did, she still refused to come out of the shell she'd become. Aurora had tried everything, including figuring out who the father was to see if his breed might have played a part in creating male offspring.

No one breathed until Luna had finally eaten. Brander said she would recover from the heartbreak of losing the babes, but it would take time. The last few days had changed for the worst, and she'd become crazed and violent, mostly against me, which we assumed was because unlike the others, I was stuck in the house until we figured out who was trying to get to me.

Death wasn't something we had ever dealt with before. People in our line didn't die. It was a blessing we hadn't realized until we'd stood there, chanting to send the souls of Luna's infant sons into a new life. It was surreal. The alphas stood silent sentinels, watching and protecting the babes until flames had consumed them. The moment the babies' souls crossed over, they'd turned on their heels, going back to the House of Alpha, all except Dimitri, who waited for me to turn, to see the anger burning in his eyes.

Knox's hand had slipped to my back, and he'd walked me to the house, leaving me at the door to walk directly in front of Dimitri, where he stood in the road, following us, taunting him openly with my scent on Knox. They'd both turned to look at me the moment they passed each other, and I'd done the only sane thing I could do; I'd entered the house, closing them both out and gone to sleep after I'd bathed.

Now with the screams and the music exploding from Luna's room as she destroyed it, I almost missed the shell version. I was stuck on babysitting duty since I couldn't go out and let loose. The others had escaped Luna's tirade, but I was being hunted by creatures, not knowing who they were or why they wanted me. Nothing had been discernible from the car bombing.

The body belonged to a human, one who had been used as an unwilling suicide bomber from what we could tell. I'd sent his family money, because what else could you do when they were mourning a loss that they couldn't explain? They had sent his human body back to his hometown, placed in the car that exploded without the explosive remnants.

When I had asked why I hadn't been informed, Lore told me Knox had handled it on my behalf. What the fuck did that even mean? He'd done the same thing with the woodland creature, and it seemed as if he was protecting me, and while he didn't like it, he still did it. The man was confusing. He was hot one moment, then ice-cold the next, leaving me with icicles hanging from my flesh.

The bounty hounds, well, they were obviously sent by whoever wanted me from within the Nine Realms, but why? I was nobody. Again, when I had gone searching for answers, I'd been told Knox was inside the Nine Realms, handling it. I could walk in the yard, and nothing tried to attack me, and I'd known Knox's brothers were outside with me, stationed around me even though they tried to hide their presence. One minute Knox had kissed me until I didn't care if I ever gained air into my lungs again, and then the next, he'd choked me, and I damn well prayed for air. Something had happened to him, and from his reaction to the babes, I had a heavy heart as I tried to add it up in my head.

Knox had been ghostly white as Luna screamed with labor pains. It was as if he had recalled something he'd been through, which made me wonder if he was a father, or had been at one time. Luna's babes had been my first birthing to witness, and it had been horrifying. Knox had turned lethal at the sight of the shrouded bodies, and I'd felt his need to sink his teeth into my throat and rip it out, and then just like Knox, he'd calmed my demons and my soul.

Breaking Benjamin's *Breath* exploded through the speaker of the stereo, and I turned from where I stood on the balcony, drenched in sweat, to stare down the street. Every night I was getting worse, as if I was fighting a war within myself, and the result was the feeling of melting from in the interior of my soul that radiated out of me. I couldn't stop the gnawing within me. I ached every day, and every night and no matter how much I flicked the bean; it didn't soothe shit.

I'd eaten copious amounts of food, and yet nothing touched the hunger I felt. The heat, the heat was endless. I spent more time making ice and dumping it into the tub before climbing in than anything else this week. Not that it helped; by the time I'd sat in the ice, it turned to water and began boiling.

Something crashed against the wall, and I gripped the railing, closing my eyes. I counted to ten and then released the breath I held and went to look in Luna's room to be sure she hadn't hurt herself. Luna tossed a lamp in my direction, and I ducked, staring at her with wide, horrified eyes.

"What the hell, Luna?"

"Get out, you slut!" she snapped.

"What the fuck did I do to you?"

"You want to know what is wrong with me. You rubbed your ass on the father of my sons, and then you fucking made out with him! I can't even bring myself to tell him that our sons died because I can't un-see you with him, you stupid whore!"

I recoiled as if Luna had hit me as I imagined her with Knox, and then frowned as the realization hit me. "Oh, Dimitri?"

"Yes!"

"Oh, my bad," I frowned. "I didn't sleep with him."

She lunged, and I backed up, watching as her mouth formed into fangs before I spun around, rushing down the stairs. The problem with this situation was that the House of Magic didn't protect us from each other.

I busted out the front door, turning to look over my shoulder as she followed on my heels.

"I didn't fuck him!" I snapped again, watching as she cracked her neck. "Luna, stop!" Her head swung toward the altar that was still covered in flowers blooming with the hold of magic we had placed on it.

"I will rip you apart!"

"No, you won't. I'm your sister, remember? Bitches before tricks and dicks? Hoes don't need hoses? Okay, I may have made the last one up, and it's utterly terrible. I didn't know you had been with him. You didn't say anything!"

"I shouldn't have had to! You are my sister."

Voices sounded behind us, and I didn't dare turn to see who it was. My heart raced, and my fingers burned. My gums were raw with pain, and I slowly stepped back, giving myself enough room to dodge her attacks.

"I heard him talking to you! He thinks of nothing else but you! What do you have, a magic fucking pussy?"

"Uh, no, but I mean, maybe?" She lunged again, and I did a backflip from a standing position, twisting to miss her other hand before glaring at her. "Luna, stop!" I shouted, swiping my foot the moment I landed, unseating hers from where she stood. "I am your sister! I didn't fuck Dimitri, nor do I intend to. You need to stop this now!" I dodged her attacks until I stepped outside the barrier, and I was shoved behind a firm back.

"*You!* Our sons are dead, and you protect your whore?" Luna snarled.

"Dick move, Dimitri," I growled, hiding behind

him.

"I didn't know she was a witch when I fucked her."

"In an alleyway behind our damn shop? She's not trash, dick. No one bends my sister over a garbage can!"

"Aria, she's about to tear you to shreds."

"Pssh, she wishes. I was just avoiding hurting her. How is it you failed to mention you were my sister's baby daddy?"

"She's a wolf, and she was oozing her scent. Luna bent over, and I just aided a bitch in heat."

"You don't get to call her a bitch." I glared at his exposed back and yelped as we both jumped back to avoid her nails.

"Aria, shut the fuck up for a moment, sweetheart."

"How do you turn it off?" I asked and then snorted when he vanished from in front of me. "Fucker!" I tripped backward as she lunged, only to watch her being pulled back as Dimitri sank his teeth into her shoulder.

She calmed, her eyes turning lethargic with a hint of lust banked in the deep blue depths as she lost focus. Dimitri's eyes matched Luna's but glowed with the strength of the alpha and his pack. Blood dripped from the bite, and yet his eyes never left mine, kissing her shoulder as he subdued her while healing the damage at the same time. She slowly began pumping her hips, rubbing against him as his hands slipped around her body, steadying her. It was erotic, and I sucked my bottom lip between my teeth as I wondered if I did that too?

"She's still healing."

He growled at me, and I frowned, dusting off my hands from the tiny pebbles that stuck to them. Slowly, I stood. I wondered if I looked like that with Knox, with his mouth against my flesh as he brought me that sweet inner peace.

Sweat beaded on my brow, my clothes clung to my body, and I peered down, realizing I was dressed in a sheer nightie that didn't cover the top of my thighs fully. Dimitri's eyes slid down my body hungrily with the alpha glow banked within their sapphire depths. I stepped back, watching as his mouth released her shoulder, and he pushed her away from him.

"Fuck," I snapped, turning and running in the property's direct line, but the moment I moved to enter it, it slammed me backward. "The fuck, I'm a witch!" The sound of feet pounded on the road, and I kicked up onto my feet, rushing toward Knox's house, barely hitting the gate when it opened, and I slid through it, slamming it closed behind me.

"Mine," Dimitri hissed.

"Nope! Not today, puppy," I chuckled. I leaned over to catch my breath as I watched him pacing right outside the gate.

"Is there a problem, peasant?" Greer asked, standing beside me as he watched Dimitri pacing in front of the large wrought-iron gates. Greer had come out of nowhere, causing me to jolt back into a fighting position.

"Jesus, Greer the Vampire! You need to announce your presence to the ladies first. I could have died from a heart attack."

"Pity that you didn't suffer one, peasant."

"You do know I'm royalty back home, right? That I'm not actually a peasant?" I asked, watching as Lore and the others strolled up the driveway, looking through the fence to where Dimitri paced, agitated that he couldn't reach me.

"You're not home, and neither am I, Aria. Here, you're just another peasant, just as I am."

"Thanks, man, love you too." I tapped my heart before flipping him deuces.

"Someone taunt an alpha and not enjoying the chase?" Lore asked.

"You fucking whore!" Luna screamed, coming toward the gate.

"Oh, damn. I should have made popcorn," Greer chuckled.

"She shouldn't be out of bed yet." I turned at someone's voice, watching Brander walking through the gravel without a shirt on. The man was built to be worshipped.

"Yeah, I know. The thing is, Luna is currently trying to murder me, so I didn't actually have time to ask her to stay in bed and be a good patient."

"Why would she murder you?"

"I didn't say she could, I said she's *trying*."

"But why would she be *trying* to murder you, Aria?"

"She thinks I slept with Dimitri, but I didn't. Turns out he's the father of her boys. I went into her bedroom because she was *throwing* shit!" I glared pointedly at her. "She threw a lamp at me the moment I opened the door, called me *nasty* names that *really* hurt, and then tried to *rip* my face off. All because I unknowingly kissed her baby daddy," I said, folding my arms over my chest.

"Because you're a whore," Luna screamed.

"Name-calling, it's unkind, asshole. You can't take them back either, so be nice!" I demanded.

"I will rip your throat out, slut."

"Really mature, Luna! I have fucked one man and one man alone in my entire life. I don't even meet the criteria for being a whore or a slut, you little bitch. I still love you, but I really don't like you right now! Sorry about the names, jerk face!"

The sound of clothing ripping drew my attention to Dimitri as he removed his shirt. My gaze slid over the rippling muscles of his abdomen, and my brow lifted. He moved his hands to his jeans, flicking the button before pushing them down. He was packing some serious swagger in his jeans. My gaze lingered on his cock before rising back to his eyes. He watched me, waiting. He was a mass of solid muscles, covered in sinful tattoos that looked pleasantly placed. Swallowing, I frowned in frustration.

"What are you doing? Put your clothes back on this minute, bad puppy!" I stomped my foot and stared up at the moon while pointing my finger at him, or in his general direction. "What the hell is he doing?"

"He's waiting for you to approve of the size of his dick," Lore chuckled.

I dug through the pocket of my nightgown and picked out my lucky dollar bill, moving to throw it through the gate. Dimitri watched it fall to the ground before lunging. "Bad puppy, bad, sit, or something!" I yanked my hand back and turned to the men behind me.

Lore covered his mouth before he bent over laughing. Brander's shoulders shook silently as Greer shook his head. And then Lore lost it, howling with laughter as I glared at him.

"I think he wanted you to exit the protection of the yard so he could fuck you with it, peasant. Not throw dollars at him like a stripper. You could have at least offered him a twenty; he's worth at least that much."

"Oh, Greer, you got a naughty side, and that was my lucky dollar bill!"

"Why the fuck is the alpha naked outside my gate?" Knox demanded, half-naked as he walked toward us. I turned slowly at the timbre of his voice, letting my eyes slip over his chest to the gray sweatpants he wore and back up to his angry gaze. "Explain, Aria. Now!"

"My sister is trying to kill me."

"Not my fucking problem, snap her fucking neck."

"Seriously, she's my sister!" I glared at him as he watched me cross my arms over my chest, digging my heels in.

"Why the fuck is there a naked alpha outside my gate, Aria?"

"I guess they're like peacocks or something?" I shrugged, scrunching up my face. Knox glared at me, and I swallowed. "I was on babysitting duty for Luna. It's been hell for the last week. Something crashed in her room, and I went to check it out. She was in a rage and informed me that I'm a whore. I unknowingly kissed her baby daddy, who happened to be Dimitri. I ran from her because I didn't want to hurt her, then he showed up to protect me. He subdued her with his bite, but I may have watched it too long because he got over her and chased me. I tried to run home, but the House of Magic bounced me to the curb, just like you did. I came here, and Greer let me in. Dimitri started stripping, I tossed a dollar at him, and now we're here."

"Get out," he said, and I frowned, nodding.

"Yeah, sure," I exhaled, turning to look at Dimitri and Luna, both who wanted me in entirely different ways. I puffed out air and started forward, watching as Dimitri smiled, inching his way directly in front of the gate I had to escape through.

I closed my eyes and started to open the gate as Dimitri's claws extended, but a hand landed over mine, holding it shut.

"Ask for sanctuary," Greer snapped.

"Greer," Knox warned.

"Sanctuary?" I peered back at Knox and watched him shaking his head.

"Sanctuary isn't something I grant to witches anymore."

"It was worth a shot, Greer." I smiled tightly to Greer, slipping through the gates before I slammed my knee into Dimitri's groin. I reached over him to grab Luna by her hair, shoving her down with him before I ran like the hounds of hell were on my heels. I broke through the barrier of our property, turning to find Knox walking directly behind me, glaring. "You're a dick, you know that, right? They could have kicked my ass together."

"You made it home, didn't you? You won't always be able to rely on other people to save that pretty little ass."

"What about my sister?" I asked, watching him as he followed me slowly.

"Luna is being taken to the medical ward you were held in, where Brander can help her."

"So, I'm safe?"

"Not even a little bit, woman."

"Oh, well…" He captured me by the arms, stopping my words as a violent tremor of need rushed through me at his touch.

"The entire pack of alphas is watching us as I speak. You will turn toward them and expose your shoulder to me and submit, understand? If you don't, I walk away, and you spend the rest of your days running and fighting them because Dimitri just broke his fucking word, and it cannot be undone now. Turn," he snapped, and I did.

I pushed my hair away, giving him my shoulder, which he took, moving the thin strap from my skin as his mouth lowered, and he kissed over the delicate curve of my throat. His breath made my nipples harden with arousal. The moment his lips touched my neck, I whimpered with a violent need. Knox slid his lips back to my shoulder, pushing his teeth through my flesh painlessly, and I moaned, instantly rocking my hips with need.

This bite was different; it was slow, methodical, and it felt like he was marking me for ownership. His hands slid down to my gown, pushing it up, before slipping his hand into my panties as the alphas emerged from the shadows, watching him claim me. I exploded violently, coming undone with two simple strokes as he held me there against his rock hard body slowly running his fingers through the wetness of my core.

He'd made me undulate against him as he pushed his teeth down further. He was hard beneath his sweatpants, and I wanted him in the most basic fucking way a woman could want a man.

"Knox," I whispered breathlessly.

Somehow I was able to make the name sound like a benediction to the gods of old. Like the heavens had opened up and touched me, but it was Satan, and I'd given him the keys to my paradise to play within my garden.

"Shut your mouth, or this turns dark real fucking quick, woman." He made a pained noise in his chest, and then the rattle started.

It wasn't the normal little one, it bordered on a loud purring noise and then turned into a deafening rattle that echoed through the streets until the alphas knelt down and *bowed*. Dimitri bowed before Knox, his naked body bare and exposed, and yet he was on his knees with his head bowed in a show of respect to Knox.

I turned, rubbing my jaw against him as he pulled his fingers out of my panties and then shoved them into my mouth when I opened it to speak. I sucked against them, feeling him tensing behind my back as my tongue worked circles around them until he withdrew them. He continued rattling until something within me followed, low at first, building until it escaped, and he chuckled against my neck.

"That's my good girl, Aria. Now make your pretty pussy stop begging me to fill it. There is only so much pheromone influence I can withstand, and you're pushing my fucking limits. This beast is fucking starving for you, little lamb."

His rattle lowered but didn't stop. The wolves lifted from the ground, slowly backing away as they watched him with me. I exhaled, leaning into his body. I wanted to stop my body, but it wasn't like there was a valve I could just shut off. Knox waited for the alphas to slip into the House of Alphas before he stepped back, releasing my shoulder. His mouth brushed against his deep bite, licking it, causing it to tingle, and I knew without looking that he'd healed the flesh with his saliva.

"Get inside, Aria. Your sister is fine, she's being tended to. You're safe again."

"Why do you keep saving me if you hate me?" I asked, watching as the tick in his jaw hammered, and his hands clenched into fists at his sides.

"Get into the house, woman."

"You saved the women from being brutalized by the House of Alphas, and you keep helping me. You could have made me dominate Dimitri, but you didn't. You aren't the monster you want me to think you are."

"No, I'm way fucking worse."

"I think you do good things because you've been hurt. I think you're still in pain, and I wish there was a way to take that pain away from you."

"You know nothing about pain, Aria."

"I know enough to see it in your eyes," I countered, and his teeth elongated as black claws slid from his fingers. "I'm not a fucking martyr, but if killing me brings you some kind of peace, do it."

"Get the fuck in the house!" I watched as his eyes filled with embers. "Get her into the fucking house, now!" he snarled, but it came out on a powerful purr, and before I could argue, Lore hefted me over his shoulder and booked it. I lifted my head, staring as Knox expanded his arms and lifted his head, rattling until it felt like the earth was shaking. Car alarms sounded as car windows shattered, and the power did a rolling blackout, keeping whatever was happening hidden in the darkness.

"You got a fucking death wish, Aria?" Lore snapped, shoving me into the house as he followed me, closing the door behind him. "Good God, you could have fucking died, and what a waste of a damn talented throat that would have been."

"What?" I asked, and he scratched the back of his neck uncomfortably.

"I just mean that when a man tells you to run, and he means it, fucking run. Don't stand around oozing that scent, because right now everything inside of him wants to toss you down and go to pound town. I mean barebones, soul destroying I-can't-get-deep-enough-into-that-tight-pussy-let-me-break-her-to-get-there kind of fucking."

"That's deep." I frowned as he nodded his platinum head, turning burning amber eyes on me.

"So fucking deep," he chuckled. "You got anything to eat? I'm hungry."

CHAPTER
46

Aria / The Creature Within

I sat on the balcony, letting the cool air calm me as the ache in my shoulder burned. It burned, the same way as I was burning from within, and yet I couldn't stop it. I had tried everything, and nothing worked. I grabbed the railing as a wave of heat shot through me, and I moaned as it ripped me apart inside. Staring down at my hands, I gasped, releasing the railing where it had caught fire. I grabbed the large cup of water and splashed it on the wooden railing.

"That can't be a good sign." I lifted my gaze to the mansion across the street before slowly looking toward Knox's house, noting the light and silhouette that stood within the room on the top floor. I hissed, shaking my head as I dispelled the image of Knox in his room, taking off that fucking shirt, while showing that dick off in those gray sweatpants that failed to hide his impressive package.

Damn, he was built, and if that wasn't enough, he was the most virile, pigheaded asshole because he knew it. The man knew he was the epitome of male sexual perfection, and he strutted and paraded it around unabashedly.

Smoke rose from my hands, and I exhaled, jumped to the ground, and then peered up at the balcony, which was three stories up. Oh wow, that wasn't okay! I could have died!

"Holy shit, why would I do that?" I squeaked, up until my body started toward Knox's mansion. "No, absolutely not! You don't get to do this to us," I growled, shouting at the creature within me, but my feet were moving, and they were moving toward Knox's house. I dug my feet in, tripping mid-step, and righted myself, rushing forward. "I better not wake up next to him naked!"

Laughter sounded in my head, and I groaned loudly.

My mind glazed over as I reached for the gate, ripping it open before walking through the gravel on his driveway in barefooted. I stopped at the door, turning my head, and all coherent thought fled and became primal as my creature moved my consciousness to the backseat, allowing me to watch, as if in a dream, while she drove us.

What is happening? Oh, my gods, give me back my body! How are you in control? Why are you in control? You just kicked in the gate; that's not nice. Apologize, or say something!

I made my way to the front door and kicked it in too, turning to sniff Greer as I entered the house.

No. No, don't sniff Greer; that's rude and just inappropriate behavior when you're wearing my face!

"That was rude, peasant," Greer snapped.

Right? I had to agree, that was totally rude. We don't kick doors in! There are rules of conduct, creature! God, what is that smell?

"You stink of dead meat."

Again, so rude! Not even what I meant by saying something. Even if someone stinks...Oh, wow, he really stinks! Plug our nose! Plug it!

"Greer, get the fuck back, my man. Aria is not in the house right now," Lore said, and I turned, studying amber eyes.

Could they sense I was different right now? If I had any control over my body, I could wave for help... Lore! It's me! Wave, wave the arm, girlfriend. I need them to know I need help. I've been taken over! Oooo, he smells...nice. God, grab him and get away from Greer, that man needs a shower stat!

He rattled, and I inhaled, hating that the dead meat-suit violated our airspace. Another rattle sounded, and I turned, inhaling. Brander watched me carefully as my eyes zeroed in on him with hunger. More rattles began to fill the air as Knox's men appeared in the entranceway. I inhaled, smiling until a louder, stronger, more defined rattle came from above.

There's our rattle...no, scratch that! Not ours! No, don't look at him...Abort before all hope is lost!

My gaze slid up the stairs, finding the male I was hunting, and I smirked as I lifted my nose, inhaling his scent deeply.

You like *the noises they make. He smells…delicious. Masculine, primal, and…Oh gods, is that pre-cum? You can smell their arousal? No wonder I'm* such *a horny bitch! We can still walk away from this. All you have to do is…*

"Aria, what the fuck do you think you're doing?" Knox snarled, and I moved. Space and time had nothing on me. I stopped in the middle of the stairs, slowly stalking him as I made my way to him. "That's new."

Wow! *We were fast! Are you hunting him? What are you doing? Turn this body around, missy! Oh, that… sound is nice. So good. His rattle is so… No! No, don't look at him. Do not look into his eyes! Don't… I'm guessing we're not leaving, then?*

"I need dick."

No. Absolutely not. No, we do not! No dick. He doesn't get to give us dick, because he is a dick, remember? We had this… talk. Oh, no. You looked into his eyes, we're screwed.

"Aria?" Knox asked, watching me carefully.

Yes! Yes, can he see me? Knox, it's me! Help!

"She is stubborn as fuck, burning shit down because you're a dick."

Jerk, I am not! I am strong, and strong enough that I don't need that penis! Unlike you, apparently, hussy.

"Brander, go check on the House of Magic."

Oh, my gods! I'd put the fire out, right? We put it out, right!?

"Amateur, she put the fire out. She is fighting me, but I won't let her anymore, and you're going to help me fix us. Do you hear me, Aria? I am fixing us."

Whew, apparently, she had been paying attention. Wait, fix us how? I didn't need to be fixed! I needed a fucking priest to do an exorcism!

"Can she see me?" Knox asked, staring into my eyes.

Unfortunately.

I moved, landing on him, ripping his shirt off over his head, then claiming his mouth in a starving kiss that stole a groan from his lungs. His hands slipped down my back, and I purred, needing more. He turned us, moving up the stairs as if my weight didn't hinder his movements. My hand slipped into his pants, making sure he'd gotten the point of my visit as my fingers wrapped around his cock. Knox chuckled, moving us into a dark hallway filled with shadows before slamming me down onto his cock as he roared for me.

Fuck! That's my vagina too! Ouch, ouch, holy shit, did you hear him roar? Yowsers! Fuck, he is too big. Climb off it, where's the reverse button on this bitch? Oh hell, he's stretching us…Ugh, make him move faster!

I whimpered huskily, my body rocking back and forth as he fucked me hard and fast, holding nothing back. He took me to the edge, forcing me to scream as he sent me sailing over the cliff, slipping into euphoria.

Oh my word, more! No, no more…There, we're good, let's go now. He doesn't need to get off, we're good to go home now.

"More," the creature growled.

Holy shit, what is wrong with you? Our vagina is happy, we can leave...Stop that shit! We talked about this. Not him and not this penis. Oh, shit, that aches! Fuck! Ugh, he's enormous. Harder! No! No, not harder, get off it! You hear me? Get off the giant cock right this...Oh, right there...fucking hell, that is amazing!

"Fucking hell, creature." He lifted me slowly, slamming me down onto him as we moved through the hallway.

Right? No, no...that's my pussy! Dick.

"Not hell, heaven. Your dick is heaven."

His dick is not *heaven! Don't build his ego up any higher! Jesus, if his ego gets any bigger, he will need his own zip code to house it!*

"Make that little witch remember that," Knox demanded huskily as he pushed the code into the elevator panel.

As if, prick. Okay, so it sorta felt like heaven at the moment, slamming into me. He wasn't wasting any time, or waiting to be behind closed doors, before ramming his dick back into me, which means anyone could be watching us!

His hips never stopped, never gave an inch of mercy as he thrust into my body as hard as he could. Using the wall, Knox slammed into me harder and harder until I was screaming and roaring as everything within me struck the chord, exploding like a bomb all at once. He chuckled, placing my flame-covered hand onto his shoulder and claiming my mouth as he stepped into the elevator.

Knox moved us to the corner, spreading my thighs

as he pounded into my body, growling while he watched me. I didn't take my eyes from his, not until the elevator beeped, and he moved us into an elegant bedroom, lavishly decorated, fit for a king.

Oh, hell, no! Not this room again. Turn this body around and get out, because nothing good happens in here!

Our fucking king, the creature thought.

Stop thinking that! We literally just talked about the size of his ego! Stop that shit, and he's not our *anything!*

Knox slammed me against the bed, sending me into a frenzied state as he withdrew. Turning me onto my stomach, he gripped my legs and pulled me to him before his hand threaded through my hair, jerking it back as his mouth licked my shoulder.

Fuck, yes! Damn, he's good at this.

"You are a beautiful fucking mess of chaos, creature."

Wow, thanks, dick. It's still my body, where's my *confidence booster? Good gods, that's my hair! Don't bite me! Don't let him leave another mark, you skank. No, really, don't let him bite us! We go stupid and needy, and that looks really bad for us.*

"You need to shut up and move, we're mad at you. You pushed us beneath the water, and it wasn't nice."

Right? Move, bitch! And about that water? That is precisely why my pussy wasn't available for penetration, duh.

He slowed, and I bucked against him.

Move fucker, now. Make him move, sweet baby

Jesus, make the bastard move. We're so close. Fuck, kick his ass or something, make him move!

"I was trying to help you," Knox said.

Psht, right. He was trying to kill us!

"You weren't trying to help us. You were trying to force me out, and that won't ever happen, Knox. Aria is stronger than you think she is. You think she doesn't know I am part of her? Wrong. She knows a lot of things. Like you sparing the women from the alpha house, yet you refuse to tell her what you did. You're not smart. She is brilliant."

Yes! You tell him! Prick was trying to end us! Wait, you're awake inside of me! Aw, you like me! And I am pretty smart.

"Aria would have carried their fucking deaths should they have been slaughtered. It would have been worse had she entered that fucking place and found them nothing but spread-eagle rutting mates to be used and disposed of when they pleased," he uttered huskily, watching us.

Damn, he'd done it for me? I hated that he wasn't wrong. I also hated that he wasn't moving. Why wasn't he moving? You move us, make him start!

"Why not tell her?" the creature asked, wiggling my hips.

Yeah, jerk? Why not? Wiggle more, own that move.

"It wouldn't matter. I didn't do it for fucking praise or Aria's approval."

"You protect us."

"She isn't evil yet. She's innocent, but her kind

destroys everything. They murder children and their own sons. They terrorize people in the Nine Realms and prey on the weak."

Ouch. That wasn't good. We should, like...leave.

Pausing, she turned to look at him. "Aria wasn't in the Nine Realms, ever."

Yeah, I wasn't!

"Which is why she's still alive," he chuckled darkly.

Uh, that isn't bedroom talk. More moving, less talking. Let's do this! The sooner we fuck him, the sooner we leave, so move bitch! Rock my hips...You know, if you could just put me back in the driver's seat, this would be so much easier.

"Mmm, not today, though, so move. I tire of your mouth, and since it's not wagging on this pussy, it needs to cease working."

Um, blunt. Oh, he's making that noise he makes right before...ooh. Damn! I think I just heard church bells and the angels singing with that thrust!

Knox growled, pushing our legs apart before he started moving, viciously between our thighs.

Days passed, and Knox never tired of our body, forgetting he needed to feed us.

Are you always awake inside me? Hello?

My eyes grew heavy, staring at him as we rode him reverse cowgirl, like the story we read last week had explained.

What the fuck are you doing? How the fuck did you do that? Hello? Are you even listening to me?

"Do you ever shut up? We sleep, I'm tired. Goodnight, Aria."

Did you just tell me to go to sleep? We need to have a sit-down and discuss stuff if you plan to drive my body...are you sleeping?

"What?" Knox asked.

Exactly! What the fuck is she even doing?

I leaned over between his legs, clamping down on him to keep him safe. After all, he was dense and could end up dead without me protecting him. He groaned and exploded within me, and I purred, closing my eyes, drifting to sleep.

Um, are you sleeping on his dick? *The fuck? Get up! No, no, no! Well, I am kind of tired. That was rough, don't you, like...Um, this is awkward. I guess you do rest...on penises. Great! Because this isn't the most awkward shit of my entire life! Who is touching me? What are they doing? There are four hands on me, hello, get up! Ahh, not cool! Give me back my body...*

"Her spine curves, like there is something beneath it," Knox sounded from behind me, and I opened my eyes slowly.

"That's not freaky," Brander replied sarcastically.

"I don't care what the fuck she is, she's fucking hot. Daddy wants one," Lore groaned.

Daddy?

Something touched my mouth, and I snarled, lifting up as my nails grew, and flames leapt from my hands that were resting on Knox's legs. I hissed, biting at Brander, who jumped back, staring at me in confusion.

About fucking time! That's what I'm talking about! My body, bitch! Did I just fucking try to bite him? *Oops, my bad.*

"She's fucking protecting you," Brander said in astonishment.

"See. Hot!" Lore chuckled. "So fucking hot."

"Mine," I hissed possessively, purring low in my chest, but it wasn't a good purr. It was a warning. My eyes narrowed to slits, and I opened my mouth as my teeth grew longer. Why was I purring at all? Why the hell wasn't it stopping?

Finally, Aria! I love you. We are going to have so much fun together...

And just like that, the creature was no longer in the driver's seat, and I was sitting on a dick, naked. *Peachy.* They watched me, slowly backing up. My eyes looked around the room, and I frowned, staring down between my legs where an entirely too large organ was pushed into my body. My head snapped back, peering over my shoulder, right at Knox, who had his arms behind his head, relaxing with a sensual smirk on his mouth.

"Hello, creature."

"No!" I groaned with embarrassment. "And my fucking name is Aria, dick. You've been fucking me for three days; you should at least know my damn name by now. You could at least get that right since you're currently buried *inside* of me. Get out!"

"Aria?" he asked, and I snorted and rocked his hips, which made my heart pound in horror.

"Please tell me you're not stuck in my vagina."

"I'm not stuck. You clamped down around me, and I can't get out unless you let me. Not without hurting you, at least."

"Well, that's not awkward at all, now is it?" I muttered while lifting to stare at the situation. "Fucking hell, you're huge. How did you even fit that into me?"

"Easy, you jumped on it, and I let you."

I groaned, remembering seeing it through a dream state but being fully awake the entire time. I'd met my creature, and it just so happened I'd done it on his dick. *Fucking great.*

I leaned my head over, banging it against the bed. "We had a deal; you fucked Knox, you should have been the one to wake up on his cock, not me! You brought us here, get your ass back out here, and fucking deal with this mess, you horny bitch." I waited, tilting my head as I clamped my eyes down and then slowly opened one to stare at Lore and Brander, who watched me cautiously. "You seriously suck at this relationship!" Knox was stretching me, viscerally so.

My flesh looked raw, ravished, and destroyed by the thing stuck inside of me. The worst part of it? I was itching to move, craving the friction and eruption I'd felt for the last three days, only feeling a water-downed version of the sensation. I wanted it.

"You good, Aria? Mental breakdown?" Lore asked. "Crazy chicks get my dick hard, just saying."

I wiggled, and fire leapt inside of me. I lifted a tad, sliding down slowly with what little of him I could. It fueled something within me, and I turned, staring back at him. I growled, but it came out as a rattle, deep and loudly, and he smiled wickedly, answering the call.

"Move, bastard."

"Get out," he ordered his men, moving me so he could get to his knees while pushing me down. He started slow, and I shook my head.

"Harder, asshole!"

"You think they sell them at the pet store?" Lore asked loudly as they walked out of the room.

Brander chuckled. "I don't think they're allowed in this realm, period."

"Get the fuck out!" Knox growled. His voice was layered and shook the room as he threaded his fingers through my hair, pulling my head back to look into my eyes. "You sure you're Aria?"

"Fuck me, asshole. Just like you fucked me last night," I demanded, watching the heat register in his eyes before he slammed against me violently. I purred, no longer caring that I was a monster because he was one too. Whatever I was, we were alike. I wasn't alone. Plus, she thought I was smart and shit, so she could stay for now.

Knox pulled me up, and his hand slipped between my legs, rubbing against my pussy, forcing me to come as if he held some magical switch that was attached to my clit. His mouth slowly kissed my neck, his other hand trailing through my hair until he held it, slightly tilting my head to give him better access to the curve of my neck.

"You make the most delicious noises when I'm inside you, sweet girl."

"You fuck me hard enough, and I'll make whatever noises you want to hear, Knox," I urged, and his dark laughter rumbled over my shoulder.

"Lift your legs, and place them behind mine," he instructed. It was awkward, but it seated him deeper into my core, and I clenched tighter than I had been, causing him to groan huskily.

"Fuck, yes!" I howled as I sank onto him, trembling around him while he purred at my reaction. "More," I hissed, meeting him thrust for thrust before rolling my hips to fuck him back.

"You're perfect. Do you feel me filling you? Every part of you is filled with me, and you take it all like a greedy little bitch, don't you?"

"I'm going to need you to shut your dirty mouth up and destroy me now, please?"

Knox laughed, rubbing his nose against the curve of my shoulder. His hands slipped to my hips, rocking them until I was breathing hard, whimpering as he touched places no man should be able to reach inside of a woman. My body held him there, forcing him to use what little I'd left of his dick unclenched in my pussy. I wasn't even sure I knew how to let his cock go, but I also wasn't sure that I wanted to either.

"Gods damn, woman. You grip me any harder, and I'm going to come before you're ready. Slow the fuck down, and stop sucking me off, Aria. When this pussy releases, there's going to be a mess," he growled huskily.

"You've been fucking me for three days, Knox. Including the times you came when my body rested, which I was fully aware of, even if she wasn't. It's all a fucking mess."

"You were awake within her?"

"Yes, now move because I need to come again."

"Greedy little bitch, you'll get to come, I promise," he growled.

My hands held his powerful thighs as he rocked me from side to side and then front to back, slowly. He was creating a wealth of heady need that built within my stomach, unfurling slowly until I dropped my head back against his chest, crying out as everything inside of me erupted like a dormant volcano, woken without warning. Explosions sounded around the room, windows shattered, and glass rained down onto the floor as my eyes popped open, staring at the flames that burned books, couches, and other things.

"Holy shit, that can't be safe."

"Those are the flames of your chaos, Aria. You could set the entire world on fire if you chose to do so."

"Yeah, like I said, not safe at all."

Knox increased the pace of my hips, slamming against me until my body finally released him with a loud popping noise that made me blush. The moment he was free, he shed whatever humanity he had in him. He started battering into me until I exploded, milking him as his hands bit into my hips. One minute I was beneath him, and the next, he had ripped me up and slammed me down on his cock as my legs wrapped around him.

"Welcome to the world, pretty girl," he purred, staring into my eyes as I purred back at him, giving him approval for his words.

"Thank you, now fucking move," I hissed, grinding against him as I captured his mouth, devoured it while gripping his hair as he rocked my hips. He slammed my clit down against his flesh on every single stroke, in and out of my body, until I broke the kiss to throw back my head and roar. Fire filled my eyes and mouth, and I turned to stare at him as he smiled. My mouth crushed against his and steam filled the air as he rolled us over, staring up at me as I rocked above him while his body jerked, and he groaned his release inside me.

"You're on fire," he chuckled huskily.

"So are you." I leaned down to run my fingers through the fire of his hair. "So is the bed."

"You're so fucking beautiful."

"Yeah, I'm not sure I want to add to your ego, but I'd totally do you, obviously." Sitting up, I stretched my arms and arched my spine. "Thanks," I stated, climbing off of him as I patted his chest.

"Where the fuck you think you're going?"

I slipped my shirt over my head and turned to study him. I bent down, retrieving my panties, and shrugged. "Home. You know, my house, where I live. I didn't bring shoes, did I? No, that's right, I jumped from the balcony. I figured I'd be all broken and shit, but it was so terrifying, but cool," I said, turning to look at him where he lay on the bed, his head resting in his hand with bedroom eyes watching me.

"Get back into this bed. I'm not finished with you yet."

"Oh, but you are. My body aches, and I need sustenance."

443

I moved to the doors, throwing them open as he growled behind me. I made it to the elevator where Lore waited, watching me carefully before he finally spoke.

"What the hell are you, Aria?"

"I have no idea, and I honestly don't care because I feel fucking great right now." I fixed my hair as he pushed the code into the elevator. Knox exited the room, prowling toward us as he slipped in the elevator before the doors could close, placing his arm against the wall as I stared up at him. "Well, fancy meeting you here, big guy."

"I didn't say you could leave yet."

"I didn't ask your permission," I said, smirking as I leaned up, claiming his lips softly before I ducked beneath his arm as the elevator doors opened. I skipped down the hallway, leaving him to follow behind me.

"She straight-up booty called you, brother."

"She walked through the fucking door, asshole."

"Yeah, but then she just zoomed on up the stairs and was like, *'I need that dick, Knox,'* and you were like, *'slide on down it, Aria.'* Meanwhile, we were all like, *'who made the popcorn, because they're about to fuck right here,'* but then you got all defensive and shit, and hid that honey pot as you plowed it."

I smiled; listening to them reminded me of my sisters. I went down the stairs slowly, sensing he'd stopped at the top.

"Aria," he called down, and I turned, staring up at him. "Did you just fucking booty call me?"

"No." I scrunched up my face as I answered, "I

mean, titles are so 90s, let's not label this. I needed dick; you got laid. It's a win for both of us. Take it, Knox. You don't like me. I don't like you, but our bodies like each other, and that works for me." He glared angrily, and I tilted my head. "I guess if you want to consider it something, it's more like a fuck and duck. I fucked you, now I'm ducking out of here." He frowned, obviously not getting the terrible reference. "You know, I came in, rode your dick, now I'm ducking out after since I got my fill. Yeah, I may be waddling a little because it was some seriously good dick, and now I'm sore— look like a duck waddling home." At his narrowed gaze and sinful smile, which revealed a dimple in one cheek, I gave up explaining and shrugged. "Catch you later, because I might feel cute and need some of that good dick again." I blew him a kiss, turning on my heel to find Greer and Brander standing by the door. "Dude, cologne! You stink like death! How are you supposed to catch the ladies if you smell like a corpse?" I messed up his hair and smiled as he watched me with a stoic face.

"I am dead, or more to the point, undead. And don't touch me, peasant."

"You don't smell undead to me. You smell dead-dead. You want pussy, you need to smell good enough to eat, and right now you smell like the dead ass meat Knox dropped into my cell, which I hope wasn't related to you, because that could be awkward. Brander!" I lifted on my tiptoes, kissing his cheek before I walked out the door, smiling at the sun as I moved toward the house. Twirling as the sun heated my flesh, closing my eyes, letting it warm my face.

I paused, twirling, staring at the glass on the ground

as it crunched beneath my feet, then peered up at the house and flinched. Ouch, that was going to cost him a pretty penny to replace all those windows. I watched him walk out on the veranda with his men who observed my dancing as I made my way through the gate and down the block.

I opened the door to my house, and everyone turned, looking at me strangely. I smiled brightly, like a fucking idiot.

"You have major fuck-me hair," Sabine pointed out. "Are you okay? The last time you woke up with him, you weren't."

"I'm great! I just rocked his fucking world, and then I walked out, leaving his mouth wide open. That's a win, or at least I'm taking it as one."

"Good God, happy Aria is almost as bad as stoic Aria. I'm kind of afraid here, you guys," Tamryn laughed, standing to fix my hair.

"Stop that, I like my hair after riding Knox." I stopped cold as Luna stepped into my path.

"I'm so sorry, Aria."

"I imagine so," I stated, watching her carefully as my body tensed and braced for a fight.

"Brander explained that I was in shock, and my body was septic. I had a fever that I knew wasn't right, but I didn't let anyone get close enough to check it. My wolf was in control, and she was in grief as well, which is a terrible combination. I wanted to go with my children."

"That's unacceptable."

"I know, I should never have attacked you."

"No, Luna. You don't get to leave us, ever. We're in this together. You're my sister, and I love you even if you tried to murder me."

"I love you too," she said, hugging me tightly as a sob rocked through her body.

"We will be okay," I promised. "Everything is going to be okay now. We have each other, and that is all we need."

CHAPTER
47

KNOX

Aria was the lace.

The creature was the leather.

Together, they were everything soft and erotic and needy as fuck.

They were polar fucking opposites that I could not wait to see melded together. Aria fought me, the creature ignited beneath me. I fucking growled, and she roared. It was supposed to be easy: deflower the little witch, fuck her out of my system, and be done with her for good. Not fucking happening. She looked at me, and shit got messy. Those beautiful, expressive eyes tore me apart, and the fire within them heated me, unlike any woman in the last thousand years had ever hoped to achieve. And that alone pissed me off.

She'd come alive on my cock, burning with a flame that danced right in tune to her pleasure. Aria was a beast in the sheets, spreading her body for me and demanding I fuck her harder, faster—and fuck if I didn't listen. It should have been fucking simple, fuck her, and toss her out. Instead, she rocked my world and shook shit up. She fucking purred, and I melted, needing to answer her call.

No one had ever fucking purred for me, but she had. Fuck if I didn't crave to hear it every time I walked into a room, only to remember she wasn't mine and couldn't be. Fuck Aria out of my system? It couldn't be done. It was, however, a challenge I was willing to accept.

Instead, I was an addict, and she was my drug. Her eyes revealed more than just a soul, and I wanted to explore the workings of her mind. Aria was brilliant and beautiful. She was a rare combination of woman, one I wanted to get lost within.

I'd watched her moving through my library, exploring parts of it that a lesser being would have passed over, but not Aria. She'd touched every part of it that I'd been in love with, as if she sensed it was part of my soul, exposed and opened for her fingers to trace over.

It wasn't just about fucking her anymore. It was more; it was deeper. I wanted to take her apart and see what made her mind work. I wanted to show her my realm just to watch her pretty eyes ignite with wonder, just like she had when she came undone on my cock for the first time.

Those pretty eyes had grown wide with amazement, her body trembling uncontrollably as I added width and length until I'd filled every inch of that tight, delicious cunt. Her head had dropped back, and her cries had awoken something within me that I'd never thought could be awoken. It had pissed me off and excited me. Those muscles had clamped around me, sucking me off as she cried my name like I was some god she worshipped, and fuck if I didn't crave more.

Aria fought me, but she gave as good as she got. I pissed her off, shoving her away the moment I'd felt my heart begin to flutter in sync with hers. I'd wanted to curl her sleek, tight body against mine and cradle her, holding her close as the sweat dried, and our bodies cooled. Even worse than that, I'd craved her the moment after I'd left her body. I'd pushed her away, needing to hurt her because it had hurt me. That need to comfort, the need to pull the little bitch against me, and take her again was a betrayal to my dead mate.

I'd never felt that way with my mate, and that had ripped open wounds. Aria had torn them wide open and poked at them without even trying. I'd wanted her to hate me so she stayed away, but the moment I couldn't reach her when she'd locked herself in that house, I'd wanted in. I'd sat with the Hecate matriarch trying to flirt my way in, but Aria wasn't available. I could smell her within the house, knew my scent was the only one on her, and yet I couldn't see her and that pissed me off. She vanished into her room and was unreachable. Un-fucking-acceptable.

I'd wanted her to hate me because hate was easier to deal with. Fucking was an emotionless act, one that I did well and often. I hadn't fucked Aria. I'd gone slowly, teaching her what it meant to be with me as she rode my cock until my balls had ached, and then she'd taken control, shocking the hell out of me.

I didn't give anyone control, and yet I'd watched and let it happen. She'd shown me what it was to be with her, and fuck if I didn't want it all. Her smile had fucked me harder than her body ever could physically. I craved her smile more than I craved her cunt, and that couldn't happen. I'd made her feel insignificant, worthless, and made sure she thought I found her body lacking, and what the fuck did she go and do? She got blown the fuck up.

That had almost taken me to my knees, but I'd watched her in the flames as she pushed off the concrete, and everything within me had tensed. She'd stared at the car and then at her sisters, noting her injuries. She'd walked out of the fire stark-ass naked and stared at me, uncaring that everyone was freaked out that she wore her flames. She'd been fucking hot, and it had little to do with the fire raging on her flesh.

Her eyes had changed, pupils blown, and she'd tilted her pretty silver head before lunging at the shooter. Aria was fierce, her mouth wrapped around her victim's throat, and those razor-sharp teeth had made me ache. The noises she made? They fucking hit me with the force of a hurricane. I'd never wanted to purr for any woman, but for Aria, I purred uncontrollably because something inside of me had demanded I return her call, giving the beautiful creature praise.

Then she'd tried to fucking dominate me, and it was the cutest shit I had ever seen in my life. Naked, sex oozing her pheromones, and that little bitch smirked, hunting me down. I'd never been so fucking turned on in my entire fucking life as when she'd walked me in a circle, fully intending to fight me so she could fuck me.

Instead, I'd claimed her, and she'd made me come unhinged with the scent of her body secreting pheromones to draw in a mate. I'd bent her over the porch and fucked her hard and fast just to ensure she reeked of my scent. Fuck her out of my system? It wasn't fucking possible with her. I couldn't even stay away from her. It was like she was connected to me in some way that either of us had yet to grasp, but it was fucking there.

When she needed to fuck, she didn't just go find some random cock to ride; she searched me out. She was a fucking hunter, and I was her prey. Soon, I would begin hunting her down, so she knew what it was like to be hunted and claimed by a predator.

I can't fuck her enough, and that was a fucking problem.

Her body was built for mine perfectly. I fucking hated her, and yet I felt the need to protect her. It was a visceral emotion that I couldn't turn off. I forced her to fight, knowing she wouldn't lose. I baited her beast, and it let Aria fight her own battles. Her beast sensed me trying to bring her to the surface and refused me.

Whatever dwelled inside of Aria Primrose was strong and intelligent, even if she assumed I wasn't mate material. That straight-up pissed me off because she damn well couldn't find better. I wouldn't let her find better, not with how much I craved her. Call it selfish; call it whatever, but that girl was mine.

I didn't save people, and yet I fucking paid the House of Alphas millions of dollars per pussy, just to send Fallon's bitches back to the Nine Realms. Why? Because I didn't want Aria to feel that pain if she entered

Dimitri's domain, and found them fighting over scraps, stretched apart from those fucking mutts tearing their bodies to pieces to breed them. Aria was soft, her heart was on her fucking sleeve, and she needed to shove it back into her chest. I sent my brother to protect her sister, Luna, to heal the little wolf before Aria felt the pain of her death. Why? I was sent here to drive the little witches back into the Nine Realms, and instead, I fucking saved one.

Aria kissed Dimitri, and it took everything I had inside of me not to rip his head off with his spine still attached. The way she danced, it fucked me inside. She taunted me, moving with her eyes on me. Aria fucked me on that dancefloor, and I felt it in my balls.

My date, if you could call her that, assumed my dick got hard for her. It didn't. I didn't even catch the little bitch's name because I didn't care. I wanted her jealous, to see me with another woman, and what did Aria do? She found an alpha and kissed the fucking mutt. He put his hands on my property, and I had every right to end his life, but I didn't. Why? Because she'd fucking feel it, and the only thing I wanted Aria to feel was me fucking her.

I'd followed her out of that mansion and watched her swan dive into that creek. She'd come up screaming. The pain in her cries tugged at me viscerally, and fucking killed me as they exploded from her. I don't care if women cry. I don't care if they hurt, and yet her screams bothered me. It made my insides twist, and fuck if I didn't want to pull her close and promise everything would be okay. It wouldn't, of course, because I was about to destroy her fucking world, and yet I still wanted to promise her that everything would be okay? No. Absolutely not fucking happening.

I was the bad guy in her story, the man who was about to destroy her kind. I had spent hundreds of years planning their fall from grace, and then she walked right in, looked me in the eye, and my insides ignited from the flames that burned within her gaze.

"You ready?" Killian asked, and I turned, staring at my brothers and the men who had helped me plan their fall.

"I've been fucking ready," I growled, standing from the couch I'd almost fucked Aria on. Her scent was everywhere here. It was on my bed, in my fucking library, and it was all over my dick—and no amount of washing it had removed her claiming scent.

CHAPTER
48

Knox

My men had noticed her scent on me, and yet they'd remained silent. They weren't stupid and had watched how she acted, and worse, how I fucking acted. I'd been locked in my library or inside the Nine Realms, looking for clues as to who her father might be. If I'm not searching for answers about her, I'm watching from the shadows for her. She was being hunted by more than just the creatures we'd been handling; she had fuckers coming out of the woodworks to hunt her, either by scent or someone powerful was pursuing my little monster.

"You need to wake the fuck up and realize what is at stake here," Brander snapped, his eyes filling with the embers of his inner fire as he stared me down. He was lucky he was my brother and not someone else.

They'd been silent until right fucking now... assholes.

"Excuse me?" I asked, watching Brander as he scrubbed his hand over his face.

"She's your enemy, our enemy."

"I know who the fuck she is, asshole. I also know that, while she may rock my cock, she is my enemy still. The plan hasn't changed."

"Hasn't it? You were supposed to see what the fuck she is, but she keeps slipping and ending up on that dick of yours."

"You don't think I've tried to get her creature to show its true form? I've pushed her creature around. I drove Aria to tears and made her feel like she's nothing after I fucked her virgin cunt, and all she fucking does is come up swinging. I have held Aria beneath the water and watched her damn near drown, and still, the beast was silent. I fucked her every which way but the right way, Brander. I fucked her hard, harder than I have ever fucked before. She took it, and she fucking *smiled* when I'd finished. She got blown the fuck up and walked out of the wreckage in flames, and she fucking owned the flames like they were hers to command. Aria made them look fucking good. She fights me, and then she fucks me. You tell me, what the fuck more can I do other than murder her to expose the beast within? You tell me what the fuck you want me to do, and I'll fucking do it."

"What if she is something we have never seen before?" Brander countered, and I glared at him.

"A phoenix, maybe?" Killian asked, and I turned, blinking before I moved my stare away from him.

Killian looked like his sister, Liliana, which was a fact I only remembered because his presence never let me forget. It was why I sent him away every fucking chance I got. The details of her image, though, have faded, even more so since the moment I laid eyes on Aria, as if she was replacing Liliana's memory in my mind. Killian's eyes were the same shade as Liliana's, his hair the exact color. I couldn't look into his eyes without feeling a punch to the gut. I frowned, turning over what he'd said, and then dismissed it.

"She isn't a phoenix, and even if she was, the only way to know would be to kill her, and see *if* she rose again."

"That can't fucking happen," Brander said, pinching the bridge of his nose. "She can't die here, none of them can."

"No one touches her yet," I replied, fighting against the urge to defend her. I looked up, staring into Killian's eyes to remind myself of what I am fighting for. "The immortals outside of this town, what's the update on them?" I changed the subject, hating the idea of extinguishing the fire in Aria's pretty blue-green eyes.

Lore snorted, watching me with a knowing look. "Dead, if they have refused to enter the Nine Realms without a fight," he shrugged. "Not many have refused once your name was mentioned. Some are hiding in the woods, but trackers are on their scent. We're on schedule."

"Good." I nodded as I scrubbed a hand down my face, smelling Aria's scent still on it. "The others will be here soon to push the original families back into the Nine Realms. Those aware and in agreement with the situation have already begun to move into their places and are ready to strike down those who are expendable."

"This house?" Brander asked.

"Will vanish once the time comes, returning to the lower level of the palace with me. Aria was in the library," I admitted, watching Brander narrowing his gaze on me. "It revealed itself to her." They all frowned, watching me, knowing the library hid itself even from them, and yet it opened and showed her its secrets.

"That's impossible. It refused to reveal its secrets to Liliana, and she was your *mate*," Killian snapped.

"Aria saw the stolen tomes on the shelves. I know because I fucking watched her run her fingertips over their spines. Her pretty bare feet walked over the frost, and every crystal within the library responded to her presence. Explain that, asshole."

"Why would it do that for her, and not your true mate?" Killian countered, anger dripping from his words.

"If I knew the fucking answer, I wouldn't be asking you. You're the scholar, you tell me. It hasn't ever revealed all of its secrets to another soul, but it chose to show her. She walked into it twice and was shown its secrets both times. She saw the white oak shelves and warmed her firm, tight ass on the flames of the Ifrit's cauldron. She draws magic from the Nine Realms, not from the nature of this Human Realm the other witches pull from. When Aria called her power to her, it came straight from our realm.

"I've felt nothing like her before. She's immune to flames, casting raw, strong magic that hasn't been tapped into since before we were born, and she's built to savage. Your sister was sweet, and I had to be gentle because of what I am and because Liliana was fragile. Aria took me, and she took it all. I fucked her every way I could, Killian. I was buried so deep in her fucking throat that she licked my balls and got pissed when I had to detach her pretty lips before I came in her throat like some fucking youth with his first maiden. I tried to break her body, it didn't break. Aria's creature looked me dead in the eye and told me I wasn't mate material. Me, I'm the fucking king who feeds an entire realm," I snapped. "I only tell you this because these facts have convinced me she is one of our kind, maybe not the same, but she is something similar to us, and we're dying out."

"And that pissed you off," Killian smirked, observing me.

"You're damn right it did. I am a provider. Your sister never fucking complained or lacked for anything she desired. Aria looked me dead in the eye and told me she found me lacking, how would you respond? Considering what we are and what we do for our women, wouldn't you be pissed?"

He nodded, frowning before he spoke again. "Aria isn't Liliana, Knox. She's a Hecate witch. The same bloodlines as the ones who helped murder my sister and your son. I watched you hold my nephew as he died a thousand deaths, cursed by those of her bloodline. I helped you bury my sister as you wept for the first time in your entire life while we mourned your family. They shot first, and I sure as fuck intend to slaughter them all, even Aria."

"You think I have forgotten our purpose here? I haven't, and the moment everything is in place, we will strike. Do not ever fucking question my loyalty to my mate and my son again. I was the one who held him as his body failed, and the light left his pretty blue eyes. I was the one who wept as he was ravished in boils and fever until he hallucinated and didn't remember who I was, didn't recognize his mother. Everything I have done and everything I do is because of them. I fucked Aria, so what. I fuck a lot of bitches, and it has never changed my endgame."

"She's not like other women, Knox. We've all seen it. I'm just the asshole with enough balls to say it," Killian pointed out.

His arms crossed over his chest as he watched me; we both knew he was right. Aria was nothing like the others. The others were just wet holes to appease the need to release the pressure in my balls. I hadn't thought of another bitch since fucking Aria. I fucked Lacey after I'd threatened Aria on the outskirts of town, but it hadn't been Lacey I'd seen as I plowed into her with anger. It was pretty turquoise eyes that defied me, taunting me. I'd fucked that useless witch long and hard until she passed out from the pain and brutality. I'd given Lacey my anger while imagining she was Aria Hecate, and I'd found her lacking. Lacey had known she wasn't the one I wanted, but she'd still gotten to her knees and opened her pretty lips for me. It had been the wrong fucking time to lip off and then open her mouth while on her knees.

I'd let Lacey wield her magic on Aria, expecting the little witch to burst into tears. Instead, she'd throat punched Lore and then went nose to nose with an alpha, begging him to fight her. Bitch had balls, that much was a given.

It was clear to me from the beginning that she was different from her sisters. I'd felt Aria pull magic to her, and I'd fucking been shocked with the sensation of the Nine Realms giving it to her. Those realms were cold and merciless, like me. Yet the moment she called, they fucking gave her everything she needed. There was no record of any creature being able to draw power from inside of the Nine Realms into this one. Her tiny little fingers wiggled, and the power was there for the taking. She made it look natural, as if she was born to wield the power. Not one of her sisters had so much as questioned why or how the fuck Aria Primrose Hecate had just yanked power from another realm to her painted fingertips. Either they were unaware and couldn't feel it, or it terrified them, and they kept it secret.

"What about the rebellion leaders that remained in the Nine Realms, any news on them yet?" Brander asked, pulling my mind back to the issue at hand.

"Gathered and ready," I announced. "Once we return, they'll march on the first stronghold, declaring war on anyone who opposes us."

"So, we move forward, and we continue with the plan," Brander said, sitting before me folding his hands and tilting his head. "Glad to know getting your balls licked didn't change anything."

"Could you imagine getting your balls licked while being buried that deep inside a woman's mouth?" Lore asked. "I've had girls take half of me, and it wowed me, but Aria fucking took it all. I watched her head push forward, and when it didn't come back, and Knox gasped, I knew she'd taken his dick all the way down her throat. And then that fucker, he says, *jaw fully extends,'* not, *'holy fuck this bitch just swallowed my dick,'* just, *'jaw fully extends.'"* Lucky bastard." Lore rubbed his hand over his mouth. "What a fucking waste of talent. It's really too bad you couldn't keep her and make her into a pretty pet."

It took everything within me not to reach over and snap Lore's neck at witnessing Aria in all her glory. The memory of her lips wrapped around my cock still got me rock-hard. It wasn't even the fact that she took all of me, but the look in her eyes as she peered up at me, giving me her attention. She wanted to please me, but also didn't fucking care if she did. I'd wanted to grab that ass, throw her down, and fuck her till she submitted, but she'd had other plans. She wanted to fight me, and she wasn't afraid to say it.

That creature had insulted my ability to provide, my ability to fuck, and my intelligence, and then, instead of admitting defeat with my superior strength, she'd sent my ass sailing across the room like I was nothing. I never got caught off guard. She wasn't supposed to be that strong, but she was. She wasn't supposed to be that hot, but she was. I wasn't supposed to crave her, but I did. It did shit to me that I hated, yet wanted to feel with her. I'd never allowed emotions to rule me, and yet I'd claimed her in front of the entire alpha pack.

I'd placed my teeth on her shoulder, staring them down as my fingers trailed through the wet mess my rattle created in her panties. She'd come hard and fast, and they'd gotten hard watching. Fuck, I'd gotten hard. I'd meant to lay claim. I claimed fucking ownership. I'd made her mine in a way she didn't and wouldn't understand, and that was another fucking problem.

Aria wasn't mine to claim, but I'd claimed her, anyway. I'd claimed her in a way that couldn't be undone, and yet I didn't want to take it back. I liked owning her, even if she wasn't fucking aware of what it meant. It was a mark of protection, but it was so much more. That mark made her need me, crave me, and it also worked the same way on me. It was a mark of mates, and yet I'd never given or offered it to my mate. So why the fuck had I claimed Aria?

I looked at other women and compared them to her, and they were lacking. Regina sucked good dick, she worked it, but the hag had nothing on Aria. Aria had dug into my cold, dead soul, and she'd lit it on fucking fire. She went to war against me, and she fucking didn't admit defeat readily. Instead, she craved me as much as I craved her, and the need to go barebones against one another won out. She was fucking wild with her need, and that wasn't something she could fake. When Aria wanted cock, she took it.

Aria fucking devoured it.

Aria was savage and enjoyed being savaged by me.

Her scent wasn't just arousing; it was consuming. Lesser creatures couldn't fight it, not even the little mutt who vowed he'd given his word. One whiff of her sex oozing with need and he'd fucking come unhinged. Fuck, I had trouble ignoring her scent, and I had never been lured to a bed by a bitch in heat until her. It was almost as if her magic was enhancing it, making her desirable to every male with a fucking pulse. Hell, even some without. Greer hated her at first sight, but that motherfucker teased her and then told her to claim sanctuary. He'd helped no female before. He hated them, preferring male company, and yet I'd watched him narrowing his gaze as I'd carried her into the house, dripping my scent from her cunt.

"Do we know who in the Nine Realms wants her alive?" Killian asked, interrupting my thoughts.

"My guess would be the asshole who fathered her. She wasn't conceived magically. Someone wanted that girl created and then made that want a reality. It's someone powerful, and with enough pull that the leaders of the rebellion counseled me to keep her alive."

"Is that why you protected her, writing your name on her pretty pussy? Or is there another reason you keep intervening on her behalf?" Killian asked, watching me for any sign of weakness. He wouldn't find it.

"Rape is violent, Killian. If the alphas had raped her, she'd be as good as dead. There are over fifty alphas alone in this town, and Fallon shared his whores with them all daily. Aria was untouched and would have fought, and we all know what happens when a woman fights a pack of alphas." I'd have slaughtered every fucking alpha here to keep her from being mauled or raped by that pack. I'd have pissed in a circle around her, marking that little witch as my prey.

"The alphas would have torn her apart," he agreed, exhaling. "Just don't get attached, she's on the kill list."

"She's also on the do-not-fucking-touch list, and I'm way past touching her. She's a fucking newborn, and she is already powerful. The creature within her taught herself to talk in a matter of minutes from emerging from her cocoon. Aria knows what she needs, but she doesn't know why she needs it. Her kind, whatever it may be, it doesn't belong here. Aria herself subdued an alpha. Not just any alpha, *the* fucking alpha. She only used her teeth and her claws, and she had Fallon coming on his own floor with the intensity of her bite. She's a fucking unicorn of mixed powers, but none of them belong together."

I couldn't have been more fucking proud of her as that piece of shit fucked the floor while she'd demanded he submit to her bite. I'd smelled his cum as it had exploded from him and watched the horror that entered her eyes as the woman mixed with predator broke apart. It fucking hurt me to see the tears swimming in her eyes as her family stared on in open horror. My little monster was all alpha, but she was still learning what that meant.

"She rattles, and she purrs. Aria also clamped that cunt down tight to keep your cock inside her body, but also to protect you as she slept." Brander rubbed his hand over his face, shaking his head. "Her flesh is clean, no scales or feathers. Her fire comes through her pores, as if beneath her flesh, there is something that ignites when she's afraid or in danger. But then fear and danger don't draw it out as it should, either. She's a fucking enigma, one I can't figure out."

"She burns hot when she comes. She damn near burned down my bedroom. The roar that escaped her throat, it blew the fucking windows out of the entire third floor. Then there's the thing beneath her spine, it moves. Other than teeth and claws, Aria shows no other physical signs of being unique or a creature. There's not a single ounce of fat on her entire body, and when she is no longer in control, her body is defined and all sleek muscles. It's almost as if Aria is the softness, and the creature is hard and lethal. She's definitely something strong, and something ancient created her."

"You forgot to mention that fact she purrs *for* you. She also answers your rattle, and no female has ever responded to your rattle, not even Liliana. You also purred to approve her actions; you don't do that for bed partners. You barely fucking did it for my sister. Why would you do it for some whore you're fucking?" Killian stared me down, challenging me again.

"Careful, Killian," I warned cautiously. "I purred to calm a newborn creature, one who could have jeopardized everything we are trying to achieve here. Don't make it into something it isn't. I have no idea what the fuck she is, but I know that if she becomes unhinged, we won't get the original bloodlines into that portal, and we won't be able to contain them if they fucking scatter to hide from a beast that doesn't belong here. Make no mistake, Aria is a beast, one that could easily be set off and destroy everything we've been working to build for the past five hundred years."

"Then snap her fucking neck and be done with her." Killian glowered at me with accusation burning in his eyes; his challenges were getting on my last fucking nerve.

"And add more enemies to the growing list? Why the fuck not?" I asked, watching him as that tidbit sank in. "We don't know who fathered her, but we do know whoever it was, they're fucking powerful, that much is clear from the little bitch that he sired, but sure, let's fucking snap her neck."

"No," Brander whispered, scrubbing his hand down his face and shaking his head before exhaling deeply.

"If her father has the ear of the council to the rebellion, he isn't just a king; he's a king over one of the beast kingdoms. If he is a king of beasts, or something even fucking *higher* than that, it means Aria's father is one of us. She's the daughter of one of our fucking allies, so whatever we do with her, we tread carefully. Killing her could cause more problems than we can handle. I'd rather not murder the daughter to one of the leaders of an entire army and lose them as we prepare to march that army on the witches."

"It changes nothing." I wasn't letting go of Aria without a fight, that much was certain. "Her father fucked Freya Hecate, and by doing so, he condemned Aria to death or imprisonment. The witches have to die, but they have to do it within the Nine Realms. Unless we find another way to achieve the end goal without ending her life, we stick to the plan—and she remains on the kill list."

"And lose an ally?" Killian frowned, shaking his head. "I don't think that is the wisest choice, Knox."

"Which is it, Killian? You wanted her dead, now you want her alive. It cannot be both ways."

"I want you not to destroy the image of my sister while you fuck that whore!" he snapped as he balled his hands into fists.

"I only told you how she responded to my cock to show you she was like us. She is just fucking like us. Our kind mates once in a lifetime, Killian. Liliana was my mate. She was also the love of my life, but she left me. Liliana also chose to leave you too, asshole. Liliana took my anchor with her, and now I grasp onto anything I can to keep from becoming the monster the rebellion wanted me to be.

"The witches took my family from me to enrage me enough to throw the first punch. I have waited over five hundred years for revenge, and some sweet as sin pussy isn't changing my mind. I became the monster the rebellion wanted me to be. The witches never expected us to rise against them, but we shall. We're about to hit them where it hurts the most. But Aria Hecate is the strongest tool they have in their toolbox. That's a fucking problem for the witches because I have Aria within my grasp, and she wears my name on her pretty cunt, as you so delicately put it. I walked in and claimed their most powerful fucking fighter, and yeah, I mounted her and fucking liked it. The thing is, I have her, and they can't stop that now."

"You're a problem solver; figure that shit out. Just know that she's your fucking enemy, and try to remember that when you're fucking her slit, *bro*," Killian said, nodding as he exhaled.

"I'm very aware of who is sliding down my cock, and that she's my enemy. She, on the other hand, has no idea what or who I am, or that she's mine now. Aria is brilliant, but she's young and innocent. I'm not. I claimed her, and yeah, she's one of them. She's also unable to deny that claim, making her something that cannot be wielded against us in the upcoming war. The fucking king took their queen, and there isn't dick they can do about it. Checkmate."

"That's true. You walked right in and slapped the little bitch with your dick, and took her from their arsenal," Lore chuckled, shaking his platinum head. "You didn't ask my advice, but here it is. Take her, keep her where they won't find her, and turn her to our side. You do that, and we've already won this war before we even marched against them."

"That won't happen. Aria isn't the type to turn against her blood. She's loyal, and that is a fucking problem; taking her, though, that won't be. I guess we will see where she lands when we lay siege to this town," I muttered, scrubbing my hand down my face with frustration.

I studied Killian, frowning as I realized that I couldn't wholly recall Liliana's face anymore, just a ghostly image when I tried, which then faded into Aria. Where her shining eyes had once haunted me, Aria's had replaced them. Where she would haunt my nightmares, I now dreamt of the sweet noises Aria made when I fucked her. I used to crave the sound of Liliana laughing, but now I craved the taste of Aria's lips and the sideward angle of her head when she was thinking hard right before she bit that sexy as fuck bottom lip.

I'd had to be gentle with Liliana, careful with her fragile body, not Aria. Aria, I fucking destroyed and went to war against in bed, and she fought back. She fucking roared for more, purring when I got harder, even before she'd been consumed by flames. It was something my kind did, but hers was rawer, and fuck if I didn't purr right back.

I had tried to convince myself that it was because I was protecting our plans, but her sexy little purr tugged at everything inside of me. Liliana hadn't ever purred, and when I did, it had been an afterthought. Something I did for her because I wanted to, not because it came automatically. Aria, I fucking had to because everything within me demanded it. I'd never bitten Liliana, but Aria took my bite, and if I didn't heal it fast enough for her, she did it her damn self.

I'd hated no one as much—or wanted them while hating them—as I did Aria. The feelings conflicted with one another, not that it mattered. I'd started a fucking war, and I had to finish it. There was no other way out of it now. Too many pieces were in play, and too many lives depended on this not being fucked before we even threw the first punch. No, no matter how much I wanted it otherwise, Aria couldn't be saved, and neither could her sisters.

CHAPTER
49

ARIA

I studied the posture of the few alphas that had invaded our house and currently stood spread out everywhere, which had my anxiety on edge. They were pointing to places on a grid map, indicating new portal holes. It wouldn't have been such a huge deal, except four of the largest holes were scattered in the backwoods on our property.

Dimitri explained the length and width of each, which was unsettling. The smaller holes were wide enough for one creature to enter, but the bigger portal holes could allow several creatures through at once. It was like someone or something was planning to invade this town en masse, and that was unsettling. Portals placed close together could indicate creatures were trying to come through as a war party, which had happened more than a few times when the original bloodlines first settled in Haven Falls.

"I'll show you where they are, but the sensors on your land should have alerted you the moment they were opened," Dimitri said. "The knowledge that the sensors failed to alert the House of Magic to the dangerous situation on the land, well, it is troubling." He folded his arms over his chest, studying me even though I had yet to meet his stare.

"It's very troubling since the House of Magic is built to detect any barrier being breached. I worry that we missed something that may have been done to my father's remains when we were gone. Also troubling is the fact the house rejected a Hecate witch when she needed it, not allowing her entrance to the property." Aurora pushed her hair behind her ear, staring down at the map. "Has Knox been made aware of the problem yet? He should be present for the search."

"Not yet." Dimitri's face reddened at the mention of Knox's name, and I had to force myself not the peek at the anger burning in his eyes, seeming to be directed at me. "I wanted you to know first since it looks really bad that the portals are hidden on your property. The situation with Amara already looks bad, but to have open portals large enough to slip an army through, well, that looks really bad."

"That is why you should have alerted him first. Knox is the one leading the investigation, and as such, he is supposed to be made aware of any problems or findings first, which definitely includes portals large enough to fit a war party through as you just pointed out," I finished and held his gaze as he snorted.

"Why? Why Knox, Aria?" Dimitri asked carefully, saying out loud what I'd been wondering from the start. "No one has asked who the hell sent him, and yet everyone falls into line because he tells them to. Who the fuck is he, or better yet, what the fuck is he?" His gaze held mine, and I hesitated with my response. He'd asked damn good questions; I mean, they were what I had asked too.

Dimitri's stare became heated, and I swallowed, dropping mine to avoid a scene before his pack. Electric-blue eyes sparkled as a subtle glow began to build, and I didn't want to feel or see the heat burning in them. Knowing what he looked like naked wasn't helping me stay out of his crosshairs. Whatever lived within me, she was a horny bitch, and she wanted one man and one man alone. Dimitri wasn't that man. Even though I liked him, liking him could potentially end his life, and that wasn't something I could accept.

"You're fucking him, and you have no idea what the fuck he is. What happens if you end up pregnant? You could die if what he turns out to be isn't compatible with your genetics. You need to stop spreading your legs for him. You're smarter than that, Aria."

"We don't even know what Aria is, Dimitri. Stop being petty because she won't let you sniff her ass and refuses to spread her legs for you," Luna growled, and the sound reverberated through the room.

"I won't get pregnant, asshole," I shrugged nonchalantly, not believing it myself one bit. "I don't know what Knox is, and I don't care. I do know that whatever he is, you bowed to him. He is a king. I know because I've seen him in his crown. He isn't from this realm, nor has he spent a lot of time within it. That is all I know. Who I sleep with isn't your concern, either."

"I think you know a lot more than you're willing to share with us. You owe this covenant your loyalty, not him. You have been fucking him for months now, and you think to lie to us and tell us you know nothing? You don't fuck someone for that long and not learn things about them," Dimitri snapped, letting his canine teeth show as he curled his lip in disgust, glaring at me. I snorted, shaking my head with his pathetic tactic to elicit fear in me with his bite. He had nothing on Knox, nor could he subdue the beast within me as Knox did.

"That is enough! You are inside the House of Magic, and a guest, Dimitri," Aurora snapped as power erupted around her, causing my hair to float with her warning. "You represent the alphas, and as their representative, you will respect the boundaries, and my home, which you are in under sanctuary. That means you do not speak to us disrespectfully or use your powers to seek to subdue one of my nieces with your dominance. You are new, which allows you some leeway, but not enough to speak to Aria in the way that you are. Witches don't ask for an entire family tree before we sexually encounter a male, you should know that. You bred one of ours, and you left her through her pregnancy without coming forth when she needed you, so I suggest you tread very carefully from this point on, young man."

"I stand corrected," he said softly, bowing his head to the matriarch of our family. "I apologize. Please accept it, Aurora. I meant no disrespect to you or Aria."

"It is not me you owe the apology, alpha."

"Aria," he whispered my name, huskily. "I apologize. I do hope you reconsider your arrangement with Knox Karnavious and consider a more appropriate match for your stature and rank. Very little is known about Knox or his men, other than they are from the Nine Realms. He could be a minotaur, or worse."

"I am not dating him, and other than fucking him, nothing is going on. I don't ask him questions, and even if I did, I highly doubt he would feel inclined to answer them."

"You're wrong, Aria. In the street, when I bowed to Knox, it was because he laid claim to you openly. The noise he made? He demanded we bow or die; that was a war cry, woman. He was willing to murder us all to place his claim on you, because he fucking claimed you as his. Do you even grasp the impact of what I'm saying? You are his, and if anyone else seeks to claim you, they must first challenge him. His scent is all over you, and that bite? It's permanent. That means you allowed him to claim you on a level so profoundly deep that no one can challenge it. You tell me, Aria, why would Knox claim you in such a way when he has no intention of remaining here after the investigation has completed?"

I blinked, uncertain what to say if anything. I hadn't realized Knox had laid claim to me. I hadn't given him permission to do that, or had I? I had given him my shoulder, but it was to allow him to show the other alphas I was off-limits. Not that I hated the idea, considering I wasn't interested in fucking others, but if what Dimitri said was true, it wasn't something we could undo easily. What I knew about claiming was limited, but something inside of me *liked* the idea of belonging to Knox. Not that it was smart to allow something like him to claim me, but because his actions had saved Dimitri's life, I'd been thankful to Knox for doing it. I knew if the alpha had tried to claim me without my permission, I'd have taken him down in a heartbeat. But why would Knox issue a challenge to alphas to fight to the death over me? That was troubling, considering he didn't even actually like me.

"Show us the portal holes, alpha. Afterward, you can tell us how you discovered them on our property, without our permission to be upon it. As for Knox, what I do with him isn't your business, nor will you tell me who I can and cannot fuck just because I denied you that right, as was my choice." I stared Dimitri down as he nodded with worry in his gaze, noting the tone of my voice. It was final, and I gave him no room to argue it without sounding like more of an asshole than he already did.

He didn't get to come into my home and make it sound like I was sleeping around. I'd had sex with one male, and while he was probably the worst choice I could have made, it was my choice and my body. I had to deal with the fallout of what came from my choices, and I would if it came to pass. He didn't have to worry about it, nor did anyone else.

However, I wasn't over the fact we'd had a lot of sex, and not once did pregnancy crossed my mind. I hadn't even considered it a possibility, but I probably should have. I needed to ensure that I was protected from creating a life with him since I wasn't ready to become a mother, nor did I want a child with a man who hated me more than he liked me.

Everyone stood and started toward the door. I followed behind at a slower pace, allowing no male behind me as they sent their pheromones into the air.

Nor was I willing to chance any alpha trying to subdue me, since Dimitri had made his intentions clear with his jealousy. Luna had explained his obsession, or the basic wolf's need to dominate and own whatever it craved, which unfortunately seemed to be me lately.

We started toward the woods that bordered ours and Knox's property, and I gazed at the darkened house that had been silent for days. I was lost in thought as I moved toward the creek, checking that the portal there was still marked and sealed. The few Knox had learned of were all marked and had a spell to prevent them from acting as an open doorway between realms.

I stopped walking and peered around the forest before pausing, noting I'd become separated from the others as I had been consumed by thoughts of consequences for what I'd been doing. Great, of course, I'd been thinking about Knox and ended up lost in the woods alone after dark. It also didn't help that the further from the house we got, the darker it became.

The hair on my neck rose as if I was being watched, and I stopped mid-step, peering around again as I moved in a slow circle. Swallowing, I frowned and noted that I wasn't alone. I was being followed.

I tripped over a stick that caught my foot, looking over my shoulder only to find one of the alphas watching me as he sauntered toward me. I got up, dusting off my hands, and started forward again, moving deeper into the woods at a faster pace.

It was difficult to watch for sticks and branches that poked up from the ground or hung from dead trees as the light continued to fade. Branches slapped my face, whipping across my flesh as I moved through them. I wasn't stupid; I realized he was sending me deeper into the woods, but what he failed to see was that we were almost to Knox's property line. The moment we entered it, Knox would be alerted. My foot crossed over the line, and I turned to face the male who watched me with darkness in his gaze. I was being hunted.

Staring at the alpha, I crossed my arms as he slowly stalked me. He growled low from his chest. The noise he created rose with a warning, announcing his intentions. He would make a play to subdue me, and I would take him down easily. It was rather stupid on his part to assume just because I was cut off from the others, I was weak.

"You think you're so fucking special, whore? You are nothing but a stupid little bitch that lies down and spreads her pussy for the bastard who thinks to rule us all. You need to be put down and put down hard, and I can't wait to make you bleed."

As if anyone could put me down harder than Knox? The man knew how to make a woman beg for it and then decide she'd bitten off a lot more than she could chew. I opened my mouth to respond, but a branch snapped in the opposite direction, pulling my attention to another alpha entering the small clearing.

Then another joined his friends, and I realized they'd separated me on purpose. I'd fallen into their trap perfectly while trying to avoid this situation from happening. I exhaled, watching each one as they started closing in on me from every angle. Fear kicked up into my throat, and I fought to calm my rapid heartbeat. Adrenaline shot through me, and I fisted my hands at my sides, waiting for one to lunge toward me.

"You don't want to do this," I whispered through the burning in my gums.

"You killed Fallon, and for what? Because you were too good for us to fuck?" one of the alphas snapped icily, malice dripping from his lips. "You will know the difference between an alpha and a wannabe king when we are finished making you scream and bleed for us, stupid little bitch."

"I didn't want to be raped, and I didn't make Fallon choose his path. It doesn't mean I thought myself better than you. I was protecting myself from being raped. I am not a wolf, nor am I bound to play by your rules!" I hissed as power erupted into the clearing, causing goosebumps to spread over my arms. I peered around the area, tasting the rawness of the power that had just entered it.

The men looked around warily, sensing something else had come into the fight. It wasn't like Knox's powers. It was undiluted, pure raw power that sent a shiver up my spine and warning bells erupting inside my skull. The men looked between each other, and then one stepped closer toward me, only to vanish before his foot had even touched the ground.

We all went still, listening to the noises within the forest. It was eerily silent, and everything inside of me said to run, now. I exhaled slowly as I started to take a step in the direction I assumed the house was located. I watched in horror as the missing alpha's head was tossed back, rolling past my feet before his body dropped from the sky.

I looked up, staring at the treetops as the other alphas began to run deeper into the woods in separate directions. I closed my eyes, breathing loud enough that it was the only noise I heard until screaming erupted from the direction one of the alphas had taken. The hair on my arms rose with fear, and my throat tightened with a scream held within it.

At the sounds of the alpha's screaming, I started running toward the house, at least what I hoped was the right direction. Whatever was in the woods, the barrier wasn't preventing it from attacking. More screaming sounded before it went eerily silent, and I turned, staring into the woods. My breathing was hard, labored, and ragged from running and trying to stay ahead of the alphas. I turned back toward the house and released a blood-curdling scream.

CHAPTER
50

Knox stood in front of me, shirtless and covered in blood dripping from his razor-sharp claws, pushing through the tips of his fingers, black as night. Blackness surrounded his eyes, which were now swallowed in obsidian, banked with fiery embers that burned within them. He looked like something out of a horror story! Power was rolling off of him in deadly waves as he took a step toward me, and I tripped backward, landing on the ground only for him to follow me down.

He didn't speak, but his nose went straight to my sex, inhaling it deeply like some wild beast before he slowly climbed my body, pinning me to the ground. He stared down at me as fiery embers continued to burn within his gaze. His mouth lowered to my neck, running his nose over the rapidly beating pulse at the hollow column where my neck touched my shoulder. Knox's teeth skimmed my shoulder, sniffing it as he boxed me in with his body and held me to the ground with his weight. His knee pushed against my core as he licked my shoulder, creating a moan within my throat that I couldn't prevent from bubbling up and escaping.

"Knox." His name came out past the chattering of my teeth as heat flooded my core. He slithered against my flesh, watching me through dark eyes. He was one hundred percent predator, and I was the prey that he watched as he played with me. His facial features were more defined sharper as he studied me.

He pushed up from the ground, staring down my body, and his mouth opened to reveal razor-sharp teeth. He growled, lowering his mouth again, running his nose against the hard nipple of my breast that responded to his mouth against my shoulder.

"So pretty, little one," he hissed thickly, nipping my nipple until I shivered with fear as his serrated teeth threatened to rip my poor nipple off.

He chuckled, watching my reaction. His clawed fingers moved between us as he held himself up by one arm, rubbing against my wetness that his close proximity had created. His claw pushed against the thin material, lifting it away before pushing his claw into my panties. In all reality, it should have torn me apart, but it didn't. The hardened curve of claws skimmed my sensitive nub, and my legs spread while his eyes lifted. "Mine?"

"Please?" I was uncertain what I was asking him for since he was all sharp edges and razors.

I should have been screaming my head off for help, but no one in this entire realm that could stop this creature if he wanted me. His deep, husky laughter created more heat in my core, and he inhaled, watching me, learning me.

Knox lowered his mouth, brushing it against mine as his scent hit me full force, causing my body to jerk with the magnitude of it. It wrecked my senses, holding me prisoner to the raw, terrifying need to spread my legs and beg him to fuck me. It was terrifying, and yet it excited me knowing that he could either fuck me or destroy me if he chose to.

Knox rattled loudly from deep in his chest, and I followed it with mine, which was feminine sounding. His men entered the clearing, covered in blood as they watched us together through heated stares. I looked away from them to gaze back up at Knox, watching the predator that held me beneath him, trapped.

He was dripping blood from his lips, and his teeth were serrated weapons that scraped over my flesh, stealing a gasp from my lungs as they touched my throat. His cock pushed against me, and I shuddered, noting it was much larger than he'd ever let me experience. He pulled back, staring at me coldly.

"You and your people brought the realm to its knees for this pathetic dream to claim another realm. I will be the one to bring them to their knees as I watch them die, burning this dream to nothing more than ashes. You, sweet girl, you will be on your knees, watching me as I rain down fire on the Nine Realms until there is nothing left. You will crawl and bleed for me, little one, but you will not die." He rattled loudly with his declaration and his men watching him as he continued to rattle until the trees trembled from the sheer velocity of it. "I will enjoy you as they cower in fear, knowing I am hunting them to extinction. You will be mine, and mine alone, woman."

Yowsers.

That wasn't ominous as all get-out, now, was it?

My hands trembled as they lifted, pushing through his hair while I brought his mouth to my throat. I bared it to him like a sacrificial lamb, and he smiled against it. His heated lips brushed against my wildly beating pulse, rushing blood to my brain with adrenaline coursing through me wildly, as he rubbed his erection against me unabashedly.

I turned my head, brushing my lips against his as he stared into my soul, devouring pieces of it slowly, meticulously. Knox had a beast, and that beast was a heartless prick who wanted to hurt me, and I wasn't sure why I wanted him to, but I craved it. I craved him. All of him, uncaring that he had just admitted he was my enemy.

Embers moved in his eyes as if there was a fire within them that called to me. His mouth dropped against mine, brushing across it carefully, without hurting me, as if it was a coherent choice not to damage my flesh. He spoke of hurting me in one breath while holding me as if I was something to be treasured with the next. It confused, excited, and called to me.

His hands pushed the hair away from my face, watching me as I took in the changes and found them beautiful. I lifted against him, inviting him to take me, without being able to ignore the visceral need for him to fuck me right here, right now. Knox was burning from the inside out as if we were alike beneath the flesh we wore. His hand drifted to my stomach as a wicked smile filled his lips, and then he leaned down, whispering huskily against my ear.

"You're so fucked, little Aria. You have no idea how much the thought of you on your knees, pleading for me, excites everything within me." He inhaled against my ear, bringing his hand up against my throat, and I shivered with need as he chuckled. "Soon, I promise."

"Knox." I shivered as he pushed his erection against my belly. The power lessened in the clearing as I exhaled, pushing myself against him as white-hot need ripped through me. His head pushed against my shoulder as the rattle sounded again, but when it lifted, and he peered down at me, his gaze was once again the color of a turbulent ocean that could sink ships with the storm raging within them.

"Do not ever fucking do that again, Aria," he uttered as his eyes turned to a deep, storm-colored blue. "Do you fucking understand me? If they had captured you, you wouldn't have walked out of these woods tonight."

"They weren't the ones that terrified me, Knox," I admitted softly, watching him as his lips curved into a dangerous grin while his gaze searched mine, but the moment he inhaled, his eyes grew heavy with lust.

"Careful, little lamb, you smell good enough to eat right now."

"I kind of like the way you devour me," I admitted.

He shivered and shook off whatever had taken control as a masculine grin lifted the corners of his mouth. Unlike mine, his wasn't all about sex. It was more about things like murder, ripping alphas apart like they were nothing more than a wispy scrap of paper, and putting them right back where he had found them because apparently, it was rude not to, but in a few more pieces than they'd been before. He moved his hips and smiled wickedly, lowering his mouth to mine before he inhaled.

"They didn't touch you." His tone held relief as he studied me, letting his gaze drift to the shirt that was still wet from where he'd grasped my nipple between his massive teeth. His hips pushed against mine, and his heated blue eyes rose to lock with mine, raw need banked in their depths.

"I never planned to let their game get that far."

He stood, pulling me with him as he picked something up from the ground and placed three tiny canisters into my palm. "They weren't planning on playing fair, Aria. They planned to rape you and then remove your head. Why are you even out in the woods alone after dusk?"

"Dimitri found portals on our property."

"And you intended to keep it from me?" He watched me as a tick in his jaw hammered, anger starting to take root as he assumed we were withholding things from him. I rolled my eyes at his reaction.

"No, of course not, jerk. The first thing we asked Dimitri was if you had been notified before us, and when he said no, we asked why you hadn't been. He said considering Amara's situation, he wanted to tell us first. We planned to figure out the location of each and then show you where they are." I left out the part where Dimitri had questioned Knox, and he shook his head.

"What else did he say?"

"He doesn't like me fucking you and thinks I should be with someone of my own stature within the Nine Realms. He doesn't like that I sleep with you and that I don't even know what breed you are, which is a violation of the covenant. I told him to not worry about who I fucked. He got pissy, but he dropped it. Anything else you want to know?"

He searched my eyes before he turned to the men. "Clean up the evidence of the kills and toss them through a portal. You, Aria, get to come with me. I thought you wanted to fuck Dimitri?"

"If I had wanted to fuck him, he'd be fucked."

"Interesting, considering every time you lose control of your beast, you end up on my dick," he said, watching me carefully.

"It's good dick, Knox."

He chuckled, pulling me closer as he nuzzled my ear before slipping his fingers through mine, dragging me toward the creek. Once he reached it, he released my hand, and I watched him as he stepped closer to the water, scooping his hands into the ice-cold section of the creek to remove the blood from his body. The moment the water touched his flesh, it sizzled and then steam curled into the air. Slowly, he scrubbed the water over his arms and chest before standing and turning to look at me.

"Come here, woman," he ordered, and I listened, because beneath the cool exterior, there was something else watching and waiting for me to disobey. And it was probably a serial killer that I'd totally almost just gotten off with. "Kiss me."

"Why?" I carefully studied the way his body pulsed with carnal power even as I stepped closer to him, doing as he asked.

"Because I need your pretty scent to hide theirs, and it oozes from you when you kiss me, so fucking kiss me like you want me, little one."

His hand lifted my shirt, exposing my midriff as he pulled me closer. I tipped my head back, claiming his lips slowly as he rubbed my body against his, creating erotic friction. My hands skimmed over the washboard abs to his chest, then down his arms, rubbing my scent over his flesh, marking him. Deepening the kiss, he devoured my mouth, pulling me closer until I was pushing my fingers through his hair as he lifted me. My legs wrapped around him, and I tossed self-preservation to the wind as I kissed him like the last few days away had left me famished, and half-crazed with need. He pushed his cock against me, and I started to undo his pants to get to what I needed.

A cough sounded behind us a moment before my sisters exploded into the clearing next to the creek. I pulled away from his kiss, staring at him, and my hands slipped off of his cock unwillingly, moving around his shoulders as I climbed down, skimming over the cock that had grown hard again to remind him he was mine. He smirked roguishly as I pushed against it, wanting it on an animalistic level.

"You're coming home with me tonight," he whispered huskily against my ear as he turned me to face the people moving through the woods into the clearing.

"You bet your ass I am, big boy."

Dimitri took in the way I leaned against Knox and his arms wrapped against my body protectively. His chin rested on my shoulder, and I was confident he had a shit-eating grin on his lips. He rumbled his growl deep from in his chest, and then the rattle escaped his lips, and mine sounded instantly, as if his beast called to mine, and it answered him eagerly.

"That explains where Aria went," Kinvara chuckled. "The new portals are larger than the first two on the property, but they are in the back and as large as Dimitri said they were."

Dimitri hadn't looked away from me. His hands fisted at his sides, and he turned his lips up, taking in the way I melted against Knox. I couldn't move, not because I didn't want to, but because there was a massive erection resting against my lower back. I was a greedy bitch, and I didn't want anyone to see the rather large package that I was going to get delivered tonight.

"Logan, Chase, and Brent have all vanished. I can't sense them or catch their scent," Dimitri growled angrily. "You wouldn't know anything about the disappearance of my men, would you, Knox?"

"I only just entered the woods and came upon a ravishing maiden drinking from the creek and decided to devour her pretty mouth. Then the impish maiden climbed on, and things got hot and heavy rather quickly, which made it rather hard to give a fuck what happened to your men. She's rather demanding when she needs to be fucked. You know how it is with Aria. Oh, wait, you don't."

"Ouch, he went there," Kinvara snickered.

"I will have her, eventually. You will be recalled to the Nine Realms, and I'll be the one to catch her when she falls. Your kind always leaves. Sooner or later, she'll welcome me instead of you."

Knox chuckled darkly like it was funny, but Dimitri's words had echoed within me. He wasn't here to stay, that much was clear. He wasn't even trying to fit in, and that was a requirement. Our races had to be kept secret from humans because it would create mass hysterics, and then they'd want to study us.

Carefully, I turned, looking up at Knox as his eyes continue to stare at Dimitri in open challenge. I stepped away, exhaling, and moved to where my sisters stood as a chilling iciness filled the clearing. I paused, hesitating, exhaling slowly as I watched my breath steamed in the frostbitten air. The men looked around as we moved closer to them.

Kinvara whimpered, remaining outside the area we'd all stood within. Her mouth moved, and sheer terror entered her eyes. Ice particles started to form on her fingers, and I frowned as I watched it growing thicker on her flesh.

"Kinvara?" Tears ran down her cheeks, turning to ice that left red marks over her flesh as they fell to the ground, shattering. "Kinny, come to me," I whispered in a plaintive tone.

"I can't, Aria," she sobbed as her skin began covering with frost, turning blue.

I rushed toward her, uncaring of the danger. Her hand lifted, and she shook her head, opening her mouth to scream in warning. The moment I got close enough to her, I felt it. It was debilitating fear, so thick and horrid that my legs slowed as I grabbed her, pushing her out of it before I started back in the other's direction, only to feel something grab ahold of me from behind. Claws slid through my flesh, and I screamed with pain ripping through me as the ice pierced my flesh. My mouth opened, and I watched Knox lunge for me, only to brush his fingertips against mine as I was ripped through something that felt as if I was being cut to shreds, screaming his name as incapacitating, all-consuming fear and pain devoured me. Knox rattled loudly, shaking the darkness that severed through my mind, fading everything around me to nothingness. I blinked past the ice that covered my eyes, solidifying in them as I hit the ground hard. The ice burned my eyes, slithering over me as I continued blinking to keep it from blinding me.

Staring up, the world blurred around me as a figure bent down, grabbed me up by the hair, and tossed me into a cart, covering my body with blankets. I was losing consciousness from the immense pain still firing through my entire body, ripping apart the nerve endings until it became too much to bear, and I finally gave in to the nothingness.

CHAPTER
51

The sound of dripping water over concrete woke me. I wiped the crusted sleep from my eyes and peered around the dark room. The horrendous smell of rotting flesh and feces filled my nose, and I gagged, sitting up on my knees to vomit onto the floor. My arm lifted, covering my eyes as they burned from the rancid smell of putrid flesh. I threw up repeatedly until everything in my stomach was spilled on the floor. Looking around the dark cell, I noted the leg of the cell's last occupant still rotting in the corner, and heaved again, even though my stomach had nothing left to give. I pushed up to my feet, staring at the bars that allowed very little light into the darkness.

I was in someplace beneath ground level. I was in a fucking prison cell? There was a pail in the corner, still holding urine and excrements from the last inhabitant. A single crusty blood-covered, blanket sat beneath me, and as I peered down as something rushed over my foot, and I screamed, standing up to hug the claw-ridden prison wall. Where the fuck was I? My ears heard very little over the sound of my racing heart, and I turned as something in the cell across from me, moaned loudly before whimpering in pain.

I shook my head to rid my mind of the fear-gripping icy claws trying to sink into it. I closed my eyes, seeing the last thing I remembered. Knox's panic eyes filled my mind, and I frowned, recalling the icy cold grip of death that had pulled me through some type of vortex that had felt like I was being torn to pieces. I'd blacked out after being tossed into some kind of cart and ended up barfing everywhere the moment I'd started waking up. I had felt the cold chill once more. The fear that had slammed against my mind had knocked me out cold, as if someone had spelled me to remain asleep.

The sound of feet moving over stone echoed loudly, pulling me from my memories. My heart beat wildly at the voice coming closer to my cell. I'd have known that singsong voice from anywhere. Moving closer, I approached the bars and peered through them, angling my head to stare down the dark hallway. It was filled with cells and cries of people. No, not people; women sobbed and cried for help from each of the cells lining the hall.

A masculine voice crooned to the singsong voice, and I narrowed my gaze. I watched my sister as she stood on tiptoes, kissing a large male before turning to look down the hallway in my direction.

"Amara," I whispered.

They started walking again, and I sagged in relief as she came into view, only to drop it as her angry glare held mine. There was madness in her blue eyes as she

493

let it slide over my crumpled frame.

"Aria," she smirked triumphantly.

My stomach rolled, flipping until I thought I would be sick again as she smiled cruelly at me. "What are you doing here?"

"I live here, this is my home. Here, I am treated like the queen I am and don't have to compete with you or the others anymore." She neared the bars, touching my hands as she smiled at me coldly. "Oh my, you thought they had taken me, didn't you? You stupid, naïve little bitch," she chuckled as the male next to her studied me, letting his lewd gaze linger on my top a little too long. "I thought my letters were pretty convincing, but you didn't bite. You just went about your day, didn't you? This would have been so much easier had you just followed my instructions and met me at the old oak tree. Now I have to make certain you hurt so much more."

"What the hell do you mean, Amara? You're my sister."

"What the hell do I mean? You are a selfish little bitch, Aria. You're miserable and insufferable to be around, and I hated every moment of being forced to endure your pathetic crying. You were everyone's favorite, and why? Because poor Aria was promised to the darkness, but you weren't, were you? No, you were just some miserable fucking bitch who acted terrified so that everyone would feel sorry for you. I am the darkness and was all along. I had it inside of me, hidden from everyone. I watched our mother try to murder you over and over again, but she couldn't. I held the darkness, and you held the light. But then you got stronger, more powerful than I was.

"You hid it from everyone at first, but I exposed you to Aurora. Everyone babied poor Aria, and no one paid any attention to me or my needs. Not until I started coming here, and they worshipped me. I searched for our father at first, and discovered so much more about our mother, and who could potentially be our father, but that doesn't matter now, does it? You took everything from me, and I know you ended up with something inside of you, but you can't access it, can you? You're too weak to control your own emotions, let alone what lives within you. It's okay, sister mine, you won't live long enough to worry about it here."

"You brought me here, why? Because you're fucking jealous? You had everything, Amara. You took everything from me, right down to the boys I liked. I never complained, never begrudged you what you did. I hid and protected your secrets. I did it because I am your sister, your twin sister."

"No, you didn't. You were the selfish one. Always poor Aria this, or poor Aria that. We moved away from my home because of you! We left everyone because you couldn't get over, almost being murdered. I lost my mother because of you, you selfish whore. I thought I was weak because we were the last twins born to Freya, but then I heard Aurora arguing with our mother, telling her what would happen to you if she brought us back here together. You took everything, Aria. You stole the power that should have been mine. I was born weak, without magic rushing through my veins because of you. I had to fight to wield it because, for me, it wasn't easy. I was a Hecate bloodline born witch with no fucking magic because of you!" Spittle sprinkled my hands, and I pulled them back, glaring at her.

"In every birth one is born weaker than the other. It is a failsafe to protect the bloodline in case one goes insane or makes a move against the coven. You could cast magic, Amara, but you never fucking cared to study it. Just because you're born with it doesn't make it yours. I earned it through learning and mastering my magic, which you refused to even try to do. I begged you to learn, but you couldn't be bothered to even crack open a grimoire. I did all of your homework for you. I warned you that if you didn't learn, you wouldn't grow stronger. Just because you carry the last name doesn't make you powerful. You have to learn to use magic and how to control it. You refused because you were lazy and thought everything should be handed to you. No one owed you anything, and neither does the realms. It gives you what you earn as everything in life does."

"I shouldn't have to learn it. I am Hecate's granddaughter. It is in my blood to be powerful," she shouted, causing the other people in the cells to groan louder. "It matters little, considering your fate."

"Amara, I am your sister. You cannot *gift* me to anyone. That isn't how it works. If you do this, they will send you to the Void of Nothingness once they capture you."

"They'll never find my beautiful bride," the male crooned, touching her midnight-colored curls while still eye-fucking me.

"You're so strong and handsome," she whispered, bringing his hand to her breast with the invitation.

I exhaled and shook my head as bile stung the back of my throat. If this was a nightmare, it was currently in the running for the most fucked-up dream in history.

Her husband's eyes never moved from me, which was freaking me out, and creepy as fuck. He breathed heavily through a nose that looked as if it had taken a sword to it at one time or another.

"She is exquisite." He let his eyes move to the saturated joggers I wore and then up further to my breasts as he smashed hers in his hand.

"If you like plain bitches that can't suck cock." She glared at me as if it was my fault he was staring. "Aria wouldn't know how to please anyone but herself."

"She isn't plain. She will look so good tied up and mutilated."

I stared at him, noting the thick tattoos that covered his arms and the discoloration of his fingertips. He wasn't ugly, far from it. He had deep sea-green eyes, midnight-colored hair, and he wore a gold crown encrusted with fingertip-sized diamonds. The only visible deformity was his nose, which held an angry scar across it.

I exhaled a shaky breath, realizing where I was. I was finally in the Nine Realms, and I just wanted to go home.

"She just needs to be cleaned and in less clothing, and my father will ruin her so brutally."

"Hold up," I said, glaring at Amara. "You're pissed off about something you assume happened in the womb. So you're willing to trade me for what exactly? Marriage? I'm not interested."

"Marriage? As if I would allow you to stand above me ever again. No, Gerald enjoys hurting pretty things. He's rather…Oh, what is the word I am looking for, baby?" she fluttered her lashes, and I snorted.

"Brutal," he supplied.

I shook my head in horror, watching Amara as her smile spread over her lips. It was nauseating knowing that I'd finally found her, only to discover that she was the one hunting me, trying to bring me here. My sister was the one who had been trying to find me so that she could murder me. Wasn't that freaking peachy?

CHAPTER
52

Amara and her husband stood in front of me, watching as I processed the horror of what they planned to do to me. Like I hadn't been having a bad enough week already? No, the world seemed to be fucking me every which way it could, and this was the cherry-flavored syrup on the top, right beneath the cherry.

"You can't do this, Amara. I have been going out of my mind searching for you. I have given you everything you have ever asked for, and now you will hand me over to be hurt because you think I stole your powers? I was an infant, you selfish bitch."

I was pulled through the bars until I feared I would be torn apart as her husband held me there, staring into my eyes while his other hand lifted up, grabbing my breast painfully hard until I screamed from the pressure he applied. He smiled coldly, enjoying the pain that threatened to make me pass out as he watched me, breathing hard against my face with rancid breath. He smashed my breast until I was afraid it would break open, and a scream tore from my lips as he chuckled, licking the side of my face as I cried.

"That is my wife and future queen you are speaking to. You will show her the respect her position gives her, whore." He didn't stop, as if my screams turned him on. His left hand held me by the hair as the other one released my breast to push into my pants. His finger entered me hard and painfully. He watched me closely, forcing himself into my body until it burned from fullness as he inhaled deeply. He breathed heavily in my face, panting with the scent of rotting flesh. "She's perfect, but I wish I could smell her cunt over the rotting corpses."

"Stop, baby. She's a virgin," she offered, patting his arm as she watched me being violated without any emotion whatsoever in her eyes. "She's a gift for your father, Garrett."

"I want to break her in, and ruin her tight little cunt, baby." His fingers stretched apart, and I screamed, fighting his hold on my hair as nausea rushed through me, causing me to dry-heave as he watched me.

"Hold still, Aria, or you won't make it to the morning without being fucked by my husband. You attention seeking bitch, you're making him crazed with your struggles."

I was making *him* crazed? I held my breath, not daring to make a move again to incite more violence as my sister stood silently, watching her husband as he continued defiling me until he was moving his hips, mimicking the movement with his finger.

"Your father is expecting a virgin tomorrow night, my love. If you breach her hymen, he will know, and will be disappointed with me."

He stared me in the eye, and then his gaze lowered to my lips. "Her mouth wouldn't be missed; it speaks ugly lies about you, my love."

"No, Garrett. I forbid you to fuck that worthless bitch. You're mine, remember? Tell her what your father enjoys doing to pretty little things like her."

"He enjoys hurting pretty girls. You will like it and everything he does to your tight holes. He makes you think you're precious, and then he breaks you in front of the guests. You will give them a good show. He'll start with your virgin cunt, ripping it open with his hugely knotted cock until it's bleeding, as all of your innocence is shattered. You will be fucked to death until he removes that pretty head of yours for his trophy case. I do hope he leaves your corpse out as he did the last one, even dead, we enjoyed fucking it until she started to fall apart with decay. She was too skinny to eat after we'd played with her for months, so we just continued to fuck her holes until she fell apart."

"That's not fucking nasty or anything," I uttered, staring at Amara, who had begun stroking his inhuman, grossly knotted cock as she watched me. "How can you do this to me?"

"It's not only you Gerald will get. They're a little medieval here, and I had no dowry to offer him. What I did have was an endless amount of Hecate bloodline witches to trade. I needed something to give him in order to marry the love of my life."

"You traded us? Your family?" I snapped. "To be slaughtered?"

"No, you see, they will only be fucked when it pleases Gerald to use them. You, my sweet twin, were my greatest gift to offer. You will be decapitated, and then they'll just be used whenever his monstrous cock needs to be fucked. I assure you, it is perfect for your first time. I hope he fucking destroys you. I can't wait to hear your screams of absolute pain, Aria. You deserve it for what you did to me, and everything you took from me. Fuck me while she watches you take me, lover," she urged, and he smiled, jumping at the invitation.

I stepped back, shaking my head at their depravity, playing out before me. He pushed her thick dress from her hips as he bent her over, and Amara held onto the bars as she smiled back over her shoulder at him. He freed his cock, stroking it as he stared at me. It was huge and deformed with knots that made bile push against the back of my throat.

"She's so pretty," he growled, moving closer. The sound of his feet made me peer down, finding hooves that clicked over the stone floor. "I wish I could fuck her too, but we promised him a virgin to torture."

He slammed into Amara as she lifted her head, expelling a scream from deep within her throat. Garrett never looked away from me, watching my breasts as he fucked her slowly, yet hard enough that she winced in pain as she held on to the bars. His hand lifted, and he sucked his finger that had been buried inside of me as I shook my head in horror.

I fought against the tears choking me as Amara watched, smiling as she opened her mouth to scream her orgasm. He withdrew his cock, watching me as he walked around her prone body and pushed her down to her knees. Shoving his cock into her throat, he turned, smiling coldly.

"I wonder if you suck cock as exquisitely as your sister does or if they'll have to rip your mouth open to fuck it."

I lowered my gaze to where Amara struggled to get past the head of his bulbous, mangled cock. Her hands worked it eagerly, and I rolled my eyes. Creatures started howling around us as he snarled his release, coming thickly into her mouth, snorting and making horrid noises as if he were half-bull, half-man.

Minotaur.

Howls erupted, baying sounded, and females screamed hysterically as I slid down the wall, covering my ears while his orgasm continued until Amara turned, dripping come from her mouth gluttonously. Her eyes held madness and pure hatred that shook me until I wanted to scream in denial.

"You'll like them in that virgin cunt, Aria. They will rip you apart the first time, but afterward, it isn't so bad as you adjust to the pain. The first time he took me, I bled so badly, and he licked it up, praising me for how tight and perfect it was as he leaked out of me. I doubt Gerald will help you, though, and my terms were you had to be in immense pain through it all. He will do such horrid things to your body. I can't wait to watch him with you, dear sister. It will be a treat for them to taste his thick cum mixed with your blood as it oozes out of you, and it will. I do so hope you bleed well."

I vomited everything left in my stomach at her words. I'd thought I couldn't possibly throw up anything else, but I was wrong.

"I will get out of here, and when I do, I'm going to take your fucking head with me." I gagged as my stomach rebelled at the images she was painting in my mind.

"How? There is no magic here, none. You're in the land of the beasts, and they forbid the use of magic. There are protection runes over each inch of this palace and the entire kingdom to prevent it from being used. Oh, I guess you haven't heard, have you? There's a war brewing, and the witches? They're on the wrong side of it. They will die for their treason. I guess I should have told you that when I came home the first time, but what would be the fun in that? The witches will pay for trying to hurt my sweet and gentle lover when he tried to court me at the age of twelve. They said I was too young, but he'd already fucked me, and I was addicted to him."

"Wipe the cum from your mouth, *sister*. We rule the witches, they wouldn't dare commit treason. They do nothing without our permission, or what we permit them to do, Amara."

"Ruled by us, meaning me too." She smiled maddeningly, her eyes sparkling with it. "I may have helped move them in the right direction since they've felt neglected by our family, making it so damn easy. You know nothing, Aria. This realm is beautiful chaos, and so fucking angry. They're so mad at us for leaving, but when I told them I shared their views, they rejoiced, gifting me with jewels and showing me their realm. Every time I came back, they ate up everything I told them, all the lies about you guys never wanting to return, and how it was such a task for everyone but me to come back, which is why it was only me going to the Witches Realm, wasn't it? They started to hate you guys more and more with every lie I told. I gave them permission to do bad things, and so they told me everything they had done without the consent of the royal bloodline.

"Did you know for the past five hundred years the witches accumulated an entire army to take over the Nine Realms? They murdered royals and have sacrificed lives to sever the connection to the Hecate bloodline. Soon, they will have everything they need, and once they do, they will weaken and cease to exist as will all magic. Garrett found me on my first summer here and wrecked me, but then he healed me and told me what I meant to him. I fell in love, but the witches thought I was too young to understand the beast that I fucked. I wasn't, and so we murdered them first.

"Garrett asked me if I was powerful, and while I wasn't powerful, I did have enough pull to help him. I came back each time to ensure our plans moved forward. Garrett told me exactly what he needed the witches to do to remove the magic from the realm, giving it back to the monsters, to which it originally belonged, before Hecate fucked them all and made them unable to wield their own magic. Now I will rule the portals, and Garrett's father will be free to hunt new victims for his trophy wall with all the magic he can ever use at my fingertips. Now all I have to do is sit back and wait for our other bitch sisters to come after you. Once they're here and discover magic doesn't work, I will give them to Garrett's father and take control of everything for myself."

"You're insane, aren't you, Amara? It is forbidden for all the bloodlines to enter the Nine Realms, leaving the House of Magic open to attack."

"You think you blessed it? You didn't. I took the stapes bone from our grandfather's ear, rendering his corpse unable to bless the house. I moved a few others, so you'd think it wasn't done maliciously, but I assure you it was." She moved her hand up, pushing the leftover cum dripping down her chin into her mouth, then smiled coldly around her finger. "Try to get some sleep. You will need it to give us a brilliant show tomorrow."

She slipped her hand through Garrett's and leaned up, kissing him. He smiled down at her proudly, licking his cum from her lips, cleaning her mouth. It was official; Amara was fucking a bull, or horse, or whatever the fuck he was, and they were straight-up nasty as it got. She murmured about his prowess and how he'd felt so good in her throat. Throat? Hell, she hadn't even managed the head. They left, and I shivered, repulsed at what my sister had become. He yelled down the hallway about how well she sucked his cock, and I rolled my eyes as he praised her for being the best.

Amateur hour, Amara. These two needed couple therapy for psychopaths.

I hugged my knees, watching as the woman across from me moved to the cell bars and peered across the hall, or she would have been if she had eyes in her head. She was young; her immortality hadn't yet healed the wounds she'd received. I stood up slowly, moving to her as blood dropped from her wrists where it appeared she had been restrained at one time.

"You're mortal," I whispered in horror as her blood

hit my nose, along with the scent of rotting flesh.

"My name is Irina," she whispered. "I'm from Italy."

"How are you inside the Nine Realms?" I asked.

"I was in Italy, giving a speech about how an author had published work I felt forced an opinion on helpless women. Others argued that fiction writers aren't providing 'how-to' guides when creating those scenes, and in most cases, have given victims an outlet to work through their own personal demons, something I hadn't considered before making the accusations. Before I could apologize to the author, something grabbed me and brought me to this place. Am I bleeding?" she asked, turning around to expose a gaping wound in the lower region of her backside, between her butt cheeks. "It aches, and the numbing medicine does little to stop the pain since he continues to fuck me there. He prefers that spot after ruining my pussy to the point that not even he stretches it anymore."

I swallowed. "It's not that bad," I lied, fighting nausea as I took in the gaping hole in her ass, if you could call it that. She'd been brutalized, raped, and from the looks of it, he'd either used something to hold it open to fit himself inside of it, or he was way bigger than his son was. "I wouldn't sit down for a while." *Or like ever again.*

"It really hurts."

"Uh, yeah," I whispered softly. "Maybe you should lie down on your side."

"I can't. The thing inside of me is eating me. Tomorrow I will go to the king, and he will release it if I am good and please him well."

I sat down, staring at her stomach, watching it move, and I leaned over, dry heaving until my body rocked with the spasms, even though nothing came up. I didn't even know how long I had been down here, or what to expect other than complete hell. My sister was worse than we'd assumed, a monster who wanted us all dead. Tears burned my eyes as I wiped my mouth off with the back of my hands. I would die here, and no one would ever know where I was or what had happened to me.

CHAPTER 53

The next morning, I was yanked out of the cell roughly and stood in front of guards that towered over me as Amara glared, stroking the fur that adorned her neck. Her dress was black with shimmering jewels that looked utterly ridiculous on her. A silver crown sat on her head, and her lips were slathered in black lipstick that had smeared on her teeth. Gone was the sister I thought I knew, and in her place was a sadistic, cold-hearted bitch that got off on fucking monsters and hurting others.

"Wash her, but do not touch her cunt. She is a virgin and must be presented as one to the Minotaur King. The ice-blue dress will work and use the glitter to entice him with her beauty, add extra to her parts that we want him to admire the most. No makeup, only a thin coat of gloss to plump her lips, so he sees how welcoming her mouth is. She must be perfect. Her hair should be down, and her breasts should be pushed up since she doesn't have much to work with. Be certain that they add the drugs, but not the pain agent. I want her to feel everything he does to her."

"Yes, Princess Amara," the guard said, pushing me forward.

The cells were all filled with women in different states of decomposition or degradation. Irina hadn't made a sound all night, and when I'd peered into her cell, something had been slithering out of her mouth. I looked away, knowing without having to touch her that she hadn't made it through the night.

At the stairs, we turned into a large room where beasts chewed grizzled meat, chomping it while grease and bits slipped down their chins. They were grotesque creatures, ones who consumed the flesh of their victims willingly. The large guard pushed me into a room, giving instructions to the women who stared at me with emptiness in their eyes.

I was washed in ice-cold water and stood naked in front of an older woman as she looked me over. Another stood behind me, brushing my hair until she was satisfied with the sheen and texture before adding a light sprinkle of glitter to it. A short, thin dress was slipped over my head, and then more glitter was added until I looked like a Winter Queen Barbie doll. They dabbed mascara on, and then a thin coat of lip gloss. Something pushed into my arm, biting as I jumped and looked at a needle emptying into my bicep.

"Slip these on," the woman ordered, staring at me before she shook her head.

She handed me thin silver slipper-like shoes, and I bent down, feeling the air on my ass as I did. I stood up, staring at the guards who had watched the entire thing, and frowned as I noticed one had drool dribbling down his chin.

They led me through a long, winding hall filled with decapitated heads behind glass, lit up and on display. Some were mummified, while others were flesh, but all had a horrified look on their faces.

Amara held her hand up at the end of the hall of trophies, and I stared at her blankly. She smiled and shook her head.

"You never noticed how unhappy I was around you after I discovered what you had done to me. Selfish, narcissistic people often never see what they do to others, even those closest to them. My sources say that you were almost charged with Jasper's death and somehow escaped the charges. How convenient for me, being it would have ruined my fun."

"Your sources?"

"Suck enough dicks promising them unlimited power, and men become nothing but bitches. What do you think I was doing there? Running that worthless store so you could all get paid? Or sitting on the council listening to the self-absorbed pricks? I was building alliances for this kingdom. I fucked so many cocks, Aria, pretending to love all of them. They're weak creatures, grown lazy in their leisure in the new realm. Garrett proved that when he grew jealous that they touched my flesh. He broke their necks, and I made it look like a sacrifice to the gods. Even poor Jasper couldn't escape his fate from my husband. I watched you, you know? I watched you sitting on the balcony, crying because you missed me. You never realized that everything I did, I did for myself. I hated you from the moment I discovered you had taken everything from me. I could have been powerful, and yet I am not. What I lack in magic, I make up for in intelligence. I guess I took yours, because you covered for me perfectly nearly every time I got in trouble, but then you refused to continue, and I hated you even more."

"That's called selfish, and you're a bitch," I growled as I was pulled out of the cell by force and stood before her.

"It's called self-preservation, Aria. That realm is about to become the hunting ground for this kingdom, and we will grow much more powerful than any other kingdom in the Nine Realms. The Kingdom of Unwanted Beasts will rule them all."

"God damn, I really wish mom would have swallowed you." I watched the anger igniting in her eyes and smiled. "You can throw me to the wolves…or, in this case, whatever the hell they are, but I won't fall, and I won't break. You will, though, Amara, that much I promise you."

"I'm glad she didn't, or I'd never have met Garrett and become his princess. I will be queen here one day, and I will ensure that it is prosperous."

"Who the hell are you, Amara?" I demanded.

"The same little girl who slept in your bed and slowly made you think you were going insane with nightmares. The noises that kept you up as you feared our mother returning, that was me too."

"You're sick. I held your secrets, and you held mine."

"Careful who you let in, Aria," she smirked as she started walking away. "Most of us just want to destroy you."

"Wow, could have used that advice in the womb," I snorted, wincing as the guard grabbed my wrist, pulling me away from her. "Bye, sis! So glad to see you again, chat later?" *Bitch.*

The room we entered was large and already filled with people. They drank from expensive champagne flutes while dressed in silk pants and matching tops of every hue of the rainbow. There were creatures from different realms, or what I assumed was different since this was the Kingdom of Unwanted Beasts, and most unwanted creatures were sent here.

I was placed in handcuffs, then watched as they attached the cuffs to a hook that had been lowered from the ceiling. I was raised up on a hook, and a light was shone onto me, causing the glitter to sparkle in the burning heat of the room. People turned around, staring at me as I hung like a slab of meat on a butcher hook.

The Minotaur King turned, rubbing his hooved hand over his mouth before nodding. I swallowed bile as he shook his hooves into hands, clapping loudly at the assembly, stopping their endless chatter.

"Tonight is a time of celebration and new alliances. My daughter-in-law, Amara Hecate, has brought me a gift: her own sister, Aria Primrose Hecate," he exclaimed, and the crowd clapped before he held up his hand for silence. "The High King and the King of Norvalla have both decided to join us tonight, let us welcome them to a new era. Norvalla is here to sign the papers of a new, stronger alliance for our people than we've ever secured before today. The High King is here to witness the signing of the alliance between our two kingdoms, how fortunate that it comes at a time during great revelry. Are you ready to celebrate with me?"

The crowd cheered as a male in armor stepped out from the protection of his guards. He was huge, his armor as black as midnight with something etched into the chest plate. His crown was etched in firestones, sparkling as the light caught them. The mask he wore was created from a skull, held together with a silver material that made it look evil and deadly. His boots clicked across the floor as he moved, following the Minotaur King until they both stood before me.

The Minotaur King grabbed my foot, staring up at me before turning to who I assumed was the King of Norvalla. He peered up at me through black eyes, and I looked away from him. Someone else stepped into the room, causing the crowd to go silent, but I couldn't see him since he was hidden by guards in armor that looked as if it was crafted from scales.

"She will break so beautifully, don't you agree?" The Minotaur King asked.

"I heard you made a woman's entrails come out her mouth one time, is it true?" The King of Norvalla asked, ignoring Gerald's question.

"Yes, but she was a mere child. Seventeen, I think. I had captured her along with her mother, so I let her mother watch me with her daughter, and then I played with her, too," he chuckled as I gagged. "Will you scream for me, pretty witch?"

"Maybe as I remove your fucking head," I preened,

watching his eyes narrow as he pulled on my leg, forcing my arms to burn, but I never screamed for him.

"Play tough while you can, but no woman can handle me for long, no matter how strong they think they are. They all break for me."

The sound of metal clinking against glass drew his attention. Amara stood, preening beneath the attention of the crowd as she pointed at me with a beaming smile on her black lips. "I give you my sister, Aria Primrose Hecate. She's a pureblood Hecate witch, and a virgin one at that, which, as you all know, is unheard of in our line. This is my gift to you, Sire. My own twin sister for you to play with, which I pray you do so violently, my king. It is a symbol of my devotion to you, and my new life here. I hope you enjoy her."

"Choke on a dick, you evil bitch," I screamed, but the words were drowned it out by the crowd clapping for Amara.

"Would you like to join me in raping her?" Gerald casually asked the King of Norvalla.

"She is a gift; you should enjoy her on your own."

"Fine, but I insist you try out my new daughter-in-law before you go. She's a gluttonous whore who enjoys pain. Amara dreams of being queen, but Garrett doesn't have the heart to tell her my reign only started ten years ago." He began stripping, and my eyes dipped to the mutilated organ that was knotted and deformed. He shed his clothes onto the floor, and I closed my eyes, praying to the beast within me to get the fuck with the program.

He reached up to touch me, and flames leapt over

my flesh. I peered up at my hands as he growled and shouted at Amara, who apologized profusely. Metal dripped down my arms as I watched him backing up, gaping as he watched the flames consuming me. The moment I was free, I jumped into the air, feeling my fangs and claws extending. I landed on his shoulders, ripping through his throat with my claws and severing his head before pulling it from his shoulders, smiling when his spinal cord came along with it.

The entire assembly was silent for seconds before total chaos ensued. Guards in matching armor swarmed around the King of Norvalla, while I turned my head, staring at him to see if he would move against me. Amara's screams ripped through the crowd as Garrett called for her from across the room. I looked between them, knowing I couldn't kill them both. I moved toward Amara with purpose, turning to miss people that jumped out of my way. Launching myself into the air, I landed on her, using my claws to pin her to the ground.

"Told you, bitch." I pushed my nails into her abdomen, slowly cutting my way through her stomach. She screamed in excruciating pain as I meticulously ripped her apart.

"I'm your sister!" Amara cried.

"No, my sister is dead, I know, because I'm about to remove her fucking head," I smiled coldly, slashing through her until her screams turned wet, and blood dripped from her mouth. "You earned this; blood of my blood, I banish you to the Void of Nothingness," I whispered, drawing my nails down her legs until I flayed them open. "I grant you eternal pain for what you have allowed to happen to those innocent women you gave to that monster."

"Aria," she sobbed, so I smiled down at her coldly as her blood coated my hands.

"Oh, calm your tits, don't lose your head over it, Amara." I lifted her by the hair as I severed her head from her shoulders. "Oops, you always were a drama queen." I stood, watching the wall of guards that were slowly approaching me.

I ran in the direction of the hallway, dripping flames as I went. People who rushed down the halls caught fire as I passed. They wailed as their silk turned into a weapon, and they cried as the flames licked their flesh. I could feel the drugs starting to enter my system and heard guards issuing orders behind me.

Turning a corner, I slammed into a body and bounced back, holding on to my sister's head, amazed that it hadn't turned to ash by now. Turned out, Amara was immune to my flames, not that it mattered now. Dismissing the thought, I jumped back to my feet and stared at the male who leaned against the wall.

"Took you fucking long enough," Lore snorted. "Is that what I think it is?"

"My sister…Well, I took her head because she was…" I said, stuttering as I began swaying on my feet.

"Was a sadistic bitch that enjoyed watching women being raped and slaughtered? Yeah, we figured that out soon after they took you."

"Why are you here?"

"Someone had to rescue you," he chuckled as feet sounded down the hallway. He pushed me into a room and bolted the door, staring at the couple who watched us inside the room. "That's a problem." He withdrew a sword and sliced through the male as the woman screamed. The doors shook, indicating the guards heard it, and I turned to look at the door before looking back as Lore severed the man's head, and then the woman's. He moved to the window, peering down and whistling. "Tell me you're not afraid of heights?"

"I'm not afraid of heights." I moved to where he stood, peering down at the drop to the next tier. "That's not realistically possible."

"Oh, it's possible. It's also our only way out at the moment," he exclaimed as more guards started beating against the barred door. "I'm going to step out, and you're going to climb on my back, understood?"

"What if you drop me?"

He smirked, staring at me as if I was cute for asking such a thing. "I will not drop you."

Lore climbed out, bracing his hands on the stone slabs etched with runes. At least Amara hadn't lied about that part. Once he was securely holding on, I climbed up and exhaled slowly before slipping onto his back. His armor bit into my flesh, and the sword on his hip was luckily secured in a leather sheath. We both looked into the room as the door gave way, and guards began rushing in. Lore released his hand, and we started falling. I screamed, and I hugged him tightly as he searched for another window to grab. When he found one, we jerked to a stop, and I slid, holding onto him even tighter.

"Aria, I cannot breathe. I'm all about you climbing

on me, or holding on, but I can't save us if I can't get air into my fucking lungs."

"Sorry," I whispered as my heart pounded, and my body trembled. He dropped again, and this time, I somehow managed not to scream as his feet hit stone, and we started sliding.

Lore gripped onto the stone roof and slowed us, but it wasn't enough to keep us from going over. His hand caught the rough edge, and I slipped, crying out as his other hand grabbed mine. I stared into amber eyes and held my breath, even though my mouth was wide open.

"Climb up," he ordered.

"I can't." I watched him turning into multiple people as the drugs grasped hold of me. "The drugs!"

"What fucking drugs?"

"They gave me something in a shot." I stared at the sky, refusing to look down.

"I'm going to swing you to the next roof, and then I want you to jump down two more. You understand?"

"You're going to throw me?" I hadn't heard a single thing he'd said after swing.

"Yes, and you will get to the lowest level and jump into the moat, Brander is waiting down there in case shit went south; it's way south, glitter tits. You understand, lowest level? Jump into the moat on the east side, and he will get you to the woods. We'll meet you there. I have to go back and murder the guards who saw my face."

"Lore!" I screamed as he sent me sailing through the air.

I landed hard, scratching my hands on the stone as I struggled to hold on to anything. I fought to hold on to the roof, but my claws refused to obey me as the drugs dug deeper, making the world spin around me. I dropped to the battlement and turned mid-air, falling on my ass before getting back onto my feet, swaying, watching as the guards who paused looked up the way I'd just come from.

Turning in the opposite direction of the men now rushing me, I started running the other direction, fighting to stay in control of my limbs and mind. I didn't stop once I reached the end, jumping and leaping over the edge, sailing through the air as I looked down and screamed. It wasn't a little fall; it was a big ass probably-won't-make-it leap I'd just taken. I could make out an ant on the side of the moat, and as I got closer, I could see it was Brander with his mouth wide open in horror. At the last moment, I sucked in air and hit the water hard. My feet touched the bottom, and I pushed up to bob over to the surface before swimming toward where he stood.

"What the fuck, woman?"

"Lore threw me."

"From the top level?" Horror filled his eyes as he peered back up from where I'd just leapt from.

"I think I was supposed to go down further, but there were guards, and shit happened. I jumped, we're here now." Something whizzed past my head, and I paused, staring at the castle. "Are they shooting arrows at us?"

He grabbed me and pushed my body to the ground as he lifted his shield, mere seconds before arrows peppered it. They were *shooting* at us! My head rested against his chest, and my eyes started to close, but an arrow shot through the shield, slicing through my arm.

"Ouch," I muttered, and Brander looked at me.

"Your pupils are fucking blown," he murmured, and I frowned as something hard rested against my belly.

"I'm on drugs. Is this hot for you?" I watched a smirk playing across his lips at my droll tone. "Are you like some adrenaline junkie?"

"You're not wearing any panties, Aria, and my hand is on your naked ass. I'm a male, not a fucking saint. Lore should be making an appearance at any moment."

I stared at the water's reflection, watching as flames erupted from the castle in a straight line, then the sound of water splashing filled my ears.

"You two coming?" Lore asked, and when Brander moved the shield, he snorted. "I'll take that pretty ass as a yes."

"Grab her, she's drugged. She also jumped from the top battlement."

Lore snorted, but whatever he saw on Brander's face stalled it. "No shit? Damn, I'm not even that brave."

I was lifted by Lore as Brander got to his feet, and we started toward the woods. Guards shouted as the gate was opened and we moved faster, or they did. Brander turned, lifting me up as we moved toward the sound of rushing water. He stopped at the edge of a cliff and peered down before looking over his shoulder.

"Take a piece of her dress and go north, send those assholes on a chase with her scent. Meet us in the passes,"

Brander ordered, and I watched as they removed a large section of the dress before Lore took off at a run. "We're jumping. You will hold on to me and don't let go. I'll tell you when to hold your breath, okay?" He set me on my feet, never releasing his hold on me.

"Got it." My head nodded as I swayed on my feet, staring at him.

"You have to hold your breath, Aria. There's a whirlpool down there, and it's going to fight to keep us in it. You can't let go for any reason. Ready?"

"I'm ready," I stated, wrapping my arms around him and hooking my hands together tightly as he stared down at me, kissing my forehead and saying something in a foreign language I couldn't understand.

He jumped, and I buried my face against his chest, listening to his slow heartbeat. Mine was hammering between the drugs and the adrenaline. I would be lucky if I didn't have a heart attack.

"Now," he shouted, and I sucked in air, holding onto him as he hit the water hard.

The water sucked us toward the whirlpool. I saw a huge, perfect tornado beneath the water before Brander pushed us off the bottom and swam with me beneath him. He pulled me onto the shore as I gasped for air, staring as more people hit the water, jumping from the cliff above us. I looked at Brander, who didn't move, and then back at the water as Knox slowly walked out of its depths while everyone else swam to shore in long, steady strokes to fight the whirlpool. Oceanic blue eyes slid over me, then locked on my face.

"Aria," he smirked as he kneeled beside me, running

his finger over my cheek. "You just slaughtered the Minotaur King in his own fucking court, surrounded by his guards."

"I murdered my sister too," I whispered past swollen lips. He frowned, letting his gaze slide down my battered body before he nodded to my words.

"So you did, little lamb. Welcome to the Nine Realms, Aria Hecate."

CHAPTER
54

We walked through a dark, shadowy valley with creatures monitoring our every move. It was unreal and my first glimpse of the Nine Realms outside of the cell. It was exhilarating, but also terrifying to see where we came from. Creatures I'd only ever read about observed me as I absently scooted closer to Knox while we moved through the darkness toward a large mountain. If he noticed me getting closer, he said nothing. No one spoke, and between the chattering of my teeth and the inner turmoil I felt, I was thankful.

Occasionally, tears would burn my eyes, but I refused to allow them to fall. I didn't need to be told that I was in shock; I felt it. Inside the cell, it felt unreal, as if it was only a nightmare, and I'd awaken from it sooner or later. Now it was settling into my soul that I'd murdered my twin, the girl who had been beside me before we'd even been born. Worse, it was sinking in that she'd hated me enough to allow me to be raped and mutilated because something she assumed I had done to her, which I'd had no more control over than her.

Amara had never once shown a darker side, and if she had, I failed to notice it or had chosen to overlook it. We all had our own problems, but in a house with sixteen females under the age of thirty, it wasn't a big deal for someone to grow distant or need space. Especially with everyone being close in age due to Freya using her magic to speed up a few of the pregnancies with spells.

Fingers brushed against mine, and I stared at where Knox's hand was touching me. Lifting my eyes, I found him observing me carefully. I dropped my gaze and continued moving forward, not willing to accept the silent support he offered. I felt like I'd just killed a piece of myself, and worse, I would have to tell my sisters I'd murdered Amara when I returned, and I wasn't sure how that information would be received. I exhaled deeply and inhaled slowly, calming the turmoil before it shifted to turbulence.

"Aria," Knox whispered, grabbing my hand and pulling me closer to him as we continued walking. "Breathe, they can't touch you anymore."

"I know that."

He slipped his fingers through mine, lifting my hand to brush his mouth against my knuckles before he let it drop. Spinning around, he paused as the others stopped around us. His head turned, staring up at the cliffs that stood high above the valley we walked through, to where soldiers stood, peering down at us. Swallowing hard, I took in the men who wore the obsidian-colored armor, and shivered violently. The man in the middle wore the skeletal mask that I'd peered into, and I shrank back, hiding behind Knox as they continued to watch us from their vantage point.

My heart hiccupped to a stop and started with the force of thunder as everything within me turned to worry. Knox was a king in his own right, but that didn't mean he was safe from the King of Norvalla. The royalty between realms could destroy one another, but only if the original bloodlines gave permission.

The problem was, the King of Norvalla was above that. He had refused to sign the covenant or even acknowledge that the Human Realm should be included in the same category, making it the Tenth Realm since it hadn't been a part of the original nine. Until Hecate had ripped through the portal she created to discover it.

Hecate was the reason the portal barriers separating the Nine Realms had been broken. To create trade opportunities among the realms, she had merged them all together as one large region, while still maintaining physical borders identifying each of the Nine Realms. This also allowed the Nine Realms to be governed as separate kingdoms but overseen by the Council of Original Bloodlines, as well as the appointed High King.

Our family was considered one of the largest and most prominent families in all the realms. Not that we exploited it, but to land a Hecate direct descendant was huge. Or it had been until we'd left the Nine Realms to live among mortals.

Aurora had told us tales of the men who wooed her, courting Hecate's daughter. My mother, Freya, had used it to mate with anything that had a cock she could physically take between her legs.

My heart kicked into overdrive as I peered up at the

male who had watched me spinning in the Minotaur's court. No one spoke as a shiver raced down my spine, and I leaned my head against Knox's back as I closed my eyes.

The image of Amara and her husband filled my mind, and I gagged. It caused Knox to turn around, staring at me. He opened his mouth to speak, and I held my hand up, shaking my head as the images flooded my mind until I turned, throwing up. No one made a noise or questioned what was wrong, as if they knew I couldn't speak about that place of horror.

Hands pulled my hair away from my face, and I heaved until nothing more would come out. Standing, I covered my mouth with the back of my hand as Brander's pained stare held mine. He exhaled before stepping closer.

"I need to examine you, Aria."

"No," I whispered as I shook my head, covering my eyes with my forearm. "I'm fine."

"You're not fine, Aria. You were in the Kingdom of Unwanted Beasts, where women are mutilated, and even if you think you're fine, I need to be certain."

"I said no," I whispered through clenched teeth, trembling as I shoved the images away from the front of my mind. "I am fine, there's no reason to check me."

I turned, staring at Knox, who watched me through narrowed eyes before he spoke in a low tone to Brander. "Once we get deep enough into the forest, we will camp for the night."

"I think it best we do. I think we could all use the rest before we go through the passes."

My stare moved to the empty cliff and then back to Knox, who had yet to look away from me. The men started forward, and I settled into their quick pace while Knox walked behind me.

It was hours more before we entered a vast forest with trees that had trunks wider than ten men standing shoulder to shoulder. My eyes stared up as I took in their height, moving higher than my eyes could see, as if they were reaching for the heavens of the gods.

All around us, woodland creatures played, jumping from tree to tree as they followed us deeper into the forest. It took another hour of moving through the woods before a group of men came into view, and I stopped dead in my tracks.

Knox moved toward the men, speaking low, in a foreign tongue as he pointed to a large clearing a mile or so away from us. I didn't rush to keep up with him and the others, preferring to remain back from the men who continually gave me a curious stare.

Large tents were set up in a clearing, but the sound of water drew my attention, and I walked away from the group, silently, finding a lovely pool. The water was crystal clear and welcoming.

Slowly, I lifted the dress from my body and stepped into the water. My hands scrubbed the glitter from my flesh, hating that no matter how much I tried, it wouldn't all come off. Footsteps sounded behind me, and I turned, staring at Knox.

His eyes lowered to the angry purple and blue bruises that covered my breast and shoulders, where Garrett had tried to pull me through the bars by force. My arms held bruises from where the guards had grabbed me roughly, jerking me around. My thighs held even more bruises, but from what I didn't know. I was battered and bruised in places I hadn't felt until the fear had left me, along with the worry of escape.

Another male entered the small clearing and paused, looking at the damage to my body. Brander groaned, covering his mouth as he took in the bruises before I gave him my back.

"Set a perimeter up around the pool. Make sure the men know to keep their distance."

"I need to examine her. When she is ready," he added firmly, placing his hands on his hips, frowning as he shook his head.

"Go do as I said," Knox ordered, and silence filled the small clearing.

My hands dipped into the water that gurgled up from the bottom of the pool. I heated it to a boiling point, dunking beneath it to close out the sounds that haunted me. I emerged to take a breath of air, and arms captured me, turning me around until I was forced to face Knox.

"What happened?" he asked with worry etched into his words.

"I can't," I whispered, looking away.

"Did they rape you, Aria?"

I shook my head, knowing he wanted to know everything that had happened, but I wasn't ready to speak about it. His arms pulled me closer, and I leaned against his silent strength, hating the tears that fell as they dripped down my face. He exhaled slowly, but it shook his body with the force of it as he placed his lips against the top of my head, kissing it.

"You rescued me again." I slipped my arms around him to lean back and peer up into his turbulent gaze.

"Is that what I did?" He smiled sadly, watching me closely.

"I can't get the glitter off."

"It's just glitter." He pushed the wet hair away from my face.

His hands cupped my cheeks, and he lowered his lips, brushing them gently across mine before he released me. He ducked beneath the water, coming up with a weird-looking shell, his eyes staring at my breast that held evidence of how large Garrett's hands had been. Knox cupped it with his free hand, and I hissed, pulling back away from him as pain ripped through me.

"Who did that to you, Aria?" he asked, but I shook my head once and turned away from him, hiding the tears that rolled from my eyes, slipping down my cheeks.

The shell slid over my shoulder, and I turned, watching as he slowly scraped the glitter off of my flesh. He was meticulous as he removed every tiny shining fleck of glitter until my arms were cleaned of any trace of it. He moved me to a flat rock, lifting me onto it, then began to clean my legs, finding my sex bruised from where Garrett had dug into my flesh while he'd used his fingers on me.

His eyes lifted, and his nostrils flared. I looked away while tears filled my eyes, and my lip slid between my teeth as my eyes overflowed with tears that trailed down my cheek as I refused to look at him.

He swallowed hard and stepped back, lowering his head. "Aria," he uttered.

"I'm tired."

He stared at me as if he'd argue and demand to know more, watching me as if at any moment, I'd break apart. He didn't push it, sensing I couldn't speak about it yet. Knox made quick work of removing the glitter from my legs and then carefully followed through with the area where they'd placed more glitter than others to make my cunt sparkly and enticing for the beast that had planned to rip me apart.

Knox didn't caress me, didn't touch me more than was needed to finish removing the particles, then he moved from the water and redressed. He picked up the soiled dress and shook it out, moving toward me as I stood on the rock, keeping my gaze on his feet. Knox slipped the dress over my head, pulling it over my naked body before he pulled me behind him, whistling to the men who had hidden in the trees, keeping sentinel. They emerged from the trees like silent warriors, falling into step beside us as we moved through the woods.

We walked back in silence, and Knox pointed to a tent that Brander followed me into. I turned slowly toward him and lifted my dress as he assessed the damage. He was clinical about it, but the moment he touched my breast, I cried out, and he looked up.

"Were you raped, Aria?" he asked, and I shook my head. "Your bruises are consistent with rape victims." I shook my head again, swallowing bile as he frowned. "Did you eat or consume anything that they provided?"

Again, I shook my head.

"There are things they put into the food…"

"I know." I gagged as the images of Irina filled my mind. I covered my mouth with my hand, and he bent down, grabbing a jug of whiskey that I accepted, gulping down.

"Slow down, if you haven't eaten, you were there for three days. I'll have food brought in for you. The shot they gave you, do you have any idea what was in it?" he asked as the wind howled outside, making the tent ruffle. I shook my head again, and he nodded. "I can't help you if you won't talk to me."

"I'm okay." I wasn't, but I would be, eventually.

"I'll have food brought in, there's a blanket in the satchel, and the brazier is being readied to heat the tent. Rest, it won't be long before we have to move again. The new Minotaur King is not happy that you murdered his wife."

I gagged again, turning away from him. He exited the tent, and I moved to the large bag that was anything but a satchel and pulled out the blanket, moving to the farthest corner before I sat down, wrapping myself in the warmth the clean blanket offered.

I could hear Brander speaking to Knox, and the sound of others joining in their conversation. The thudding of hooves beating against the ground made my head lift, and I tilted it sideways, listening. It was several riders, and no one seemed worried about it, so I pulled the blankets around me and lay my head on the bag, closing my eyes.

CHAPTER
55

Something touched me, and I screamed, jerking and jolted away from it as I crawled back to escape whatever it was. Knox watched me, his mouth opened, and he growled at my reaction. I fought to control my body, which shook violently, trying to calm myself down and rid my mind of the nightmare that had haunted my dreams. My hands pushed through my hair, and I released a shuddering breath before the scent of food caught my attention.

"Eat," he said, and I grabbed the plate from him, sniffing it before I forwent the silverware and consumed the meat with gusto. I hardly chewed as I devoured it, and when I finished, I closed my eyes. I hadn't even realized I was starving until the scent of the meat touched my nose.

Knox grabbed a jug of water and handed it to me, and I gulped it down until it was running down my chin. I swallowed, wiping my mouth off with the back of my hand, and I realized the brazier had been brought in as

I slept. Scooting closer, I shivered as the heat warmed my flesh.

"There aren't enough blankets for everyone, and this forest is rather cold at night. You will share with me," he said, and I nodded silently.

He sat behind me, pulling me against him. "Can we sleep by the fire?" I asked, unable to stop the tremble that never seemed to stop.

"Yes," he agreed, scooting his body against mine until we were as close as we could get. I stared into the flames.

We didn't speak for a long time. We just sat together in silence with his arms around me, reassuring me I was safe. His lips would occasionally brush against my shoulder, where he had claimed me. The flame danced hypnotically as I watched, noting that it danced toward us as if it knew we needed its heat. I replayed what had happened and tried to detach it from my mind, but then my mouth opened, and I spoke barely above a whisper.

"My sister traded me to that monster to be raped and mutilated."

He didn't speak, but his mouth kissed the arch of my neck and didn't pull away; he just left his lips against it as he felt my pulse.

"She planned to give all of my sisters to him as well, and all because she assumed I took her powers from her in the womb. Hecate witches are born unequal. One is always much stronger than the other, like a failsafe in the event it was needed to obtain balance. If one turns to the dark arts, the other one can either pull her back or end her life. It's just balance, but Amara didn't care. She traded us as her bride price; her fucking dowry was her sisters. The others were to be used as Gerald deemed, but I was to be beheaded after being tortured and raped. She hated me that much."

Tears rolled down my cheeks as I said what had been consuming me out loud to the silence in the tent. His arms tightened, and his breathing slowed as I continued.

"She let her husband hurt me. He pushed his fingers into my body as she watched him," I said as my sob filled the tent. "She fucked him in front of me, and together they stared at me the entire time. He hurt me, and she just watched him doing it. She did nothing to stop him, and I'm her sister. He tasted me as he fucked her, pushing his fingers that had been inside of me into his mouth as he watched me. The only thing that prevented him from raping me was that I was a gift for his father, and they couldn't smell that I wasn't still a virgin over the rotting corpses of their other victims. She said I was to be a grand gesture of her devotion to her new life, the virgin witch of the Hecate bloodline as a trophy for his hallway," I whispered, staring at the dancing flames for strength.

"I saw such horrible things there. Irina, a human, had something inside her. It was consuming her, eating her from the inside out. They had ripped apart her rectum, and something inside of it kept it open, I think. In the morning, she was dead, and the thing inside of her was escaping through her mouth. The others, they were missing limbs or pieces, like they were slowly being taken apart as they ate their bodies. My sister walked right by them, and she did nothing to help, and that isn't something we do. We are supposed to protect the weak. She bragged about their torture and explained in vivid, disgusting details what would happen to me. She *wanted* me to die like the other girls had died. She hated me enough that she was crazed and excited to watch me be raped and brutalized in front of that crowd of people.

"Brander said it was three days that I have been gone, but I can only recall waking in the cell the day Amara appeared, and maybe one time before that, but I couldn't stay awake. I could feel hands touching me. I could feel hands touching my face, and other parts of me, yet I don't remember any of it. It was as if I was in a dream state, and it was happening to someone else, but I know it was me. I felt everything that happened, and yet I couldn't see their faces, and I couldn't wake up from the nightmare. When I first awoke, I smelled their scent on my flesh, as if they'd touched me enough times to leave their scent on me as I slept. Everything before I awoke in the cell is a blur, and yet their taunts continue to echo like they're speaking down a tunnel, and I am on the other end of it, trying to make out what they're saying.

"Then there's what Amara said she had done and was planning to do in the Nine Realms. Amara said that she has been moving pieces around, granting the witches permission to wage war with other factions of immortals within the Nine Realms. She said that the witches have been doing it for over five hundred years without us knowing or suspecting a thing. I don't know if it is the truth, or if she lied to make herself sound more powerful. I don't even know who the hell that evil woman was because she couldn't have been my sister. That would mean I have lived my entire life with evil right beside me, and I never even noticed it. How stupid would that make me?"

I leaned back, letting his heat take away the bone-deep chill while he remained silent behind me.

"I once asked my aunts how we could enforce the laws if we weren't a part of the realm, and Aurora said that to trespass against the ones we had in place was treason. Now…now, I have to wonder if maybe we were wrong. I don't think we should have left anyone else in control of our realm. If what Amara said is true, then the witches are doing whatever they please without us knowing it. If it was happening five hundred years ago, that would mean my aunts were knowingly a part of it, because we hadn't entered the realm of humans yet. I guess I could see some of the need to take down monsters; if any of them were akin to Gerald, they deserved to die by whatever means necessary. Some beasts don't deserve to live, not if they terrorize others, or can't listen when told to do something, I guess. I could see their reasoning for trespassing against laws and attacking creatures, but then it is still treason, is it not? I don't think we should have ever left the Nine Realms to go claim the tenth one. It seemed to me that they are far too innocent for our kind to live among. I wonder what we will find when we return to the Witches' Realm, now that we are being forced to see if they have trespassed against the laws. I wonder if I will agree with them because of what I have been through and be glad they slaughtered others within the Nine Realms." I had begun rambling, and he'd gone stiff behind me.

I turned to peer at him over my shoulder, and then faced him only to find him glaring at me through an angry stare. A shiver snaked down my spine as I opened my mouth to speak, but he moved, crushing his lips against mine until I moaned from the intensity of it, but it was a different kind of kiss. It was violent, as if he was kissing me to end my mouth from saying anything else. He pushed me down to the ground, moving my legs apart until I cried out when he touched my flesh. Knox paused, breathing angrily as the tick in his jaw hammered wildly. While he fought to control his anger, I lay silent, staring up at him as he shook his head, glaring down at me as if he was fighting something I couldn't see. He turned me abruptly onto my side, curling against my back, and hissed out his next words coldly.

"Go to bed, now," he snapped gutturally. "We ride the moment the sun rises."

CHAPTER
56

I awoke alone, shivering against the cold morning air. Sitting up, I stared around the empty tent. It held only me and the blanket I'd slept in. I'd felt Knox leave in the middle of the night, but he hadn't come back, and I'd been too exhausted to go after him. Standing up, I slid my hands down the ruffled dress and rolled up the blanket, pushing it back into the satchel, which, in reality, was the size of a large duffle bag. I exited the tent, staring at the armed soldiers and the skeletal mask of the King of Norvalla.

My heart jerked against my chest as I watched him stepping closer to me. He paused, tilting his head in the mask he wore, studying me. Unlike the last time, his eyes were oceanic waves that rushed over me. He laughed coldly as my breathing grew labored, and I dropped the bag onto the ground.

"You didn't rescue me," I whispered as I sensed the other men closing in around me. I stepped closer to the tent, watching his eyes studying me as the realization of who he was sunk in.

"I told you, little lamb, someday you'd get eaten. It's someday."

I turned, running with everything I had left in me, zigzagging around trees as branches snapped beneath the thin shoes I wore. I could hear them giving chase, the sound of men calling out orders and directions as I rushed headfirst into a forest that led to…I had no idea. A branch crunched beneath a boot close to me, and I veered the other direction, slipping beneath a fallen tree only to slam into something hard.

I stared up at Knox, who watched me in his armor with something dark in his gaze. He started to bend down, and I kicked out, knocking him down before I got back up to my feet. I started to run away, only for his hand to wrap around my ankle and pull me back down onto the ground hard enough that it knocked the wind out of me. I turned onto my back, kicking against him, and I screamed with frustration as he got to his knees, settling between mine, watching me fight him.

"Let me go!"

"I can't do that, Aria."

"Knox, let me go." I stared up at him in his armor, his power rushing through the woods from his pores, which he no longer hid, making me realize just how fucked I was.

"If I let you go, you're as good as dead."

"The Council of Immortals will never let you get away with this!"

He smiled coldly, pushing his hand against my throat

before he brushed his lips across mine and whispered against my ear. "What council would that be, sweet girl?"

"The one that rules over the Nine Realms while we are gone!"

"I don't think they care anymore," he smiled wickedly. "Not since I took their fucking heads and mounted them on stakes outside my palace. You and your kind abandoned this land, and you left those who ruled in your stead to brutalize the people of the realms. You and your kind, my sweetest little lamb? You're the worst of them. You murdered entire families because they wouldn't bend a knee to the Queen of Witches. It's a new day, Aria Hecate. When the dawn comes, the Nine Realms will no longer be yours, but they will be bathed in your bloodline."

"You can't do this, you have no right!"

"I have every fucking right! I watched my people being slaughtered by magic from your fucking people. I held my son through one thousand deaths that the Queen of Witches bestowed upon him because I wouldn't bend my knee to that whoring murderous bitch! After my son died, my wife went to a witch, and she begged her to take her immortality away so that she could join him in death, so they did. Only they gave her a potion that ended her soul forever, destroying any chance she had to join our son in the next life or find me in mine. They took her away from me, and they did so in a way that she would never escape death's torturous grasp," he snarled as his grip tightened on my throat until air wouldn't pass through my airway. "You say I have no right? I have every fucking right to end the witches' reign, and anyone who would oppose the new leaders of the realms."

Knox watched me gasping for air and pressed his forehead against mine as lights exploded in my vision, and I stopped struggling. Knox's lips brushed mine, and he pulled away, watching my body jerk violently as my brain starved for air. My body seized, and his hands released me.

"Fuck!" he snarled, taking his hand from my throat as I gasped for air, turning onto my stomach as I gagged, crawling through the dirt to escape him. "Where the fuck do you think you're going?" he asked coldly, slowly following me as I crawled on my hands and knees, slipping through the wet, frost-covered leaves.

"Home," I whispered gutturally, barely able to make words leave my tongue past the damage of his hands.

"You have no home left to escape to, Aria." He watched me struggling, following me soundlessly for several moments before using his foot to push me onto my back. "As we speak, Haven Falls is being captured, and all inhabitants are being rounded up and brought back to the Nine Realms to face charges by the High King of the Nine Realms for treason against the realms they abandoned. They are to be put to death so that their magic will return to where it belongs, to the people they left behind."

I stared at him in horror and shook my head vigorously. I sat up slowly, staring at him as he watched me absorbing the news of what he had done. Using my claws, I clasped my hand together and closed my eyes before his power pushed against me, forcing them to open. He smiled, kneeling down to stare into my eyes as he lifted his mask, watching me.

My eyes locked with his as I drew the Celtic symbol for sisterhood in my palm and smiled up at him sadly, slamming my hands together as magic roared through the land. It shook the trees, and Knox grabbed my palm, staring at it before he stood, issuing orders as his men rushed away from where we stood. I watched him, amused as he bent down and ripped me up from the ground.

"What the fuck did you just do?"

"You will never find my family, Knox." I smiled, and he shook me as his men watched in silence around us.

I laughed soundlessly, ignoring the tears that rolled from my eyes with how stupid I had been, but I had taken precautions against him. He'd fucked up, he'd told me he would ruin me, and I wasn't about to go down without a fight.

"You will pay for that, Aria."

"How, Knox? How can you make me pay any more than I already have? What the fuck can you do to me? Beat me? Violate me? Rape me? Destroy me? Fucking bring it, motherfucker. I am no one's bitch! You want me dead? Fucking do it and get it over with. Do it!" I screamed with tears running down my face as I stared him down in open challenge.

He watched me, holding my dress, glaring at me through cold eyes before he released me abruptly. He stared at me silently, stepping back as someone came up behind me, pushing me down to my knees. On the cold ground, steel touched against my neck. I smiled sadly, staring him in the eye as I stretched my neck across the blade, ready to die knowing my family was safe. If this was the cost to protect them, I'd pay it a thousand times over again.

"Any last words, Aria?" Knox asked softly.

"Yes, I'll say my prayers," I smirked, preparing to whisper the witches' prayer. "I am the fire of the cauldron that heats the realms. I am the wind that fills the land and sails the ships upon the rough seas. I am the earth that grows the crops and feeds those within the Nine Realms. I am the water that bathes the soul. I am of Hecate, created from within her soul. I am the magic that creates the land and feeds it power. I leave neither child nor a mother behind who will grieve me, only my magic to be returned to the land from which it was given. I give it back on this day. I now go to my grave without regrets. I go to where pain cannot touch thy soul. I leave this vessel of flesh and go to lands of plenty, and land of promised peace. Blessed be, for the ones who will go on, do not weep or grieve for me, for I am finally free." I lifted my eyes to his and smiled wickedly as I held my arms out with my palms held up. "I am ready to die—go time, fucker."

He stared at me through mere slits and shook his head. "No, no, I will burn down your fucking world, and you will watch me do it." He kneeled down, staring at me as he grabbed strands of my silver hair, rubbing it through his fingers.

"That's anticlimactic, Knox."

He shook his head, and a dark smile tugged at his lips. "Your sarcasm won't work, Aria. You're wrong, you know. I will find your family. Just as I found your mother and took her head. Your Aunt Hysteria and her daughters? Their skulls are what I have built my throne with. We covered my throne room walls in the skulls of your people. A reminder of what my purpose is, and soon, my entire kingdom will be covered with them."

"You killed my mother?"

"Before I came to your shitty little town, I took her head."

I laughed, and then threw my head back, laughing even more as he watched me. His lips pulled into a tight line at my response. "Oh, is this where I'm supposed to cry because you killed my mommy? Nah, wrong bitch, Knox. If you hadn't done it, I would have eventually; but my sisters? You won't find them, because no matter how strong you are, I don't fucking bend my knee either."

"You will bow for me."

"Hard pass," I chuckled as my arms were grabbed and put into cuffs behind me. "I only get down on my knees when I want to, and I don't fucking want to for you anymore."

He studied me as if his mind went back to that room with me, and his thumb traced over my lips as if he were imaging them around his cock. "You will break the moment I deliver your sisters' heads to you and make you clean their skulls for my throne. Only pureblooded Hecate witches adorn my throne, the rest only get to line my walls. I wouldn't sit on anything less, little lamb."

"Knox, I don't plan on sticking around long enough to clean shit for you. You need help cleaning shit, hire a maid service."

"You won't escape me," he said, touching my throat where it felt bruised. "You're mine now, Aria. You will see none of your family again. You will never taste freedom, nor feel the sunshine glowing on your pretty flesh unless I decide to allow it."

"You're wrong, King of Lies," I said, smiling impishly. "I am no weakling, and no matter how far you bury me in chains, I will fucking rattle them until they break, and I am free of you. You want to burn my world down? Fine, but you will watch me rise from the ashes. Legends always rise from the ashes."

"You will rise. But only to be captured by me, Aria Hecate, because you're mine from this moment on," he smirked, standing up. "Get her up, and let's go home."

I was lifted painfully and shoved forward, only to land face-first on the ground with my ass in the air, exposed.

"Pretty little ass," Killian growled, reaching down to grab it. I moved, turning to glare up at him as my body trembled violently from his touch. My skin lost color, turning a ghostly white with memories of my time in the cell. He watched, stepping back as if realizing what he had done by touching a witch he loathed, and instantly looked as if he regretted it.

"Enough," Knox snapped, pulling me up until I whimpered as pain burned on my arm where the cuffs were too tightly placed. "I love the sounds you make when you're manhandled," he chuckled.

"Yeah, there wasn't much difference between being fucked by you and my body being abused; both were brutal. Shows what you know about the noises a woman makes when fucking, doesn't it?" I smirked, walking past him as blood dripped from my fingers onto the ground from where the cuffs had torn my flesh.

"Brander, tend to her wrists. Can't have her broken before I even begin playing with her."

I turned, looking back at Knox over my shoulder, lifting an eyebrow. "Don't worry about me; I'm fine with pain and betrayal. I'm starting to expect it. My sister said something before I took her head, y'know. I actually fucking get it now. She said to be careful who I let in because most people just want to destroy you. I wonder if she would find the irony in this situation. My lover, the only man I ever allowed to actually fuck me, is also the one who wants to break me. If that isn't fucking irony, I don't know what is." I turned to watch as Brander approached slowly.

He moved behind me, and I started forward, heading for the horses and dismissing him outright, along with his offer to tend to the wounds.

"Aria, your arm is cut," Brander stated.

"Yeah? Isn't that the entire point of this? You want to hurt me, and so I am. Do not touch me, asshole."

"You're riding with me," Knox whispered softly, stopping me as I peered into his eyes. "Believe it or not, Aria, I'm trying to save your fucking life by claiming it."

"You should have let them take my head, it would have been kinder." I winced as the cuffs were removed, and my arms were placed in front of me.

"Brander, tend to her. She doesn't get to bleed out," he said, watching me as he lifted his hand, touching my cheek.

I pulled away from his touch, staring at the horse. Brander approached and looked at the small wound on my arm, peering over at Knox curiously when he found a tiny cut. He placed an ointment and gauze around them. Once done, he wrapped transparent material over the gauze and then replaced the cuffs around my wrist in front of me. He tested them and looked up at me.

"You remember the last time we did this, sugar?"

"Yeah, I only sort of hated you then, now my hate is genuine."

Brander smiled tightly, and I turned, watching as Knox produced silk and placed it over my eyes. My shoulders drooped as he leaned closer, whispering huskily.

"And then we played this part, and you screamed my name, remember that?"

"Yeah, I remember. I remember thinking you were someone else, but you were just fucking me over then too. I was just too naïve to realize how much or how hard you planned to fuck me back then. More fool am I, bastard."

CHAPTER
57

The ride was insufferable, and no matter how much distance I tried to keep between Knox and me, it didn't work. I'd scoot up until I was damn near riding on the horse's neck, and he'd pulled me back against his body, wrapping one arm around my waist as he directed the horse with one hand on the reins.

He'd talk, and I'd block him out as fear for my family entered my mind, controlling my thoughts. His arm slipped further up my chest, and I cried out in pain as it pushed against my breasts. He lowered it immediately, exhaling while I fought the silent sob of pain from the accidental brush.

"You always said you wanted to see Norvalla," he whispered against my ear huskily.

"Yeah, not anymore," I answered in a clipped tone. "I have it on good authority that the king is a treacherous prick. Turns out, I don't give a fuck about seeing it after all."

"It's a wild and untamed realm with the strongest creatures that the Nine Realms have ever created or produced. It seems fitting that something such as you would end up here, fucking its king."

"Cool, can you stop touching me now?" I asked icily.

"I couldn't leave you to die in the Human Realm, Aria," he said, his voice hard and cold. "I made a choice to protect you, and I don't regret it. If I had sent you back, you'd have fought and died. I couldn't live with that choice."

"Who says I would have died?"

"I do. I sent in my best assassins to bring your sisters and the others back, and if they fight, they will die in that cold, selfish realm that they chose to become a part of."

"You assume we were not prepared for treachery, Knox. We were created from a land where everyone wants to kill each other. You think my sisters will be there when your assassins breach the portal to the Human Realm, but I assure you they will not. They were gone the moment my body ignited, and the House of Magic vanished from its current location."

I prayed that it was what happened. I'd created a spell on my own and tested it on smaller objects in order to perfect it, but a house was another issue. If it had worked, the house would still be there, along with my sisters. They would be hidden behind a shroud on invisibility; no one would be able to see it or breach the house, but my family also wouldn't be allowed to leave it, either.

To an outsider, it would look like nothing but a vacant lot. The house itself was straddling the portal and had been since it was built, but it was also able to be moved to sit over the creek where crystals were embedded into the surrounding land. They'd picked a location where the portal was the weakest. Witches were resilient like that, always prepared to bug out if shit got bad.

We always had a backup plan, but where Aurora had planned to seal the house and leave it visible, I knew Knox would figure out how to breach it sooner or later. So, I'd used my blood, slowly draining it, and then replenishing it to drain it again in the months I'd hidden in that house from Knox. I'd added my blood, along with the ingredients, onto the altar that the bones lay upon, shielding them from everyone.

The spell would release a single piece of vellum from the ceiling, warning my family that trouble was brewing, and so it would begin. We would come back to the Nine Realms through the portal and take back what was rightfully ours.

"You think you will beat me, little girl?"

"That just depends on what you consider being beaten?"

"I have you, Aria Hecate. You're my prisoner; that's a fucking win I'm willing to take. I walked in and took the strongest fucking witch from right out from under their noses."

"Technically, my evil bitch of a sister took me. I was just the idiot who fell for the whole *'save the damsel'* routine. Guess I should have known you weren't the saving type. Lesson learned. It's a good thing I don't make the same mistake twice, right?"

His lips brushed against my neck, and I shivered as he kissed the hollow column gently. "Take Aria and ride ahead, seal her in my room, and post guards outside of it. Do not leave her alone, Lore."

I turned my head, listening as hands slipped around me, screaming out as he touched the wounded breast that had still yet to heal as he'd wrapped his arms around me. My body trembled with the pain, and I clenched my teeth as I swayed against the new body.

"Careful of her wounds, she is hurt more than she's letting on. Tell no one who she is, not until we're ready to protect her if they move to murder her for the blood that runs through her veins."

"On it," he said, pulling me against his body. Leaving me blindfolded, Lore started the horse at a gallop as we moved away from the voices. "Sorry, Aria."

"No, you're not. Don't even try to say you're sorry. It was his plan since the moment he set foot into Haven Falls to slaughter us all, and you were in on it."

"Yeah, that much is true. You were supposed to be brought back with the others to face charges, but he couldn't bring himself to kill you."

"Magical pussy, I guess."

"Nah, Aria. You're something special, but you also have someone powerful protecting you. But, you have Knox too, and he isn't willing to let you die yet."

"I wish I knew who. Maybe he'd go to war against Knox to get me away from him."

"Just don't piss Knox off—and no one is crazy

enough to go to war against him," he warned. "You have no idea what he has been through."

He was wrong. I was more than willing to wage war against Knox.

"Knox told me about his wife and his child, but I also know I wasn't a part of what happened to them. I know that by the blood that runs through my veins, I am his enemy. He forgets that I wasn't raised here, none of my sisters were either. That wasn't by choice. That was because Hecate and the council demanded we remain in the Human Realm."

"It doesn't change anything, Aria. It doesn't change what happened here. Imagine watching your child die a thousand deaths, each one worse than the first. They weren't pretty deaths either. Imagine the most violent deaths that you could envision unfolding before you, and all you can do is sit there and hold your tiny child through each one. It took Sven four years to succumb to the last death, and Knox held him through each one. For four entire fucking years, he sat holding his dying child. No matter what form of death came for Sven, Knox held him until he succumbed to it. Liliana couldn't bear it, so she hid in her room and refused to come out for the duration of his life. She forced Knox to live through that terror alone, and I wasn't her biggest fan because of it.

"On the day Sven died his final death, we were called away to settle a fight for one of the high lords of the nearest town to the palace, but when we got there, he told us he'd never called us, to begin with. We rushed back to the palace, but it was too late. Liliana had found a witch hidden on our land and begged her to provide a spell that would send her into the afterlife with Sven.

It did the opposite. It banished her to the one place she could never be reborn, or find eternal rest. It consumed her soul and sentenced it to the Void of Nothingness.

"We later discovered that the witch had sent a message to Liliana with the location of her cottage. It was an offer of help to ease her grief; she had never found her, but had been called to her. Add it up, Aria. Your bloodline ended his family's lives. Imagine losing everything and knowing that the only way to prevent it from happening to other people is to cut off the head of the snake that is striking us down."

"And so you started a war?" I asked, but he tightened his hold against me, and I held the cry in as it pushed against my breast.

Noise erupted around us, and people called out to Lore as the sound of a large gate opening met my ears, scraping over the ground. I could see nothing past the thick silk that covered my eyes, but I could smell dried meat, and the earthy scent of mead being placed into barrels to be stored. Wheat was being ground with cinnamon as someone else added yeast into the mixture. They argued over portion, and I inhaled the taste of the cinnamon in the air. Children laughed in the distance, and a baby squealed with hunger. Women catcalled to Lore, offering him their bed for the night as, somewhere close to them, someone beat against a carpet, clearing it of dirt. My hands were bound before me, and Lore's arm had replaced Knox's, shielding me from those around us. If I had to guess, I'd say Knox had brought me to his palace, and that meant my chances of escaping him were slim, all things considered.

"Keep your mouth closed, or I will cut that skilled

tongue off myself, and that would be a fucking tragedy."

I didn't speak as he entered what I assumed was a courtyard, calling out that the king was en route and that the people should assemble. My heart hammered in my chest as he stopped, pulling me down with him carefully.

"Open the doors," he demanded, and we went through quickly, or I tried to until my foot struck a stair, and I started to trip. "Steady." He rushed me through the inside of what I assumed was the palace, helping me up countless sets of stairs, which he finally gave up on, hefting me into his arms, moving faster as we ascended them.

My heart raced as heavy footfalls sounded around us. The smell of freshly polished steel hit my nose as Lore adjusted me in his arms, issuing quick, rapid orders to men, who answered in the same strange language they spoke. Once we stopped moving up the stairs, he walked slower as the sound of a doorknob turning and hinges clicking into place met my ears. We were finally at what was to be my prison cell.

CHAPTER
58

A door opened and closed, and then the blindfold was yanked off, and I blinked to adjust to the light of the room. Lore frowned, moving to a large box. He opened the lid and removed a shirt, sniffing it before pulling it over my head and down my body, covering the cuffs. Next, he pushed me toward an open balcony door and stopped me before I was through it, turning to stare down at me.

"Watch, but don't make a fucking sound, or I'll choke that pretty throat until you're a fucking mute, understood?" he asked. I nodded, turning to watch the large party that we'd been with earlier enter the gates. Lore pushed me to the corner of the balcony, concealing us in the shadows.

The soldiers obscured Knox's presence, but the moment they parted and spread out in the courtyard, he came into view. I closed my eyes against what he held in his armor-clad fist. Amara's head was held by the hair, a trophy that made the cheers for their king's return go silent.

"I give you Amara Hecate, the daughter of Freya Hecate. An original bloodline witch," he roared, and the crowd went crazy.

And just like that, he claimed my kill, fucker.

Knox wore full armor, but gone was the obsidian that matched his men's. He wore a silver chest plate that was covered in ravens, with a larger one etched into the middle. His skull mask was more silver than bone this time, proving he had many. His crown was gone, replaced with horns that stuck back instead of forward. He looked like the legends of the knights of old, and yet his armor was more advanced and easy to move in. Metal protected his neck, and underneath was a wicked covering of thick chainmail. The shield on his free arm was also etched in ravens, with the initials *SK* in the middle of the design, reminding him of what he had lost.

Knox dismounted from the warhorse, walked to a statue of a beautiful woman and boy, and placed my sister's head at their feet, like an offering. I watched him peering up at me, staring as I shook my head, feeling as if I was intruding upon his sacrifice. I backed up, I turned to look at Lore, who smilcd, slipping an arm around me to cover my mouth as he held me there, forcing me to watch Knox.

"You will watch and listen, because the king demands it," Lore uttered, barely above a whisper.

"As I speak, those from the original bloodlines that followed Hecate to the Human Realm are being collected and brought here to face charges of treason, as are the leaders of these bloodlines that remained here, in the Nine Realms, watching as the rest of us suffered at the hands of the witches and their supporters. They will be brought here and given a traitor's death. Soon, we will prepare to march on the first of the House of Witches castles and take their heads for our walls!" The crowd exploded, and I closed my eyes, silently praying that people got out before he reached them. "Tonight we feast! Tomorrow, we prepare for war on those who murdered thousands of our people, and our beloved queen and our prince!" His voice held hatred, and worse, it held the hope of victory. Hope could kill and win more wars than any other emotion. Hope made them believe they could win, even against insurmountable odds.

Knox left Amara's head sitting on the base of the statue as people cheered him on, touching him as he passed by them, staring directly at me through the slits of his armor. Lore pulled me from the balcony the moment Knox vanished beneath us and walked me back into the room.

It was the same room as in the library with books piled on tables, and pillows covering the white bed where he'd watched me flicking the magic bean while withholding the stock. I shivered as the sound of heavy footsteps walking over granite floors echoed as they closed the distance to the door. Lore stepped away from me, staring at Knox as he came through the door. I refused to meet his eyes, hating that he'd taken me from one prison only to hold me in another.

"Wait outside, Lore," he growled, not moving from the doorway as I stood with my hands in front of me, staring away from him.

The moment Lore was gone, Knox started toward

a large dresser. I closed my eyes and listened as he removed his armor and then stood in front of me. My eyes were mere slits that were glued to the floor when his hand brushed my cheek. I snapped them open wide, glaring at him as I stepped away from his touch.

"Sit down, Aria." His eyes narrowed, emphasizing the demand, so I moved to the couch and took a seat. He snorted, looking around the room before turning back to me, "You're alive because I decided you can be useful."

"Like the other witches, you control? The ones you turned into mindless zombies? Pass, mowing down on bones and brains is a hard limit for me. As is being your little bitch, Knox," I snorted.

"You witnessed Gerald and his depravity. That is who people left in charge of taking care of the Nine Realms. In fact, he is tame compared to most of the monsters that rule in your absence. Your people gave the power to corrupt leaders, and they, in return, tore this fucking place apart. I intend to rebuild it."

"Yeah, in fire and blood sounds like an amazing place to live," I stated, looking at him dead in the eye.

"I want you to help me fight this war, Aria."

"Pass."

"If I bring you the head of the witches to clean for my walls, I bet you change your mind. It changed the witches who served me in Haven Falls, minds. I'm guessing you don't want to find your sisters' heads among the pile?"

"You won't find them," I stated confidently.

"Oh, but I will." He held his arms out wide, watching

me. "Look around you, Aria. You're in the same library that stood in Haven Falls."

"Noticed, but even so, you won't find them." I crossed my arms, staring at him blankly.

"I can torture you to find their location."

"Get to it then, big boy," I stated firmly, smiling wickedly at him. "You think I didn't foresee this as a possibility, Knox? I spelled my body to contain my secrets; even in the event of death, my soul will hold them. Break me, rip me apart, do whatever you think will work, do it. I assure you nothing will come off my tongue. The anger I saw in your eyes was raw, but the unguarded glimpses of pain? They were debilitating. You wanted to hurt me, but you also didn't want to hurt me, and that pissed you off the most. You were at war with your demons, and in the end, the demons won, because those types of demons always do. I planned for it, and so I took steps to protect my family from my foolishness.

"You were let into my home because of me, but you messed up. You came in too soon when I still suspected you were an enemy. The House of Magic showed me all the cameras you installed to watch what was happening inside the house and throughout the property. The video you saw? With a simple spell, you only saw what I wanted you to see. The trackers you placed inside the house in our things? I found those too, and I disabled them. The piece of vellum you added to the grimoire room when you shoved me against the desk? I rewrote it. I planned for betrayal, Knox, because my life has been one big letdown after another, and you're just the newest one in a long line of disappointments. My mother taught me that no matter who you let in, they weren't always on your side, and more often than not, they would seek to destroy you the hardest. She would say that those we let get too close to us, are often led there for a reason. If not for a reason, then they sought you out and did so with a motive that shouldn't be trusted. So, you see, I trusted no outsider even if they're fucking me. I may not be as strong as you, Knox, but I will go toe-to-toe with you in intelligence."

Knox turned to face the gargoyles at the top of the shelves lining the library walls. "Cyan, Ker, and Lars go watch the spot where the House of Magic sits, and if you see any movement in the house or anyone on the property, snap their fucking neck and bring them back here to me."

I turned as the gargoyles left the top shelf, nodding before they shifted from their solid form and vanished. I smiled sadly, slipping my gaze back to his as he watched me, still covered in chainmail.

"You may be smart and capable of waging logical warfare, Aria, but the thing is, we don't play by your rules. We have our own, the first rule being there are no fucking rules in this war. Get up and get out of that dress, now."

I stood, holding my hands out, hoping he would remove my cuffs. Shaking his head, he walked over and ripped the dress off, brushing his hand over my breast in the process. A whimper of pain slipped from between my lips at his roughness, and I tried to turn away from him, holding my wounded breast with my arms, but his hands caught my shoulder, holding me in place.

His eyes lowered, and he scrubbed his hand down

his face, then he moved to a drawer and withdrew a white silk nightie. Carefully, he placed it onto my shoulders, tying the shoulder-straps into delicate bows as he pushed the fabric down, covering my naked body.

"We're going to war, Aria. One way or another, you're in it. You can either be on the right side or the wrong one."

"My sisters?" I asked, and his eyes lifted as a frown tugged on his lips. "Which side are they on?"

"You are being offered sanctuary, only you are allowed to choose a side."

He leaned down, touching his nose against mine, glaring into my eyes as the chainmail touched my flesh through the nightie, creating a chill that settled into my bones as he held me there.

"Don't make me fight you," he whispered before tilting his head to brush his nose against my cheek.

I stepped back, gazing at him. "I will not willing wage a war with you while my sisters are on the other side of that war. I won't do it. I get that this place needs a reboot, I do. I get that we dropped the fucking ball, and I even agree with you. I understand why you are doing this, Knox. The laws state that if a queen or king oversteps and commits treason, then they are to be held responsible for their actions. You want to remove them, okay, fine. But that isn't what you want. You want to slaughter the original bloodlines and end their reign in the Nine Realms. You want to put new people on our thrones, and the only way to do that is to kill us all. You intend to commit genocide on the witches, for the deeds of a few? No, absolutely not. That is like finding one bad apple and tossing away the entire batch because of it."

"One bad apple?" Snorting coldly, he shook his head, glaring at me as the room exploded with raw, undiluted power leaking from his pores. "There are entire fucking castles filled with covens that are using people as shields on their walls. They're also sending unsuspecting people into crowded towns, spelled to drop potions that erupt, killing everyone inside the barrier erected by the witches the moment their victim is deep enough into the town. Another coven is filled with debauchery, only anyone who joins in the revelry is spelled and not there willingly.

"When the witches created life with anyone other than human, and if a male child were to be born, they fed that child to the father as punishment for giving them a son. The witches are destroying the Nine Realms, and they're doing it because they can. Freya and her sisters were the molds from which the witches of the Nine Realms followed, but somewhere, they got off-course and adopted their own fucked-up rules. No one has intervened in over five hundred years, allowing them to go unchecked." He watched my chest rise and fall with anger, with fury at his words. "That's it; get mad. Your house betrayed you, not me, little girl. Not until they forced me to choose between saving your life and removing that beautiful fucking head of yours."

"If that is true, then it is our bloodline's job to clean our house. When your house is messy, you don't ask another to come clean it for you. You handle it yourself. I *will* clean my house, but I won't do it on your terms."

"My army is fifty thousand strong and growing

daily. I am the head of the fucking rebellion, Aria. If you're unwilling to help me, I will chain you to my bed and protect you from those who crave your pretty head be removed. I will keep you, as I have claimed you in a way that can never be undone. You are mine forever. There is no way out of this situation for us now. Not for you, not for me, not for anyone."

"You won't keep me, Knox. I am Aria fucking Hecate. I am a survivor. War is in my veins, and I assure you, if you do this, I will escape you. I will fight against you. I will always fight for my family. It's in my *blood* and burned into my *bones* to protect them. You're fighting for the memory of your ghosts, but I'm fighting for the lives of mine who are still here."

"There is no escaping me, Aria. And I, too, was created for war, and I have declared war on you personally. That rattle you hear? That's my beast calling to yours, and she answers him. The purring? That's rare, very rare for them to purr to one another in this day and age. I may hate you, and you may hate me, but the things inside of us? They enjoy one another *immensely*. Not to mention, I branded that sweet flesh of yours, and I left my mark on you. My scent clings to your flesh, warning other males that you are mine, and mine alone. There's nowhere that you can hide from me that I won't find you. You can't run from me, because I know the taste of you, the scent of your flesh, and every secret inside your beautiful soul. If you get free, never stop running because I will be in every shadow and dark corner, waiting to get you back, and I will because I never fucking lose."

"I'm okay with running; you no longer scare me."

He smiled, moving his fingers as chains slipped around my ankles, while the others dropped from my hands. I stared at the blood-covered bandage and back up at him. He had used *magic*. Swallowing hard, I studied the way he watched me, knowing that he'd wanted me to see he could use it as well. Our studies had informed us that only witch's wielded magic, but he wasn't a witch. He was something else, and he'd just used it too.

"Do you plan to keep me in your bedroom for the entire time you have me here?" I asked, watching as he reached into the fire and pulled out a piece of red-hot metal.

Knox walked over to me, staring through emotionless eyes while he stopped in front of me. He grabbed my arm and pushed the branding rune against my skin, causing the flesh to sizzle as I screamed out in pain, fighting against him. He held my arm firmly, watching me as the metal painfully burned a design into my red, raw flesh. Knox placed the branding rune back into the fire and grabbed a pitcher of water, pouring it over my arm as tears ran down my cheeks.

"That will prevent you from casting, and where else would you be held? You're mine, remember? I prefer you inside my bedroom, in my bed, where I know you are safely hidden from the world. No one can trace you here, or use a spell to detect your location. If you leave this room, I will know it. You're in my realm now, little girl." His hands came up to touch my cheeks. "I am the wolf that hunts the lambs, and you are fucking delicious," he whispered raspingly.

"I'm not a lamb that you can hunt. I'm the woman

who rattles your beast. I intend to shake your entire fucking realm, Knox."

"You think you can rattle me, little girl?"

I smiled past the tears that flowed from my eyes, watching him as I closed the distance between us and rattled from deep in my chest as his beast answered the call loudly. I leaned up on my toes, brushing my lips against his as the purr sounded from deep within me, and he answered it with his own as he lowered his mouth.

"Let's go to war, asshole. I'm about to rock your fucking foundation and rewrite history. War is brutal, but so is love. Let's rattle the realms, monster, and see which one of us ends up burning in the ashes of the fire we set, and which of us will rise as a legend these realms will never fucking forget." I nipped his lip moaning against it, stepping back slowly with the challenge burning in my stare.

"Love isn't brutal, and it's nothing like fucking war."

"You're wrong; it is the exact same thing as war. And don't assume I speak about loving you, Knox, far from love as a comparison to war, as both are brutal and bring you to your knees. If you've never gone barebones or felt your soul being rattled right down to the very thing that makes it burn, you did it wrong. Love should rattle your soul, but so should war. There's a very thin line between love and hate, but also between war and peace."

"Elaborate, woman," he stated, watching me through narrowed slits as he folded his arms across his chest, glaring at me.

"If love isn't brutal, then you're doing it wrong. It is barebones banging together beneath the full moon, stronger and more forceful than any storm could ever hope to achieve. The sound of flesh hitting flesh, and the feeling it leaves when the body cools and the sweat dries but the soul continues to slowly burn, lit from the connection it shared with another. It is the brutality of ripping apart a soul, learning what is within it, and accepting it at face value without wanting to change a single thing. Love is a fucking battlefield, and you fight because you want it with every fiber of your being. It's the exact same as war, which I assure you, Knox, you'll learn to love war with me. On the other hand, you may decide you hate it, but either way, you will know the difference between the two."

"What the fuck would you know about love, Aria?"

"That when I find it with the perfect mate, it better be exactly like that," I whispered, smiling sadly. "I don't want no basic bitch romance, I want to rip it apart and watch it grow from the ground up. I want to build it so fucking fortified that no one can ever touch it because me and my guy? We'd fight the entirety of the Nine Realms to keep it safe. That is what I want, and I won't find that here, and sure in the hell won't be with you. You live with ghosts and are fueled by the need to avenge them. I live in the now, here, right now."

He stared at me through narrowed eyes as if my words had found their target. I bowed my head, exhaling. His chest rose and fell as he scowled, unwilling to look away as I challenged him to go barebones with me, only I didn't want his love; I wanted the war he promised.

"I will fight you, Knox. Not because I want to, but because to stand beside you, I have to choose between my family and a man who doesn't even like me. You made this decision easy for me." I dismissed him, giving him my back as I walked toward the bed, dragging chains across the floor. I crawled onto the bed, peering at him as I rested my head on my hand. "I'm about to become your worst fucking nightmare, so go and enjoy the party below. I will rest, as I have a war for which to prepare."

"I hope you're ready to lose because losing isn't an option for me. I've had five hundred years to plan; you've had five fucking minutes, little one."

"I'm a woman, Knox. We only need a few minutes to rain hell down upon men. I wish you luck because you will need it. I'm about to rattle your fucking soul and bring you to your knees."

CHAPTER
59

I felt a body pressed against mine as hands roamed down my curves in a slow exploration. Lips touched my neck, and I moaned, turning to claim them in a demanding kiss. My body arched off the bed, rocking against fingers that pushed through the naked heat between my legs, and I heard a dark chuckle at my response. I spread my legs, giving more access until my eyes popped open, and I sat up, wide awake, and pushing Knox away from me before he could hold me down with his weight. My body flushed with a raw, brutally aching need that soaked into my bones.

Closing his eyes, Knox leaned into me, inhaling deeply, savoring my scent while releasing a low, husky growl that made the smoldering flame inside of me ignite and catch fire. "Your body wants me, woman."

"Yeah, well, my body makes awful decisions occasionally, and you're its current worst mistake," I muttered through sleep that clung heavily to my words.

"Ride me, witch." Knox rested on his back, exposing

his cock, which was hard and ready to use. I shivered at the explosive need to do as he said and hated that my body wanted him. It was bipolar, and it took everything I had in me not to straddle him and do just as he'd wanted.

My body flushed, purring huskily as I jumped out of bed and moved away from him. Distance was needed, because if I didn't get some, he was going to end up getting some of me, and that, he didn't deserve. I shook my hands out as I stretched my neck, inhaling slowly.

"It is right here, Aria," he taunted huskily, slowly stroking his cock as he watched me warring against my needs. "All you have to do is take what you need."

"Hard pass, literally. You don't get to have me anymore, Knox." I shivered again, fighting the need to inhale his scent and cave to the baser need that was driving me. "Put it away," I warned, unwilling to look at him as he lay in the bed, pointing it at me.

"Oh, it is hard; that's what happens when some sexy little nymph rubs her pretty ass against me all night, whispering my name like I'm a saint when she knows damn well I'm a fucking sinner."

"Nightmares happen." I didn't turn toward him, uncaring that he couldn't see the heat flaming my cheeks, or the anger burning in my gaze.

"If you won't fuck me, we can do this your way, Aria. There are clothes on the couch for you to wear. Get dressed. I have a present for you downstairs."

"Is this where you set yourself on fire, and I get to roast marshmallows on your cock?" I asked, adding a hopeful note to the latter part.

"I'm fireproof, little one," he murmured behind me, and still, I didn't turn around.

I could feel the heat of his body from his proximity, soaking into my bones even though we hadn't touched. His breath fanned my shoulder, and I turned, looking into his eyes with the fire and lust I felt burning in my eyes and soul. I wanted to rip him apart, but worse, I wanted to ask him to remove the feel of Garrett from my flesh, to erase the taint that had been burned into my memory. I wouldn't, but the urge was right there in my stare, and I couldn't remove it.

"Say it, and it's done, Aria."

"Pass," I whispered through the tightening in my throat.

"Get dressed then." His hand scrubbed over his mouth as his shoulders stiffened. He turned to leave, but my words stopped him.

"I can't get dressed with chains around my ankles, jerk." I crossed my arms, watching the struggle in his eyes. He dropped his heavy gaze to my raw ankles and then lifted it slowly over my body before pausing at the pink, pebbled nipples that pushed against the nightie.

He bent down, grabbing my ankle, causing me to go off-kilter, and I dropped back onto the couch. Knox smirked, skimming his fingers over my calf before magic pushed against the cuff, unhooking the clasp. He released the other cuff, and I stood, uncaring that my hip rubbed against his cheek or that my ass was in his face as I grabbed the dress, looking at it with a frown.

"No panties?" I questioned, turning to stare down at him where he was slowly breathing while his stare remained on my bruised, naked flesh.

"You don't need them," he stated unevenly, as if he was struggling with my body being so close to his in the tiny nightie he'd given me last night. "You won't be out of this room long enough to warrant wearing them. Who fucking touched you?"

"Does it matter? Why do you care?"

"Tell me so I can end them."

"That's not your fight, asshole. It's mine. You're not my protector or my mate. I'll deal with him when I escape you. So, I am to be kept in your bedroom, naked?"

"No, you'll be watched when I am gone for extended periods. You'll get clothes, Aria. Just not today," he growled thickly as he stood and peered down at me. "Strip, I need to see the damage to know if it is healing."

"As if, Knox. That also isn't your job," I snorted, but before I could argue, he reached up and snapped the straps apart without hurting me. I shook my head, frowning as he stepped closer, brushing his fingers over the angry bruise on my breast.

"I will kill him for this," he whispered angrily.

"Why? You plan to kill me one minute and then say you want me alive in the next. Now you want to kill someone for groping me? I don't get you at all, Knox. You hate me, yet you protect me. You saved me so you could enslave me. You kiss me awake in the morning, and yet you promise to destroy me. You hate me because you want me, because admitting that to yourself is a slight against the memory of your wife. You don't get to put that guilt on me—that is not fair." I turned away from him and grabbed the dress to pull it over my nudity.

He didn't speak, and I wasn't even sure he was still there anymore. I dropped my head back, closing my eyes before spinning around to look at him, but his eyes were cold, merciless when they met mine. I stepped back, shivering at the intensity that watched me.

"When we leave this room, you will say nothing to anyone. I don't care if they speak to you; you don't say a word. When we get outside, you will stand beside Killian, and you will remain silent, or you won't like what happens when we get back to this room."

"Why take me at all then?" I asked curiously, continuing to step away from him as he prowled closer. "Why not just leave me locked in your bedroom naked? Isn't that what you want from me? To have me at your mercy, cut off from the world as you slowly destroy who I am to rebuild me into what you want me to be?"

"Because you're not missing this," he uttered as his hands balled into fists at his sides. "And I think you're fine the way you are, but your views need to be cleared. You haven't seen this place or the results of what your bloodline has done, but sooner or later, you will."

He moved across the room, slowly and meticulously putting on each piece of armor. It was as if he was making a show of it, and it caused the hair on my neck to rise with the silent warning. My heart clicked into overdrive as he turned, smiling wickedly once he was fully armored, holding his hand out.

Whispering through the dryness in my mouth, I started to tremble with the look burning in his eyes. *Victory.* "What did you do, Knox?"

"Exactly what I said I was going to do, Aria. Come, it's time."

"Knox, don't do this." My voice held a plea of desperation, but his eyes held no mercy as he moved to me, pulling me against his armor, staring into my terrified gaze. "I am begging you."

"You won't change my mind," he breathed, lowering his mouth to mine as he brushed against it. "You will hate me for this, but maybe one day, you will see it from where I stand, Aria Hecate. This is their fault, and they must pay for what they have done to us."

He didn't wait to see if I followed him. Instead, he grabbed my hand, jerking me against him as he started out of the room. I had to run to keep up with his long, angry strides as he moved through the empty hallways with only a few guards behind us who had been posted at the door. I memorized the layout silently, staring down hallways as he took me down long, winding staircases and through more halls until I realized he was confusing me on purpose.

Once we were down the staircase, I pulled on his hold, staring in horror at the walls lined in skulls carved with pentagrams. We emerged in a large room with tall cathedral ceilings and stained glass windows, decorating the room in every shade. A throne sat on a raised platform, built from skulls of the Hecate bloodline, as indicated by the pentagrams that were magically bestowed to them at birth, instead of those that were carved into the skulls along the walls. Hecate witch skulls sat at the base of the throne, while femurs and high witch skulls created the backrest. I swallowed denial, turning tear-filled eyes to him as my chest rose and fell with the realization of how many witches he'd slaughtered. I trembled visibly as he watched me fighting the sob that built in my lungs.

"I did not lie to you, Aria. I have built my life over the past five hundred years around murdering witches. I will never stop, not until the last one bleeds their magic back into the soil of the Nine Realms. Come," he said darkly, pulling me behind him again until sunlight touched my face. "Maybe now you will see that you cannot escape this fight. You will either be at my side or against me one way or another, little one."

CHAPTER
60

Knox pushed me toward Killian, who grabbed my arm painfully, jerking me closer until I was standing between him and Lore silently. I scanned the courtyard, seeing familiar faces from my childhood as I noted the line of prisoners being brought in through the gates. I searched for my family, and relief washed over me until they shoved Dimitri into the courtyard with Aurora beside him.

The world went silent around me. My heartbeat pounded in my temples as the air sat stuck in my throat. Everything around us stopped and moved in slow motion as my hands lifted, covering the cry that fought to escape my throat. Tears burned my eyes, slowly rolling free as fear ripped through me and pushed icy claws around my heart, squeezing it painfully.

I turned to Knox, who watched me for a moment before he looked away. His shoulders pushed back, his neck stretching as he refused to look at where I stood in silent horror. He'd found Aurora and Dimitri somehow, and he expected me to remain silent as he slaughtered them?

My throat swelled and burned with tears. Dimitri caught sight of me and opened his mouth to speak, but Aurora touched his shoulder. Her gaze moved between us, and then to Knox. Slowly, she turned, staring at the statue that was inches from where she stood, where Amara's head remained still upon it. Aurora's mouth opened, but Knox beat her to it, shouting to incite the crowd.

"I give you the leaders of the original bloodlines! Those who betrayed the Nine Realms and will now face charges of treason against us!" he shouted, and the crowd howled in applause. "How do you charge them?" he demanded, and the crowd erupted with screams of guilty or worse.

Nausea swirled through me as he stepped to the first original in the line and used his swords to crosscut the head from the body before he used his foot to kick the body back. I sagged in shock, still covering my mouth as tears poured from my eyes. I couldn't do this. I couldn't watch the only mother I had ever known, or would ever know, die like this, as part of his sadistic show. It wasn't justice. It was a fucking slaughter. A low growl rose from my chest as my body rattled with rage.

"Give me one reason to take your fucking head, witch," Killian growled beside me, tightening his hold on my arm. "One fucking move and you end here and now, and no one will stop me."

"Careful, Killian. You were told to guard her, not goad her," Lore warned through clenched teeth, helping me to stand back up where my knees were refusing to hold my weight. "Close your eyes, Aria." I jerked my arms away from him and covered my mouth once more.

Close my eyes?

I continued to stare between Aurora and Knox as he continued slaughtering leaders of the original families of the Nine Realms. Her eyes pleaded for me not to interfere. My breathing grew ragged with anger and denial as I turned, watching the bodies being stacked into a pile while the heads were collected and placed as an offering to his dead wife and son. Every time he killed one, Aurora moved closer to his blades. He refused to look at me, refused to see the silent plea in my eyes.

I watched Knox in silence. Slowly, I lowered my hands together, staring at Aurora as more screams erupted, and the chaos of the crowd turned frenzied with bloodlust. Fear and anger collided within me, and I reached for my magic, forgetting briefly about the runes that had been burned into my flesh. Power from the Nine Realms rushed through me, answering my call, and I gasped silently, relieved that the runes had failed to bind my magic.

Through the noise and commotion, I mouthed the words, no one hearing the spell leaving my lips. My finger worked over my palm, giving warning to the others within the House of Magic. I watched Aurora as she stepped closer and closer, time inching toward her death with every tick of the clock as Knox picked up speed, covered in the blood of the originals. My teeth grew with the need to act, covered by my lips as I fought to contain the growl and purring that was building into one furious vibration as it built within my lungs.

My palm itched, and I turned my eyes to Knox, who paused as they removed the bodies, looking at me and then to Aurora, tears blinding my vision. He turned back, waiting for the last of the bodies to be removed, and I shot forward without warning, shouting the spell as power ignited and erupted into the courtyard. I slammed against Dimitri and Aurora, taking their entire section of originals with us through the portal I'd created with the spell.

"Run!" I screamed as men fell through the portal, and my hands clapped the moment Knox moved to lunge through it. "Gargoyles!" I watched in horror as I took in the chaos. I watched the men who had slipped through the portal with us go down, unable to escape the brutality and efficiency of the gargoyles who slaughtered them. "Faster, Dimitri, Aurora, move now!" I screamed as I threw my hands up, sending the gargoyles that shot toward us, flying backward with a blast of energy. The house appeared, and we fell inside the moment Kinvara opened the door.

I jumped to my feet, turning as the door creaked and shivered as something slammed hard against it. My hands lifted, slapping together, and a barrier erupted around the house. I slid down the door, sobbing as everything hit me at once.

"He killed Amara," Aurora whispered thickly.

"No, I killed Amara." I held her gaze while the others went silent. "She traded me to the Minotaur King. She gave me to him so he could rape and murder me. She traded us all as her dowry as if we were something she owned. He was horrible." A sob exploded from my chest as I wrapped my arms around my stomach, shaking my head. "He had a hallway full of trophies and pictures of the results of his use and brutalization of women," I said, wiping away tears that refused to stop falling.

"She wouldn't do that." Sabine stared at me, horrified by what I'd said.

"But she did, and I was hung up on display to be raped and mutilated as she announced to the entire party that I was her gift to her husband's murderous father. Amara hated us. She hated me the most. She thought I stole her power while we shared a womb. She fucked her husband as he stared at me. Amara let him abuse me as she watched, and then she told them what to dress me in so I could be tortured, and then beheaded."

"That's insane." Aurora pushed her dirty fingers through her hair, staring at me as tears filled her eyes. "Then she was already lost to us. To do something so horrendous to blood is the same as treason. You did what you had to do in order to survive. What the hell is happening at home?" she murmured through chattering teeth, shaking off her horror at what we were currently facing.

"Aria, we do not blame you, and the answer to that question, Aurora, is the entire world has gone mad," Kinvara said, tossing her arms up in the air, kneeling before me. "We have to go now. The shield you placed around the house won't hold for much longer, and the concealment spell was broken when Dimitri stepped into the house."

"I know." I stood up, pushing my shaking hands over my skirt before eyeing each of my sisters to ensure they were all accounted for. "I need the map I told you to get." I fought for calm, shaking internally as I felt something prodding against the shield I'd placed. Something slammed against the house, and I closed my eyes as Knox screamed my name before another earthquake shook us. "Now, that isn't a knock, ladies. Grab Hecate's grimoires that can be removed, as well as grandfather's skull. Where are my clothes and my things?" I asked, and Kinvara handed my bag to me as she nodded at the map on the table. "Start a five-minute timer; grab anything you want because we will not be back. Make sure it is small, and only something you can carry because we're entering the Nine Realms without anyone knowing we are there."

"Why? The house will hold; it was brilliant, Aria." Aurora smiled, hopefully. "You saved your sisters from ending up with me when I rushed out to help Dimitri as men invaded the town."

"It won't hold because it isn't blessed and hasn't been since Amara took a bone from grandfather's ear, the stapes, which is literally the smallest bone in the body. She made sure we couldn't hide from her husband." I grabbed my leg as pain burned where Knox's name was written upon it as he shouted my name again. "Go, we don't have long before they penetrate that shield, and then we all end up on our knees, getting a haircut with his blade."

Everyone moved into action as I went to the window, throwing open the curtain to stare at Knox, who waited by the door still dressed in his armor. An entire army stood at his back, awaiting his orders. His gaze slid to the window, and he moved, slowly strolling over to tilt his head against the glass as he stared in at me. He was still covered in blood, and Dimitri growled from beside me as I turned my head subtly, staring up at Knox as my chest rose and fell rapidly from adrenaline pumping through my veins.

"Turn around, Dimitri," I stated, slipping the dress off, over my head, not bothering to see if he had listened.

I walked to the coffee table, slipping on the black silk panties, and grabbed the pleather pants that hugged my curves enticingly. I strolled back to the window, peering out with my cheek against the glass as Knox snarled, glaring over my shoulder at Dimitri. Three witches were slamming energy magic against the house as other creatures added to their power. Obviously, Knox hadn't planned to murder *all* witches, or at least not the ones who were helping him—yet.

"Move it!" I screamed, turning my face away from the window as I pulled on the pentagram top, then slipped my arms around to secure the buttons behind my neck, only for hands to grab it first.

Dimitri snapped the back together, adjusting the clasp before his lips brushed over my shoulder, and I smiled, glaring at Knox, whose eyes had turned black, filling with fiery embers as he watched us through a murderous gaze.

"Ready," Aurora stated. "Where are we going?"

I slipped on the black leather jacket and turned away from Knox. "You're going to Hecate's tomb, to take her skull. After that, you are going to the sanctuary to bless the lands and add our blood to it, because we are going to war."

"You can't do that. Aria, we cannot take my mother's skull from her place of rest."

"We can, and you will. The House of Magic is compromised. We need something strong to safeguard the house we are about to conquer and take back the control in our realm. Hecate is the strongest power to which we have access. I know she is your mother, but she would want you to survive, and we won't against Knox unless we're smarter and willing to play as dirty as he is. His army is over fifty thousand strong and growing, Aurora. He just walked into Haven Falls and took the fucking original families from their homes and slaughtered them in front of us. We are all that is left! If we don't survive, they will win."

"Aria, my father's skull…If we remove it from this place, the barrier which protects Haven Falls is gone, and the entire town will start to fall to erase any proof that we were ever here. It will set off the magical detonation built into the foundation, and each and every house will be erased from this realm, one by one."

"The failsafe, I know. I'm counting on it." I shivered as power slithered through me, knowing that we had to do this now, or what little power I had left would wane before we all got out. Knox's brand hadn't worked on me to prevent my use of magic, but it was weakening me slowly.

"This place will be gone, and we won't be able to come back," she insisted carefully. "The portal will be gone, and we can never come back again because only Hecate had the power to open it."

"I know, but we can't stay here either. We cannot hide for the rest of our lives. The Kingdom of Witches is in chaos, murdering thousands of creatures in the name of Hecate's bloodline; that's us. We didn't give them permission to slaughter creatures or build an army for war. The entire Nine Realms hates us because of their actions. Our house is messy, and what do Hecate witches do when it is messy?"

"We clean the house," she stated firmly, dropping her eyes. "So, we will go to the tombs and take my mother's head while she slumbers." Tears filled her eyes. "Then, we do what we need to do together."

"I can't go with you." I closed my eyes as they began arguing all at once. "I am marked, and if I go with you, Knox will find you immediately. I will go elsewhere while you prepare the items we need to secure a new, stronger House of Magic. I will keep Knox busy for now. I will keep running until you send me word that you are ready to raise the new house in the Nine Realms. You must stay in the shadows and draw no attention to you once you are there, do you understand?"

"And me?" Dimitri asked.

I turned, staring at him as Knox watched through the window, unable to breach the barrier even though it was weakening. He was stuck outside the shield protecting the house unless it fell. For now, my magic held firmly against the assault his witches were throwing against it.

"Welcome to the family, Dimitri. There is nowhere else you can go, so if you want to be wicked with us, let's get wicked, shall we?"

His eyes smiled even though he shook his head. "They slaughtered the pack. They slaughtered the entire alpha pack the moment they engaged in battle."

"I'm sorry, but if you're bordering on hysterics, you will need to hold it for a little while," I said, moving to the wall to clear it of pictures and adornments. I sliced deeply into my palm, drawing a symbol onto the white paint as everyone watched in silence. "I love you guys, see you soon," I whispered, slapping my palm against the wall, watching as it turned into a wind tunnel that would send them through the portal, straight to the sacred tomb where the dire wolves lived.

I stepped back, watching as one by one, as Dimitri and my family jumped through the portal. When the last one was through, I slapped my hands, sealing the portal before I whispered a spell, disengaging the blood and pulling the droplets from the wall, forming a ball of blood in my palm. Slowly, I turned around to stare at Knox, who watched me, along with the witches.

"Open the fucking door," he hissed. "If you run, I will find you, Aria." His chest rose and fell as he glared at me, noting every single movement I made with his predatory gaze. "When I catch you, because I will, I will punish you for running from me. Come out now, and I'll go easy on you. If you make me chase you, you will regret it."

"I know you will catch me eventually." I smiled sadly. "That doesn't mean it will be easy, Knox, King of Norvalla. I have no plans of making anything easy for you, all things considered. You just tried to kill the only mother I have ever known. You tried to neuter my magic and to enslave me. No, catching me won't be as easy as you want it to be." I pressed my head against the cool window as my hands went flat against the thick glass, the ball of blood hovering in the air beside me. Sweat beaded on my brow as his hand lifted, copying mine as if he could coax me out. His purring slithered through me, and I moaned, opening my mouth to let mine escape, watching as his gaze heated from the needy timbre of mine.

My eyes closed even as another eruption sounded, shaking the house. I had to wait out the timer. The time between portal spells was crucial to altering locations. I had to be sure I ended up far away from my family since the burning reminder on my thigh was humming with warning. I slowly opened my eyes, staring into black orbs filled with flecks of red flames. It unnerved me, not the chaos I witnessed burning in those fiery depths, but the excitement. He was deadly calm, his eyes focused on me in a way that made me shiver with trepidation. He wanted to hunt me down, and I wasn't sure if it was the beast or man that craved the hunt more.

I started to step away, but the witches slammed the window with magic, and I lifted my fingers, snapping them once as all three fell to the ground, dead. Knox peered down at their corpses, then at me with a narrowed glare before his lips curved into a sinful smirk.

Peering over at the timer, his gaze followed mine as it ticked down minutes until I could open another portal into the Nine Realms, deep within the Wicker Forest. I was going straight to the first castle he intended to storm and see if what he said was true. I made it three steps away from the window before my leg jolted with pain, and I dropped my knees, throwing back my head to scream in the worst agony of my life.

"Get the shield open, now!" he shouted as I crawled toward the wall, painting the blood in a different design for the new location, through blinding tears and debilitating pain. "Now, before she fucking escapes!"

Once I'd painted the portal, I sat on my knees, sobbing as more pain ripped through me. My eyes lifted to his, and he covered his mouth with his hand, staring as he continued to apply pressure and pain to my leg until it was almost too much to take. Sweat dripped from my hair as I slid my arms through the backpack Kinvara had prepared for me. I grabbed the hammer from the coffee table and then the skull with my bloodied hand, centering it.

Slowly, I stood up as everything within me screamed to curl in a ball in the fetal position. My hands trembled, and my eyes lifted to Knox, watching as he realized what I was about to do.

Knox turned, staring at his people before he issued orders in rapid command as I brought the hammer down, shattering the ancient skull. I tumbled to the floor, screaming as pain burned against my flesh, and I arched off the floor, explosions sounding in the background.

My body jerked until I was seizing, realizing that when the explosions got to my house—when the last house had been demolished to erase proof of our existence—I would die if I didn't make it through the portal. It wasn't something I could live through. It was ancient dark magic, cast by the goddess herself.

Knox pounded on the window, and I continued to flop around the floor, unwilling to let him in to save me. I'd saved my family. I'd protected the witches who could rewrite the future without bloodshed, and I was ready to die if my life was the cost. I'd done what I needed to do and had given the Nine Realms the best chance, they had to fix the wrongs.

The pain in my leg eased, and I exhaled, laying

there staring up at the ceiling as I fought to get air into my lungs. Knox continued to slam his palms against the window. I sat up slowly, staring at him as he watched me. Turning to look at the wall, he veered around, watching as the House of Alphas imploded, sending wood sailing through the air like weapons.

"Get the fuck up and get through the portal now. Now, Aria!" Knox ducked as a board impaled beside his head, sheering the siding as it stuck into the house. "Get up and get through the portal!"

I turned, staring at the wall as I summoned magic to me, crawling on hands and knees to where the portal slowly turned black and violet, spinning in a circle. I slipped through the portal as the House of Magic began to scream in protest.

Getting to my feet, I stared through the other side of the portal at the empty window where Knox had stood, and beyond it, where Haven Falls fell to flames. There was no sign of Knox, but I knew he'd made it through somehow.

I stepped further into the portal, closing it with one last look at the Human Realm. Moving deeper into the Wicker Forest, I slid down a tree, staring at the air where it was solidifying, to erase proof that the portal had ever existed. My leg throbbed, and I pushed my hand against it, knowing he'd already begun hunting me. I had to give it to him, he was persistent.

Knox wanted revenge, and I agreed we owed him retribution, but it didn't give him the right to remove the leaders by force. There were steps they could have taken, failsafes that were in place to protect them, should a king or queen become corrupted by power. He had chosen another route, one that ended in the slaughter of all witches and all rulers.

I wouldn't let him win. I would stop him, even if I died doing it. Life wasn't black and white; there were hues between both, hues in which people walked in every shade that existed. He'd started a large-scale rebellion that had given him the power to take control of the Nine Realms. That didn't mean he would win; it just meant he had a headstart on us.

I would clean the Kingdom of Witches and take control of the Witchery, where we ran and directed all witch-controlled strongholds and palaces. I would bring a new dawn to the Nine Realms, and wash away the eternal night he wanted to create.

Knox would find me, but how he found me was my decision. I held control of my life, and as long as I continued running and never stopped, he wouldn't find me as easily as he thought he could. I'd find him when I was ready, and we'd start this war on my terms because I'd just thrown the first punch, and I wasn't about to back down.

I stood, moving from the cover of the woods to stare down at the large castle lit against the night. It was time to get started, and the clock was ticking because Knox already knew where I was. I was in his realm now, but it was mine too. My bloodline had created in the Nine Realms, and as Hecate's granddaughter, I was finally home. I'd known I belonged here my entire life, and now that I was in the Nine Realms, it was time to fight for what we wanted—and to right the wrongs of those who had betrayed us.

I would rattle the realms, and bring that man to

his knees, even if it was the last thing I ever did in my lifetime. I guess it was a good thing we were immortal since neither of us planned on losing. I wouldn't bow to him, nor would I let him win this war. Not with what the cost would be, not with the finality of death, he craved to deliver to those I loved. No, I'd rattle him until he shook, and then I'd bring that man to his knees and make him bow to me. This war was just getting started, and I had been born to wage it against him.

Knox

And so it begins. I will catch her, and when I do, she will wish she had never met me.

The End for Now

Ashes of Chaos
coming 2020

Nine Realms' Compendium

Key Players in the Series

Knox Karnavious – King of Haven Falls

Brander – Brother of Knox, full-blooded

Lore – Brother of Knox

Fade – Brother to Knox, full-blooded

Killian – Lilianna's brother and Knox's best friend

Greer – Friend and butler to Knox, vampire

Hecate Bloodline Introduced So Far

Freya – Daughter of Hecate

Aurora – Daughter of Hecate, sister to Freya who raised the twins.

Hysteria – Daughter of Hecate

TWINS OF THE BLOODLINE

Aria Primrose Hecate / Amara Other half unknown

Kinvara / Valeria – Succubi

Aine / Luna – Alpha werewolf

Sabine / Callista – Nymphs

Reign / Rhaghana – Unknown

Tieghan/Tamryn – Witches, born of human fathers

ALPHA PACK

Dimitri – Pure-born alpha werewolf

Jasper – Pure-born werewolf, Fallon's son, and Prince of the Alpha wolves.

Fallon – Pure-born alpha wolf, King of the Alpha Pack

MINOTAURS

Gerald – King of the Kingdom of Unwanted Beasts

Garrett – Son of the King of the Kingdom of Unwanted Beasts

ITEMS AND MORE

Grimoire – A book of ancient spells

Scrying – The ability to search a map with magic to find a location.

White Oak Trees – Grown only in Norvalla in the Arcadian Forest of Knowledge

Frost fire – Ice from the Dark Mountains, appears as regular ice until it swallows up anything, or anyone it can touch. Unbreakable by anything other than witches fire, a spell that only rare witches can use. It was used to protect Norvalla from the Kingdom of Unwanted Beasts.

Midnight Blooming black roses – Grown in the darkest passes in the Dark Mountains. A rare type of rose that blossom's in the icy snow caps of the mountain, holding a unique essence that witches covet.

Gargoyles – Protectors of the Library of Knowledge

THE VISITED LANDS WITHIN THE NINE REALMS TO DATE

Dorcha –The Darkest Realm, realm in which Norvalla sits as capital

Norvalla – Knox's Homeland

Kingdom of Unwanted Beasts

The Dark Mountains –The Mountain range bordering The Kingdom of Unwanted Beast and Norvalla's high passes.

Library of Knowledge – An ever-changing room that only reveals its treasures to those it finds worthy of the knowledge it holds.

About The Author

Amelia lives in the great Pacific Northwest with her family. When not writing, she can be found on her author page, hanging out with fans, or dreaming up new twisting plots. She's an avid reader of everything paranormal romance.

Stalker links!